AN
UNQUIET
HEART

A POET IN LOVE AND REVOLUTION

A Novel

MARTIN SIXSMITH

SCRIBNER

LONDON NEW YORK SYDNEY TORONTO NEW DELHI

First published in Great Britain by Scribner,
an imprint of Simon & Schuster UK Ltd, 2019
This paperback edition published by Scribner, an imprint
of Simon & Schuster UK Ltd, 2020

1 3 5 7 9 10 8 6 4 2

Simon & Schuster UK Ltd
1st Floor
222 Gray's Inn Road
London WC1X 8HB

Simon & Schuster Australia, Sydney
Simon & Schuster India, New Delhi

www.simonandschuster.co.uk
www.simonandschuster.com.au
www.simonandschuster.co.in

A CIP catalogue record for this book
is available from the British Library

Paperback ISBN: 978-1-4711-4981-8
eBook ISBN: 978-1-4711-4982-5

Typeset in Palatino by M Rules
Printed and bound by CPI Group (UK) Ltd, Croydon CR0 4YY

Martin Sixsmith studied Russian at Oxford, Leningrad and the Sorbonne. He was a Slavics Tutor at Harvard and wrote his postgraduate thesis about Russian poetry. From 1980 to 1997 he was the BBC's correspondent in Moscow, Washington, Brussels and Warsaw. From 1997 to 2002 he worked for the British government as Director of Communications and Press Secretary to several cabinet ministers.

He is now a writer, presenter and journalist. He is the author of non-fiction titles including *Russia – the Wild East*, *Putin's Oil* and *The Litvinenko File*. His bestselling 2009 book, *The Lost Child of Philomena Lee*, was adapted for film and became the multiple Oscar-nominated *Philomena*, starring Steve Coogan and Judi Dench.

Also by Martin Sixsmith

Ayesha's Gift

Philomena

Russia: A Thousand Year Chronicle
of the Wild East

Putin's Oil

We almost always forgive that which we understand

MIKHAIL LERMONTOV,
A Hero of Our Time

Sergei Yesenin

CHAPTER 1

The boy was lost to the world.

In his grandfather's house, he was bent over the pieces of card that would make the face of the tsar.

He found Nicholas's eyes, his beard, and the jewelled star on its crimson ribbon. But some pieces had been lost over the years and he feared the puzzle would defeat him.

The tsar's dark hair was there, his broad forehead and manicured eyebrows – the boy thought he looked handsome. In Petersburg, Nicholas himself was welcoming the twentieth century with the confidence of a dynasty that would reign forever.

Sergei was four and the world he'd inhabited since his parents abandoned him was full of puzzles with no answers. Jigsaws that nursed him in their embrace of image and imagination were an escape. When he looked up, he didn't know where he was.

In the moment it took for the room to coalesce, he sensed the house was empty. Panic gripped him. He ran out to the meadow.

'Dedushka! Dedushka! . . . Where are you, Dedushka?'

From somewhere in the woods Romka the dog barked and Sergei ran towards it. In a clearing, his grandfather was pointing his rifle. A shot; then the dog whimpering.

'Dedushka! – Romka? – Why?'

His grandfather waved him away. 'He was no good. Get back in the house.'

Sergei hardly knew it – it had become his mind's familiar – but deep within him, where thoughts congeal in the forest we must never enter, the absence of his parents lay in wait like a hunter with a snare.

After Romka died, his grandmother comforted him. But she had no answers to his questions.

'Babushka, why does Mother stay away? Is Father angry with me?' Was he such a wicked child that even his mother didn't want him?

He woke in the night. A dream had left him covered in sweat. From the top of the stairs he heard his grandparents talking.

'Well, I saw our Tanya—'

'Oh, God be praised! What did she say?'

'She didn't want to talk. She hasn't seen the boy's father for months. He's away in Moscow with some job in a butcher's shop. Doesn't send her money, won't see her—'

'God have mercy! It's because of the little girl, isn't it? He thinks the child isn't his—'

'Be quiet, woman! You know how they'll talk in the village—'

On the landing, Sergei burst into tears.

'Babushka ... Dedushka ... I want my mother ...'

Tsar Nicholas II in 1899

Sergei's grandmother was a good singer. She taught him the old songs and folk poems passed down by generations. On long walks from village to village, she took him to services at churches and monasteries. Sergei loved the prayers, the chants, the hymns. He imbibed the ancient rhythms of Russian life, breathed in the music of lakes and forest and steppe.

His childhood was beauty, cradled in pain. His grandfather, calloused by life, set out to make him a man. In the spring, he rowed Sergei to the middle of the lake and threw him from the boat. The shock of the water squeezed the breath from the boy's lungs, sucking him down, writhing in darkness. The memory of suffocation would stay with him, waking him gasping and screaming in the night. But he clawed his way to the surface. He fought his way to the shore and collapsed on the shingle. When his grandfather picked him up, Sergei thanked him.

Later, he sat the boy on an unbroken horse and whipped it so it fled across the steppe. Sergei clung on. He was small and when he was bullied by older boys, his grandfather made him fight. He said he was grateful, but the terror of the water, the horse and the bullies never left him. Years later he would write that his grandfather had made him strong. But the trauma of abandonment was in his soul. He would live on the edge.

In 1895, the year of Sergei's birth, Russia had mourned the old tsar – Alexander III, dead from kidney failure at forty-nine – and was about to install the new. Sergei had been six months old when crowds stampeded at Nicholas II's coronation, trampling a thousand people to death. It took a day for the news to reach the Yesenins' village, Konstantinovo, a hundred miles south of Moscow. 'There was a howl of horror,' wrote the journalists. 'Those at the front were being crushed. Death, terrible death, was all around. Blue, sweating faces, people vomiting, gasping for air, the cracking of bones, corpses held upright by the crowd with nowhere to fall.'

In a superstitious land, the tragedy cast a shadow. Neighbours whispered to Sergei's mother that it was 'a sign from God' and 'no good will come from the reign of this tsar'. The Yesenin family fell apart soon after.

Yesenin's parents, Alexander and Tatiana, before their separation

Sergei was beautiful, with blond curls and cornflower blue eyes. When his grandmother walked him through the village, her friends stroked his cheeks. The boy smiled, dropping his gaze with a shyness that delighted them and made his grandmother proud. He enjoyed the company of women. He responded to their gentleness and they returned his affection.

School was hard. The hubbub overwhelmed him. On the first day, he came home in tears. His grandfather was about to beat him, but his grandmother intervened.

It took a week for the teacher to persuade him to speak. At first, he just nodded or shrugged. But she encouraged him.

'Sergei's a clever boy,' she told his grandparents. 'A sweet, lovely boy; very polite, very eager to please. If I ask for volunteers, he's the first to raise his hand. He's way ahead of the others – I've had to bring him books from the older children's class.'

His grandmother beamed.

'I knew it! And such a hard life he's had without his mother—'

'I was going to ask about that,' the schoolteacher said. 'Because there are times when I see another side to him. He finds life intimidating; he's scared of many things, but he won't let it show. He refuses to cry when he's hurt. And he's really quite aggressive if he feels he's being challenged. You know about the bullying and how he dealt with that. There's a ferocity, a violence about him that can be alarming . . .'

It was a time of famine. The harvest had failed for two years in a row and the grain silos held only dust and mice. Much of Ryazan District, including Konstantinovo, was suffering. Deaths from starvation were reported from outlying settlements.

In the taverns where peasants gathered to drink and argue, voices were raised against the tsar. 'The calamity at his coronation was an omen. Why does he sit there in his palace while the people suffer?'

Strangers with answers began to appear among them, students and intellectuals from Moscow.

'The tsar is no friend of the people,' their leaflets said. 'On his orders, workers and peasants are beaten, shot and exiled to Siberia. All to reinforce the crumbling bastion of autocracy. It may seem that justice has been driven from the face of the earth and the reign of iniquity in Russia will last forever. But the power of the people is great. The thunder of the people's anger will strike the contemptible tyrants responsible for the misery, the robbery, the torture and deaths of millions!'

His grandfather used Sergei as a hunting dog.

'You loved that Romka,' he said. 'And now he's gone.'

When his grandfather shot a hare or a duck, Sergei would race through the field or swim out in the lake to retrieve it.

It made him tough. It made him nimble. It made him a part of the Russian land, closer to nature than to people.

The animals were his siblings; the sun and rain, the moon, the night his interlocutors.

He spoke to them and they spoke back.

Yesenin's grandfather, Fyodor

On a Sunday in January 1905, a column of workers approached the Winter Palace in St Petersburg. They were carrying icons and portraits of Nicholas II, singing 'God Save the Tsar' and waving a petition.

> Sire! We ask you for justice and protection. We are in deepest poverty, oppressed with labours beyond our strength. We are treated like slaves. Despotism and arbitrary rule are suffocating us. Our strength is exhausted, our patience run out. We would prefer death to the unbearable torment we are forced to suffer.

On the advice of his ministers, Nicholas II was not there to hear the marchers' plea. He had taken his beard and his manicured eyebrows to another palace, fifteen miles outside the city. Soldiers opened fire and a hundred people died.

Nature consoled Sergei and confounded him in equal measure. He loved its mysteries and rejoiced in its beauty.

He mastered the trails that meander through the Meshchory woodlands, climbed the trees to peer into birds' nests and followed the horse traders as they took their animals to water at the Oka.

They were grizzled, life-hardened men, who looked on the blond child with nostalgia for what they might have been and unspoken hope that he might become it. They took him with them at night as the horses plashed in the shallows, drinking up the river's blackness and all the stars reflected in it. They laughed when he cried out that the stallion was drinking the moon and would plunge the world into darkness.

In winter he skied through the forests and skated on the Oka's ice, returning after dark to his grandfather's house, clambering into bed above the stove, a foot below the ceiling, in his private heaven of warmth and dreams.

In the morning, he told his grandmother that he had seen Christ on a donkey riding through the firs and pines and the Mother of God flying through the night with another baby for the world to crucify.

In spring, when the ice cracked with furious cannon shots that exploded in the night, his grandfather picked up the litter of puppies the Collie bitch had produced in the hay barn and stuffed them in a sack. Sergei followed him to the Oka and watched as he dropped them in the current that would wash them from God's world.

That evening when the bitch bayed at the moon, she was weeping for her children. That was when Sergei began to rewrite the merry endings of his grandmother's stories.

Bloody Sunday made little impression in Konstantinovo. Demonstrations and massacres seemed far removed. But an event the following month brought things closer.

The tsar's uncle Sergei, the military governor of Moscow, was blown to pieces in the Kremlin. On seeing his severed head on the cobblestones and his blood and fingers on the walls, Nicholas went into shock. For the next eight years, he and his hysterical German wife, Alexandra, would not be seen in public.

The assassin, a young poet and Socialist Revolutionary called Ivan Kalyayev, was sentenced to death. News that his hangman was from a settlement just ten miles from Konstantinovo filled the locals with pride. They traded accounts of how 'our man' had carried the offer of a royal pardon to the death cell, only to be sent packing by the obdurate martyr.

The assassin, Ivan Kalyayev

CHAPTER 2

In 1909, Sergei finished the village school with a record that persuaded the rector of Spas-Klepiki seminary, sixty miles to the north, to take him as a pupil. It was an honour for Konstantinovo.

In Spas-Klepiki, he was a peasant boy among sons of merchants and landowners. On the first morning, he stood in the corridor struggling to breathe, his fingers opening and closing on his thumbs.

When a boy in a smart jacket brushed against him in the yard, Sergei demanded an apology. The boy laughed and Sergei hit him in the face. In the afternoon, the boy returned with two others and left him in a pool of blood.

That was how Grisha found him.

Grisha Panfilov was fifteen, a year older than Sergei. He'd been at the seminary long enough to know what was worth picking a fight about and what wasn't. He took Sergei to the washroom and cleaned him up. When Sergei's nose wouldn't stop bleeding, Grisha held a handkerchief to it for over an hour.

The emotion of their meeting created a bond; empathy reinforced by the knowledge of each other's shyness and a shared, reticent sadness at being parted from home and family.

They rearranged the beds in the dormitory so they could

be beside each other. At night, their conversations went on after lights-out. When the other boys complained, Grisha would climb into Sergei's bed and huddle with him under the blankets.

Grisha Panfilov and Sergei Yesenin as
pupils at the Spas-Klepiki seminary

Like all Russian teenagers, they talked about politics. They read the pamphlets that Socialist Revolutionary recruiters left at the school gates. When they discussed the growing demands for change, Grisha was categorical.

'Things can't go on like this. The people are suffering and the nobles just carry on with their banquets and balls. The people aren't going to put up with it!'

'But the aristocracy have their uses, don't they?' Sergei said. 'The Romanovs have ruled for three hundred years and Russia has done all right. The peasants worship the tsar. They call him their Little Father. I don't think there's going to be this revolution that everyone keeps talking about.'

Grisha squeezed Sergei's hand.

'Listen! I've decided what I'm going to do. When I leave here I'm going to qualify as a doctor. Then I'm going to join the SRs. Come with me!'

'I don't know,' said Sergei. 'Of course it would be good if

we could make life better. But I can't see how a revolution that destroys the whole of society would solve anything.'

Grisha frowned and Sergei saw he was offended.

'I've got a joke,' he said. 'Do you want to hear it?'

Grisha nodded.

'All right. Two of the tsar's secret policemen are having a drink after work. The first one says, "Tell me. What do you *really* think about this regime we live under?" The second one says, "Well, the same as you do." So the first one thinks for a minute then says, "In that case, it is my duty to arrest you . . ."'

Shared laughter eased the tension.

'If you're not joining us in the revolution,' Grisha asked, 'what *are* you planning to do?'

'You want to be a doctor. People will always need doctors.' Sergei looked at his friend from the corner of his eye. 'I want to be a poet—'

'A poet!' Grisha said. 'Have you actually written anything? Or are you just hoping the muse of poetry will descend on you?'

They laughed again.

'Of course I've written,' Sergei said. 'Listen':

Beneath my window
The silver birch
Is haloed in snow,
Light silver aglow.
Sumptuous branches
Snow-trimmed;
Buds float
Velvet fringed.
The birch tree
In the sleepy silence;
Snowflakes blazing

In golden fire.
Dawn,
Lazily strolling,
Throws more silver
On the quivering pyre.

When Sergei looked up, Grisha had his eyes closed. Sergei feared it might be from embarrassment, but the older boy held out his hand and pulled him into an embrace.

'Splendid,' he murmured. 'Beautiful. The soul of the Russian language in your words. But why do you write about things, rather than people? Why don't you write about the subject that unites us all – feelings, affection . . . love?'

Sergei shrugged. 'Nature's easier; it doesn't hurt you. I've been trying one poem – about a farmer's dog I once knew. But it won't come together':

The bitch gave her babies life
In the snow. In the hayshed
Dawn silvered the row
Of hessian sacks on the wall.
All day she nursed them,
Licked their soft fur neat, as
Meltwater trickled
From her body's heat.
At dusk, she saw the master
Throw them in a sack; then,
Bounding on beside him,
Eager to match his stride,
She saw the water quiver . . .

'I can't get any further. It's frustrating!'

Sergei Yesenin and Grisha Panfilov spent three years together in the seminary. They were rarely separated, always sparring, joking, laughing. They disagreed about many things, but agreed about more. The eternal questions of God, love, art and beauty filled their minds.

They acted in school plays, learning the poetry of the Russian greats – Pushkin, Chekhov, Lermontov and Griboyedov. Because of his golden curls, Sergei got the women's roles. He enjoyed the drama of it, the make-up and the glamour.

Grisha had never been strong and as the months passed Sergei saw his friend's health was weakening. He ate well enough, but never put on weight. On their country walks, he was becoming tired earlier, halting to lean on a gate or a stile.

Sergei's own body hardened and grew. A peasant vigour kept him always in motion, contrary, provoking, full of opinions. A devilish energy threw him into every ruckus and brawl.

Grisha reproached him for it. He didn't like his friend's tough-guy streak; he found it ugly, unpleasant, verging on the bully. He understood that aggression was Sergei's defence against life. But it was in danger of taking him over, submerging his true nature as ivy engulfs the oak.

'I like you better when you are my sweet Seryozha,' he said. 'The kind, affectionate boy I know you to be, with all your feeling for poetry and sincerity and love. Don't let the world make you callous.'

Sergei looked away. 'If devils lodged in my soul,' he said, 'it was because angels dwell there too.'

On his seventeenth birthday in October 1912, Sergei received a letter from his estranged father. There was little in the way of paternal affection and no suggestion of financial help. But there was an opening for an apprentice in the Moscow butcher's shop where his father worked and he thought his son might want to take it.

'God knows, I don't want to be a butcher,' he told Grisha. 'But it's a chance to move to the city. I'd get a Moscow residence permit and I'd have an income to spend on books.'

Grisha nodded. 'Yes,' he said. 'Or you could stay here and finish your studies, as I'm intending to do.'

The train from Ryazan to Moscow was crowded with traders carrying boxes of potatoes, oily crates of perch and pike, hessian sacks that wriggled with life. It was November and the carriage filled with smoke from the stove; the stench of sweat and urine flooded Sergei's lungs. There was fear in his stomach.

Disembarking at Kazansky station he was swept into a jostling, shouting tide. Peasant women in colourful headscarves, mothers with babies strapped to their chest, powerful, bearded men spitting and cursing, forlorn families squatting on bundles that held the sum of a lifetime's toil, waiting for a train, a comrade, a revolution.

Sergei pushed through the crowds. With his father's directions, he found the tram and jumped on as the driver whipped the horse. He recognised the Red Gates with their gilded, trumpeting angel. In the Chistye Prudy district, blackened plane trees scraped at the windows. Nature was diminished here, he thought; tamed and caged.

When the tram rattled over Krasnokholmsky Bridge, he knew to get out at the next stop. He asked for directions. No one had heard of Krylov's butcher shop, but they knew where Shchipok Street was.

Alexander Yesenin showed an interest in the son he hadn't seen for a decade. 'Welcome,' he said. 'You've been costing me four roubles a month. Now you can work for a living.'

For six days a week, from seven in the morning until seven at night, Sergei sawed and chopped at the carcasses of calves and sheep that arrived before dawn on the carts of farmers from the suburbs.

He didn't like the work, but he didn't complain. On his rest days he walked the streets, peering into churches, visiting museums, always ending at the bookshops on Okhotny Ryad and Arbat. His father took half his salary, rent for the curtained-off corner of the room where Sergei slept, and what was left went on books. He was such a hungry reader that he could barely keep himself supplied. He read on trams, in his work breaks, late into the night. The booksellers all knew him and all had suggestions for more.

Relations between father and son were not warm. Alexander had made contact with Sergei's mother, Tanya, but the couple agreed it would be hard, probably impossible, for them to live together. In conversations over the butcher's block, Alexander asked Sergei about his memories of his mother. He was a jealous husband, keen to enlist another's support for his rancour; but Sergei sensed a longing in him for a past that had slipped from his grasp. His father wanted him to condemn the maternal grandparents who had brought him up, but Sergei stayed silent.

He got to know the customers. Old man Krylov rarely served at the counter, and Alexander was surly to the point of rudeness. Sergei, young, articulate, attractive, was an asset. Women of a certain standing, ladies who came with a servant to carry the meat, seemed to visit with greater frequency when 'the young man' was on duty.

Others came for purposes less transparent; men in dark overcoats with collars raised, who brushed past him into the back room. Sergei tried to make out the muffled conversations punctuated by eruptions of argument or laughter. He was tempted to look inside the brown paper parcels they left under the counter for collection. But he sensed these matters were freighted with danger. When he asked his father, he was told to hold his tongue.

In the summer of 1913, workers at the Moscow Metalworks went on strike. Unrest had been brewing since the previous year, when government forces massacred 270 striking miners in the Lena goldfields. News of the walkout spread quickly; more factories and textile mills downed tools, demanding a shorter working week, civil rights and an end to punishment beatings. The police used rifle butts to disperse a workers' rally in Trubnaya Square. Rumours exaggerated the extent of the injuries and by nightfall there had been incidents of looting, tramcars overturned and police stations attacked.

In the butcher's shop on Shchipok Street, the men in dark overcoats came with increasing frequency. Ambivalent about the cause, Sergei was thrilled by its drama. He wrote to Grisha Panfilov about the clandestine activities he had witnessed and intimated that he played a part in them. 'I remember our conversations, Grisha, when we spoke about change and revolution ... Here in Moscow I have seen things beginning to happen. And I have myself been active among the workers.'

Grisha's reply brought news of rebellion in the countryside. Groups of Socialist Revolutionaries from Moscow had been encouraging the peasants to rise against their masters. In a village not far from Konstantinovo, a local landowner had been lynched and his property torched by peasants angry at his refusal to cancel their agricultural taxes. The landowner's wife and two daughters had been raped and tortured before having their throats cut.

The news tempered Sergei's revolutionary feelings.

'Clouds have gathered over me, Grisha,' he wrote. 'I am revolted by the dark passions of the blind crowd ...'

Snow fell early that year. Moscow became a wasteland of rutted streets and garbage-littered slush, blackened by the smoke of furnaces and abattoirs.

On Tverskaya, where a row of cabs was waiting in front of Yeliseev's food hall, a volley of curses made Sergei look across the street. A cab-horse had sunk to its knees and was being berated by its owner.

The cabbie was beating the animal with a whip, yelling at it to get to its feet. A small crowd was urging him on. A bystander picked up a stick from the sidewalk and joined in the beating. Others threw stones.

Sergei ran towards them. The animal was emaciated and looked half-dead. He grabbed the cabbie's whip and shouted at the others to stop; but the crowd was beyond reason, propelled by the frenzy of collective cruelty. A man punched Sergei hard in the mouth.

He came to with his face in the snow. The shouting had stopped and the crowd was gone. The horse was motionless, stayed from falling by the wooden shafts of the vehicle, but unmistakably dead. The cabbie was hugging its neck. 'Mikolka! I'm sorry! I didn't mean to hurt you ... Come back!'

Sergei saw that the man's face was covered in tears. 'He was my horse,' he said. 'My only horse. I loved him ...'

Sergei found Moscow oppressive. The scale of the place was unnatural, the drudgery dehumanising. He dreamed of Konstantinovo and the beauty of the countryside. Nature was his consolation and the city had none of it.

'I have witnessed terrible things here,' he wrote to Grisha. 'Man in the city is cut off from his roots. It makes human beings inhuman ... For me, Christ is the example of a man of true perfection, but I don't *believe* in Him. I cannot discern the true purpose of our life on earth; yet all the same, we need to know why we are living. You yourself once said, "I believe there is another life, after death." Yes, I think so, too. But why do we have this life? Why do we live?'

Sergei had done enough butchering. He wrote to Sytin's and asked for a job.

Ivan Sytin and Co. was Russia's biggest publisher, with a

catalogue ranging from Tolstoy and Chekhov to almanacs, calendars and picture books that sold in millions. The company's printing works, on the corner of Pyatnitskaya and Monetchikovsky Lane, had been burnt in a clash between police and workers in the 1905 revolution, but Sytin had rebuilt it bigger, a splendid five-storey peach-and-white art deco landmark covering two city blocks.

At his interview, Sergei shone. He was intelligent, well-read. He asked for an editorial post, but was told he'd need to start at the bottom, as a messenger in the dispatch department.

His fellow workers didn't know what to make of him. The boy from the sticks turned up in a modish brown suit, a starched high neck shirt and a bright green tie. Where was the deference?

Sergei Yesenin was cocky. But he was beautiful and his beauty stilled tongues. Blue eyes that had lost their childish diffidence, high Slavic cheekbones, straw blond hair. The women fluttered in his presence; the men backed down.

Within a month he was promoted to assistant copy editor, checking proofs and reading passages aloud for the editor to verify. He liked the reading. And his female colleagues liked to listen. The more he threw himself into the spirit of it, the more they gathered round. He was eighteen and life's possibilities were unfolding.

Anna Izryadnova worked in typesetting, four years older than he was, a city girl from a liberal intellectual family. Sergei read her his poems. He told her that the copy-editing was just a prelude to his literary career and one day he'd be as famous as the authors Sytin now published.

Anna liked it that Sergei was trying to impress her. She was small, self-effacing and unused to men showing respect. When he asked her to dinner at Krynkin's, he came for her in a cab. The driver took the scenic route to the top of Sparrow Hills and they looked back on the city through the restaurant's telescope. Krynkin himself brought them their starters of cured sturgeon. Sergei drank a glass of vodka.

The bill for the meal came to more than Sergei's monthly salary and Anna knew it. When he told her that he had the keys to a friend's vacant apartment, she nodded and squeezed his hand.

Anna watched Sergei undress with a shiver of desire. He had the muscles and complexion of a sun-blessed country boy. He said it wasn't his first experience, but she knew it was. He was pushy and shy, eager and clumsy, tender and attentive all at once. When she urged him to slow down, he didn't object. He did as he was told and the moment lasted.

Sergei was eighteen, Anna twenty-two, and it gifted her a subtle authority. She had seen more of life. She found the city and people easier to deal with than the boy whose existence had been spent in the fields.

She wondered if Sergei resented the advantages she held. Previous men had insisted on putting her down. She expected him to do the same, but he didn't.

He knew he was not Anna's first lover. She didn't talk about her past, but in bed she was the teacher, he the pupil. He could have blustered, but he didn't. He wanted to learn. He was eager to love and eager to please.

Anna told her friends about the beautiful boy from the Russian provinces whose innocence and trust had made her so happy. 'Pure and bright,' she said. 'His soul unblemished and good . . . a radiant being.' Her friends were pleased for her. And jealous. Later, she would discover another side to Sergei – a boy who had been hurt and who dealt with it by hurting others.

In the first flush of togetherness, they enrolled at the Moscow Public University. It was a philanthropic institution, founded by an aristocratic family to educate the people, hoping perhaps that education would temper the people's wrath. At Anna's suggestion, they studied history and philosophy. When term finished, she introduced him to her family.

Anna's father liked the boy's quick mind, the provincial burr that leavened the spikiness of his conversation, and the respect he showed for his daughter. At her request, he spoke to a friend at Sytin's and the following month Sergei Yesenin's first poem was published.

'The Birch Tree' appeared in a Moscow journal for young people. It was four stanzas in a magazine with a handful of subscribers, but Sergei was delighted. The sense of validation through artistic success was a thrill that would become an obsession, marking the rest of his life.

Anna's validation came from love. She spoke to her parents. Her father mumbled something about waiting to get settled before getting married, but Anna convinced him. He offered to find them a flat.

When Anna told Sergei, she was surprised to see him

hesitate. She cried when he said he would have to think about it. She asked if she had misjudged the love that existed between them. He apologised. Of course he was grateful; of course he wanted to live with her. Within a month, they had set up home.

Anna Izryadnova

CHAPTER 3

Nineteen-fourteen dawned. The world, and Russia, were stumbling towards war. Sergei, full of the energy of youth, didn't notice. At Sytin's he worked without thinking, his mind elsewhere, turning words and rhythms in his head. He wrote about the mysterious beauties of nature and life in the Russian countryside. They were sweet, lyrical verses. Poetry was all; the rest of life was just the rest.

He devoured the books that Anna brought him. She told people that her Seryozha lived in the world of the spirit; he had no understanding of practical things. When they signed their marriage papers at the wedding palace, he entered his profession as Poet. That afternoon, he completed his poem about the bitch and her puppies.

> Back from the river, lifting her eyes
> To the moon above the trees,
> She saw her children's souls
> Glide darkly through the sky.
> Keening at the deep-blue void,
> She watched them – the moon, the souls –
> All shimmer, slide and vanish
> To a place unseen, beyond the hill.
> And now, when men mock her,

Throwing not meat but stones
In her face, her dull eyes flow
With tears that are wrought from stars.

When Sergei said he was thinking of quitting his job to become
a full-time poet, Anna didn't protest. She was pregnant.

My dear Grisha, Forgive me for so long a silence. So many
things have happened to me; so many events in the world ...

Sergei felt guilty about his neglected friend. In his letter, he
described his work at Sytin's, then – in great detail and with
some exhilaration – his successes in the world of literature.

His marriage to Anna and her pregnancy were a footnote.

He was still working at Sytin's in February when the owner
announced a visit by Russia's great writer and thinker, Maxim
Gorky. Charges against him for his anti-tsarist novel, *Mother*,
had forced Gorky into exile in Italy. But Nicholas II had munif-
icently, foolishly, declared a general amnesty in honour of the
Romanovs' 300th anniversary and Gorky had returned.

The hall was packed. Sergei and Anna had to stand. Ivan
Sytin, angling for the copyright of Gorky's collected works,
gave him a rousing introduction and the audience erupted. At
the end of the evening, they carried him on their shoulders to
his waiting car. Sergei could barely contain himself. 'Writers
are the most famous and most admired people in Russia,' he
told Anna.

The next day, he enrolled at the Mlechny Put' poetry

collective. Its name, *Milky Way*, conjured a vision of the stars, but its headquarters were not celestial. At the end of an alley-way in the Kitai Gorod district, Sergei found a low-ceilinged room with a group of young men smoking and drinking tea. One of them, dark, gangly and big boned, leapt to his feet.

'Come in! We're arguing about the magazine. The Futurists won't agree to appear if the Acmeists are given the front page. And the Symbolists have already walked out. It's a complete disaster! Bobrov's the name – call me Volodya. What's yours?'

Grisha greeted the news of Anna's pregnancy with caution. He wrote to ask if Sergei were certain this was what he wanted. Did he really want to be tied to a life of domesticity with a woman?

Sergei was reassuring.

Dearest Grisha, You are my closest friend and confidant. You will always be the person most dear to me. As for Anna, she adores me so completely that it is almost comical. There are times in bed when I can hardly restrain myself from bursting into laughter!

Volodya Bobrov was amusing, bewildering, at times over-whelming; an inextinguishable force, charging back and forth making extravagant plans, urging others to follow him, refus-ing to be thrown by life's reverses.

Sergei mocked him. 'You'll never make it as a poet with your hair all over the place and a smile on your face, Volodya. You need to suffer and sigh. Try acting a bit strange. Be a wild man. I am always pretending . . .'

It was a miracle every time *The Milky Way* rolled off the press. The magazine attracted calamities. Established authors would promise contributions, only to renege at the last minute. Young poets would deliver manuscripts four times the length they'd been allocated, then furiously refuse all suggestions for cuts.

The editorial team, poets themselves, lacked business sense. The association's finances staggered from collapse to crisis and back again. Only the beneficence of a wealthy patron kept them afloat. But they were young men who believed in themselves and in the sacred calling of poetry.

After Sergei quit his job at Sytin's, he spent his days writing. In the evenings, he and Anna invited friends. Volodya came regularly and when Anna, visibly pregnant, became tired, she would leave them talking.

'Did you hear about Mayakovsky and Burliuk? They were on one of their Futurist tours down in Odessa, doing their "Slap in the Face of Public Taste" routine. They'd hired the local urchins to run through the streets shouting *Priyekhali footooristy!* – the Futurists are in town! – only, the lads got it wrong and went around shouting *Priyekhali footbolisty!*'

'And what about that "Rite of Spring" bust-up in Paris? People booing and throwing seats; the police called in to break up the riot. A real Russian scandal – carefully staged to make the headlines!'

Art was in the public domain and in the public's face. Rival groups competed to create the biggest noise, the biggest self-promoting outrage. Poetry was a living force and Sergei loved it.

Grisha's health was in decline. Sergei was not to worry, he wrote, but the doctors had diagnosed consumption. They were gloomy fellows and they feared the worst, but Grisha was determined to prove them wrong.

Sergei spent a long time drafting his reply. Grisha's optimism was a pretence; he had known since their time in the seminary that God had numbered his friend's days. But Sergei's letter made light of it.

He wrote instead about his own exploits, listing the poems he'd had published, poking fun at his colleagues at Mlechny Put', inventing a series of revolutionary adventures he claimed to have taken part in. Only at the end did the mask slip.

Grisha, my dearest, I feel sad. I'm so alone, and there is no one to whom I can bare my soul. The people here are shallow. You are far away from me, and there are things one cannot express in a letter. How I'd love to see you! I grieve deeply at your illness. Whatever happens, be assured of one thing: I love you; you will always be in my heart. Your Seryozha.

When Anna, tidying the house, picked up a discarded draft, she read it with alarm. The letter raised questions that she couldn't bring herself to ask. She said only, 'Why do you lie to your friend about all these so-called revolutionary activities?'

'Because he is unable to live them himself,' Sergei said. 'He wanted to be a revolutionary and now he never will be. I am living life for him. That's what poets do!'

Anna gave birth to a son. They christened him Yuri. It seemed like a new start, a chance to move on from the misunderstandings of the past.

Sergei took Yuri with him to poetry recitals and editorial meetings, boasting to all who would listen about the glittering future that lay in store for his beautiful boy. His delight in fatherhood cheered Anna.

'It makes me happy to see the two of you,' she said. 'I doubted you, Seryozha, but now I know your love for me is real. We can look ahead to wonderful times.'

Anna was already planning the wallpaper they would have in the house they would buy in the country.

Evenings were unpredictable. The baby meant fewer visitors. Most nights they ate dinner and spoke of trivial matters. Conversation was polite.

But there were other nights, when wine and nursed grievances ballooned into acrimony.

In the summer, the assassination of an Austrian archduke in Sarajevo sent a tremor through Russian society. The Austrians wanted revenge and their target was Russia's ally, Serbia.

'In my opinion, it's an opportunity,' Anna said. 'The tsar's already talking about going to war if the Serbs are attacked. He'll need the support of the people for that. So now's the moment for the people to demand reforms.'

Sergei disagreed. 'Russia is in peril. Internal divisions are the last thing we need. National unity is crucial at a time like this.'

'So, you've become a monarchist all of a sudden?' Anna's tone was sharp. 'And just a few weeks ago, you were telling Grisha how you were rallying to the cause of revolution—'

Sergei stood up and pushed his plate away. He made to leave the table, but Anna wouldn't let him.

'What's the matter, Seryozha? Can't I have opinions of my own?'

'Of course you can. That's not—'

'So, what are you angry about? Doesn't our family, our baby, give you joy?'

'Yes, of course it does—'

'Is life with me so terrible? Am I not enough to make you happy?'

'Anna ...' Sergei hesitated. 'Can you be content with this?' He gestured to the narrow room with its rented furniture and smoke-blackened ceiling. 'Don't you understand, I need more.'

'Well, start paying for it then!' Anna's bitterness spilled over. 'How do you think we've been living for the past year? Your poetry doesn't earn a penny! It's my father's money we've been living on. Why should he pay for someone who treats his daughter so badly!'

They didn't speak for a week. Sergei felt insulted, but the wound was deeper because the words contained the truth. He knew how worthless he was.

At the end of July, hostilities broke out between Austria and Serbia. Nicholas II ordered the mobilisation of the armed forces and twenty-four hours later Russia was at war.

Sergei was sleeping in the Milky Way. He had slammed the door on Anna and he wasn't going back.

Volodya, a devoted father, asked him how he could walk out on his marriage and his child.

'I'm eighteen,' Sergei said. 'There are things I need to do with my life.'

There were other, unspoken reasons that he hid from himself. It was easier to talk about poetry. Volodya was working on a patriotic drama, invoking the heroes of Russia's past to stiffen her present resolve.

'Why do you keep writing about nature?' he asked Sergei. 'At a time like this, with the world on the brink of catastrophe? Even the Symbolists, Blok and Bely and the others, are writing about Russia.'

'Another friend used to ask me why I don't write about love and emotions,' Sergei said. 'I told him that I write what I know and what I think I understand. Maybe when I've created my own life, then I shall turn it into poetry . . .'

Some of the boys were talking about joining up. Volodya spoke of Russia's historic mission to protect civilisation and the threats she had seen off in the past – the Polovtsians, the Mongols, the Ottomans, the Teutonic Knights, Napoleon's invading armies.

'It's all right for you,' Sergei said. 'You know what you believe and what you want. Your life is destined to run easy.'

The Milky Way held a poetry evening in aid of the war effort. Russia's need had revived national pride, patriotism quieted the demands for revolution. Volodya read from the twelfth-century 'Song of Igor', a rousing call to defend the motherland.

Then Prince Igor gazed upon the sun and said, 'Brothers! Better would it be to be slain than be a slave! Let us mount our swift horses, that we may look upon the blue waters of the Don. I want to break a lance at the limit of the Polovtsian steppe, with you, O Russians. I want to lay down my life, or else drink of the Don from my helmet!'

The audience applauded and Volodya's eyes shone. 'Igor's Song' was a reminder of the ruin that faces Russia when her sons do not unite.

Then Prince Igor steps into his golden stirrup ... but the wolves stir up a storm in the ravines; the foxes yelp at scarlet shields; the screeching of eagles summons the beasts to a feast of bones. O land of Russia, you are already beyond the hill! The black earth beneath the hooves is sown with bones and watered with blood: a harvest of sorrow has come upon the land!

The audience leapt to their feet. There were chants of *Rossiya! Rossiya!* and a hired band played Tchaikovsky's 'Slavic March'.

Volodya Bobrov volunteered that same evening.

He was part of the Russian army that entered East Prussia on 17 August. As Russian forces were routed at Tannenberg ten days later, a bullet entered his left eye and blew away the back of his skull.

Russian prisoners,
August 1914

War fervour had rallied support for the monarchy. But defeats at Tannenberg and then the Masurian Lakes spread apprehension. Autumn was a time of uncertainty.

The revolutionary movement split into those who agreed with the war and a hardcore who declared the enemy of their enemy to be their friend. A young agitator named Vladimir Lenin, in exile in Switzerland, believed collaboration with the Germans was a price worth paying if it helped remove the tsar.

Backing the status quo was no longer without risk, but Sergei did so. He knocked on Anna's door and told her he was leaving Moscow. He was going to St Petersburg, because that was where the best writers and critics were based, and where the royal family lived.

'I can't be satisfied with poems in obscure Moscow journals. Moscow is not the centre of the literary world; it takes everything ready-made from Petersburg. If I am to be successful, I need to be there.'

He would conquer the literary salons, win over the critics

and enchant the aristocracy. He would become the most celebrated poet of the age.

Anna looked at him. 'Really? Is that how poets conduct themselves?'

'Poets write stories,' he said. 'Then hope that people believe them.'

Grisha wrote again.

When you married Anna, I asked if you were sure this was what you wanted. Now I ask if you understand what you are doing leaving her.

You told me long ago how you suffered when your parents abandoned you, how it robbed you of your life. Do you want to do the same to Yuri?

Are you scared of happiness, Seryozha? You could have it with your wife and child. Long ago, you could have had it with me. Why do you reject those who care for you?

I have little time left. I would love to see you. But I know you are far away and you have your own troubles.

CHAPTER 4

He arrived in St Petersburg with a single suitcase, full of poems.

Yesenin had composed the sentence on the train, the opening line of the biography he imagined appearing in his old age.

He had nowhere to go and nowhere to stay. He knew no one. He had staked everything on his talent.

It was almost true.

He had presaged his arrival with a letter to the nation's greatest living poet, Alexander Blok. Blok had replied with a patrician diffidence that others might have taken as a rebuff. Sergei, who needed the world to acknowledge him, took it as an invitation.

He hauled his suitcase along Nevsky Prospect, past the Yusupov Palace and the Haymarket, down to Blok's apartment on Ofitserskaya. From the window of the great man's study, he watched the barges on the Pryazhka. He struggled to breathe, clenching his fists until his nails drew blood from his palms.

'The master will return shortly,' the servant had said. It was an hour before he came.

'Yesenin? I received your poems. Peasant verse. Talented. You and I have little in common.'

'But, master . . .'

Sergei's deference softened Blok.

'Your way will be hard. All of us must answer sooner or later for our actions and in Russia today, literature is the harshest path. It is hard to tread so that the wind does not sweep you away or the swamp suck you under.'

Sergei proffered an anthology of Blok's work and the poet graciously signed it.

'On reflection, you might go to see Gorodetsky. I shall write you a note.'

Sergei Mitrofanovich Gorodetsky, poet, recognised the handwriting.

> Dear Gorodetsky, I am sending you Sergei Yesenin. I attach
> six of his poems. You will understand him better than I.
> Do all you can to help. Blok.

Gorodetsky invited him in. Compared to Blok's, the apartment was shabby. A living room, a bedroom and a study, in which for the next three months Sergei would sleep on a couch whose wayward springs made him toss and turn.

Gorodetsky had standing. Not of the first rank, but a competent lyricist and willing to help a younger colleague. He took Sergei to the Stray Dog.

In the basement of the Dashkov mansion on Mikhailovsky Square, the Dog was the *haut lieu* of Russian poetry. The greatest names gathered at its smoke-filled bar to hear the satirical cabaret and recite their poems with the ink still damp. Akhmatova, Mandelstam, Tsvetaeva, Gumilev and Blok himself. Poetry, power and celebrity ricocheted from its walls like the wild electrons recently netted by the scientists of the Petersburg Polytechnic.

It was a Futurist evening. Velimir Khlebnikov declaimed his 'Incantation by Laughter'; Kruchenykh chanted verses from his 'Victory over the Sun'. Then Vladimir Mayakovsky rose, head shaven, hands thrust into his pockets. With eyes cast down, in a voice gripped by emotion, he recited three poems excoriating the war, 'Mama and the Evening the Germans Killed', 'Napoleon and Me', 'War Is Declared'.

There was silence, followed by quiet approbation. The months of hostilities, with hospital trains ferrying back the dead and wounded had changed public attitudes. People were tired of it, but hesitant to speak out.

Vladimir Mayakovsky

Sergei climbed on to the stage. Something about him – the fire in his eyes, the beauty of his face – stilled the room. He took a breath and began.

I have tired of my native land, of her
Endless fields and buckwheat fragrant.
I shall leave my home forever,
To live a thief and vagrant.
I'll walk the silver curls of life,
Seek out the humblest dwelling.

My dearest friend will turn his knife
On me, the reason not for telling.
My winding yellow path will measure
The sunlit fields of flowers;
The girl whose name I treasure
Will chase me from her bower.
And when I come back home to live
And see the others smiling,
I'll hang myself with my jacket's sleeve,
On an evening greened in gloaming.
The willows by the fence will bend;
The dogs will bark. Unwashed,
I shall be buried by my friends
In a shroud of unbleached canvas.
And the moon will float up in the sky,
And drop her oars down in the water.
And as ever, Russia will get by
And dance and weep in every quarter.

He woke in the morning with the memory of applause. The audience had responded to his peasant rhymes and folk rhythms. They liked his enthusiasm and loved his golden curls. The management had invited him back.

Yesenin and Gorodetsky, 1915

When he returned to the Stray Dog, the doors were locked. A notice explained that the establishment had been 'closed by order of the competent authorities'. Tsarist agents had reported the anti-war sentiments aroused by Mayakovsky's poems and the Petersburg governor had decreed that subversion must be repressed.

A vision had dissolved in a change of light; Sergei was an addict deprived of his drug. Gorodetsky tried to put things in perspective, but Sergei wouldn't listen.

'You don't understand,' he said. 'For you, poetry's a job. For me, it's everything. My parents, my wife and child, my friends – I've sacrificed them all. The other night seemed like the start ... but it's gone!'

A letter reached him via Moscow.

Esteemed Sergei Alexandrovich,
    My son died yesterday. He suffered much, but his end, when it came, was peaceful. Grisha fell asleep and his soul passed into eternity.

He spoke of you every day. He said how sad he was that his Seryozha was not with him. He would read your letters many times over. He had your portrait on his wall.

Sergei Alexandrovich, my son died a martyr. His illness had so diminished him that only skin and bones remained. His mother and I are so afflicted by sadness that we cannot speak. We cannot live.

Your letters are safe. I have collected them in a file and sealed it with wax. His diary lies locked in a casket, in memory of our darling boy.

Dearest Sergei, the loss of our child is unbearable for us. Our souls are burdened with sorrow.

Andrei M. Panfilov

The move to Petersburg, the false hopes of the Stray Dog, the strain of living among strangers, and now the loss of his friend. It was a blow too far. Gorodetsky found him weeping. Sergei showed him the letter.

'Grisha Panfilov was the person I loved most in the world. I knew he was dying but I didn't go to him. How could I have let him die alone!'

Gorodetsky offered comfort, but Sergei didn't want it.

'There is no excuse. I told myself I was busy, but I could have made the time. There's something wrong with me. I'm cruel; I hurt the people who love me . . .'

That night, on the cusp of sleep, he glimpsed his reflection in the mirror on the study wall. It was black and deformed: he saw himself. His diary entries charted his self-loathing.

I can't imagine what's the matter with me. If things continue in this fashion, I will kill myself. I'll hurl myself from the window.

I'm a real bastard. I'm covered in lies and deceit. I think I've buried my soul. Or, more like, sold it to the devil. And all for the sake of my talent.

I lust for fame and recognition ... more important than family, love, decency and truth itself.

Self-awareness and self-reproach were twin torturers. They would draw him to a relationship that would shape his future.

When Sergei wrote to Nikolai Klyuev, the older man knew who he was. His appearance at the Stray Dog had not gone unnoticed. People were speaking about the young poet with the radiant eyes.

> Highly esteemed Klyuev!
> I have read and admire your poetry and feel compelled to write to you. Like you, I am a peasant poet. I appeared recently at the Stray Dog, where my verse was highly appreciated. There are many things I would like to discuss.
> S.A. Yesenin
> PS You may write to me at Gorodetsky's.

Klyuev's reply was unctuous.

> Dearest Sergei,
> I was at the Stray Dog and was moved by your appearance! I loved the freshness of your poems – they struck me as the true voice of the countryside – and I admired the physical beauty of your person, which I regard as an earnest of the inner purity of your being.

Russian poetry has been swamped by artifice and
insincerity. Natural poets like you and me must take up
the cause of renewal and spontaneity. I am burning to
speak with you. Klyuev.

Sergei showed Klyuev's letter to his host. Gorodetsky read
it through.

'Nikolai Klyuev is powerful,' he said. 'And clever. Russia
has had enough of sophisticated poetry – all that mystical,
foreign-sounding Symbolism we've been fed on. Since the war
came, people have wanted something more down to earth,
more Russian. So Klyuev's been serving up his peasant verse –
"poetry of the people for the people", he says. And dried-out,
intellectual Petersburg has lapped it up. Klyuev is popular. The
critics, the public, the aristocracy love him.'

'But that's perfect,' Sergei said. 'I can do all those things!'

'Yes, I think you can.' Gorodetsky hesitated. 'The problem is
that Klyuev is . . . difficult. He has a gift for poetry, and also for
self-promotion. His poems are full of religion, but his personal
behaviour is scandalous. He writes of innocence and belief, but
he's a cynic. He's sincere and duplicitous, loving and scheming,
generous and predatory. People fall under his spell, and once
they're in his power he doesn't let go.'

Sergei laughed. 'Don't worry about me! I'm as tough as they
come. I grew up in the wilds. My grandfather used me as his
hunting dog. I can deal with Nikolai Klyuev.'

The war was a year old and Russia was suffering. The
Germans had used poison gas at the Battle of Bolimov, where
forty thousand Russians were killed or wounded. On the
streets of Russian cities, young men blinded and with lips

covered in froth began to appear alongside the limbless and the disfigured.

When the Germans broke through Russian lines in Galicia and advanced into Russian territory, the war menaced the home front. Thousands of square miles were lost; refugees fleeing the fighting poured into the cities. What had been a distant combat became immediate and threatening.

The tsar took personal control of the armed forces, but defeats continued. Nicholas seemed strangely detached. Writing from the front, his letters to Alexandra were filled with news of social occasions, games of dominoes and queries about the children's health.

Young Russians, who had rushed to enlist in 1914, were now refusing to serve. There were conscription riots and prominent figures, including Vladimir Mayakovsky, tore up their draft papers.

Sergei received his and hesitated. He wasn't against the war; but there were other considerations. He was a poet. Dying in the trenches would be absurd; but making a show of pacifism might harm his reputation. He found a helpful doctor who certified a problem with his eyesight.

The threat remained. The call-up demand would return if the situation worsened. Like many young Russians, Sergei spent the autumn of 1915 wondering how long he would be free.

He met Nikolai Klyuev in October, when the older poet returned from a summer composing exalted verse in a northern retreat.

'I am dying to see you,' Klyuev had written. 'If you are able to come, then come at once without even replying to this letter.'

He found Klyuev's apartment in the shadow of St Isaac's

Cathedral. Drawn blinds, dark wallpaper and thick Turkish carpets gave it the air of a shrine. The only light was from an iconostasis illuminated by candles that smelled of incense.

Nikolai Klyuev

Klyuev, stocky and balding, wore a peasant blouse with red-embroidered collar, wide blue trousers and knee-length boots. His greeting was effusive.

'Such meetings as ours are the miracles that make life worth living. It is a joy to know you, little brother. Your fame goes everywhere!'

Flattered, Sergei submitted to his embrace.

'You are too generous. I am a novice and you a master. I hope one day to emulate your success.'

Klyuev gazed at him.

'I have read enough of you to recognise your talent, but sometimes talent does not suffice. Everything is changing in Russia, Seryozha; everything is in turmoil. In such times, we must shout to make ourselves heard.'

Sergei nodded.

'Every day I go into the woods,' Klyuev said. 'I sit by a white-washed chapel amid age-old pines and feel myself an inch from the eternity of the Russian sky. When the azure-feathered dawn alights on my notebook and the hare nibbles the hay from the rick, I know the paradise of the spirit is in me. I am the vessel through which God will speak to His world.'

He paused.

'But a poet must convince his public that he is giving them what they desire. Even if that means debasing oneself before the unworthy. Do you understand, Seryozha? Do you know what I mean by debasing oneself . . . ?'

The balance between them had tilted. Sergei had come as a supplicant, but now the master wanted something from him.

'Debasing oneself? I fear I don't understand.'

Klyuev's eyes were knowing and ashamed. Sergei smiled to prompt him, but he drew back.

'What I mean is that you may have been surprised by some of my actions. You may feel that my behaviour in public – I mean my recitals and so forth – does not always correspond to the seriousness of my work . . .'

Sergei laughed. The moment had passed.

'You mean the peasant act? The clothes and the country accent and all that palaver? To be honest, it does seem a little – extraordinary!'

Klyuev burst into laughter.

'Precisely! *You* can see through it, because you're from the country yourself. But the toffs and the intellectuals simply love it. They've been crying out for the authentic voice of the Russian people ever since Tolstoy told them the peasants are the fount of God's truth and wisdom. So I'm giving them what they want! They've no idea what I've invented to stoke their fantasies!'

Klyuev read the admiration on Sergei's face.

'It's astounding, Seryozha; I've never been so popular in my life. The critics praise me to the skies and I've got so many bookings for recitals that I can barely fit them all in.'

Sergei took his hand. 'But, that's what I want, Nikolai. That's what I want for myself.'

CHAPTER 5

Inflation was eating at the Russian economy. Prices rose daily. Family budgets that had kept people in comfort no longer made ends meet. When the rouble was taken off the gold standard, coins disappeared to be melted down. The war was dissolving the glue that held society together.

Publishing houses continued to function, but writers and poets struggled. Some of them wrote political poems, supporting or opposing the status quo. Sergei was reluctant. His time in Moscow and now in St Petersburg had exposed him to the ways of the city. Themes of alienation and loneliness had begun to appear in his verse, alongside memories of childhood and the village.

At Gorodetsky's suggestion, he carried a notebook to record his impressions as he walked the streets. Neither of them was writing commercial poetry, the sort of polemical verse that commanded fees from publishers with vested interests. Gorodetsky found satisfaction in the creative act, but Sergei wanted more.

'It's fine for you to say that beauty is its own reward. But what's the point of beauty if no one sees it? We'll be two more neglected poets who went to their graves without changing anything. At best, we'll be a footnote at the end of a book about some untalented charlatan who got himself noticed!'

When Gorodetsky asked what he intended to do about it, Sergei shrugged.

'Klyuev has invited me to recite with him.'

The audience at the Tenishevsky Theatre on Mokhovaya Street was an assortment of shabby students and smartly dressed couples, artists and shop-girls rubbing shoulders with aristocratic ladies attended by liveried servants. Nikolai Klyuev opened the evening.

> Love's beginning was in the summer,
> Its ending dusky fall.
> In a maiden's simple guise
> You approached me with a greeting.
> The woods, watchful, mute,
> Turn to the blue of smoke.
> Winter thaws, imperceptible
> Through the patterned lace.
> But the heart senses: mists,
> A vague movement of the forest,
> Irrevocable shades
> Of violet-tinted evenings.
> Oh, do not flee to the branches
> Like a trembling little bird!
> The years will fade into the
> Grey haze of time.

The familiar material with its vague, infectious yearning couched in the language of nature drew applause. After an hour, Klyuev ended with a new poem describing the journey of the human soul through the regions of the body. The audience seemed puzzled by the explicit physicality of it, the references to intestines, stomach, guts and the burning sexual organs. But it sounded as if it was imbued with the wisdom of the people, so they applauded anyway.

Klyuev held up his hand for silence. He waved to the wings. It was Sergei's twentieth birthday and he was going to make an impact. In a Russian blouse of pink silk, gathered by a tasselled golden belt over aquamarine pantaloons, he was exactly what the audience expected from a peasant poet. Rouged cheeks and darkly pencilled eyes gave his natural beauty the theatricality of outrageous artifice.

> She hobbled on a shattered foreleg,
> Then curled in pain outside her den.
> Thin stitches of blood
> Marked out her circles in the snow.
> The memory of the shot still
> Filled her ears with pulsing smoke.
> The forest swayed now in her eyes;
> The wind quickened, made her drunk.
> The mist was upon her, a black woodpecker,
> The evening sticky, wet and crimson.
> She raised her head in anxious query
> As her tongue went cold on the blazing wound.
> The vixen's yellow tail fell like fire in the storm;
> The taste of rotted carrots on her lips;
> The smell of hoar-frost and the fumes of
>   burning clay;
> The blood seeping slowly in her tight-shut eyes.

Sergei hardly slept that night. In the morning, he went to buy the papers but there were no reviews. Gorodetsky found him uncommunicative and tense. A week later, the *Monthly Journal* published an appreciation by the critic Boris Lazarevsky:

> I heard two poets last night – and what poets they were! Nikolai Klyuev is a genuine Russian bard ...

Sergei skipped several paragraphs.

> ... Klyuev's companion, Sergei Yesenin is a 20-year-old cherub, blond and curly, and he amazed me. His verse is as simple as air, as fragrant as grass, and as tender as the new moon. In a quarter of an hour, he taught me to respect the Russian people and above all to understand that which I had not understood before – the music of the people's language.

Sergei was gleeful. The glimpse of public recognition seemed a promise of vindication against those who had doubted him, a reassurance in the face of his own uncertainties.

'Russia is ready for me,' he told Gorodetsky. 'Ready for the new poetry I represent – I and Klyuev, of course. People are tired of poets plumbing the depths of the soul, ascending the Golgotha of mysticism. Russia yearns for the ice water of simplicity; the precise, concrete image; unmediated contact with the tangible, visible world. We must reject the mystical past and celebrate raw reality!'

The peasant boy who had come seeking shelter and advice was dispensing unshakeable prescriptions of wisdom. Gorodetsky praised him, but Sergei sensed hesitation.

'What? You don't think this is cause to celebrate?'

'No, of course it is—'

'So, what then?'

'I just wonder if there isn't something ... unreal about it. Poems about nature and animals are well and good, but what about your own emotions as a poet, as a man, living through the greatest changes in human history—'

'But there are emotions!' Sergei said. 'What do you think the vixen poem is? Or the bitch and her puppies? They *are* emotions – my emotions . . .'

Klyuev laughed when Sergei showed him the review.

'What did I tell you! They love our poetry. You and I must always appear together. I shall make sure your name is on the posters.'

With every recital, their audiences grew. Klyuev said the public wanted optimistic verses about the beauty of the land and the purity of the folk. He advised Sergei to omit the sorrow and regret, and concentrate instead on sweet memories of his village childhood.

Sergei did. His poetic landscape melted into an idealised Russia that had never existed. He used his art to rewrite his life, removing the pain and terror, omitting the anguish of his broken family in an idyllic love song to a happiness he'd never known.

Like Klyuev, he adopted a provincial accent that metropolitan commentators proclaimed the true voice of the Russian people. He would recite his poems then sing unaccompanied *chastushkas*, folk songs he had learned as a child. He danced the *trepak* and played the accordion. His outfits became more outrageous, his make-up thicker. The audience cheered when he stepped on stage and applauded after he left it.

Gorodetsky, who had been reporting on Sergei's progress in weekly letters to his own mentor, Alexander Blok, was dismayed.

Klyuev has dug his claws into Sergei. He has cast Yesenin as his young brother and seeks to dominate him. He has taken possession of the boy – I can find no other word for it. He fastens his belt for him, strokes his hair and follows him with his eyes.

Klyuev is charming in his insidious humility. He says he is a religious poet, but he believes less than an atheist. When he is accused of lying, he says 'deceit is the only weapon we peasants have against the intelligentsia'. He pretends to be illiterate, but it's all an act. He lives in luxury and reads Heine in the original. Why does Sergei prostitute himself? Why does he do what Klyuev tells him?

After a recital at which they had worked the audience into a frenzy, the two poets had been forced to flee from crowds of admirers. They ran through the blacked-out streets, roaring with laughter, yelling verses at the top of their voices. Klyuev took Sergei's hand. When they found themselves at Klyuev's apartment, Klyuev invited him in.

'Time for champagne!' he said. 'How I love to tug at your curly hair, Seryozha! I won't tell you what you are for me, because you know it yourself, my dear beloved one.'

They drank and talked, drunk on success.

'Nikolai . . . Kolya . . . ?' Sergei said.

'Yes, dear one . . .'

'You do admire my poetry, don't you?'

'Of course I do—'

'And you're not . . . ashamed of me?'

'How could I be ashamed of such a—'

'Then tell me – why don't you take me with you when you recite to the toffs?'

'To the toffs?'

'Yes. I know you go to their salons. You get invited into high society . . . to the lords and ladies.'

Klyuev thought for a moment.

'Well, Seryozha. Not everyone is granted access to the world of the aristocracy.'

'But *you* are! And that's what I want, too. I want to impress the people who matter.'

Sergei had drunk too much.

'Seryozha, let's not argue,' Klyuev soothed. 'We're tired, and it's too late for you to go back to Gorodetsky's. I'll make up a bed for you in the lounge.'

'But if you want to stay my friend,' Sergei said, 'you'd better think bloody carefully about what I'm saying.'

Klyuev smiled and turned out the light. At three in the morning, Sergei felt a hand caress his cheek.

'Seryozha, dearest heart. Come and sleep with me in the big bed,' Klyuev said. 'We'll be snug in there. And if you let me hold you, I'll take you with me to the toffs.'

Sergei Yesenin was a sensation in Petersburg's salons. The city had renamed itself Petrograd in a spit of anti-German pique but the literary passions of Catherine, the great Prussian tsaritsa, lived on. Aristocratic ladies paraded fashionable writers and poets at *après-midis* and soirées, hosting gatherings in gilded drawing rooms, with canapés and tête-a-têtes sometimes *très intimes*. Those who pleased the arbiters of high society were invited back, fêted and rewarded, taken on trips to stately homes and stylish resorts. It was an enchanted circle, at odds with the reality of the war-blighted city.

Sergei's first appearance had been nerve-racking. In the salon of Countess Zubova, he had stood clenching and unclenching his fists, waiting his turn to perform. Klyuev, there to introduce him, stroked his hair and squeezed his waist.

Leaning on the marble fireplace, he began without waiting for silence. Muscular, incantatory rhythms, rising and falling with the drama of the verse, verging on the histrionic, always hypnotic, hushed the hubbub. Men put down their drinks; ladies eyed him through their lorgnettes.

His poems drew applause and smiles. But he wondered if they were smirks.

'I have one more thing,' Sergei said. 'Something I am working on at the moment. It's in prose. I'm not sure how the story will end.'

He looked at Countess Zubova.

'May I read it, your highness?'

The countess nodded. The boy was beautiful.

'It's called "By the White Water" and it's set in the countryside where I come from. The characters are peasants, true Russian folk. I want to show that they have emotions and dreams and desires as vivid and as moving as any of us – any of you – here today.'

The room was listening.

'Perhaps it was the intense heat or the water lapping on the shore. Pelagia could think only of her absent husband, of lying naked with him in the hayloft, of the memories that excited her.

Her blood stirred. Her lips were red and moist. Her breasts swelled. When she stroked them, carefully, gently with her open palms, she felt her legs tremble and her cheeks begin to burn.

She pictured her husband's powerful chest, his strong arms and soft lips; she felt the warmth of his breath and the press of his mouth on hers. Her body arched with desire. She knew it was a sin.

"The satanic one!" She crossed herself. She plunged into the water to drown her longing, lit an icon candle with her wet hands and fell to her knees. She prayed. But at night, naked beneath the sheet, the heat ran through her body and her thighs pounded.

She walked to the chapel to pray for salvation. On the way home, the heat made her take off her shoes. Walking barefoot in the long grass she felt dewdrops sparkle on her calves.

A young man caught up with her and spoke rudely, insinuatingly. Her eyes measured his muscular body.

"Do you think I am afraid of you?" she said; and as she spoke, her breasts filled and her eyes grew dim. Her resolutions from the church were forgotten.

When the man took her hand, she didn't pull away. She pressed herself against him, leaned her head on his shoulder and walked with him. Her blouse came open and her scarf fell to the floor.

"Must be bad without a husband," the man said. "Maybe I'll come and see you."

"Come!" she said.

The sun was setting, casting long shadows from the bushes. The heat was intense and filled with the fragrance of buckwheat. Pelagia dropped to her knees.

The earth was pulling her down. The man was upon her, clutching her by the neck. She felt no fear, no regret at what was happening. She lay on the grass and closed her eyes. His blazing cheeks were caressing her breast, his tobacco-scented lips and his rough hands.

"Don't!" she said, struggling to lift herself. "Don't!"

She hit him hard in the face and ran. Hiding in the wheat, flat to the ground, she held her breath, fearful her breathing would betray her. The day died and the moon rose with white horns in the sky.

When she reached home, the night was blue and dark. She opened the door and the man was there. He seized her arms.

"What are you up to?" he said. "First you tease and then you scream. This time I won't let you go. Scream or don't scream, I'm going to have you!"

The weight that had oppressed her lifted from her heart. Her body flooded with warmth. She realised it wasn't him she was running away from; it wasn't from him that she hid in the wheat field.

She pushed his hands off her arms and lay on the floor. He buried his face between her knees. She bit hard into her lip and a stream of blood ran down her chin.'

Sergei looked up. Ladies were fanning themselves with black lace *éventails*.

'I said I don't know how the story will end, but I have a draft that I've been working on since I met my friend, Nikolai.' He gestured to Klyuev, who smiled and bowed. 'Would you like me to try it on you?'

There was a murmur of assent.

'When Pelagia's husband returned from his year away, she hardly recognised him. He was a skeleton. His chest was sunken, his shoulders fallen, his face gaunt.

She asked him what the matter was, and he answered with a bitter smile.

"I got ill. I went downhill. Who can tell?"

There was sadness in his voice. He lay on the bed and closed his eyes. Pelagia lay down next to him, her heart racing. She knew it was wrong of her, but she pressed herself against him; she couldn't stop herself.

Her husband lifted his head. "I can't, Pelagia. The illness. I don't have it in me any more."

He looked longingly at her full breasts and soft cheeks, stroked her hair and touched her bare neck.

In the spring they took on a helper, Yushka, the son of the village policeman, who came to live with them. Sometimes, when Pelagia was sitting at her husband's bedside Yushka would brush against her shoulder as if by accident.

One night she crawled into the bed where he was sleeping. Yushka looked surprised, but then understood. He wrapped himself around her and didn't let go. She burned and trembled with a powerful fever.

In the morning, when she was lighting the icon lamp, she thought, "There is emptiness in my soul," and the lamp fell from her hands.

On the porch, she burst into tears. The dog came to comfort her, but sensing the depth of her mistress's sorrow, she cried too and their keening rose in a bitter howl of grief.'

Gorodetsky wrote to Blok.

Yesenin has decamped. He packed his suitcase this morning and has moved in with Klyuev. When I asked why he was going, he said it was because it is a bigger apartment with proper heating and electricity.

It is certainly true that Klyuev lives well. The man pretends to be an itinerant monk, but he lives like a prince. He has introduced Sergei to the nobility. He parades him in salons and drawing rooms, where he's fawned over by society ladies and by gentlemen of an aesthetic bent.

Sergei has become the *haut monde*'s darling. People have been waiting for a genuine poet of the village, and this one has brought his verse wrapped in a rustic kerchief. He offers the idealised village that our soul-sore society has been thirsting for – a prelapsarian idyll to restore our faith in mankind. The result has been a joyous festival of mutual admiration.

But Sergei is smart. I think he's using his peasant guile to outwit the townies, to offer the intellectuals what they want to hear and seduce the countesses. Blue eyes, curls and a shy smile can go a long way.

Before Sergei left, Gorodetsky had given him a note of recommendation to the publisher M.V. Averyanov, and Sergei went to see him as 1915 drew to a close.

Delighted by the prospect of publishing the new young poet that everyone was talking about, Averyanov told him to select thirty or forty poems that could be made into a debut collection.

When Averyanov asked if he had a title in mind, Sergei said, '*Radunitsa*, the day of all souls. Because it will remind me to pray for mine.'

CHAPTER 6

The war had divided the arts in Russia. Popular culture rallied to the tsarist banner with songs, paintings and plays glorifying the national struggle. Caricatures of Kaiser Wilhelm appeared. Postcards, lithographs, children's comics and films showed the enemy as beer-swilling murderers.

The avant-garde, already at odds over the legitimacy of tsarist autocracy, was less certain. Some artists and writers refused to renounce the revolutionary cause. The vast majority simply ignored the conflict. Theatres served up escapist fare, farces and light operettas, or – at the other extreme – plays about death and decay. After an initial enthusiasm for Glinka's patriotic 'Life for the Tsar', opera houses decided it was enough simply to play the national anthem and avoid German composers.

The closure of the Stray Dog had left Petersburg's poets homeless. A new venue appeared in early 1916, in the shape of the Actors' Camp, another basement cabaret, this time on the Champs de Mars between the Moika and the Neva. More spacious than the Dog, it had two high-vaulted rooms painted with figures from the commedia dell'arte and a proscenium stage, on which the director Vsevolod Meyerhold had been engaged to mount a series of deliberately provocative plays.

Mikhail Kuzmin's *Two Swains and a Nymph*, an imbroglio of same-sex lovers disquieted by an undertow of heterosexual desire, topped the bill. The confusion of war had weakened the grip of the tsar's censors, but the management were nervous. They asked the author for cuts, but Kuzmin refused.

Kuzmin's former lover, Nikolai Klyuev, bolstered his resolve. Since they had parted, almost a decade earlier, they had maintained a regular exchange of caustic commentaries on literature and sex.

'I say you should stay firm, dear heart,' Klyuev said. 'Meyerhold will stand by you. Remember how brave he was when we insisted on a female Dorian in his film of dear Oscar's comedy?'

'I dare say,' Kuzmin replied. 'And if the play is a disaster, I shall just go back to writing poetry. I see you have been keeping busy, yourself – quite the celebrity nowadays . . . you and your little peasant boy.'

Klyuev laughed.

'He's so sweet. And so naïve! I told you about my charade of not inviting him to the *haut monde*? He got so annoyed and stamped his little feet. So of course, when I said he could come after all, he was ready to do anything I asked of him – and I mean *anything*, my dear!'

'And what did you do in return?'

'I took him to all the salons – Countess Zubova, Ignatieva, Kleinmikhel, Bukharova, Gippius and Merezhkovsky. It was a hoot. One lady told me she was surprised our little peasant was so clean. She'd been expecting a dirty-faced yokel with shit on his boots. Another said how nice it was that he knows how to use a fork and spoon! But he has this unwavering faith in his own genius. He uses incomprehensible dialect words that intrigue his audience. When the ladies ask him to explain, you can see the mischievous cunning in his eyes. I'd say there's a lot of calculation in young Sergei. Behind that guileless face, there's a determined, practical mind. At times, I think he despises us all!'

'We are fools for beauty,' Kuzmin said. 'A comely face, shapely thighs and a cute smile – we are dough to be kneaded in their hands. And if they hate us, it makes it even more piquant to keep them bound to us despite themselves!'

'I am a little concerned about that,' Klyuev said. 'Sergei has written something that troubles me. It's a heterosexual romance, "By the White Water", and it describes sexual desire from the point of view of a woman attracted to men. What do you think that can mean?'

'Heaven knows!' Kuzmin said. 'But why worry? Beautiful boy, beautiful prose. What more could one wish for?'

'For clarity!' Klyuev said. 'I just want to know – is he a self-loathing homo who hates himself for letting himself be seduced? . . . Or some calculating hetero ready to do whatever it takes to further his career?'

Photo dedicated by Sergei Yesenin to Nikolai Klyuev,
'I shall carry your love with me forever', 1916

The war clouded people's minds. The spectacle of proximate death led them to ask unfamiliar questions and seek answers in unfamiliar places.

Booksellers struggled to sell their usual wares – editions of the classics lingered on the shelves – but a new genre of sensationalist, often violent pornography found buyers in all sections of the population, including the most respectable.

The nationwide bestseller was Mikhail Artsybashev's novel, *Sanin*, with its advocacy of unbridled sensual gratification in the face of nihilistic despair. Newspapers were swamped with small ads for obliquely described sexual services and for their corollary, a rash of patent medicines for gonorrhoea and syphilis.

Russians were nervous, unsure, vulnerable. The search for meaning took people beyond the traditional Church to séances, table-tapping and theosophy. Extreme religious sects overlaid pagan sensuality with the trappings of Christianity and prophecies of the apocalypse.

Several peasant communities, convinced that the Antichrist was loose in the world, elected to cheat the devil through acts of collective suicide. Others flocked to visionaries who promised salvation through mortification. The Skoptsy sect declared that the way to avoid sin, and hence eternal damnation, was self-mutilation, specifically castration, sometimes forcibly administered.

The Khlysty – named from the Russian word for *whip* – offered a road to redemption that combined flagellation with sexual licence, denial with ecstasy. Their worship took the form of hypnotic, circular dances with participants turning faster and faster until a state of frenzy was reached and the Holy Spirit entered their hearts. Thus cleansed, they were ready to perform the 'holy sin', a collective orgy of copulation.

The Khlysty elders were the living God, whose behaviour, however extreme, was beyond sin. An elder could work miracles and foresee the future, attracting disciples by his secret, holy power. Followers obeyed his will without question. When he demanded sexual favours they were granted, for these were 'the love of Christ', 'the sins that drive out sin'.

By the spring of 1916, Petersburg smelled of fear and decay. Religious depravity that had begun in the countryside had spread to the city. The Khlysty were finding converts in the capital.

Anna wrote from Moscow. Life was hard without her husband. Sytin's publishing business had been affected by the war and she was able to work only part-time.

She included a photograph of their son. Yuri was eighteen months old now, very independent and already able to write five letters with chalk on his slate. His talking was delightful; his favourite word was Daddy.

Sergei gazed at the curly hair and the bright, wide eyes that were unmistakably his own. He rummaged in his suitcase for a photograph of Anna.

The joy they had known suddenly outweighed the bitterness.

When Sergei told Klyuev that he was thinking of going to Moscow to visit his wife there was silence. Over dinner, Klyuev returned to the subject.

'Seryozha, my white dove, there are dangerous temptations for people such as you and me. You and I are goats in the world's orchard. We are tolerated there only by grace. There are many venomous, thorny plants in this orchard, which you and I must avoid for the health of both our body and our spirit.'

'Maybe,' Sergei said. 'But Anna is my wife and I want to see her.'

Sergei was about to leave the table when Klyuev rose abruptly and threw himself to the floor.

'You're not going!' His voice ascended to a scream. 'You're not going! Not going! Not going!'

He was writhing on the ground, arms and legs flailing. Sergei tried to step over him, but Klyuev grabbed his ankle.

'Don't go, Seryozha! Don't go!'

The telegram arrived two days later. Sergei Alexandrovich Yesenin was being summoned for a further interview and physical examination to determine his suitability for military service.

It seemed improbable that the call-up could be avoided a second time. The doctor who had certified Sergei's weak eyesight had been struck off for illegal practices.

When Sergei showed him the summons, Klyuev frowned then tried to make light of it, reciting the terms of the military oath with mockery in his voice:

'I do solemnly swear that I shall give loyal and faithful service, not sparing even mine own life, to the very final drop of mine own blood, sacrificing all in the cause of His Imperial Majesty, even though I shall suffer and perish—'

Sergei told him to stop; it wasn't funny. Klyuev said there might be a way out.

'There is something I could try. You may have to do some things that seem strange to you, but you know I always have your interests at heart. You trust me, don't you?'

Sergei nodded.

If he was going to see Anna, it would have to be soon. His military examination board was scheduled for the following week.

Klyuev was writing letters and attending appointments; he wouldn't explain what he was doing, but his attempts to keep Sergei safe appeared genuine. When he asked if he could come with him to Moscow, Sergei couldn't refuse.

They took the overnight express, sharing a sleeping compartment with two grain merchants who drank vodka and played cards until the early hours then kept them awake with their snoring.

Anna's letter had led Sergei to picture her exhausted and careworn, but she was splendid. Her face had the freshness and candour that had attracted him to her at their first meeting. Sergei took her in his arms and kissed her.

The apartment that he remembered as cramped and dirty struck him now as cosy and agreeable. When he asked to see his son, Anna laughed.

'Well, he's here somewhere,' she said, pointing to the bookshelf in the corner and raising a finger to her lips. 'But I certainly don't know where he is. I wonder if his daddy might be able to find him ...'

Sergei took up the challenge, rustling curtains, looking behind chairs, loudly declaring his perplexity. When eventually he peered behind the bookshelf, Yuri shrieked with excitement then covered his eyes. Anna had told him Daddy was coming, but this wasn't how Daddy should look.

Sergei set about winning the boy's confidence with a childlike enthusiasm of his own, singing songs, making faces, dancing little jigs until he had coaxed his son out of his reticence. When Yuri stretched out his arms in a gesture of trust, Sergei felt a surge of love.

Anna and Klyuev had greeted each other warily. When they sat down to lunch, Klyuev insisted on serving.

In the afternoon, Klyuev said he had to go out; there were old Moscow friends he hadn't seen for years.

Alone with Anna, Sergei enjoyed a freedom he hadn't known since he left for Petersburg. He told her about his literary successes, his triumphant recitals, the promised publication of his first book of poems. She was happy for him. She missed him, she said, but she understood that he needed time to establish himself. If he wanted to come back, she would welcome him with sincerity in her heart.

Yuri Yesenin, Sergei's son

In the evening, Klyuev began to make the sleeping arrangements. He was perfectly happy to sleep on the floor of the living room – he was an old peasant, he said, with no need for luxury – and in that way Sergei could have the spare room to himself.

'Nonsense,' Sergei said to Klyuev. 'You take the spare room. I'll be sleeping with my wife.'

They heard Klyuev prowling the house after they had gone to bed. When Anna asked what the matter was, Sergei took her hand. Her arm felt warm against his. He moved his leg towards hers and brushed against her flesh.

They made love for the first time in a year. In the morning, Sergei thought how foolish he had been to give all this up, to renounce such affection for the pursuit of fame.

Klyuev was already awake, rattling dishes, setting the table for breakfast. As soon as Sergei appeared, he said, 'We should go back. I need to see someone who has promised to help keep you out of the army. Shall we get the afternoon train?'

'I think we should stay another day,' Sergei said. 'The poets I worked with – the Milky Way – have a recital tonight and I think you and I would do well to appear at it.'

For Klyuev, the prospect of a Moscow recital was tempting; the city's reading public was a big target.

'All right,' he said. 'I will organise things.'

By lunchtime, Klyuev had been to the market and returned with a bundle of swatches from the cloth merchants. He laid them on the floor. He told Anna how to cut the cloth, how to embroider the decorations and how to fit the blouse and pants. She did as she was told with good grace.

The recital was well attended, but the audience seemed nonplussed by the two visiting peasants, their garish costumes and village poetry. There was none of the rapturous applause they had grown used to in Petersburg. They returned to the apartment subdued and gloomy.

Sergei found the failure hard to deal with. Perhaps he was wrong to define his life by his work, to pin validation to the vagaries of acclaim. He fell asleep wondering if he might stay with his wife.

At 5 a.m., Yuri woke him with his crying. He told Anna to quieten the child, but she said they must leave him so he would learn to sleep through to morning.

At breakfast, Sergei was irritable. The bread was stale; the butter tasted sour.

When Klyuev said they must return to St Petersburg, Sergei shrugged and told Anna they had to leave.

The salon was unlike others he'd attended and Sergei was puzzled. Klyuev had said he would not be expected to recite. There was the usual gaggle of Petersburg ladies milling in the drawing room, but from what he could hear of their conversation it was not literature that had brought them here.

Half an hour went by.

Two servants opened a double door. From the far end of a corridor palely lit by gaslight, a figure approached. The women froze as he made the sign of the cross.

'Bless you, my sisters.'

The man was tall, bearded, with long, dark hair that looked unwashed; wearing the sandals and coarse brown robes of a monk.

'Salvation is in God,' Rasputin said. 'But you, my sisters, you do not see God. The mansions you live in, your affairs, your thoughts, your friends – all hide God from you.'

There was silence. The speaker's eyes, deep set and cowled, glowed with otherworldly intensity.

'What then must you do to see God? You must go from here into the fields. Leave the city behind you and walk until there is only open horizon ahead. Then stop and think about yourselves. Think how insignificant you are.'

He paused.

'Think how helpless you are. What then of your pride, your power, your riches and position? You are pitiful. You are unwanted. You are nothing.'

Sergei heard a sob from the back of the room.

'You must look up and seek for God with all your heart.'

Rasputin's voice was hypnotic.

'The Lord God is your only father. To the Lord God alone does your soul belong. To Him alone must you surrender it. He alone will support and help you. You must give yourself up to the joy that is the first step to knowing God.'

A woman's voice murmured, 'I shall!'

'The kingdom of heaven is within you. You must cherish it like the pupils of your eyes.'

Rasputin's homily was reaching its climax.

'Therefore shall you come unto me. Each of you here shall come to me. For I shall lead you into the fields of God!'

There was a sound like the fluttering of small birds on whom a hawk has descended. The room shrilled with cries of assent; women raised their hands and bowed their heads.

When Sergei glanced at Rasputin, he thought he caught a conspiratorial wink.

Sergei asked Klyuev what the point had been.

'Rasputin barely looked in my direction. As soon as he finished his sermon, he took three of the women and disappeared into the other room. What was the benefit of me being there?'

'Don't underestimate Our Friend,' Klyuev said. 'Rasputin has the gift of sight. His eyes penetrate the soul. He sees through pretence.'

'Then he certainly sees through his own pretence,' Sergei muttered. 'He is the most transparent charlatan—'

'Be quiet!' Klyuev said. 'It took me a lot to have you admitted.

He is a *starets,* an elder of the Khlysty. I have been a Khlyst for many years and I have never met a more powerful leader, or one with more influence over the temporal authorities of this country. Rasputin will judge you. And if he finds you worthy, he will summon you again.'

CHAPTER 7

A series of German advances had disrupted the railways. Food supplies to Petrograd and Moscow were severely reduced. The government commissioned the secret police, the Okhrana, to report on public morale.

Growing disorganisation threatens to tip the country into anarchy. In many regions, law and order has collapsed. There is pillaging and swindling by shady operators in all branches of commerce and industry. State and local representatives issue mutually contradictory orders. The result is an inequitable distribution of food products and essential goods, an alarming rise in prices and a diminution in food production. While wages have risen by 50 per cent, prices have increased by between 100 and 500 per cent. The economic condition of the masses is deplorable.

The crisis is producing a troubled mood among the people. An exceptional intensification of animosity has been noted among the most diverse sections of the population. Complaints about the administration and condemnation of government policy are on the rise. The spirit of opposition has reached levels higher even than in 1905–6.

Sergei had sensed Klyuev's unhappiness about his 'White Water' story. He didn't explain and didn't apologise, but he did refrain from attempting to publish it. When the subject arose, Klyuev made out that his concern was for Sergei's reputation, that a poet should stick to poetry and avoid writing prose.

Sergei disagreed. The form of the story was highly poetic, he said, a sort of 'poetry in prose', polished as painstakingly as any verse. Sergei read him another one, a story titled 'Absence'.

'I spent the final years of the century just ended in the provincial town of N—. An affair of the heart had persuaded me to leave Moscow, a matter that had caused me much pain. Giving up my old life, abandoning my practice as a commercial artist and retreating from the world seemed the only way to retain my sanity.

N— was not beautiful; it may have been the plainness of the place that convinced me to settle there. I was not looking for beauty or consolation, but rather to bury myself in the provinces and forget the past. The apartment I found on the outskirts was small and dark, but it mattered little. I spent the days drinking coffee and the nights vodka.

My contact with the townsfolk was negligible. It would have remained so, had my funds not begun to run low. Obliged to find employment in order to feed myself, I placed an advertisement seeking work as a decorator and was engaged by a handful of local families.

I did the work and was generally paid on time. I avoided detailed conversations. When they asked about my past, I gave non-committal answers; I said nothing about my former career or my life in Moscow. Only when my employers requested the most tasteless, most offensive colour schemes did I fail to hold my tongue.

I found myself offering advice, suggesting alternatives to the dreadful, fashionable melanges of purples and bottle green they all seemed to love, nudging them in the direction of something less vulgar. I counselled against the drab flock papers that the bourgeois plaster on their walls. I proffered sketches of fresher, less predictable décors and blended commercially available paints into aesthetically pleasing shades.

It was a slow process, but one or two families accepted my prescriptions and word began to spread that olive was not the only colour. I found myself unexpectedly in demand. Work flowed and my finances recovered. I could have afforded to move to a better apartment closer to the centre of town, but I didn't. My heart had been frozen by the affair that had driven me from the city of my birth.

The economic revival prompted by Prime Minister Witte's reforms brought N— a modicum of prosperity. I had been living there for four years when the railroad arrived in 1899. Hotels and restaurants sprang up around the railway station and that in turn created work for me. I was called on to advise the new establishments on their interior design.

I was working at the Hotel Bristol when I received the telegram that made my heart race. Count T— would be passing through N—, it said, on his way to Kiev. He requested the favour of a consultation.

The telegram, unanswered, sat on my mantelshelf. The date suggested by Count T— was two weeks ahead and I passed them in a state of agitation, torn between a desire to flee and a nagging compulsion to meet the man.

I watched from the hotel's upper storey as the train pulled into the station. A middle-aged, slightly corpulent fellow with grey curly hair and a neat beard summoned two porters to carry his luggage to the Bristol. I watched him check in then go to his room. He had left me a message.

'Count T— expects the pleasure of your visit. Please call at your convenience. Room 51.'

The note was peremptory; my mind skittered through the possibilities. Did he know? Had he come to confront me? And if so, did that mean that *she* had told him?

I hardly slept. In the morning, I gathered my catalogues and price lists and set off for the Bristol.

'Come in, dear fellow.'

Count T— was full of bonhomie.

'I don't believe we have met. Do sit. We have much to discuss.'

I was convinced he knew. He talked about renovating his country house, said I had been recommended to him, but I was sure he was mocking me.

The tension gnawed. I was about to challenge him when I heard him say, 'My wife, of course, is behind this. She is the reason for my visit.'

I braced myself. Count T— was explaining that Vera, his dear spouse, had issued instructions that he absolutely must engage me for the job, that he must not accept no for an answer.

I left the Bristol with a request for an estimate and a sickening feeling of unease.

Vera, Countess T—, was the reason I had fled from Moscow. For the past four years she had been the constant subject of my thoughts; she was the woman I loved.

I had sat with her husband, uncertain if he knew the truth. And he was coming back. In a week's time, on his return journey from Kiev, he expected me to bring him my plans.

I wavered between fear and hope. Had Vera really told him to come? And if she had, was it for revenge ... or for love? Had he come with her blessing to humiliate me? Or was it her way of saying she still cared for me? Had he guessed about me and come to test his suspicions?

Or, worst of all, perhaps T— was simply telling the truth: he and Vera needed a tradesman and neither had even thought how hurtful that would be. It would mean Vera was indifferent; she had forgotten me.

I returned a week later, hardly knowing what I intended, fearing what I might be capable of. T— was there, placid, smug, full of self-regard. How could my sweet, lovely Vera be content with such a person? Content with him when she had known me, a man of originality and imagination? I was agitated; Raskolnikov would have taken an axe.

'Count T—,' I heard myself saying, 'I decline your commission. What you have requested is hideous, so lacking in taste that I am revolted by the thought of it. You should find someone else to pander to your philistinism.'

Count T— looked at me.

'May I ask,' he said, 'why a person of your refinement happens to be living in this backwater?'

I had expected anger or scorn. I felt an urge to talk.

'I am here, sir, because of a woman. A married woman that I loved and still love. A woman I gave up and have yearned for ever since.'

I spoke at length. About the nights of passion and the depth of our affection. About the emotional and spiritual understanding that bound us. And about her sorrow when I told her I was leaving; how she had begged me to stay, offered to give up her home and husband to come with me.

I told him of the years since we had parted, how I had thought of her, dreamt of her, longed to return to the paradise I had given away. I told him everything except the name of the woman who haunted my life.'

When Sergei finished, Klyuev smirked. 'Beautifully written, my dear. In a style that I would say is quite worthy of Turgenev! May I ask – is this Anna that you are writing about?'

'No, not Anna. But it is about making choices. In this life we get just a handful of chances for happiness, and we need to seize them. I have a feeling I may write more about the characters in this story.'

People's nerves were frayed. Anger at the war, the hostilities getting closer, the shortages and the time wasted standing in queues led to confrontations. The slightest incident provoked brawls. There were daily fights outside shops and banks.

Some parts of the system had not broken down. The arrest warrant was promptly issued and promptly delivered:

Yesenin, Sergei Alexandrovich; peasant; born 21 October 1895; District of Ryazan; having failed to attend a mandatory interview with the Imperial Military Recruitment Office, is deemed to be in breach of Article 34(ii) of the Russian Penal Code and therefore subject to detention at the pleasure of His Imperial Majesty, Tsar Nicholas II.

In a country where rail links were shattered, where rotting meat piled up in railway depots, trains continued to run between Petrograd and the royal estate of Tsarskoe Selo, fifteen miles to the south.

In April 1916, in the week that the thirteen millionth Russian was called to the colours, Klyuev and Yesenin travelled there not knowing if Rasputin would receive them.

They had an appointment with Countess Vyrubova. Klyuev had recited for her and she had promised to do what she could. Petersburg gossip had it that Vyrubova was Rasputin's lover, a title she shared with others. It was she who had introduced the holy monk to her friend the empress, and Alexandra too had fallen under his spell.

Vyrubova's cottage on the Tsarskoe estate, within sight of the palace, was dainty, in the English style, with chintz curtains and lacquered furniture. Vyrubova was not dainty; big boned and ungainly, with the innocent face of a slightly challenged schoolgirl. When Klyuev reminded her that they had come to see Rasputin, she glanced around nervously.

'Yes. Yes, of course. I spoke to Grigory Yefimovich. He is with the empress at the moment. He often comes here afterwards. I cannot guarantee it.'

Anna Vyrubova and Rasputin

They drank tea. An hour went by.

Klyuev asked if Madame Vyrubova might telephone the palace and she left to make the call. At once the door flew open. Rasputin walked in, treading mud from the garden.

'I know about your petition. I know about you.'

He spoke rapidly, his voice low and hoarse. Sergei noticed that he avoided eye contact.

'You – come with me!' He pointed to Sergei.

'And you' – he gestured to Klyuev – 'remain with the woman. I have no wish to see her.'

Rasputin grabbed Sergei by the arm and dragged him out. A chauffeur snapped to attention as they climbed into the back of a black Mercedes Phaeton.

'To the Villa Rhode!' Rasputin seemed angry, staring out of the window, refusing to answer Sergei's questions.

The doorman at the Rhode ushered them into the club's dining room. Rasputin, familiar with the place, beckoned Sergei to follow him through a green velvet curtain. In a private room, female dancers were fixing their hair. A gypsy band was tuning up. Their leader clapped his hands and the air filled with music.

Rasputin called to the musicians to play 'Along the High Road' and began to rock in time, moving and stamping his feet. He danced unexpectedly gracefully. Dressed in his monkish robes, he glided across the room. As the music quickened, he squatted and kicked out his legs then rose and approached the women. One after another, he beckoned them to join him. A tall brunette fluttered a brightly coloured kerchief and pressed herself against him. No one seemed surprised.

A waiter brought a bottle of fortified wine. Rasputin gestured to Sergei to pour. When the music finished, he took a swig. He bit into a pickled cucumber, twirled the rest of it in his fingers and summoned the woman who had danced with him. She smiled and allowed him to push it into her mouth. He dipped his fingers in a plate of caviar and indicated that she should lick them.

Buoyed by the wine and the music, Rasputin was ready to talk.

'I left your friend at Vyrubova's because he is a *goluboi*,' he said to Sergei. 'A man who sins with the flesh of the male. But you and I are different.'

Sergei looked surprised; Rasputin smiled.

'I see into people's souls. I know what you wish for. As for your petition – your trouble with the army – I shall think about that tomorrow.'

Rasputin poured more wine.

'You and I are brothers,' he said. 'Peasants making our way in the world by the sharpness of our wit. All we possess, all we have achieved, is the result of our cunning.'

The wine was rough, the music loud.

'I have achieved nothing,' Sergei said. 'Whatever I shall achieve lies ahead. But you have come from nowhere and changed the world.'

Rasputin acknowledged the flattery.

'I give people what they need, then they are grateful. The shirt I am wearing' – he opened his robe to reveal a singlet decorated in blue cornflowers and stitched with golden thread – 'was embroidered by the hand of the empress. Alexandra made it for me. Why? Because God has given me the gift of curing the sick. I heal her son and I comfort her.'

'If God sent you to the tsar,' Sergei said, 'then surely He has a purpose in mind? A purpose for you and for the country . . .'

'My purpose is to save Russia,' Rasputin said. 'I warned Nicky against entering this war; now I tell him to get out of it. Only immediate peace with Germany will save us. People say it's because the empress is German – that she and I are dealing with the enemy – but they are wrong. We must end the war now, or the revolutionaries will kill us all.'

He was drinking more quickly, finishing the glasses, the bottles, calling for more. He spoke of 'Mama' and 'Papa' – the empress and the tsar – boasting how they loved him. He was the only one who could cure the tsarevich. He was sent by God. A dancer came to sit in his lap and he pushed another into Sergei's.

Rasputin was repeating words – God, prayer, wine – mixing everything up, torturing himself, shuddering with convulsions. He rose with a cry, threw himself into the dance as if plunging into a burning house. When he returned, he took Sergei by the arm. He dragged him and the two women into another room where there was a wide, unmade bed.

They drove back to Tsarskoe Selo at dawn, Rasputin huddled in the corner of the back seat.

'Do not speak of what happened tonight,' he said. 'Alexandra would not understand. She does not know the appetites that drive us, or that we may worship God in the body as well as the soul.'

'Why do you risk everything?' Sergei said. 'Why do you gamble all you've achieved by behaving the way you do?'

'*Khochu, mogu!* If I want it, I can do it! You are a peasant; you understand. I do it because little time remains. I see the future and Death is on his horse. God has decreed that I must suffer for Russia.'

'What future do you see for me?' Sergei asked.

'I see that we have much in common. Each of us hungers for respect. Each of us is playing a role. For you, I see both joy and pain, success and ignominy. I see you in a dark place struggling to breathe. Does that mean something?'

'Yes,' said Sergei. 'When I was a child, I almost drowned. Even now I have nightmares of suffocating. It happens when I am awake, too – fear that makes me panic until I cannot breathe.'

Rasputin nodded. 'There is darkness ahead – many people

tortured in Russia; piles of bodies; the rivers running red. I wish only to save the tsarevich. Then I must devote the time that remains to pilgrimage, to wandering the land and saving my soul.'

Sergei told him about the military call-up papers and the warrant that had been issued for his arrest.

'I deal with a hundred petitions every day,' Rasputin said. 'I have the power to grant them or refuse them. My own son had the same problem. I brought him to Alexandra and she liked him. She found him a posting far from the fighting. I will take you to the empress. You can recite for her. If she likes your poems, I will ask her to help you.'

Petrograd had run out of firewood and was close to running out of food. The streets were filled with garbage, the people afraid, the times neurotic. Crude rumours spread panic, as refugees brought tales of barbarism from the front. Two million armed deserters were roaming the land, seeking vengeance on the tsar who had sent them to an unwinnable war.

Hopelessness bred outlandish hopes; a disturbed society found disturbing remedies. The more clearly they saw the fate that awaited them, the more desperately Nicholas and Alexandra clung to Rasputin. Knowing the game was up, they convinced themselves he was God's messenger – obey him and all will be well; Rasputin was right, the evidence wrong.

'Hearken to Our Friend and believe in Him,' Alexandra wrote to her husband. 'It is not for nothing that God has sent Him to us – only, we must pay more attention to what He says. His words are not lightly spoken and the balm of having not only His prayers but His advice is great. It will be fatal for us and for the country if His wishes are not fulfilled.'

In April 1916, it was Rasputin's wish that the empress should meet a young poet. Sergei Yesenin was a true Christian, he said, a friend of the monarchy, a believer in Russia's holy destiny.

Alexandra was magnificent. Slim and elegant, her chestnut hair set with a diadem of two rows of diamonds and, on a *ferronière* across her brow, a ruby-encrusted Orthodox cross. Long ruby chains, like enormous threads of fire, flowed from her neck to the front of her bodice and thence to her waist.

Panic gripped him. Rasputin told him to bow and he felt his head spin. The water was drawing him into the depths where breath fails and the heart falters. He steadied himself. The first poem was crucial. He chose a song of grief and pride.

> On the edge of the village, a poor peasant hut;
> An old woman prays, her weary eyes shut.
> The old woman prays, she prays for her son,
> Her boy who has gone to fight for his home.
> She sees foreign lands, they're the fields of war,
> And on them her son, in death's darkling maw.
> To his muscular breast, by bullets brought low,
> He clutches the flag that he seized from the foe.
> And filled by her vision with sorrow and pride,
> Her grey head in anguish falls to one side.
> Her eyes are closed tight on her thoughts
> and her fears
> And from her lashes like pearls falls the stream of
> her tears.

Sergei kept his own eyes closed. The poem was a sentimental trifle, but well crafted and – he hoped – tailored to its audience. He heard the empress sob.

'I should like my girls to meet you, Mr Yesenin,' Alexandra said.

A servant hurried out and returned with four young women in white dresses.

'Olga, Tatiana, Maria, Anastasia – this is Sergei Yesenin. He is going to recite for us. Please pay attention.'

The girls giggled and sat by their mother. Like her, Sergei thought, they had an ethereal beauty – Olga, the eldest, with Alexandra's chestnut hair; Tatiana tall, serious, reserved; Maria chubby and smiling; Anastasia, the mischievous tomboy who would barely reach seventeen before bullets would tear her to pieces.

Sergei watched them as he read. He chose poems with religious, patriotic themes and saw Alexandra concentrating, as if at prayer. The girls sat with their heads on one side, nudging each other with the hungry air of young women closeted from the world, deprived of men. He offered an unrehearsed encore.

> The sunset froths in crimson glow,
> And the crowns of the birches burn white.
> My muse salutes you, young princesses,
> Your maiden beauty, your sweet souls alight.

The verses were a response to the unexpected moment. He was suddenly the anxious boy in the village schoolroom, eager to please, hoping that earnestness might stave off the threat of life's horror.

> In the hour of our nation's trial,
> You bless us with your steady hand.
> You see the dreams of life before us,
> Comfort those who suffer for our land.

He paused. The final verse swept him to a conclusion he feared and could not avert.

But fate, harsh fate sweeps you onwards,
To the place where sorrows stain your brow.
Oh, pray for them! Pray for our dear sisters;
Pray to God for our princesses now!

There was silence. Had he misjudged the moment? Had he referred to anxieties that must not be acknowledged? Rasputin whispered in the empress's ear and she left without a word. A servant ushered Sergei into an antechamber.

A clock ticked. Footsteps came and went.

A knock at the door brought him to his feet, and a smiling Princess Anastasia waved him to sit down.

'I hope you don't mind,' she said. 'I wondered if you needed anything.'

Before he could stop himself, he said, 'I'm starving! I haven't eaten since last night.'

She laughed.

'I can do something about that.'

In the kitchen, she opened the lids of pots until she discovered a freshly made borshch that she poured and heated on the stove. The warmth of the bowl in his hands, the sweetness of the soup in his mouth, the ray of sunlight through the grill of the window and the doomed princess in her white dress were a moment of enchanted stillness. Neither of them would forget it. Much later, Sergei would tell it in different versions, all with the borshch, some with details of their conversation that varied in the telling, others with hints of kisses exchanged.

It was the empress's adjutant, Brigadier Lohman who found them. The empress had told him to offer the young poet a safe posting for the duration of hostilities. Would a billet on the royal hospital train serving the military infirmary in Tsarskoe Selo be acceptable?

Empress Alexandra with princesses Olga, Tatiana, Maria and Anastasia

Sergei ran the quarter mile to Madame Vyrubova's.

'The empress was beautiful! All of them! A princess making me borshch! The empress taking me on her train!'

Klyuev told him to slow down. He asked how the recital had gone. Sergei listed the patriotic poems he had read.

'And the empress listened with tears in her eyes. She loved my poetry; they all did. They are such clever, lovely people—'

'The royals are in the condemned cell,' Klyuev said. 'The war and the people's anger will determine their fate. So of course they love poems about eternal Russia and the eternal beauty of the countryside. They can tell themselves that things have been like that for centuries . . . so that's how they'll remain forever.'

'So we are just play-acting?' Sergei snapped. 'Do you think our poems are just make-believe? Maybe that's true for you, but not for me! I believe in my poetry. I believe in the monarchy!'

He woke. Yesterday's elation was gone.

Klyuev could barely coax a sentence from him.

'My grandfather taught me to fight,' Sergei said. 'What am I doing taking the coward's way out, when millions are dying for Russia?'

Klyuev said a poet had a duty to protect his genius; he was too important to die as cannon fodder. 'And poetry is power, Seryozha. The power to charm people, to shape their choices and mould their lives. It was poetry that convinced the empress to help you. Russia is the country, of all countries, where poetry matters. Don't belittle that, Seryozha.'

Sergei shook his head.

'I'm a coward,' he said. 'A despicable coward.'

Sergei Yesenin and Nikolai Klyuev, 1916

He was assigned a billet in the Tsarskoe Selo barracks, issued with the uniform of a hospital orderly – khaki jacket, wide black trousers, high Russian boots – sent to have his head shaved and told to wait for orders. There was little in the way of training.

Sergei was not the only one who'd had strings pulled on his behalf – there were others there with connections in high places – but he felt more than once that people were looking at him. There were whispered conversations that he half heard, arguments about the military situation and the legitimacy of the war that flared up and were quickly hushed.

The royal train had been equipped as a mobile hospital, travelling back and forth to the fighting, collecting wounded officers and men to be brought home for treatment. A posting on board wasn't risk-free, but it was better than dying in the trenches.

Sergei found the waiting hard. Separated from his friends and uncertain what lay ahead, he moped in the day and lay awake at night. The anxiety that had been his companion since the time of earliest memory stiffened its hold.

The spring thaw brought a new offensive. The Russian Eighth Army under the command of General Alexei Brusilov advanced along a 200-mile sector of the southwestern front, probing the Austro-Hungarian positions, taking large areas of territory. The winter stalemate gave way to daily skirmishes; fluctuating fortunes redrew the frontline with bewildering rapidity. Casualties were high and the hospital trains busy.

Train No. 143, *Her Imperial Majesty The Empress Alexandra Fedorovna,* was dispatched to western Ukraine under the command of Brigadier Dmitry Lohman. In the absence of civilian traffic and with the railways now run by the military, progress was rapid. They passed through Belgorod and Poltava, stopping in Kiev to take on supplies. The train's twelve carriages, previously occupied by the royal household, held four hundred bunks and an operating theatre. Sergei and the other orderlies spent the journey mopping floors, starching linen, sterilising the racks of medical equipment.

Brigadier Dmitry Lohman

In Kiev, they were given a day's leave. In the evening they attended prayers at the city's Pecherskaya Lavra, the Monastery of the Caves, where monks had kept vigil for nine hundred years, venerating God, compiling the chronicles of ancient Rus'. After the service, Brigadier Lohman read a message from the tsar, thanking the armed forces for their part in a campaign that would determine the future of the war and of Russia herself. The train would proceed westwards, Lohman said, towards the town of Lutsk, where Russian forces were advancing. Conditions from now on would be perilous; the fighting was unpredictable and territory gained today could easily be lost tomorrow. It was uncertain when and where they would come across the front. The German air force was flying daily sorties, attacking Russian targets.

Sergei listened with a sense of detachment. The war felt unreal. The routine of the train had a feeling of permanence; the fighting was extraneous, hard to picture, obscured by childhood memories of chivalrous knights and decorous formality, a jewelled gauntlet thrown down in gentlemanly challenge.

An explosion shook the speeding train in the early hours of the morning, tipping him from his bunk. The carriage was in darkness, filled with acrid smoke. Officers were shouting incomprehensible orders amid noise and confusion. Sergei struggled to understand where he was.

A shell from an Austrian howitzer had exploded within twenty metres of the track, churning the earth into mountains of black mud. The train had ground to a halt, the duck-egg blue of its coachwork riddled with shrapnel. In the distance, on the far side of a reedy meadow, a Russian infantry detachment was engaged in combat with a troop of Austrian cavalry.

Sergei watched as the Russians fell like swathes of harvested wheat, then began to flee. Puffs of smoke rose in the air. Men running towards the train unfathomably started to lie down before they had covered even a fraction of the distance. Sergei willed them to get up and run, but they continued to lie there. Fewer and fewer were on their feet; fewer still reached the train. By then, Brigadier Lohman had re-established order. Engineers were assessing the damage, medics preparing the operating theatre.

Lohman handed field glasses to Sergei and another orderly. He told them to observe the Austrians and report immediately if there were any sign they were preparing to attack the train. What had seemed a distant puppet show became real. Seen through the glasses, the meadow was suddenly, distressingly close. Sergei scanned the site of the battle, the Russian bodies mutilated by Austrian bullets and sabres. A couple of the wounded were trying to crawl away, but their injuries were severe.

An Austrian officer, tall, elegant in his red uniform, prodded one of the wounded men. The Russian stirred as the Austrian lifted his chin, very gently, with the toe of his boot. It seemed a gesture of compassion. The Austrian looked towards the train, aware of the eyes that were trained on him, and smiled conspiratorially. Then he stamped with all his force on the wounded man's throat until blood and spittle spurted from his mouth. Sergei wanted to drop the binoculars and look away, but couldn't. He watched as the man struggled vainly to breathe, his features contorted in a grimace of panic and despair.

CHAPTER 8

The rest of the mission was a blur. Lohman's report would confirm that Medical Orderly Yesenin had carried out his duties with a soldierly attitude, but Sergei remembered little. After repairs, the train had continued westwards to Lutsk, where thirty-seven wounded officers and two hundred other ranks were embarked. The most serious cases were treated on board; Sergei helped to hold them down as wounds were stitched, arms and legs amputated.

It was distressing work, but the pain inflicted on the men had a purpose. The cruelty of the Austrian officer was more disturbing. It remained with him, souring his dreams; he wanted to talk about it, to see if others felt the same or if his reaction were somehow unreasonable. On a cigarette break, he sought out the orderly who had watched the murder beside him.

The fellow was tall, with black hair and lowering eyes. He could have been only nineteen or twenty, but he seemed unperturbed by what they had been through. When Sergei asked him about it, he shrugged and muttered something incomprehensible. Sergei thought he must be a simpleton. He asked his name and the man said, 'Dmitry Rasputin. My father knows who you are.'

Dmitry Rasputin (left), with mother and sisters

Hospital Train 143 returned to Tsarskoe Selo. It was met by a military band and crowds with Russian flags. Officials came on board to say that the empress would be distributing medals to the heroes of Lutsk. But when the list of recipients was read out, Brigadier Lohman shook his head. Eleven of them had died on the journey; replacement heroes would have to be found.

Wounded and able-bodied were lined up beside the train for Alexandra to review. She greeted them with handshakes and gracious remarks. She gave Sergei a particularly warm smile, but he turned his head away.

Hospital Train No. 143: Sergei Yesenin (front)

The Brusilov offensive was among the most effective of the war. Between June and September 1916, the Russian army carried off a series of victories. The Austro-Hungarians lost nearly a million men, including 400,000 taken prisoner, and around 25,000 square kilometres of territory. German troops were diverted from France to shore up the front, weakening the forces available to counter the British advance on the Somme.

In the autumn, Hospital Train No. 143 left Tsarskoe Selo to ferry wounded men from Petrograd to the sanitoria of Ukraine and Crimea. It was to be a leisurely lap of honour through safe territory. Councillors from the sanitoria resorts were on board, angling to enhance their reputations. War artists and journalists were engaged to record it for posterity. Madame Vyrubova came along to represent the empress.

But the mission coincided with a reversal of Russian fortunes. Brusilov's forces had run short of ammunition and food; the arrival of the German battalions had strengthened the enemy. Russian Army Command gave the order to retrench and, sensing a moment of weakness, the Central Powers moved to retake the territory they had lost in the summer. Germany's ally, Bulgaria, saw its opportunity, seizing Serbian territory in the west and Rumanian lands in the north. Warships operating from Bulgarian ports began to harass Russian shipping in the Black Sea.

Sergei found the journey tedious, the company irritating. Madame Vyrubova spent whole mornings in earnest conversation with the lugubrious Dmitry Rasputin, trying to persuade 'our young poet' to join them. The train travelled south, via Moscow to Oryol, then on to Kursk. Disruption to the rail network meant a three-day halt in Kharkov, the first sign that disorder was spreading from the front to the southern heartland.

They arrived late and tired at the Crimean resort of Yevpatoria. The town council was undaunted. The visitors were fêted with provincial pomp. Before unloading at the station, they were treated to speeches by the mayor, Semyon Duvan, the head of the Yevpatoria Evacuation Committee, Colonel Vilchkovsky and the governor of the Empress Alexandra Fedorovna Military Sanatorium, Colonel Kryzhanovsky. Flags were waved, marches played and 'God Save the Tsar' sung three times.

There was bunting the length of Duvanovsky Boulevard. Along the corniche, the town's population had been deployed with instructions not to stint on the hurrahs. The war seemed to have been won.

The heroes were wheeled to their wards and given a reassuring lecture about the healing properties of sunshine and sea air. The train's crew, from Brigadier Lohman to the lowliest private, were invited to a celebratory dinner at Yevpatoria's smartest restaurant, the Beau Rivage.

The meal dragged on. It was late. Bored and tired, Sergei asked Lohman's permission to return to the train. On Primorskaya Street he was overtaken by a group of soldiers running towards the port and decided to follow them.

There was a glow in the sky over the docks that grew brighter as they approached. The police had erected barricades, but the soldiers were ushered through and Sergei went with them.

A navy corvette moored a hundred metres from the quayside was in flames. Burning oil was spreading over the surface of the sea and charred bodies – evidently men who had jumped overboard – were floating in it. Police and soldiers were exchanging feverish whispers about 'enemy action' and 'sabotage'. No one knew what to do.

Sergei ran to the railings. A flash of light from the burning ship lit the water. He saw heads bobbing. He turned to the police commander, but the man shrugged. 'All dead. We'll get them in the morning. No point in risking more lives.'

A moment's hesitation was followed by a flood of emotion – fear, cowardice, drowning, suffocation, life, redemption . . . He kicked off his shoes and dived in.

The water shocked him. Things were clearer at this level, and more confusing. He brushed against something below the surface and pulled it to him. Soft; warm. A human face; half a face; charred black flesh stripped from a clenched white grin. Sergei pushed it away, but others took its place, brushing up against him like needy cats seeking comfort. The water was a charnel house.

He wanted to turn back, but the face of the dying infantryman from Lutsk stared him down. He swam through the bodies; shaking them, shouting at them, willing them to live.

An arm lifted from the water and fingers clutched his neck. Horror; hope.

'It's all right,' Sergei said. 'It's all right.'

The man wasn't listening. To save himself, he was pulling Sergei down.

Sergei thought of his grandfather. The lake. Retrieving his wounded ducks.

He hit the man on the side of the head and the grip on his neck loosened.

Now Sergei could hold him, clasp him close.

In reckless, desperate embrace they slid through the oil-anointed water. The man was solid weight. Sergei fought his way to the shore and collapsed on the shingle.

'Here! Help!'

He turned the man on his side and felt for a pulse. Nothing.

He pushed his fingers into the man's throat, cleared his airway, turned him on his back and pressed on his chest.

There were no wounds, no burns, no mutilated flesh. He was a boy. Seventeen, eighteen, blond. Blue eyes beautiful and staring. His face perfectly untouched. Why didn't he breathe?

Sergei put his mouth to the boy's lips.

There were voices now, people running towards them.

He blew life into the boy.

Breathe! For the sake of Our Saviour's holy blood! Breathe!

A medic took charge. Sergei reassured him.

'It's all right. He's all right. Just comfort him. He's only a boy.'

The medic turned the body over and shook his head.

All the gains of the Brusilov offensive were lost. Russian casualties were on the same inhuman scale as the enemy had suffered in the months before. The commander of the Galicia front wrote in desperation:

> We have neither cartridges nor shells. The German artillery roars without cease, blowing away our trenches and all in them. We barely reply, for we have nothing to reply with. Our exhausted men are beating off German assaults with little more than bayonets. Blood flows endlessly; our ranks grow thinner; graveyards expand by the day.

Brusilov's name was vilified. The war was tearing Russia apart. In November 1916, the moderate centrist party in the Russian parliament, the Constitutional Democrats, withdrew its support for the monarchy. The party's leader, Pavel Milyukov, made a speech accusing the tsar's German-born wife of being an agent of the enemy, together with 'certain persons' who had a malign influence over her.

'There are rumours of treachery at the highest levels,' Milyukov said, 'rumours of dark forces working in the interests of Germany. Shady personalities grouped around the empress are manipulating the affairs of state – motivated by treachery or stupidity, you can take your pick; the results are the same!'

The empress and her acolytes became the target of patriotic indignation.

Rasputin and the empress caricature, 1916

On the evening of 16 December 1916, Grigory Rasputin was in his private room at the Villa Rhode when a servant knocked politely, apologised for interrupting and informed him that there was an urgent phone call.

Rasputin took the call and spoke for around ten minutes. Then he summoned his driver and left for an unknown destination.

The following morning, when Rasputin failed to appear for his daily meeting with the empress, Alexandra asked Anna Vyrubova if she knew where he might be.

Vyrubova said Rasputin had phoned her late the previous evening. He had been summoned to the palace of Prince Felix Yusupov, where Yusupov's wife, the attractive young Princess Irina, had asked to see him.

Irina was the tsar's niece and Alexandra knew that she was not in Petrograd. Alarmed and suspicious, she asked Vyrubova to contact Yusupov and find out what had happened.

Yusupov claimed he had spent the evening with the tsar's cousin, Grand Prince Dmitry, and Dmitry backed him up. But Vyrubova felt the two men were hiding something. When she told the empress, Alexandra had them arrested.

Yusupov's story crumbled. He offered to explain things in person, but Alexandra refused. She told him to make a written statement that she would read.

Yusupov confessed everything. The invitation to meet the beautiful Irina had been bogus, an excuse to lure Rasputin to the Yusupov palace on the Moika Canal. A group of right-wing noblemen – patriots for Russia, he said – gave the vile charlatan wine laced with cyanide. The doctor who provided the poison said it was enough to kill ten men, but the diabolical figure in his monkish robes drank it and asked for more.

In a panic, Yusupov suggested they pray together while they waited for Irina to come.

Rasputin stood before me, his head bent and his eyes fixed on the crucifix. I slowly raised the revolver. Where should I aim, at the temple or the heart? A shudder swept over me; my arm grew rigid, I aimed at his heart and pulled the trigger. Rasputin gave a wild scream and crumpled on the bearskin . . . The doctor declared there was no possibility of doubt: Rasputin was dead.

Our hearts filled with hope; we were convinced that Russia and the monarchy would be saved from ruin and dishonour. But a terrible thing happened: with a sudden violent effort Rasputin leapt to his feet, foaming at the mouth, rushing at me and sinking his fingers into my shoulder like steel claws!

Yusupov and his accomplices pumped more bullets into the evil madman, stove his head in with iron bars then drowned him in the icy canal.

His last words were, 'Tell Nicky that my death shall be his also.'

Prince Felix Yusupov and Princess Irina

The corpse turned up three days later. Felix Yusupov and Prince Dmitry had hacked a hole in the ice and pushed him into the Moika, where tidal currents from the Gulf of Finland dragged him with the rest of Petrograd's garbage through the canals and underground rivers of Peter the Great's swamp-built city, to surface under the Petrovsky Bridge. In life he had been a giant; now, swollen by water, Rasputin was a bloated leviathan.

Discovery of Rasputin's corpse, arms aloft, 19 December 1916

The empress sent for Anna Vyrubova. In the Chesmensky Almshouse, the pathologist was already slicing her lover's flesh. His heart was in a steel dish; in his forehead, two bullet holes from Yusupov's revolver.

Vyrubova and Alexandra wept in each other's arms. The popular mood was menacing – there had been celebrations at the news of Rasputin's death – but they needed to see him. At midnight on 21 December, dressed in identical hooded cloaks, they drove to the Chesme Church with an oversized zinc coffin and four muscular servants to load it on to the back of a military transport.

On the drive to Tsarskoe Selo, they debated what to do with him. Taking Rasputin to the Imperial palace was an unnecessary danger, so they decided on Vyrubova's cottage. The coffin was too big to fit through the door, but a resourceful servant removed the doorframe of the scullery and it was taken in by the tradesman's entrance.

Rasputin was buried in a corner of Vyrubova's property,

visible from the empress's bedroom. Nicholas and Alexandra were there, as were the four royal princesses, Brigadier Lohman and some of the dead man's friends. The tsarevich, whom Rasputin had nursed through the worst crises of his haemophilia, was too ill to attend. As the coffin was closed for the final time, the empress, pale and close to fainting, pressed a holy icon to the chest of the man she knew to be the emissary of God and the saviour of Russia.

The tsar was pragmatic. His ministers had told him that Rasputin's demise would help assuage the people's anger against the monarchy. Alexandra was heartbroken, demanding retribution against his killers. Nicholas decided on banishment. Yusupov was exiled to his remote country estate and Grand Prince Dmitry sent to a posting with the Imperial army in Persia.

When family members pleaded for the men to be pardoned, Nicholas scribbled a curt refusal. 'Nobody has the right to kill on his own private judgment. I am astonished that you should even have applied to me.'

In the first weeks of 1917, Hospital Train No. 143 was out of commission with damage sustained on a visit to the front. Sergei was in Tsarskoe Selo, working in the royal infirmary. Eating his lunch in the canteen, he was joined by a familiar figure.

'Forgive me disturbing you,' Dmitry Rasputin said. 'You knew my father. I wanted to talk to you. Do you mind?'

Sergei motioned to an empty chair.

'Only, you know, there is so much being said about him. So

many terrible things. They're not true, but people believe them. I just wanted to hear you say that my father was not a bad man.'

Sergei hesitated. Dmitry saw it.

'He was a good father – he really was. He loved me ... he loved all of us. When I was growing up, he looked after me and helped me. Many people loved him – the tsar himself. But I knew some people were jealous. Once, a madwoman came to our village accusing him of all sorts of things and tried to kill him with a knife. My father said she'd been sent by the corrupt politicians. I helped save him. I know people say he did bad things; but he was my dad – I loved him. You can understand that, can't you?'

'Yes,' Sergei said. 'There was good in him. And he was good to me.'

Rasputin, post-mortem photograph

CHAPTER 9

A letter arrived with a familiar seal – the Milky Way poetry circle was evidently still in existence! His former colleagues had thought to write to him.

From the members of the Mlechny Put' Poetry Collective

To Sergei Alexandrovich Yesenin

Unanimously approved

You are a traitor to your class and to the cause of the peasants and workers you so speciously claim to embody! Living in the high society of Petersburg, your psyche has become split. Your outrageous touring of the aristocratic salons, your toadying to the nobility who have brought Russia to her knees, has distanced you from your roots. You are an individualist, absorbed in yourself and your unprincipled search for fame. We declare that we reject you and hereby break with you forever.

There followed the signatures of all the young poets Sergei had considered his friends in the early Moscow years.

He stuffed the letter into his pocket. It was three weeks before he replied.

When I first came to Petersburg, I was young and unknown. Like all of you, I was anxious to make my name as a poet and I was lucky. The capital's *littérateurs* raised my reputation to the roof. It was they who took me to the salons, and they who insisted I recite to the aristocracy. But while all these people were praising me, I spent the nights on the streets and in doss-houses. I pushed away what they were offering me. I could have taken as much as I wanted from their purses, but I despised them. With all their riches and all they had, I considered it vile even to touch them.

When Klyuev came to visit him in the Tsarskoe Selo barracks, Sergei spoke at length about his dead friend Grisha Panfilov. He didn't mention the letter from the Milky Way poets, but he pressed Klyuev to say what he thought Grisha, the revolutionary idealist, would think about the signs that his long-awaited revolt was finally in the making ... and about Sergei's own willingness to serve the tsarist institutions he had so detested.

Nevsky Prospect, St Petersburg's main boulevard, was the city's forum. Women gathered there to exchange news at the butchers, bakers and fishmongers. It was in the bread shops of the Nevsky that discontent turned to insurrection.

In February 1917 the war was in its third year, the economy had collapsed and housewives were spending hours queuing for bread that often never came. Their anger came to a head on Thursday, 23 February, International Women's Day. Thousands of women left their places of work and joined forces with the bread queues. Delegations went to factories, banging on doors, pelting the windows with snowballs, urging the workers to down tools. They wanted bread, free-dom and an end to the war.

Men from the Putilov engineering plant went on strike. Workers at the Lessner munitions factory declared they would refuse to fight for Russia until the regime accepted their demands for civil rights. What had begun as a protest about bread acquired an ominous momentum. By late afternoon, shop windows had been smashed. Women took what food there was; men pushed over tramcars and built barricades from paving stones.

In Tsarskoe Selo, they were preparing for the winter ball. A special train was bringing guests from the capital. Men dressed in knee breeches, buckled shoes and plumed hats, women in evening dresses and diamonds were collected at the station then whisked through the park in sleighs piled high with furs, through the swirling snow, past the frosted trees to the gates of the palace, illuminated by a thousand lights. Ethiopian guards in turbans offered the guests mulled wine as they stood in the receiving line. Carriages with beautifully groomed horses in the crimson and gold Imperial livery waited in the courtyard.

Sergei watched the comings and goings. It was common knowledge that the empress would not be there – she hadn't been seen in public since the death of Rasputin – but the men were saying that Nicholas too would be absent, detained by the more pressing task of saving the country. There were reports from the city of clashes between demonstrators and police and of machine guns being deployed on the roofs of buildings. Detachments of Cossacks, the most feared of the tsarist troops, were patrolling the streets.

For Sergei, the music, the shouts of the revellers, the glare of the illuminations seemed a provocation. Life was not here. Life was on the streets.

When the music died down after midnight, he followed the

line of departing guests. In his medical orderly's uniform, he had little trouble finding a place on the train to Petrograd.

Nevsky Prospect, February 1917

The bridges were closed. In an effort to keep striking workers out of the city, the authorities had lifted the crossings over Petrograd's rivers and canals. It was eight o'clock and the sun was rising before Sergei arrived at Nevsky Prospect. A crowd of men and women who looked as if they had been there all night were huddling round bonfires, sharing food and bottles of beer. A soldier in the uniform of the Semyonovsky Regiment gave him a mug of tea.

'Here,' he said, handing him a length of red ribbon. 'You'll need one of these.'

Sergei saw that the soldiers in the group had tied ribbons to their lapels. He did the same.

'How long have you been here?' he asked.

'Since yesterday. We're waiting for the men from the Vyborg Side, strikers from the factories. They tried to come in over the Liteiny Bridge, but the police stopped them. They're meant to be coming over the ice.'

As far as Sergei could see in both directions, the Nevsky was in the hands of the people. He asked where the troops were.

'Ha! They were here yesterday, all right. Cossacks with whips, riding up and down trying to scare us. But when it came to it, they backed off; seems they didn't want a fight. People have heard about it, so there'll be even more of us today.'

Sergei said he was going to have a look around. The side streets leading off the Nevsky were filled with groups of serious-looking men and women, workers for the most part, almost certainly from the outlying factories, who had crossed the frozen Neva. Others – students, shopkeepers, office workers – had come as spectators but were drawn into conversation with the demonstrators and fired by their enthusiasm. For such a large gathering, there was very little noise, just a whispered hush of anticipation.

Sergei walked west towards the Admiralty. There were sandbags on top of the Singer Building and the stock exchange, but no sign of the machine guns people had been talking about. He was surprised by the absence of police; in normal times there were uniforms on every corner. There were plenty of soldiers, all with the red ribbon of insurrection in their buttonhole. When the crowd spotted one without a ribbon, they called out, 'Brother! Come and join us! Be with the people!'

The noise began at lunchtime. The streets were packed and people sensed a tipping point. Individual voices were raised, men shouting jokes or humorous obscenities; then the women joined in. 'I'm hungry, comrades! What about you?' 'I'm hungry, and so's my baby!' 'What're Nick and Alix eating – that's what I'd like to know!'

Police observers on the Nevsky and the Liteiny told their commanders that 150,000 people were on the streets. The mood was threatening; only the army would have any chance of keeping them in check. The message was relayed to the palace, but word came back that the tsar was away, visiting military headquarters at the front.

There was a hiatus and the people seized on it. The raised voices were shouting orders now, giving a shape and a purpose to the inchoate human mass. It wasn't organised, there were no professional revolutionaries, no dogma, no -isms; the crowd stirred organically and became a unified force. One group went north along Liteiny towards the Russian parliament in the Tauride Palace, while the main body continued east to Znamenskaya Square, congregating at the huge equestrian statue of Alexander III, the brooding symbol of immovable autocracy.

Orators climbed on to the statue's plinth, whipping up the crowd's anger at the death and sacrifice 'the tsar's war' had inflicted on the nation, denouncing 'Nick and Alix' as blood-sucking leeches, sneering at their stupid, stuck-up bitches of daughters. A hunger march was becoming a revolution.

There were thousands in the square and not everyone heard what was being said, but it didn't matter. All of them shared the same grievances and the same demands. Calls to overthrow the monarchy were being aired in public and the police were powerless to stop it.

When the crowds dispersed, late in the evening, there was more looting; more trams and carriages overturned, more skirmishes with the Cossacks. The statue of the old tsar, Alexander, was toppled and beheaded. The air had changed in Petrograd. It was the air of hope, the air of freedom now, and Sergei took in lungfuls. He wandered the streets, sat at bonfires, broke bread with his brothers and sisters. When they sang, a people's version of the Marseillaise with ferocious new Russian words, he sang with them.

> We renounce the old world!
> We shake its dust from our feet!
> We hate the golden idols,
> We hate the palace of the tsar!
> Arise, arise, you labouring masses!
> Rise against the foe!
> Forward! Forward!
> Let the people's vengeance go!
> The greedy rich exploit your work,
> They take your last piece of bread.
> The tsar, the vampire, drinks from your veins;
> The tsar, the vampire, drinks the people's blood.
> Arise, arise, you labouring masses!
> Against thieves, the dogs – the rich,
> Against the evil vampire tsar!
> Kill the cursed the criminals!
> Bring on a better life!

In the early hours of the morning Sergei returned to barracks. No one had noticed he was missing. The Russian state was in chaos, surprised by the events on the streets.

For the rest of that day, Saturday 25 February, Petrograd was in the hands of the people. Perhaps remembering the consequences of allowing troops to fire on the Bloody Sunday marchers twelve years earlier, Nicholas II played a waiting game, hoping the protests would fizzle out.

They didn't. The following day, a quarter of a million people converged on the capital chanting 'Long live the revolution!' Troops intercepted a column of marchers at the Moika Canal. As the crowds approached, the soldiers knelt and aimed their rifles. The people at the front saw what was happening and stopped, but those at the back were pushing them onwards. The soldiers fired two volleys and the front row of marchers fell to the ground. People fled, slipping in pools of blood.

With disorder escalating and no instructions from their political masters, Petrograd's military commanders told the troops to fire at will. Two thousand people were gunned down.

The massacre disgusted many soldiers who'd been rushed back from the front to deal with the insurrection, and defections increased. On Monday, 27 February, the Petrograd garrison mutinied, murdering those officers who tried to stop them. Tsarist insignia were torn down, police arsenals looted and guns handed to the crowds. Even the Cossacks began to desert.

The Russian parliament telegraphed the absent tsar:

> The situation is growing worse. Measures must be taken at once; tomorrow will be too late. The fate of the country and the monarchy is being decided. The government is powerless to stop the disorder. The garrison is in the throes of rebellion. They have joined the mobs. They are marching on the Interior Ministry and Parliament. Your Majesty, do not delay! If the agitation reaches the Army, the destruction of Russia is inevitable.

Nicholas seemed strangely detached. His letters to Alexandra, written in flawless English, made no reference to the fate that was descending on them:

> Military Headquarters, 24 February. My sweet, darling sunshine! My brain is resting here – no ministers, no troublesome questions demanding thought . . . I got your telegram telling me of Olga and Baby having measles. I could not believe my eyes – this was so unexpected. At dinner I saw all the foreign generals – they were very sorry to hear this sad news. For all the children, and especially for Alexei, a change of climate is absolutely necessary after their recovery. We shall think this out in peace on my return home. I greatly miss my half-hourly game of patience every evening. I shall take up dominoes again in my spare time. Your loving little hubby, Nicky.

Tsar and empress, family snapshot

When the tsar finally plucked up courage to return to Petrograd, the railways had been cut by striking workers. His train was diverted, then shunted into a dead end. A delegation from parliament found him in a siding near Pskov. It was already 2 March, and in the intervening days Alexandra had been sending telegrams playing down the seriousness of the situation, urging her husband 'not to sign any paper or constitution or other such horror'.

But the deputies told Nicholas he had no choice: only his abdication could defuse the people's anger. The Romanov dynasty that had ruled since 1613 and celebrated its third centenary with great pomp just four years earlier came to an end with a royal proclamation written in a railway siding.

In the days of the great struggle against foreign enemies who for nearly three years have tried to enslave our fatherland, the Lord God has been pleased to send down on Russia a new heavy trial. In these decisive moments, We believe it Our duty to facilitate the consolidation of all national forces. We have thought it well to renounce the

Throne of the Russian Empire and to lay down Our supreme power.

As We do not wish to part from Our beloved son, Alexei, We transmit the succession to Our brother, the Grand Duke Mikhail. We call on all faithful sons of the fatherland to fulfil their sacred duty and obey the new tsar in this heavy moment of national trials. May the Lord God help Russia!

Nicholas's portrait was ripped from the wall of the parliament chamber. A provisional government would run the country until elections could be held.

Later, when revolution had altered the country's history, Sergei would compose a new version of his role in it:

The revolution found me at the front in a disciplinary battalion. I had been sent there as a punishment for refusing to write poems in honour of the tsar. When the February revolution happened, I refused to serve in the army of Alexander Kerensky's Provisional Government and threw down my rifle. I lived as a deserter, working with the Socialist Revolutionaries. I was in their combat brigade.

A poet's metier is to reinvent reality. Sergei's greatest verse would be wrought from the reimagining of his own life, Yesenin the man refashioned into a complex lyric persona, walking the paths of joy and despair. So fully would he embrace this nexus of life and art that the former would come to be valued merely as material for the latter, until in the end he would feel compelled to live out the destiny his poetry foretold.

But that was in the future. In February 1917 there was no evidence of any Sergei Yesenin in the tsar's punishment battalions or, indeed, in the ranks of the Socialist Revolutionaries.

There was, on the contrary, evidence that he returned to army life in Tsarskoe Selo, that he helped to treat casualties from the fighting in Petrograd and that the experience deepened his anguish. Things that had been dependable were falling apart. The scared little boy raising his hand, eager to please, had been awed by the splendour of the empress; a princess in a white dress had made him a bowl of borshch; he had fallen for a vision of eternal beauty, but it had been an illusion.

He was forced into a brooding reappraisal of his life, of his feelings for Russia, patriotism and justice. The old order was lost; the thought of the future screwed his stomach into a knot.

> The puddles shine blue today
> And the breeze whispers in my hand;
> But like you, I know that no one
> Needs the firmament's green land.
> In the world of material things,
> We live all times alone.
> You, like the oak in the springtime,
> Drink the white of your days 'til it's gone.
> You love, I know, I know,
> You love the gentle soul's caress.
> But the way to heaven is barred

By the seal of our earthliness.
There's eternal distance before us,
The way there thought-filled and hard.
Beyond the hills our shelter –
A dirt-filled village churchyard.

When he sent his poems to friends, they read them as letters of farewell.

Listen to me, my filthy heart!
Listen to me, you heart of a dog!
I'm on to you, on to you like a thief;
And in my hand I have a knife.
Sooner or later, I know it,
I'll stick the cold steel in your ribs.
I've no longer any yearning to travel
The eternal, stinking distance ahead.
Let fools and charlatans chatter,
About dreams and goals and rewards.
If there's anything on earth or beyond it,
It's emptiness. And that's all.

When Klyuev tried to talk to him, Sergei pushed him away.

'My life will be short,' he said. 'You know how to battle against life, but I shrink before it.'

A provisional government was formed, led by liberals, moderate socialists and Constitutional Democrats, all well-intentioned, all committed to freedom and democracy. But these were the men who had previously agreed to collaborate with the tsar's ideas for a constitutional monarchy and that didn't go down well. A minister sent to address a rally of railway workers heard his government denounced to his face.

> What do we think of this new Provisional Government, comrades? Does it have representatives of the people in it? Fat chance! Look, it's led by a prince. I ask you, why did we even bother making a revolution? We've suffered at the hands of princes and counts for long enough ... and these new ministers, they're all landowners. Maybe we shouldn't let this fellow out of here – what do you say, comrades?

The minister fled. The Provisional Government was on shaky ground. Another, more radical centre of power was emerging – the Soviet of Workers' Deputies.

Factories all over Russia had elected councils known as soviets, as had many army units. Most of the revolutionary groups were represented in them – Mensheviks, Socialist Revolutionaries and a handful of Bolsheviks. Where the Provisional Government wanted a parliamentary democracy, the Soviets wanted a revolutionary dictatorship, land to the people and an immediate end to the war. For much of 1917 the Provisional Government and the Soviets vied for power.

The war continued. Sergei was still in the army. But by mid-March the army was no longer the one he had joined. The Provisional Government was weeding out unreliable elements and selecting new officers. On 17 March Brigadier Lohman handed him an official document.

> Attestation. Yesenin, Sergei Alexandrovich. Military Orderly, Train No. 143. Has fulfilled all obligations and duties with soldierly integrity. Present notice confirms that soldier Yesenin is suitable for promotion to the rank of Ensign.
> Signed: Guchkov, Minister of War

Sergei hesitated. The collapse of the old world and a future pregnant with cruelty and reprisals filled him with dread. On 20 March, he laid down his rifle and walked out of barracks for the last time.

CHAPTER 10

The year of revolution, 1917, tore up history. The nation was breaking with its past and Sergei did the same.

Before he left Petrograd, he threw the gifts he had received from the empress – a gold watch and an embroidered kerchief with the Imperial crown and two-headed eagle – into the Neva. He went to his publisher, Averyanov, and told him to burn his recently printed collection of poems, *Azure*, 'Dedicated with reverence to Her Imperial Majesty, Alexandra Fedorovna'. Then he headed to Moscow.

In 1914 he had walked out on Anna; in 1917 he was walking out on himself. For a second time, he arrived in a city with no plans and no place to go to; the difference now was that thousands of others were in the same predicament. Moscow was overflowing with the homeless, whole families sleeping in public parks and under bridges, their possessions crammed in cardboard suitcases or tied up in sheets that held all they had rescued from the wreck of war.

Uniforms were everywhere; tens of thousands had rejected the summons to serve the new government. For the first three nights Sergei slept in makeshift shelters, bedding down with his fellow deserters. Most were passing through, waiting for transport to take them back to their villages. They talked of their wives and children in voices buoyed by anticipation.

When they asked Sergei where he was from, he said, 'Ryazan, but I'm not going back.' If he was walking out on himself, he was walking out on everything, and that included his home.

On the fourth day, he read a poster glued to a lamppost.

REVOLUTION! MOBILISATION! THE SOVIET
OF LEFT ART HAS BEEN ELECTED! JOIN
US IN TEATRALNAYA SQUARE, 4 P.M.

Moscow streets were full of announcements – official ones about food rationing and identification papers; rival notices from the Soviets countermanding the orders of the Provisional Government; Church bulletins decrying the godless new regime, requesting prayers for the royal family; and eccentric, hand-printed posters like the one that caught Sergei's attention. He didn't know what it was about, but he went.

A crowd had gathered. On the steps of the Bolshoi Theatre, a man in a double-breasted blazer with a striped scarf and a top hat was waving his arms, declaiming poetry. In the beleaguered city it seemed unreal; there was very little Soviet about it.

After a few minutes, a voice from the crowd called out, 'Comrade! Enough of this rubbish! Let us have a poem about the revolution!'

Another man, wearing an immaculate white tunic and crimson cravat stepped forward.

> Savage, nomad hordes of Asia
> Poured fire from the vats!
> Razin's execution is avenged
> And the pain of Pugachov,
> Whose beard was torn away.
> Hooves
> Have broken

The crust of the earth,
Heavy with the chill of centuries;
And the supernal sky, like a stocking
With a hole in its heel
Has been rescued from the laundry-trough,
Wholly clean!

The audience looked puzzled; the poem sounded like a provocation. There were murmurs of discontent. A third poet took the stage, but he too was jeered. Sergei pushed his way to the front and raised his hand for silence. His army uniform helped quiet the crowd. Slowly and deliberately, he began to recite the narrative poem he had been composing since he left Petrograd:

My tale's of a worker's son, Martin,
Meek blue eyes and hair dark as night.
His father slaved to feed his family,
With the help of a comrade, Lord Jesus Christ.
Christ the child in Mary's arms
From the icon on the wall,
Looked down on the family table
And smiled to bless them all.
Outside their window
The wind of change was blowing;
The Russian people rising,
To take back what was owing.
The trees are roaring,
Storms are raging.
Through the mist,
Eyes are blazing.
Blow follows blow,
Corpse falls on corpse;
Terror breaks

Its fearsome tooth
And the world explodes
In shrieks and shouts,
A stream of pain
From a screaming mouth.
Jesus heard the people's cries,
He heard their guiltless plea;
And here on earth, and arm in arm,
He walked with you and me.
Our dreams of freedom blossomed,
Eternal hopes of joy,
Nurtured and encouraged by
The winds of February.
But cannons barked
And bullets flew;
A fatal dose of mankind's lead
Pierced the infant Jesus through.
Oh, hear me now and hear me well –
There's no hope of resurrection since
Our Lord Jesus fell.
Only words outside the window
Come and go like magic,
And people seem to listen up,
And mutter *our republic!*

Someone in the crowd called the police. These poets were
insulting the Church ... or insulting the revolution ... or insulting the people ... They had to be stopped!

Sergei felt a hand on his neck. He swung around and hit
the constable full in the face. At once, the crowd rushed up the
steps, engulfing them in a melee of violent humanity. When
the military police arrived to march them away in handcuffs,
the poets were grateful.

In the communal cell of the Petrovka Street police station, a mob of petty criminals mocked their theatrical elegance with whistles and jeers. The man in the blazer waved his hand in flowery acknowledgement. He handed Sergei a business card with the words, 'Anatoly Marienhof, poet', and introduced his friends as Vadim Shershenevich and Alexander Kusikov.

'That seems to have gone rather well,' Marienhof said.

'What do you mean, *well*?' Sergei replied. 'I've got a black eye and we're in jail!'

'Yes, but think of the publicity. Our names will be in the newspapers. People will read about the revolution we've unleashed on the world!'

'*Revolution*? *Soviet of Left Art*? What the hell is that about? None of your poetry's in the least bit Soviet. It doesn't even mention the revolution. It's all images and clever wordplay.'

'Precisely!' Marienhof said. 'That's what's so brilliant! It's a *poetic* revolution. And, to be honest, there are so many poets around at the moment that you've got to do something dramatic or you'll never get yourself noticed.'

'So it was a publicity stunt?'

'A happening, I prefer to call it. A provocation. A poetic incident . . .'

'And all this dressing up – your blazers and scarves and top hats? Is that a provocation, too?'

Marienhof nodded.

'It's a means to stand out from the crowd. But it is more than that. You are a poet; I'm sure you've read Baudelaire?'

Sergei shook his head. 'I am a peasant poet. I read the poetry of the people. Your fellow sounds like a Frenchman.'

'Baudelaire is the prophet of the dandy,' Marienhof said.

'We follow his lead in that. And we believe in the redemptive mission of poetry that he proclaims.'

In the grimy prison, amid the thieves and prostitutes and vagrants, a Socratic dialogue of the strangest order unfolded. Marienhof spoke of the transformative role of art and the power of poetry to remake the world.

'Do you know what Baudelaire called his greatest collection of poems? *Les Fleurs du Mal*. That is the essence of poetry. It takes the stinking dirt of life and turns it into beautiful flowers.'

Marienhof gestured to himself and his extravagantly dressed companions.

'The dandy uses art to correct the blemishes of nature. He fashions an image of perfection and immortality. It is an expression of what we believe as poets – that art is the sorcery which transmutes God's pitiful creation.'

Anatoly Marienhof

They were interrogated by a puzzled police sergeant, who demanded to know why they had sown panic among the population with posters proclaiming revolution and universal mobilisation. He listened to their explanations of the divine role of culture and their denunciations of rival poetic movements, and concluded they were mad. The poets, Anatoly Marienhof,

Vadim Shershenevich, Alexander Kusikov and Sergei Yesenin were formally admonished, fingerprinted and released.

On the sidewalk outside they celebrated, throwing their hats in the air. Marienhof beckoned Sergei and they ran to Tverskaya Street, where they tumbled into a bar and a bottle of Pertsovka vodka.

Two hours later, they had drained a second then a third and toasted every poet, every philosopher and every beautiful woman they could call to mind. By midnight they had sworn friendship for life and Marienhof had invited them back to his place. Expecting an apartment to match his new friend's lavish wardrobe, Sergei was surprised to wake the following morning in a garret with a leaking roof. When he opened a window, slurred voices yelled at him to close it and go back to sleep. It was lunchtime before they assembled, still buoyed by the excitement of the previous evening.

'Dearest Sergei Alexandrovich,' Marienhof said, 'welcome to our home. And welcome – if you so wish it – to our movement, to a school of poetry that will shake the foundations of Russian literature!'

'. . . but which doesn't pay the bills or keep the rain out,' added Vadim Shershenevich, to laughter.

Sergei liked the good-natured freedom of the group and the intellectual focus of their conversation. Shershenevich was bluff and open, Kusikov small and dapper. Marienhof, tall, distinguished and unmistakably aristocratic, was their natural leader.

'So, what do you say, young Seryozha? Do you throw in your lot with the future? Do you join us in the quest to remake the world?'

Sergei raised his hands in surrender.

Marienhof's attic on Bogoslovsky Lane extended across two adjoining buildings. The floors were uneven and you had to duck to avoid the roof beams. There was no heating and only an ancient water heater. It was unclear if the place was legally occupied, or if they had simply moved in amidst the chaos and lawlessness of revolutionary Moscow. In a city filled with homeless people, even the humblest accommodation was seized on.

Sergei's bed was a mattress behind a partition and for the first few weeks he rarely left it. The violence of his recent experiences had shaken him. He was disturbed by the disintegration of his infatuation with the Romanovs, filled with a sense of shame and personal loss. He had broken with the old world, his old life and friends; his disenchantment with the past had left him bereft. He was eating little, reading less and writing nothing.

They all drank. For the others, drink was a celebration. For Sergei it was an escape.

Marienhof and Shershenevich, who had both seen action in the war, attempted to comfort him. He thanked them, but things didn't improve. When they asked him questions about his previous life, he shook his head.

At mealtimes, the poets took it in turns to read aloud the compositions they were working on, asking for opinions and advice. Sergei contributed little, but he listened. The earnestness of their belief in poetry's redemptive power, their love of words as sounds, as music, and the veneration of the poetic image as an end in itself intrigued him. When Marienhof said they should pick a name for the movement they were intent on founding, Sergei said, 'It's obvious – Imagism. You're Imagists!'

Shershenevich, who was translating Baudelaire, saw Sergei's interest in his readings of poems from *Les Fleurs du Mal* and offered him one of Baudelaire's essays he had recently translated, 'The Painter of Modern Life'. In the days that followed, Sergei read and re-read it so often that he knew passages by heart.

> The dandy aspires to cold detachment. His delight in clothes and material elegance is the symbol of an aristocratic superiority of mind ... A dandy may suffer pain, but he will keep smiling, like the Spartan under the bite of the fox. The dandy represents what is best in human pride, the need to combat and transcend life's meaninglessness. Dandyism is the last flicker of heroism in our decadent age ...

At the next mealtime discussion, Sergei asked the others if they shared the French poet's vision of art triumphant over the pain of life. Marienhof said he did; Baudelaire's obsession with clothes and make-up was a metaphor for art's power to correct the world's flaws. He read out a passage from the essay's praise of women.

> Nature can teach us nothing. It is artifice alone that creates beauty ... When a woman uses make-up to disguise the blemishes nature has sown on her skin, she rises above nature, she transforms nature, she becomes magical and surreal. All art is at its noblest when it reforms and perfects the imperfect world.

Marienhof combined poetic sensibility with the energy of a delinquent child and the untroubled cynicism of a businessman. He had plans for promoting the newly coined Imagist movement. No stunt or provocation, no public scandal to get their names and their poetry in the newspapers was beyond his imagination.

He came home with a bulky parcel wrapped in brown paper and announced 'a night-time, guerrilla operation, involving screwdrivers'.

Sergei, gripped by melancholy, excused himself, but Marienhof put his arm around him and said, 'No, Seryozha. This is an order.'

After midnight they walked down the hill to Kuznetsky Bridge. Marienhof was beginning to unwrap the parcel when a policeman appeared.

Marienhof froze. 'Put the thing on the ground!' he said. 'Sit on it! Pretend you're drunk!'

The four of them huddled together as the constable approached. He poked them with his boot and concluded they were harmless. 'No homes to go to? Half the city's sleeping on the streets nowadays. Anyway, it looks like you've got enough anti-freeze in you to keep you warm.'

He walked off and Marienhof sprang to his feet.

'Vadim, get the screws and the hammer. Alik, you pass me the first one from the top of the pile. And Seryozha, give me a leg-up ...'

Marienhof took what looked like a steel plate from the parcel and with Sergei's help climbed to the top of a lamppost. With unexpected dexterity, he unscrewed the street sign attached to the post and replaced it with the one that Kusikov had handed him. Sergei saw that Kuznetsky Street had been renamed, 'Sergei Yesenin Street, the Imagist Republic of Moscow'. The four of them burst into laughter.

The following morning, Muscovites found other locations bearing unfamiliar names. Everyone knew the Provisional

Government was removing public references to the discredited tsarist regime, but Marienhof Street, Kusikov Avenue and Shershenevich Boulevard caused widespread head-scratching. As did a plaque attached to the Pushkin statue on Strastnaya Square, bearing a purported quote from Russia's national poet.

I AM WITH THE IMAGISTS!
LOVE, A.S. PUSHKIN.

Marienhof, Yesenin, Kusikov and Shershenevich

Marienhof said ink on paper was outmoded, a remnant of a discarded age. Now poetry needed to be written on the streets.

He bought three tubs of red paint from a builder's merchant, a ladder and a set of housepainter's brushes. They would all agree on the verses and he – Anatoly Marienhof – would select the canvas. He had considered the walls of the Kremlin, but concluded they would be arrested before they could begin.

'So I asked myself what would most horrify the bourgeoisie and decided it was the Church. Tonight we shall sanctify the walls of the Strastnoi Convent, the Nunnery of the Holy Passion, with the divine alchemy of art!'

Sergei went along with a heavy heart. He knew the world had changed, and he understood the motive for Marienhof's stunt. But respect for the Church – and fear of the punishments that awaited those who mocked it – was part of his upbringing. Daubing slogans on the walls of a convent felt like a blasphemy so wild that it would cut him off forever from a past his mind rejected, but his soul still clung to.

Marienhof went first:

> Citizens, change the underwear of your souls!
> Mary Magdalene, today I too shall come to you, in
>   clean drawers!

Kusikov climbed the ladder:

> Behold the fat thighs of this obscene wall!
> Here the nuns at night remove the trousers of Christ.

Shershenevich could not bring himself to go through with it. Yesenin hesitated, then picked up the brush:

> Oh Lord, I sing to you. Oh Lord, I appeal to you –
> Oh Lord, give birth to a calf!

It worked. The newspapers fulminated. *Izvestiya* was outraged:

> It has become fashionable to talk about bringing art on to the streets and the Imagists have taken this literally. On the morning of 28 May, Muscovites discovered that the walls of the Strastnoi Convent had been daubed in so-called poetry, with a purportedly joyous message: *Lord, give birth*

to a calf! . . . Citizens, change your underclothes! and other such monstrosities, signed by a group of poets calling themselves Imagists.

Those who gathered to witness this outrage were overcome with indignation. This was the act of hooligans, whose art is nothing more than bad language, cynicism and foul manners. Serious measures must be taken to protect our city from the malicious behaviour of this new breed of young people!

Marienhof, Kusikov and even the reticent Shershenevich were cock-a-hoop. The wrath of the bourgeoisie had exceeded their expectations; the names of the Imagists were on everyone's lips.

Sergei alone was gloomy. In his makeshift bedroom, behind the partition that screened him from the world, he began a poem of contrition:

> A Village Psalter:
> O mighty sun,
> You golden pitcher lowered into the world,
> Scoop up my soul!
> Draw me out of the well
> Of torment of my native land.
> Every day,
> Grasping the chain of your rays,
> I clamber skywards.
> Every evening
> I slip back and fall into the sunset's jaws.
> Sorrow afflicts me,
> My lips sing forth blood.
> They are tearing to pieces
> The virgin snows,
> The shroud of my mother country –

Her body hangs
Upon the cross.
The shins of her mountains
Are smashed.
And from the west, the wolf-wind howls.
Night, like a raven,
Sharpens her beak on the eyes of the lake
And dawn is nailed to the hills
Like an inscription on the cross:
Jesus of Nazareth, King of the Jews.
O moon!
May my grandfather's nut-brown hat,
Hurled by his cheeky grandson up on the branches
     of a cloud,
Fall once more to earth
And shield my quavering eyes.
O, where are you now!
O, where is my motherland!
O, red glow of evening!
Forgive me my cry to you.
Forgive me
My mistake,
For what do we know?
I studied only at the village school;
I know only the Bible and fairy tales.
I know only that the barley sings in the wind,
And how to play the accordion
On holy days and holidays.
And yet I understand.
I know it is
Better to die
Than to live
When your skin's been flayed.

Perish, my country!
Perish, my Russia,
My poor land
That has witnessed a third coming.
O stars!
You slender candles
Pouring waxen drops of red
On the prayer book of the dawn,
Bend down closer!
Incline your flame,
That I might
On tiptoes,
Rise up and snuff it out.
He who lit you
Could not conceive
Of the death
My verses sang.
Sing, o Volga,
Sing and seethe!
In your blue manger
Will she swaddle
Her child.
Do not tell me
It is the full orb
Of the moon
That rises . . .
No! It is He!
It is He
Who shall thrust forth
His head
From the womb of the sky!

Marienhof read Sergei's manuscript.

'I think you need a drink,' he said. 'And you definitely need a woman. When did you last have one?'

'I don't know . . .'

'Was it that mythical wife of yours? All those years ago?'

'Anna? No, there've been others. I haven't seen Anna for—'

'What you need is a woman who will make you feel like a man. Come on, I'll show you!'

War and revolution had filled Moscow with human flotsam, the homeless and the dispossessed, willing to do anything to stay afloat. In the streets behind the Central Telegraph Office, connoisseurs could find services to suit every taste. Marienhof took Sergei on a tour. In Kamergersky Lane and Gazetny Passage, he pointed out the goods like a guide with a tour group. There were women of all types, tall, short, garishly dressed, elegantly gowned, with make-up and without; there were men for women and men for men; and there were children, boys and girls barely in their teens, with deathly, knowing faces.

Sergei wanted to leave. Marienhof laughed.

'Give it a chance, Seryozha. Don't be so strait-laced. It will be good for you. Look, here's a couple of beauties. We can take them home.'

Anatoly Marienhof

After that first night, with the Ukrainian girls in Marienhof's attic, something loosened in Sergei. The vodka, the sex, the knowledge that the flesh pressed against his came with a price in roubles, not in emotions or responsibilities, felt like a release. He sensed for the first time that he was not beholden to the past, no longer bound by vows to God or country, to friends or family, to outdated notions of goodness. He was in Moscow, in the eye of a revolution that was shaking loose the keystones of the world, and he, too, was free. Marienhof's friendship was a promise of fulfilment in a universe that might be conquered.

They went back to Kamergersky. Marienhof continued the tour, lauding the other wares on offer. How about some of the young men? They were so beautiful, so feminine. Or the little ones? Think how soft and warm they must feel. Sergei refused.

Marienhof joked that whenever they took two girls home, both of them wanted to sleep with the blue-eyed, flaxen-haired Yesenin and neither wanted to sleep with him. What if they were to take just one girl and share her? How about giving it a try?

Sharing brought them closer. It was an expression of the unwritten pledge that bound them.

In search of even sharper pleasures, they would draw lots for who would sleep with whom. At times, the girl was dispatched to the single bed.

'I don't know what to make of you,' Sergei said to Marienhof. 'In your black cloak and your top hat, one might take you for a benevolent Mephistopheles.'

Anatoly Marienhof

Marienhof and Yesenin were rarely apart. The others retreated, ceding the attic to them and their night-time activities.

They shared their money and published their poems under one cover. When the nights grew colder, they slept under one blanket.

They were Imagism's undisputed leaders; Marienhof and Yesenin were the names that appeared at the head of the movement's Manifesto:

> We laugh when people talk about the content of art. The only purpose of art is the revelation of life through the image and the rhythm of images. The image and nothing but the image! We have no philosophy; the logic of our certitude is much more powerful than that. In these days of bitter cold, only the heat of our poetry can warm the souls of the people!

Poetry was magic. It justified everything, from immorality to cruelty to pain and shame.

Sergei never treated the girls brutally. In bed, he was selfish, perhaps, but never violent. When Marienhof fell asleep, a young woman who had spent the night with them asked Sergei if he would sit with her.

'You seem a good person,' she said. 'I mean, someone who hasn't lost his humanity in this inhuman city. And I recognise your accent . . .'

She was from Ryazan Oblast, born an hour's walk from Sergei's village. When her father was killed in the war and her mother died in the cholera epidemic, she was sent to an orphanage, where she was raped by the director and most of the staff. On her seventeenth birthday she had fled to Moscow.

Later, after the girl had gone, he told Marienhof about her.

'Yes, it's hard,' Marienhof said. 'The times are hard. We must make a choice, Seryozha. We can give in to pity and weakness. Or we can stay strong and harden our hearts. Only the strongest among us – only the man with the iron will – can emerge from this. Only the strongest can write the poetry that in its beauty will redeem the people's suffering. You must ask yourself, which way do you choose?'

'I want to be strong . . .' Sergei hesitated. 'I want to be a great poet . . .'

'Then we must swear an oath. And we must write it in blood . . .'

Marienhof took a knife from his pocket. 'So stab thine arm courageously,' he said, 'and bind thy soul with the flowing stream of blood, that thou might truly be numbered among the gods!'

CHAPTER 11

The Provisional Government was teetering. Its leader, Alexander Kerensky, was committed to justice, liberty and the rule of law, but events had outrun him. Lenin, back from his Swiss exile, sneered at the liberals' attachment to democracy. He understood the people's anger and promised to meet their demands – land, bread and an end to the war. When it emerged that Kerensky had pledged to continue hostilities against Germany, Lenin pounced:

> There must be no support for the bourgeois Provisional Government! We must expose its capitalist, imperialist nature as the enemy of peace and socialism. No! to a parliamentary republic. Yes! to the dictatorship of the people. An immediate end to the imperialist war! Demobilisation of the army!

In July, a Russian offensive was beaten back with heavy losses. When angry soldiers and workers took to the streets of Petrograd, Kerensky gave the order to gun them down and dozens were killed. The Bolsheviks denounced the Provisional Government as worse than the tsar. A quarter of a million people besieged Kerensky's headquarters calling for him to go.

The chairman of the Petrograd Soviet, Leon Trotsky,

assembled Red Guard militias ready to seize power, and on 25 October a salvo of blank shots from the cruiser *Aurora* in the city's harbour signalled the start of the coup.

The terrified ministers of the Provisional Government, holed up in the Winter Palace, offered little resistance. Their troops had abandoned them. The revolutionaries simply walked in and helped themselves to the tsar's wine cellars. Alexander Kerensky fled to a lifetime of exile in Paris and New York, but his ministers were cornered in the imperial breakfast chamber and forced to write their own arrest warrants.

Unlike the genuinely popular February revolution, October was a putsch. The majority of people in Petrograd barely knew it had happened. It was over in twenty-four hours with only two recorded casualties.

The Bolsheviks had seized power and were determined to keep it. Their secret police, the Cheka, rounded up and imprisoned the Party's opponents. When the Constituent Assembly, a freely elected, democratic parliament bequeathed by the Provisional Government, met for its inaugural session in January 1918, the Bolsheviks sent armed troops to close it down. Red Guards opened fire on demonstrators who protested.

'Everything has turned out for the best,' Lenin wrote. 'The dissolution of the Constituent Assembly means the complete and open repudiation of democracy in favour of dictatorship. This will be a valuable lesson.'

The Bolshevik dictatorship would be harsher and more pervasive than that of the tsars. Russia was declared a republic,
her cities and streets renamed, her alphabet recast and her
calendar recalculated. The capital was moved from Petrograd
to Moscow, foreign and domestic debts disowned, religion
persecuted, independent newspapers banned. The Bolsheviks
controlled people's private lives. Marriage was declared a bourgeois relic and free love official policy; divorce was facilitated,
abortion legalised. Titles and ranks were abolished, social
etiquette rewritten; instead of 'sir' or 'madam', people were
instructed to call each other 'citizen' and Party members to
address each other as 'comrade'.

But the regime was fragile and beset by powerful enemies.
Civil servants, the banks and the treasury, railway and communications workers all went on strike. Wages were unpaid;
the economy collapsed. At home, anti-Bolshevik forces were
preparing armed opposition; abroad, the Western powers were
growing ever more hostile.

Lenin sent Trotsky to negotiate a peace treaty with the
Germans, recognising that an end to the war would be

immensely popular. But the Germans insisted on punitive conditions. The Treaty of Brest-Litovsk, signed in March 1918, brought big territorial losses. The new Soviet Republic forfeited a quarter of its population and vast swathes of its coalfields, agricultural land and heavy industry. Supporters of the old order were spoiling for revenge. Civil war was brewing.

Sergei struggled. He had spent his life seeking the approbation of schoolteachers and grandparents, of God and the tsar; calculating his worth as a person in accordance with their fickle signals of approval. But their authority had been exposed as worthless. He had wasted his life bowing to shadows.

Easter tipped him over the edge. There were the usual processions, led as always by the gold-robed priests parading the holy icons of Christ crucified, chanting the joyful mystery of Christ resurrected. But this was 1918 and believers were sparser, more hesitant in their expressions of faith. The Red Guards shepherding them hesitated, too. Some mocked and spat, but others crossed themselves as the icons passed. The revolution was young, the Church venerable.

Sergei followed the marchers down Tverskaya towards the Kremlin. The new Patriarch, Tikhon, had been appointed by the casting of lots as the revolution unfolded, and Sergei saw the tension in his face; the pale nimbus of martyrdom tightening round the Patriarch's brow rekindled his childhood awe.

An army unit halted them at the Resurrection Gates. Centuries of Easter marches had passed through into Red Square, but the Party had decreed that this year would be different. A young lieutenant engaged the Patriarch in conversation. It was official policy, he said, that no expressions of religious faith, of whatever denomination, were now permitted on the territory of the central government. Sergei saw Tikhon summon his courage. He was a short man, but he gained in height as he made the sign of the cross.

'The square is the territory of God,' Tikhon said. 'The Cathedral of the Blessed Saint Basil is upon it. And in the Kremlin, where the godless ones now sit, there are churches and cathedrals of Our Lord, bearing witness to a millennium of Orthodox faith. Who are you, my son, to forbid the people their right to pray?'

The lieutenant tried one more time to convince him, then shrugged and waved to his men. From the street behind the State Historical Museum, a squad of Red Guards with batons emerged at the double, charging into the procession, smashing heads and legs, sparing neither the elderly nor the infirm. Most of the marchers turned and ran, but a core of believers stood their ground, refusing to defend themselves. One after another, they were knocked to the floor, faces covered in blood. The soldiers kicked them and beat them until the officer gave the order to desist. Sergei turned away in horror and despair.

Patriarch Tikhon

He drank for a week. He wandered from one bar to another, slept on the street, shared the *samogon* that the tramps distilled from corn mash, potatoes, furniture polish and cleaning fluids. He could not have found his way home if he'd wanted to. He was in a world where fixed points had been erased; the earth had trembled and he'd fallen off.

On the eighth day, a hand touched his shoulder. He opened his eyes and saw the outline of a face.

'Seryozha, what are you doing in the gutter?'

The voice came from a great distance; he thought it might be that of Grisha Panfilov, come to rescue him after he was beaten up in the seminary at Spas-Klepiki.

'Why have you come to rescue me again?' he said.

'We have a pact. Remember? We swore it in our blood . . .'

'In our blood . . . Yes . . . But it's too late, Grisha. I don't want to be rescued . . . And . . . anyway, I think you are dead – forgive me, my friend; forgive me!'

The face smiled.

'Look at it this way,' Marienhof said. 'Life can be good; life can be bad. Detach yourself. Life is just fuel for your poetry. Art is the philosopher's stone that transmutes existence. Do it and you will find meaning.'

It was the year of hunger, house-searches, typhus and lies. For Sergei, it was the year of debauchery. Alcohol and carnality were the reckless helmsmen of his existence. His behaviour was wild, dangerous and uncaring. Idealism ceded the field to contempt, innocence to blasphemy, good intentions to sneering depravity.

He wrote little and, when he did, it was dark. The celebrant of the village, the proclaimer of nature's beauty, became the Virgil of the urban underworld, the Moscow of taverns, prostitutes, thieves and scoundrels. He wrote of his own debasement:

Play, accordion! Boredom, tedium, ennui;
The player's fingers flee.
Drink with me, you mangy bitch!
You're so randy; drink with me!
You've been fingered and soiled so often –
It's all too much.
Why do your blue sparks glare so softly?
Are you looking for a punch!
They should sit you astride the orchard
To frighten off the crows.
Just how deep in my guts you torture me
God only knows.
Play, accordion! Play for the lousy bar!
Drink, you skunks, drink!
I'd be better off with the one with the
          tits;
Her sort don't think.
You're not the first I've handled thus ...
Your kind's not scarce.
But with one like you, so scandalous,
This is my first.
Pain and passion together –
You know how it makes me feel swell.
I'll never kill myself, never!
So you can go to hell.
It's high time for me to be leaving
You and this lousy crew.
My love, I'm weeping.
Forgive me. Forgive me ... do ...

Sergei was troubled by the poetry he found himself writing.
Marienhof reassured him.

'Callousness and despair are grist to poetry's mill, Seryozha.

There's no such thing as a moral or an immoral poem. Poems are either well written, or badly written. That's all.'

Opposition to the Bolsheviks was growing. The October Revolution had divided the country. Millions had defected from the tsar's army, but millions had not. Former tsarist generals were assembling their forces – Whites, because of their cream-coloured officers' uniforms – bent on driving out the Reds.

Lenin's newly named Communist Party held Petrograd and Moscow, but the Whites controlled vast areas of Russia and Ukraine. The tsarist generals Kornilov and Denikin were advancing from the south; Admiral Kolchak's army from Omsk in the east; and from their base in Estonia, General Yudenich's troops were threatening Petrograd itself.

Britain, France and America sent thousands of men to help the Whites in the struggle against the socialist menace. Anti-British songs swept the Red cabarets.

> Our former tsarist masters begged the foreigners
> To save their land and their banks.
> So the crafty old English sent in troops and tanks!
> To the bourgeois devils our people say:
> We'll take death over slavery any day.

The Whites were within a hundred miles of Moscow and even closer to Petrograd. The Bolshevik Minister of War, Leon Trotsky, introduced conscription and shot those who refused, dashing from battle to battle in his own armoured train, haranguing the troops, executing deserters.

Russians fought against Russians, neighbour against

neighbour. The closeness fuelled the ferocity of the fighting and the enormity of the atrocities.

General Kornilov instructed his men not to take prisoners, pledging to restore the monarchy even if it meant burning half the country. Captured Red soldiers were executed and Jews murdered in White-backed pogroms. 'There are no rules and no limits! God is with us,' cried the White Cossacks. 'Slash left and slash right!' Villages were razed; inhabitants who refused to feed White troops hanged. To save White bullets, two thousand Red prisoners were buried alive.

The Bolsheviks were equally brutal. The Cheka secret police tied White officers to planks and fed them into furnaces or vats of boiling water. Crucifixions, scalpings and flayings were commonplace. Eyes were gouged, tongues torn out and flesh ripped from prisoners' backs. In Oryol naked prisoners were doused with water in sub-zero temperatures and left to freeze to death.

Sergei averted his eyes, refused to read the newspapers, refused conversations about the war.

Marienhof had fewer scruples. His poetry revelled in the horror:

> I shall make the sky
> Abort its foetus
> And squeeze the milk
> From the tits of the moon.
> I shall spit blood
> At the stupid face of God
> And watch the wind
> Sweep up
> Heaps of human flesh.
> Blood, blood, blood
> Splashes in the world
> Like water in a bath.

Who cares about the dead!
I just walk on by.
One more hour
And the meat of our souls
Will turn a putrid green.

It was a provocation too far. The Imagists were reviled. There were renewed calls for them to be banned. The Bolsheviks' Commissar for Education, Anatoly Lunacharsky, was asked to take measures.

Sergei was unnerved. The months of alcoholic bewilderment, the horrors of civil war, the misery of life in the starving city had left him fragile and disturbed. He told Marienhof he was going home.

Bolshevik victims of the Whites

The Ryazan train was overflowing with desperate, sweating humanity fleeing from something to somewhere, barely knowing what they were seeking or what to expect when they found it. Smartly dressed men spoke of aunts in the country and how it would be safer to live 'out there' than on the coming battle-field of Moscow; peasants caught in the capital were bolting for their villages; the homeless and the uprooted heading for yet another place of desolate exile. Sergei found a space on the floor.

After two hours, the train halted. Rumours flew through the carriages – the line had been cut; the Reds had blown up the tracks; the Whites were waiting in ambush; there was fighting in the next village. The engine shuddered back into life. The train moved forward then stopped, started again then pulled into to a country station with no nameplates. There was a crowd of people on the platform, some of them trying to board, others looking anxiously for friends or relatives due from Moscow.

An official arrived with news. There had been fighting three miles ahead; scouts had been dispatched and the train would be held until they returned. Several hours passed. Passengers with seats were reluctant to vacate them, but afternoon turned to evening and hunger forced them out. Peasant women selling onions and cucumbers outside the station were able to double their prices.

It was a risk to go beyond the station forecourt, but the train showed no signs of moving and Sergei walked into the village. On the street beside a clapperboard inn, a young woman asked if he needed anything. There was music from inside and enough light from the half-open windows to make out the blond braids and blue eyes beneath her patterned headdress.

Sergei lifted the woman's scarf and looked into her eyes.

'Perhaps I do,' he said with a smile. 'We may not have long, though. How much?'

The woman recoiled.

'You've got it wrong,' she said, pulling away. 'You are a stranger here and the Bible enjoins us to show kindness to strangers. Do you not know the hospitality of bread and salt? Do you not know Russia?'

Two blasts from the engine whistle had summoned him back. The train set off into the darkness; the click of the wheels eased him into sleep. He dreamed of the girl and of the women selling onions. The old woman, the *starushka* from Dostoevsky's Karamazov Brothers, was proffering him her single onion, the one act of kindness that might save her from hell after a life of greed. But when he lifted the woman's headscarf, he saw she was not old at all. She was young and pretty, and she was offering her bare breasts for him to fondle. Shame came over him. He woke to the half-light of the carriage.

When next he slept, he was in the burning lake of hell beside the *starushka* and God's angel was extending the onion down to her, urging her to grasp it so she could be pulled into heaven. The old woman seized the onion and was lifted out of the fire. But as she rose, dozens of other sinners began to hold on to her legs and ankles, and as they were pulled up along with her, thousands more grabbed on to *their* legs until it seemed the whole bowels of hell were hanging from a single woman's body and the onion to which she clung.

Sergei was the last to see what was happening. He realised that he was being left behind. At the very final moment, he grasped the ankle of the last person in the chain. He felt himself rising up, and a wave of joy swept over him. He was part of the gigantic, swarming beehive of humanity, millions upon millions of the living and the dead, being plucked from the depths of damnation.

But as he clung to the ankle above him, he sensed that something awful was happening. His weight was tipping the balance, adding the fateful few pounds that would stretch then break the onion. They were falling now, falling forever, deeper into the blackness of the abyss.

It was after midnight when the train dropped him at the halt by the level crossing and he walked the four miles in darkness, seeking familiar paths, stumbling over stiles, navigating by touch, by memory, by instinct.

He arrived in Konstantinovo as the dawn broke. In his grandfather's meadow, the sun was rising from behind the aspen copse. The dew glinted on the feather grass and the velvet buds of Sergei's silver birch floated in the light.

He put off going to the house. He took the trail that sloped down through the fields to the Oka. The river was in spate. Timber from the mills was careering downstream, whole trunks swept along by the current.

He paused on the grassy bank where once he watched the horses drink the moon, then stood at the spot where his grandfather drowned the puppies under the ice. He found the lake where he, too, was nearly drowned.

Nature lifted him; the stillness, the air, the brightness that washed away the dirt of the city. Words stirred:

> I'm home among my people now,
> My land of dreams and tender feeling
> Where days shine bright as fields of snow ...

The lines came easily:

> I walk the valley, my cap pushed back
> And hands in gloves of kidskin ...
> I have no cares, no deeds to do,
> But sing the song that fills my heart
> And hope the lightest breeze should blow ...
> I leave the road, descend the slope
> Where scythes are whistling in the field.
> My youthful body, tall and straight ...

It was the old inspiration, bubbling up from before the time of corruption, from the days when life's sweetness lay in sun and snow and elderflowers in the hedgerow. He sensed an augury of escape in them, a casting off of the city, of the darkness and confusion.

He ran to the house. His grandfather was sawing firewood in the meadow. Without a word, Sergei took the saw's second handle and they worked in tandem, pushing forward, pulling back in the heartbeat rhythm of shared exertion. He found comfort in it, a sense of physical integrity after the months of debasement. Shavings flew, unlocking the honey perfume of the sap. Neither of them spoke. When the log fell from the trestle, Sergei saw his grandfather's tears.

'Seryozha,' the old man said, turning away. 'We thought we would not see you again. Wait ... wait here ...'

He came back with Sergei's grandmother. She hugged the boy she had raised in a trembling embrace.

'Thanks be to God!' she said, over and again. 'Thank you, Lord! Thank you for saving my boy!'

His grandmother loaded the table with dishes of salted perch, plates of fatted veal, dried fruit from the cellar beneath the haybarn. She fussed; the samovar whistled; the room filled with steam and talk.

His grandparents' welcome overwhelmed him. A sense of belonging he had thought forever lost.

'Thank you,' he said. 'Thank you ... It hasn't been easy since I left ...'

'It's all right, Seryozha. It's all right. Everything will be all right,' his grandmother said.

She spoke of his childhood, of their walks together to

churches and monasteries, his successes at school. She sang the songs she had taught him and laughed at the folk tales he had taken so seriously.

His grandfather made a sign to his wife. She nodded; she would go and prepare Sergei's old bed on the shelf above the stove. He would be warm and safe there.

His grandfather sat.

'Seryozha,' he said finally. 'I want to tell you something. When you were young, I think I was harsh on you. I cannot tell the motives for this. I told you it was to make you a man, and that is true. But there were other things. Your mother had upset us, me and your grandmother. She had left her husband, and left you, because she had feelings for another man. I do not know the details. But what I want to say is that perhaps this contributed to me treating you badly. And if it did, then I want to say I am sorry . . .'

'I don't blame you for anything,' Sergei said. 'You did well to do what you did. It prepared me for life. I never hated you . . .'

His grandfather held up his hand.

'There is something else. I know it has been difficult for you. I know you and your mother have not seen eye to eye over the years. I don't know if you have forgiven her for abandoning you. Perhaps you haven't. But what I want to say is that circumstances weren't easy for her—'

'Grandfather, I don't want to think about it . . .'

'But I fear you will have to,' his grandfather said. 'Your mother is back. She and your father are living with us . . .'

Sergei was in bed when his mother got home. He heard the whispered conversation between her and her anxious parents. But he didn't get up. And she didn't come to him.

His grandfather had told him how Alexander Yesenin, fired from his butcher's job in Moscow, had swallowed his pride and made it up with the wife who had borne a daughter he doubted was his. 'Our Tanya' had split with 'whoever it was she was living with', was all his grandfather would say, and had accepted her husband's terms. Times were hard, neither of them had a job, so they'd come to live here. Tanya had found work as a cleaner in Fedyakino, five miles away, and rarely got home before midnight. Alexander was away visiting his parents and wouldn't be back for some time.

Sergei had hoped for a restful night after months of insomnia, but the thought of his mother troubled him. In the bed above the stove he lay awake, reliving the past, scratching at old wounds still unhealed.

In the morning, his grandmother brought him tea. She took his hand and stroked his hair. When the four of them gathered awkwardly at table, his mother's appearance took him aback. The fragile elegance he remembered from his first years had gone; her face was lined, her youth vanished.

His grandparents said they had something they had to attend to. Mother and son sat on, not knowing how to begin.

'Have you read my verses?'

'Yes.'

'And?'

'I liked the ones about Konstantinovo, about animals and nature ...'

'But?'

'Why do you write all those poems about drunkenness and women of loose morals?'

Part of him had hoped she would throw her arms around him; that she would explain, apologise, offer a new beginning.

She, too, was nervous, troubled by his reputation and by his behaviour. She listed his pranks and debaucheries, asked why he brought the family name into disrepute.

Sergei bristled.

'That's not for you to say, Mother. A mother who loved her son, who was there for him when he needed her ... such a mother has the right to say those things!'

'Don't judge me, Sergei! Don't judge me!'

'Judge you? But didn't you judge *me* all those years ago? You judged me when you left; you judged me when you walked out!'

'Seryozha! Don't speak of what you don't understand. You don't know me. You don't know about your father—'

'I worked with my father. In Moscow. I worked with him in his stinking butcher's shop. And if he was such a monster that you had to leave him, how come it's suddenly all right for you to take him back?'

Tanya sobbed.

'We are adults, Seryozha. And the past is the past. Can you not find it in yourself to understand what happened ... ?'

She extended a hand, but he didn't take it.

'You never thought about rejection and how it corrodes a life,' he said. 'Rejection not just by anyone; rejection by the most important person in the world – the person who gave you life, then judged you unworthy of love!'

Alexander and Tatiana, Yesenin's parents

He announced he was going back to Moscow. His grandparents tried to dissuade him, terrified by the rumours of impending conflict.

He hesitated. But his quest to find refuge in the idyll of the past had been vain. He left an envelope for his mother.

A Letter to My Mother

Are you still alive, my *starushka*?
I am too, and I wanted to write.
I hope the evening still bathes the cottage
In the same inexpressible light.
They tell me you try to hide it,
That I'm causing you pain and distress.
That you walk out on the road after supper
In your tattered, old-fashioned dress.
And when you go walking through twilight,
What you brood on is always the same:
There's a bar-room fight, and deep in my
      heart
Someone plunges a slim Finnish blade.
It's nothing, my dear! Calm yourself.
It's only a dream born of dread.
I may drink, but I'll see you again
Before anyone lays me down dead.
I'll come back when our garden is white
With the blossoms that I used to know;
But this time don't wake me at daybreak,
As you once did, all those years ago.
Don't awaken the dreams that are gone;
Don't rehearse what can never come true.

The grief that living can bring
Fell to my lot when life was still new.
And don't ask me to pray. Don't do it!
What is long past cannot be made right,
Though the evening may still bathe the cottage
In that same inexpressible light.

Sergei Yesenin and his mother, Tatiana [nee Titova]

The journey to Moscow took three days. The train was halted, diverted, shunted into sidings. Armed men came on board, claiming to be security patrols. At times it was hard to tell if they were Whites, Reds or merely brigands.

On the second day, they stopped at a burned-out station and Sergei recognised it as the place where he had accosted the young woman. The village looked deserted, damaged by fire.

The unlikely coincidence of a second stop at such an out of the way location filled him with foreboding. His act of disrespect towards the girl appeared to him as the mark of his sin, the manifest of his life's guilt.

The train was being held until engineers could repair a damaged bridge twelve miles ahead. Passengers were permitted to disembark, but were told to be ready to depart at the sound of the engine whistle. It seemed a chance to make amends, to offer an apology.

He found the village littered with abandoned carts and broken furniture. The inhabitants of the charred cottages that lined the streets had evidently struggled to save what they could. There were half-burned timbers in large puddles of water, where efforts had been made to douse the flames.

An old woman sitting with two suitcases on a bench told him what had happened.

'It was to do with that *prodraz* thing, dearie ... *vyorstka* or whatever they call it ... when they come with guns and take away all the grain. Well, last spring they came here and they went through everything. We had a big trunk in the house where we keep bits and pieces of food. But they even found those things in the trunk and took them away, too. This was all in May, after that Vladimir Ilyich promulcated his degree. Well, we heard they were coming back again. And our menfolk weren't going to stand for it. They got together with what do they call them? – those Green Armies, full of peasants like us who won't stand for being robbed. And they lay in wait for the *prodraz* people to come – this was at the end of last week – but the *prodraz* men must have been tipped off, because they brought cannons and guns and set fire to the whole place, like as you can see. And all our menfolk either got shot or they've run away now to join the Greens.'

Sergei thanked her.

'I'm looking for someone,' he said. 'A young woman. Very pretty. Around twenty or twenty-five. Blue eyes and blond plaits that she winds around her head under a green-and-blue scarf. Do you know who I mean?'

'That could describe half the young women in our village,' said the old woman. 'Don't you have a name for her?'

He shook his head.

'No, I don't. All I can tell you is that she has something to do with the inn on the main street, the one with the clapperboard front – I've just been there and it's been burned down.'

'Why didn't you say so? That'd be Lydia Anisova . . .'

'Yes?' he said eagerly. 'Where can I find her?'

The old woman sighed.

'In the cemetery, dearie. Along with all the others.'

CHAPTER 12

Marienhof was unsurprised that Sergei had returned. In the Poets' Café on Tverskaya Street, they drank vodka and talked about happiness.

'I thought I could escape,' Sergei said. 'I thought there was a way out . . .'

Marienhof nodded. 'Escape is a slippery thing. We can escape from the world perhaps, but we can't escape from ourselves. Griboyedov was right when he said happiness is *where we are not*.'

'Then what must we do with our lives?' Sergei said. 'Changing scenery, changing beds, changing bodies. What's the point? The time for dreaming is short. There's no love; there's no place left to live or belong. I shall have passed like a whisper and I shall sleep like the ice. Is this how men live?'

'Yes,' said Marienhof. 'And there's only one way to avenge ourselves on the whole stupid joke. We must take our life and squeeze its neck until it sings. Art is our revenge.'

'So we accept the tragedy? We embrace the role?'

'Yes,' said Marienhof. 'I'm working on my memoirs and I'm going to call them *The Cynics*, with an epigraph from Leskov, *The poet must disfigure himself for his art. It is a sacrifice that demands a special heroism.*'

Marienhof had forged his reputation from scandal and Yesenin followed his example. He would be a hooligan now. It would furnish his verses with a striking lyric persona, a doomed hero who would haunt his poetry for the rest of his life. He marked the turning point with a poem-manifesto, titled 'A Hooligan's Confession':

Not everyone can sing; not everyone can be
The apple that falls at others' feet.
Here goes with my hooligan's confession,
The swaggering avowal of a deadbeat.
I'm down and out, my hair's a matted mess,
My head's a gas lamp, flaming on my neck.
From the murky depths, from the city's bowels,
It lights the barren autumn of your souls.
The abuse, the stones you hurl at me,
All your belching thunder, I just don't care.
I clasp my head and cling on tighter
To the reckless, swaying serpents of my hair.
I try to think of aspens and the leaf-greened pool,
Of my mother who won't give a damn for my poems,
Yet loves me like the rain that slakes the soil.
Poor, poor peasants, if you only knew it:
Your son, who once went barefoot in the rain,
Your Sergei is Russia's greatest poet.
The boy who stroked the horses, bowed to cows
Strolls in top hats now, wears patent leather shoes.
Good night! Good night to all!
On twilit meadows,
The red sickle of the sun

No longer falls.
The light's so blue, so blue!
To die in such blueness might not be too soon;
Or else through the open window
I could maybe piss the moon ...
O, who cares if I speak like a cynic!
I'm the Orpheus of the city's rats.
My skull, full of the wine of August,
Steadies me to breathe my last.
Let me be the yellow veil
That shrouds the land,
To which all of us must one day sail.

The Whites were closing in. They already controlled the south and most of Siberia. By July 1918, they were approaching Yekaterinburg in the Urals.

Nicholas II and his family had been sequestered in the sixteen months since his abdication. The Provisional Government had promised them safe passage; Alexander Kerensky had personally asked Nicholas's cousin, King George of England, to take them in. But George had refused, fearing that the presence of a monarch deposed by his rebellious people might turn an already strife-riven Britain against him.

The Bolsheviks had none of Kerensky's compassion. The royal family were taken from the palace at Tsarskoe Selo, where they had been under house arrest, and sent eastwards, first to Tobolsk and then in April 1918 to Yekaterinburg. They were held in a confiscated merchant's house. Red Guards remained with them night and day, mocking and insulting. Alexandra and the four girls were the target of particular abuse. The

tsarevich, Alexei, was suffering from recurring attacks of haemophilia. Nicholas reassured them, but his fears grew.

Captivity in Yekaterinburg

For the Bolsheviks, the Romanovs were a danger.
Yekaterinburg could fall to the enemy and a rescued royal
family would be a powerful weapon, rallying support for the
anti-communist cause.

On the afternoon of 16 July, Nicholas took a stroll in the
garden with his daughters. The family went to bed at 10.30 p.m.
At midnight, they were woken by pounding on their bedroom
doors. Two secret policemen told them they were being taken
to the cellar, where they would be 'safer'.

The tsar and the empress were allowed to wash and dress,
eventually emerging from their rooms at one in the morning.
A guard reported later that 'the tsar was carrying young Alexei
in his arms, father and son dressed in matching soldiers' shirts
and caps. The empress and her daughters followed Nicholas
down to the cellar. None of them asked any questions. They
did not weep or cry. It seemed as if they all had guessed their
fate, but not one of them uttered a single sound.'

The secret policeman in charge of the operation described
what followed:

Nicholas put his son on a chair in the cellar and stood in front of him as if to shield him. I said to Nicholas that the Soviet of Workers' Deputies had resolved to shoot them. He said, 'What?' and turned towards Alexei, but I shot him and killed him outright. Then we all started firing. Bullets ricocheted off the walls. The shooting intensified and the victims' cries rose. When it stopped, the daughters, the empress and Alexei were still alive. Alexei was sitting there, petrified. I killed him. The others shot the daughters but did not kill them. They resorted to a bayonet, but that didn't work either. Finally they killed them by shooting them in the head.

When the executioners examined the princesses' bodies, they discovered why they had been so hard to kill. The women had sewn the royal jewels into their corsets, which had deflected their bullets.

The murder chamber after the killings

After a brief hesitation, the Bolsheviks announced the deaths of the royal family. The Russian people were instructed to rejoice. The bloodsuckers and whores who had brought Russia to her knees were no more.

Many did rejoice, but others were distraught. Some sought revenge on the regicides. There was shooting in Petrograd and Moscow. Snipers opened fire from the upper storeys of town houses, killing Red Guards in the streets.

At the same time, a disaffected faction of Lenin's own party, the Left Socialist Revolutionaries, staged a putsch from within. An SR hitman named Yakov Blumkin assassinated the German ambassador to Moscow in an attempt to sabotage the Bolsheviks' peace accord with Berlin. Blumkin used forged papers to bluff his way into the German embassy and shot the ambassador through the eye. It was the signal for the putsch to begin. Two thousand rebel soldiers bombarded the Kremlin with artillery shells. They seized the Central Telephone and Telegraph Office on Tverskaya Street and for more than forty-eight hours, they controlled much of the capital.

There was fighting in the city centre, with casualties on both sides. The Left SRs sent proclamations to all parts of the country, declaring that they had taken power, triggering similar insurrections in Petrograd, Vologda and Yaroslavl. The Bolsheviks put down the revolt, but were left in no doubt that their hold on power was tenuous.

Their response was to intensify the campaign of class hatred. The cellar where the tsar's family had been murdered was preserved, with bullet marks left in the walls and markers on the floor to show where the tyrants had met their bloody ends. When the White forces were pushed back from Yekaterinburg, guided tours were organised for Party workers.

Bolshevik officials shown the murder chamber

Sergei told Marienhof he was having nightmares about Princess Anastasia. He kept seeing her in a bloodstained white dress opening the lids of pots, looking for borshch, but instead pulling out human hands and bloody lumps of flesh. He had started to glimpse her in the daytime, too, hiding in corners, mingling with the crowds, eluding his pursuit. He asked if he was going mad.

Marienhof said he should stop worrying. Tsarism was yesterday; the future was socialism. And the Imagists were going into business.

'Look,' he said, 'I've got a lease on a basement on Tverskaya Street. And I've got official permission to turn it into a café!'

He placed a letter on the table, stamped with the word 'Approved'. Under the heading 'People's Commissariat of Enlightenment', was a single paragraph:

I fully approve the aims of your undertaking and hereby authorise you to proceed.

A. V. Lunacharsky,
People's Commissar of Enlightenment.

Sergei let out a whistle.

'How did you get the Commissar for Enlightenment to authorise us opening a café?'

'Well, to be honest,' Marienhof smiled, 'it's not exactly permission for a café. It's more what you might call a socio-scientific, artistic and political association ... Here's the application I sent':

Esteemed Comrade Lunacharsky,

I have the honour to request your official endorsement and approval of The Association of Progressive Thinkers of Moscow. The Association is an educational body that brings together leading activists in the fields of culture and politics. Its aims are the intellectual and economic furtherance of progressive thinking among cultural figures loyal to the spirit of world revolution, in order to encourage the widest possible dissemination of revolutionary idealism in art and literature. The Association counts among its membership prominent figures from the fields of poetry, *belles-lettres*, music, theatre and painting. It will be funded by revenue from its public-minded activities, including recitals, concerts, plays, the publication of books and journals, and the operation of a collective canteen.

Yours respectfully,

The Supreme Soviet of the Association of Progressive Thinkers of Moscow,

Marienhof, A.

Yesenin, S.

Shershenevich, V.

Kusikov, A.

Sergei laughed. 'What a weighty undertaking! And all for the sake of that last sentence ... Would I be right in thinking our "collective canteen" will have booze, women and dancing, and will stay open all night?'

'Of course. But it will also have nightly appearances by Russia's greatest poets, two of whom happen to be sitting here right now! Moscow won't be able to resist it. And there's another thing – they've given us permission for "the publication of books and journals". We're going to have our own publishing house, Seryozha; we're going to be rich!'

Anatoly Lunacharsky, People's Commissar of Enlightenment

Marienhof was a showman, but he was also an operator who saw the potential for profit. The Bolsheviks' state monopoly on trade had proved a disaster. The civil war had cut off supplies and the cities were suffering. A new class of black-marketeers stepped into the breach, shady dealers in commodities that the regime was manifestly incapable of providing. The speculators were reviled, but people needed them and they got rich.

The Moscow of 1918 offered few opportunities for joy. The spivs had money to spend and a *café dansant* with music, cabaret and alcohol was just what they were looking for.

'The key thing is to keep it above board,' Marienhof said.

'The Red commissars are keeping an eye on us and it seems to be a kindly one, but that can easily change. So, no politics on stage, no offences against public decency – not on the premises, at least – and a good dose of poetry and art.'

They engaged the Armenian Futurist painter Georgy Yakulov to decorate the walls with vivid, angular figures, bright friezes and quotations from Imagist poetry. A polished dance floor was installed and a raised stage for a small orchestra. Low-level lighting gave the room a conspiratorial air. Under the glass on the tabletops there were inlaid spaces for new poems that would change each evening.

Marienhof took charge of the publicity. He was about to commission posters when he realised the café didn't have a name.

'We need to call it something classy,' he said. 'And arty. The paying clientele may be philistines, but the place will be a magnet for poets and a platform for us. How about "Mount Parnassus"?'

'More like "Mound of Venus"!' Shershenevich said, 'the number of tarts we'll get coming in here. I'd go for something less pretentious – "Bacchus' Retreat", maybe?'

The others shook their heads. Kusikov rattled off a list of ideas – The Poets' Den, Image and Imagination, The Flight of Fancy – but all were rejected.

Sergei found the solution.

'We need a name that says art, but something full of energy and élan. Pegasus was the steed of the Muses, right? – everywhere his hoof touched the earth, a fountain of poetry erupted. We should call ourselves "The Pegasus Stable" . . .'

The opening caused a stir. Marienhof had done a good job with the posters. Crowds gathered on Tverskaya. By evening, a hundred people were milling at the entrance.

In the darkened basement, Sergei panicked.

'How can we do this?' he said. 'How can we expose ourselves to a public that hates us? These people have come because they detest us and everything we represent . . .'

Marienhof laughed. 'Maybe you're right. But who cares? Let them come to see the delinquent boys; let them boo and throw things. They'll pay their entry fee and they'll buy their drinks. We don't need them to love us!'

But Sergei did need people to love him. He was convinced that almost no one did.

On 30 August 1918, Vladimir Lenin addressed workers at an engineering plant in the Zamoskvorechye district of Moscow. His speech drew applause; a throng of well-wishers cheered him to his car. But in the factory yard, three shots rang out. Lenin slumped to the ground. His bodyguards bundled him into the car and rushed him back to the Kremlin. In the crowd, a young woman slipped a revolver back into her handbag.

Doctors summoned to Lenin's bedside found him close to death. The bullets had pierced his arm, his jaw and his neck. Blood was leaking into his lungs and he was struggling to breathe. They decided that removing the bullets could kill him, so they dressed his wounds and prayed that infection would not set in.

At the factory, police units seeking clues to the assailant's identity rounded up those who had been present, but there were contradictory accounts. No one knew who had fired the shots.

The Bolsheviks were in the middle of a civil war, menaced by foes at home and abroad. They concluded they were facing an enemy conspiracy.

A few hours later, news of another attack confirmed their suspicions. The head of the Petrograd secret police, Moisei Uritsky, had been shot dead. The order was given to lock down both cities. Scores of suspects were rounded up, tortured or shot.

The Pegasus Stable filled with cigar smoke and noise. At the best tables, expensively dressed men with greased hair pulled blonde Ukrainian girls on to their laps, clicking their fingers to summon food. Waiters ran in carrying plates of caviar and trays of beer. Ladies of the night leaned on the pillars to the right and left of the stage, adjusting their stockings. In the shadows at the back of the room shabby poets chatted nervously and fingered their manuscripts.

Gypsy music gave way to cabaret songs then to satirical monologues. A voice yelled, 'What about the poetry!' Sergei mounted the stage. He raised his hand to quiet the cheers and the boos, called for silence and introduced his fellow Imagists.

Kusikov and Shershenevich recited to a mixed reception. Marienhof declaimed a few stanzas then handed back to Sergei.

'Please welcome,' he said, 'a poetic phenomenon – former peasant, former monarchist lapdog, now a fully fledged degenerate and hooligan of our fair city, Mr Citizen-Comrade Sergei Yesenin!'

There was a smattering of applause, a few whistles and catcalls. Sergei unfolded a sheet of paper, looked it over and dropped it to the floor. With his eyes closed and his left hand beating time, he began:

> So that's it then, no way back now;
> Quit my home, dumped my friends.
> My old poplars with their leafy brow

Won't shield me from these winds.
The house will sag without me;
My dog, God love him, is dead.
The twisted streets of Moscow
'Til death I now must tread.
I'm an inmate of the city,
With its cupolas and elms,
Where the golden sleep of Asia
Has suborned us to its ends.
At night, when the moonlight sways
And spreads its demon glow,
I hang my head through the alleys
And down to the bar I go.
It's a dive, a creepy, seedy hangout,
With such a racket, and scams to break your heart.
All night I drink with the pimps and touts
And shout my poems to the tarts.
I can feel my heart rate rising,
My speech is slurred and slack:
I'm just like you, I say at random:
Lost! Like you! With no way back! . . .

A volley of curses interrupted him. At a table next to the stage, a man in a dinner jacket struggled to his feet.

'What the fuck are you talking about, you jumped-up little prick? – "*Like you*"? – "*Like me*"? You're *nothing* like me – you're a fucking nobody!'

A beer glass flew at them through the air. The room erupted. The man in the dinner jacket, swaying unsteadily, grabbed Sergei by the throat.

'You're a piece of shit, little poet boy! Why didn't you get us a real poet? Why don't you get us . . . you know . . . Alexander Blok!'

Sergei pushed the fellow, who fell to the floor.

'Blok! Blok's a nobody!' Sergei shouted. 'He isn't worth the varnish on my nails!'

Chairs were being thrown now.

It was a riot about poetry, because poetry mattered. Poetry was the nation's voice when political discourse choked.

Poetry defied repression; offered Russians a better vision of themselves.

But poetry was dangerous. In the new Russia, just as in the old, stray words could be a death sentence.

When Sergei sobered up in the early hours, he was choked by shame. Had he really spat on the name of Russia's greatest poet?

Lenin's assailant had tried to escape. Fanny Kaplan was a member of the disenchanted Socialist Revolutionaries, the group that had shelled the Kremlin a month earlier. She had volunteered for the assassination, but she was short-sighted, almost blind, and physically weak from beatings received in tsarist jails. A policeman spotted her running away. When he challenged her, she gave herself up.

Lenin was barely clinging to life, but the Bolshevik press played down his injuries. 'Lenin, Shot Twice, Refuses Help!'

declared the Pravda headlines. 'Continues to Guide Locomotive of World Revolution!'

The Soviets accused the British of masterminding the plot against them. Red Guards ransacked the British embassy and shot a British official. The acting ambassador, Robert Bruce Lockhart, was dragged from his bed and driven to the Lubyanka prison.

Soldiers brought Fanny to his cell, hoping for a sign of recognition between them that would confirm their collusion. But Lockhart and Kaplan remained impassive. After an hour she was taken away to be executed, not knowing if her attempt to alter the course of history had failed or succeeded.

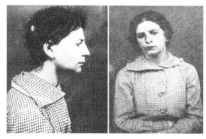

Fanya Yefimovna Kaplan

The Pegasus Stable was a *succès de scandale*, talked about in shocked tones with exaggerated accounts of the nightly disorder. It was a place of screaming foxtrots, empty-hearted, red-lipped clients reeking of wine, powder and cheap passions from Tverskaya. The spivs and their tarts drank until they were red in the face. Pale, badly dressed poets sat at empty tables, arguing about who was the greatest.

The Imagists gained a reputation for provocative verse; the clientele gained a reputation for provocative behaviour. The

Pegasus stayed open until 3 a.m. with the poetry beginning at 11.30 p.m. Yesenin was the main attraction. His appearance entranced the women; his chutzpah enraged the bourgeoisie.

When someone from the floor accused him of plagiarising Klyuev and Blok, Yesenin jumped down from the stage and punched him. A noisy customer so enraged him that he seized the man by the nose and dragged him across the dance floor.

Drink had always been a presence in Sergei's life. He had had periods of drunkenness in the past that left him dazed and lost. Now, with Pegasus providing access to alcohol round the clock, it swamped him. He drank at breakfast; by lunch he was slurring his words; most evenings were a blur.

One night, visibly drunk on stage, he looked around the room.

'Do you think I've come here to recite to you? Really? To this crowd of spivs and whores! Well, you can think again – I've come to tell you . . . that you can all fuck off!'

An outraged customer called the police. Yesenin, Marienhof and Shershenevich were held in a cell until the following morning. They were expelled from the Union of Russian Poets. An editorial in the *Literary Herald* accused them of bringing the profession into disrepute. The Pegasus Stable was an apt name, it said, because the place was full of literary horseshit, bad coffee and pies, for which they charged truly poetic prices.

A fellow poet sent Nikolai Klyuev a report on his former protégé.

Yesenin appears nightly. He is unfailingly charming. His smile is constant. It does not change according to whom he is addressing – a friend or a stranger, a woman or a man. This is disconcerting and unreal. However courteously he speaks to everyone, it is clear he regards them solely as a pedestal to his future glory. For Yesenin, fame is everything; obscurity means worthlessness.

The August shootings made the Bolsheviks even more brutal. The Central Committee declared it would unleash 'merciless mass terror against all opponents of the revolution', the suppression of those who had tried to murder Lenin and anyone suspected of supporting them.

Red Terror meant indiscriminate slaughter. People were executed for their social origin. Former officials, priests, lawyers and bankers were seized and held as hostages. Being well off made you guilty; soft hands could get you shot. Recovering from his injuries, Lenin himself signed the execution lists.

'Terror is a necessity,' said the head of the Cheka. 'We judge quickly. We don't need justice.'

Half a million people would be liquidated in the name of Lenin's Utopia. Nine million would die in the civil war, from combat, typhus and starvation. Another two million fled abroad.

In Moscow, people sold their possessions for scraps, bartered family heirlooms for firewood. Dogs and cats disappeared from the streets to be made into civil war sausage. Before he starved to death, the philosopher Vasily Rozanov wrote in his diary, 'With a clank, a squeal and a groan, an iron curtain has descended over Russian history. The show is over.'

The show at the Pegasus Stable went on. Sergei's reputation as a drunken brawler grew. People visited the place in anticipation of thrown punches and hurled beer glasses. But they listened to his poetry. His fame as a poet rose in line with his renown as a hooligan.

Outside the smoky basement, winter descended. The writer Yevgeny Zamyatin described Russia's devastated cities as the preserve of mammoths and icebergs, a wasteland where cavemen, swathed in hides and blankets, retreated from cave to cave. The threat of starvation sent thousands fleeing to the countryside. Moscow lost 53 per cent of its population, Petrograd 72 per cent.

Not content with imposing revolution at home, the Bolsheviks were exporting it. Wars flared with the Baltic states, Finland, Poland and Ukraine. Popular opposition to state terror served only to entrench it. Lenin built labour camps for those who disagreed with him.

Yesenin tried to look away, but Marienhof courted controversy by deriding the bloodshed. Controversy was his weapon. When it slackened, or the outraged headlines dried up, he would think up new ploys to revive them.

'How would you feel about wearing a top hat and tails?' he asked Sergei. 'We have to give people something to fume about . . . Patent leather shoes, too, maybe . . . They'll pillory us, but it will get them talking. And we'll just smile – Baudelaire would approve!'

'You've been right so far,' Sergei said. 'You spotted the market for debauchery. Why not try the clothes?'

Nikolai Klyuev's informant sent him another letter.

Marienhof has catered to the demands of a desperate city, and it will make him rich. But he has thrown Yesenin to the wolves. He knows the boy mustn't drink, yet he puts him in a cabaret where people endlessly ply him with vodka. He has turned him into an alcoholic and now he's exposing him to mockery and outrage by dressing him as a ludicrous dandy. The Pegasus is truly the home of nihilism and spit-on-everything corruption. Yesenin lets himself be dragged into it because his Mephistopheles Marienhof tells him so.

An envelope arrived, addressed in a hand that Sergei recognised. It was the first time Klyuev had written to him since they parted. Thirty lines of poetry made clear that the older man's feelings still smouldered.

> I don't want to be a poet famous
> For top hats and lacquered shoes.
> I face the world dressed only
> In my song; for props I have no use.
> No topper to hide my wood-demon horns,
> No shoes or tails to plug the gaps of *my* soul;
> Just a tear in my eye and a crown of thorns.
> To Russia I'm true, to the Russia of old,
> Where cherubim float like finches ascending
> In the spring-time tide of my love unbending.
> I don't want to be some gloss-lacquered poet
> With apish fame stamped on his brow.
> Let tormented Yesenin brawl and run riot
> And seek for a joy that's lost to him now.
> I don't want to be some horse-mare poet
> In some stable laden with shit and fog.
> In my dreams I see heaven, in my ears
> Peal the bells of the coming of God.
> I danced for you before the Romanovs' throne,
> In peasant attire and sly boots of leather;
> Weighty words that you knew were mine own
> Joined your fate and my fate to each other forever.

But with the broom of forgetting like a storm in
     your hand,
You swept out our history like footprints from sand.
So curse you! A curse on your shoes,
Your top hat and hollow madness.
Golden-horned Klyuev will never use
Lacquer to shroud *his* soul's proud sadness.
I may be far, but I shall return.
Then my words like pearls
On a virgin bride's breast . . .
All of Russia shall learn!

Sergei crumpled Klyuev's poem into the waste basket. He got it out, smoothed it down then threw it back in. He folded it into a square and stuffed it in his pocket. He showed it to Marienhof.

'I don't know what you want me to say,' Marienhof said. 'I thought you had broken with that dreadful man. He's a predatory pederast. He wants to get his claws and God knows what else into you. Surely you're not going to reply?'

'No. And yet, I don't know. Of course Klyuev had evil designs. But he was good for me . . . good to me. As for the top hat and patent-leather shoes, I think he may have a point—'

Marienhof interrupted. 'The clothes are the mark of the dandy, Sergei. They're the symbol of our nobility, our moral superiority . . .'

Sergei had sacrificed much to the scandals and the provocations, clinging to the promise of fame that would redeem the sacrifice. But his world was empty. He needed someone to comfort him.

Seryozha, dearest! I cannot tell you what heavenly joy swept over me when I received your note! You cannot imagine how distraught I have been since you left!

Klyuev's letter burned with desire and pleas for the prodigal to return.

I love you, Seryozha. Why have you fallen under Marienhof's spell? Do you not see how he exploits you? His unclean hands have soiled your muse with beer stains and nicotine. A dandy's costume cannot hide the tavern's slime.

Your new persona – doomed hero, *poète maudit*, or whatever you choose to call it – is dangerous. It may feed the stuff of your poetry, but beware! It is not a pretence you may throw off like an actor's costume.

For Marienhof and the others, hooliganism is a pose, a provocation. But you have assumed the role so completely that I fear you may not escape it.

CHAPTER 13

With factories closing and wages unpaid, even the proletariat was deserting the Bolsheviks. 'Down with Lenin and horse-meat,' read the graffiti on the walls. 'Give us the tsar and pork!'

When strikes broke out, the government crushed them with arrests and executions. The Bolsheviks imposed a regime of War Communism, harsh, enslaving and repressive. The state was turned into a militarised machine, in which workers obeyed orders from the top. Forced labour was introduced, breaches of discipline punishable by death. Prisons overflowed.

A siege mentality drove the Bolsheviks to ever harsher measures. The incitement of class hatred, the requisitioning of property, the punishment of independent thought were the tools of a new autocracy more ruthless and more dogmatic than the old.

Members of the former middle classes were 'bourgeois para-sites' and 'non-persons', their homes confiscated, their furniture and clothes seized. They were put in the lowest category for food rations, on the border of starvation, forced to do cruel, often deadly labour. Begging and prostitution were rife. City streets filled with orphans and child thieves.

Starving street children

Sergei did not reply to Klyuev's letter, but he brooded on its contents.

The old Yesenin, good-hearted boy-celebrant of nature's consolation, had perished in the century's cataclysm. The caesura in Russia's life was the schism in his. With civilisation dying, it was no longer enough to sigh for Arcadia.

Klyuev had questioned his sincerity and it disturbed him. He found himself examining his own behaviour, puzzling over reasons he had overlooked or wilfully suppressed.

If the world is suffering, he told himself, the poet must suffer with it. Being a hooligan was an act of defiance, a brawling statement acted out in life, an acquiescence in personal destruction in the name of poetry.

But where did it come from, this compulsion to don the garb of the damned? From the need to feed his poetry? From the yearning for fame? Was he a fraud? Was he ready for Calvary?

Lenin blamed the peasants. It was their greed, their grasping refusal to hand over the grain so desperately needed by the cities that was crippling the Bolshevik state, thwarting the people's dream of a socialist utopia.

> The wealthy peasants hate socialism! The bloodsuckers grow fat on the suffering of the people; they rake in hundreds of thousands of roubles by pushing up the price of grain. These leeches have sucked the blood of the working class. They grow richer as the workers starve. We declare war on them! Death to them! We shall crush them with an iron fist!

Lenin delegated the crushing to armed food brigades, sent into the countryside to force the wealthy peasants to hand over their crops. Those who resisted were shot, their homes burned and their families deported. In retaliation, the peasants murdered fifteen thousand food-brigaders. One village impaled their decapitated heads on spikes, until government artillery razed the place to the ground.

For Sergei, poetry was the measure of his life, and Klyuev's letter had shaken his faith in it.

Of course his behaviour was an act; the hooligan and the doomed poet were roles he played. But they were also his way of transmuting brute reality into art. He played roles to re-create himself, to become a character in his own poetry.

In the end, he showed Klyuev's letter to Marienhof, who read it with growing anger.

'I'm going to see him!' Marienhof said. 'You stay here!'

The more grain the Bolsheviks seized from the peasants, the less grain was left for the peasants to sow. The more peasants the Bolsheviks murdered, the fewer peasants there were to do the sowing. Crop failures increased, famine spread. In the Volga region, twenty million cattle were lost; ten million people were starving.

Lenin's response was more repression:

> We need to set an example. You need to hang – I repeat, hang, without fail, in full public view – the wealthy peasants. Then publish their names and take away all their grain. Execute the hostages, in accordance with my previous telegram. Do it in such a way that people for hundreds of miles around will tremble. Use your toughest men for this!

They met in the Poets' Café, neutral ground.

'You accused me of debauching Sergei,' Marienhof said. 'You said I exploit him, that I have besmirched his poetic gift. Do you think Sergei is a child? Yesenin is his own man. How do you think he survived all those years in Petrograd? He hobnobbed with courtiers and aides-de-camp; got himself spared from the trenches, introduced to the empress and her daughters. And all the time, he knew what he was doing. How could we, poor little Imagists, manipulate such a person? More like he manipulated us!'

'You have turned him away from me!' Klyuev said. 'You have destroyed the boy and created a monster. For you and your friends it's all just play-acting, but Sergei takes it seriously. If he suffers, it will be your fault!'

'Then you simply don't know him!' Marienhof said. 'If you think he is that easy to influence, you are stupid. *He* is the one who wants the scandals and provocations; *he* is the one who wants the charades and the role-playing. He wants it because that is the way he will be famous. And for him, fame is *all* that matters. It matters to him more than anything in the world – more than friends, more than family, more than truth or honesty!'

When the Patriarch protested against the closure of churches and the confiscation of Church property, Lenin resorted once more to terror.

> We must put down all resistance with such utter brutality that they will not forget it for decades. The greater the numbers of clergy we succeed in executing the better!

The regional directors of the Cheka took him at his word. Tens of thousands of priests were murdered, publicly crucified, thrown into boiling tar or forced to take 'communion' with molten lead.

Yesenin had always been an actor. The priests' robes and golden chains, the incense-soaked drama of the sung masses of his childhood; the women's dresses and garish make-up of school plays at Spas-Klepiki; the gaudy peasant shirts of his early days as a poet; the top hats and tails of his incarnation as a dandy – all were part of his need for life to be bigger and more colourful, for the world to be better and more inspiring than it was.

As a poet, he gave the public what it wanted – naïve peasant, monarchist darling, debauched libertine or doomed hooligan – because acting a part furnished the material of his poetry.

Marienhof would say later, 'I never knew which Yesenin transmuted the more often, his life into verse or his verse into life. His mask became his face; his face became a mask. His life burned unevenly. On one side. Like a badly smoked cigarette.'

A critical remark about Sergei's writing was a slight on his value as a person. How could someone who had never created anything presume to judge someone who had given his life for it?

The dandy's elegance and the make-up on his face were ways to conceal the hurt; a pretence of serenity, a refusal to flinch at pain. There was pride in it; swagger and defiance.

> Living beings all are scored
> With a sign that marks them in fate's book.
> If I had not become a poet,
> I'd've been a brawler and a crook.

I was scrawny as a child,
But I fought my corner with the big guys.
When I came home with cuts and bruises,
Or a bloody nose, it was no surprise.
If my mother would sob to see me,
I might smile and mumble through the pain:
It's OK, Ma, I just fell; believe me,
Tomorrow I'll be right as rain.
My fiery temper's cooled a little
Since those days of restless youth.
Now, with my soul still proud and brittle,
I forge my poems with love and truth.
I pour myself into my verse,
My heart's exposed for all to see.
My former reckless, blustering courage
Expressed these days in poetry.
Just like the old days, I'm bold and proud;
Just like the old days, I still get hurt.
Back then they hit me in the mouth;
Now it's my soul they trample in the dirt.
Now it's not to Mother, but to laughing,
Mocking strangers I say to hide my pain:
It's OK, I just fell; believe me,
Tomorrow I'll be right as rain.

The November Armistice returned much of the territory that the Bolsheviks had ceded to Germany at Brest-Litovsk. For some of its inhabitants the prospect of reverting to rule by Russia was less than appealing. Fighting broke out in Armenia, Bessarabia, Ukraine and the Baltic states.

In Russia itself, civil war intensified. Allied intervention had bolstered the Whites. The French established a foothold on the Black Sea by landing troops in Odessa. Britain engineered the installation of Admiral Alexander Kolchak as Supreme Ruler of the White armies, hoping to unite the disparate factions in a renewed assault. Kolchak's manifesto echoed Western aspirations:

> My aims are the overthrow of the Bolsheviks and the re-establishment of law. I pledge that the Russian people shall have the right to choose a government in accordance with their wishes. I am committed to the ideals of liberty and freedom. I call upon all citizens to make every possible sacrifice in the deadly struggle against Bolshevism!

The Bolsheviks retained control of Russia's major cities, but their grip on power was uncertain. Whoever won would inherit a country in ruins.

Admiral Kolchak inspects White Army troops, November 1918

Sergei had survived the war, survived the revolution; come through displacement, homelessness and upheaval. In common with most Russians he had expected things to be better, to see at least some reward for the suffering. Instead, that winter the nightmare worsened.

He found Christmas difficult. It rekindled memories of his childhood faith, the years when belief was easy and consoling. On Christmas Eve he felt himself sinking. He told Marienhof he wanted to cancel the evening's appearance at the Pegasus Stable.

'Seryozha,' Marienhof said, 'come and recite. It will make you feel better.'

Sergei was still agonising over Klyuev's letter. *Of course* poetry was a game of artifice; he knew that. But there was something damaging in Klyuev's pointing it out. Like the magic trick explained, or the childhood fairy tale mocked, it made belief hard to sustain.

Marienhof pressed him.

'You are young and healthy, attractive and talented. You should be grateful for the gifts you have, but you think only of the problems. Come and lose yourself in the Pegasus!'

CHAPTER 14

December 24th, 1918. In his memory, the evening glowed;
the Pegasus suffused in beauty, the smoke from a hundred
cigars the perfumed incense attendant on the mystery of
the moment.

He began slowly. He had the habit of picking poems to
match his mood.

> The puddles shine blue today
> And the breeze whispers in my hand ...

Another.

> Listen to me, my filthy heart!
> Listen to me, you heart of a dog!

Another.

> I'll stick the cold steel in your ribs ...

Then, something that hadn't happened for a long time; a poem
swam up from his youth, from the years before the wormwood
lodged in his throat.

Beneath my window
The silver birch
Is haloed in snow,
Light silver aglow.
Sumptuous branches
Snow-trimmed;
Buds float
Velvet fringed.

A voice from his past, reciting a poem long forgotten.

The birch tree
In the sleepy silence;
Snowflakes blazing
In golden fire.
Dawn,
Lazily strolling,
Throws more silver
On the quivering pyre.

He looked up and didn't know where he was. He saw the mouths moving, the plates rattling. But he heard nothing.

He scanned the room. That must have been the instant he glimpsed her. A pair of eyes in the crowd; nothing more.

He was searching for the next poem but not finding it. He didn't know what was happening; his mind never went blank.

The verses came, all at once, from memory:

I believe. I believe – in happiness!
I believe the sun yet shines, that rays
Of daybreak like a crimson book of prayers
Proclaim the joyous news. And yes, oh yes,
I believe – in happiness.

Ring out! Ring out, you golden land!
Rage on, you wind, still fierce and unabated!
For blessed is he who with fondness celebrated
The sadness of your lonely fields, your hope forlorn ...
Ring out! Ring out, you joyful, golden Russia!
Ring out and sweep us on!

He thought his lines had fallen on silence.
  Then he saw her and she was applauding.

Zinaida Raikh

His readings soared. The evening became a shiver of elation.
  Was it the intensity of her look? The gaze that held him was
for him alone. Her flickered, conspiratorial smile? A spark
had passed between them. The lips that said she understood
him and wished to know him? The intelligent, serious beauty
directed so openly, so knowingly at *him*?
  Sergei made an effort to address the room, to encompass

the poets, the spivs, the tarts. But his eyes returned to her. And when they found her, she was looking at him.

At the end of the evening he hurried from the stage. Well-wishers, critics and drunks held him back. When he freed himself, she was gone.

He ran to the lobby. He asked Marienhof if he had seen the beautiful girl with the radiant eyes, but Marienhof shrugged, 'There are so many of them ...'

He found her in the corridor, where fans congregated, waiting for autographs or inscriptions. He signed, shook their hands, watching her always, worried she would leave.

When the last of them departed, she introduced herself.

'Zinaida Raikh, *Delo Naroda*. May I ask you some questions? It's for the arts pages ...'

It was the last thing he'd expected. A journalist. From a newspaper he barely knew.

'Yes,' he said. 'Yes, of course. *Delo Naroda*, "The People's Cause" – what sort of paper is that?'

'Political. Like every paper nowadays,' she said with a laugh. 'I do the culture section. I keep out of the politics.'

She asked him the expected questions – How long had he been a poet? Whom did he admire? Where did he come from? Then the unexpected ones – What was his favourite colour? Was he superstitious? Was he married?

'It sounds like you're interviewing me for the society pages – if society pages still exist ... No, I'm not married,' he said, glossing over the fact that he was, 'and I'd better say my favourite colour is red, hadn't I?'

'All right. How old are you?'

'Twenty-three,' he said. 'How old are you?'

'It's not me we're interviewing here ...' Then, after a pause, 'A year older. Tell me what you're working on ...'

Sergei spoke about his writing, about his connection with

the Imagists, his previous incarnation as a peasant poet, his views on Futurism and the other literary schools vying for precedence in post-revolutionary Russia.

'We should do something about politics,' Zinaida said finally. 'Can I say you are a fervent believer in the ideals of the revolution?'

Sergei shrugged. 'I suppose you can write that ...'

'I don't want to write something if it isn't true,' she said. 'If not the revolution, what can I say Sergei Yesenin believes in?'

'I don't know,' he said. 'Perhaps my problem is that I don't believe in anything ...'

'Really?' she said, surprise in her voice. 'How can someone believe in nothing? I don't see how that could be possible.'

'Well,' he said. 'Perhaps you can write that I believe in poetry ... You can write that poetry for me is not an act. That it is real and true. That it is my life!'

He felt deflated. Had she wished to see him only for an inter-view? He realised he had not asked for her address.

He found the number for *Delo Naroda* and rang the editorial office. The voice that answered sounded like a policeman. The People's Cause had been shut down.

Later, an envelope was delivered to the Pegasus Stable. It contained an apology from Zinaida. The newspaper's demise meant her article about him would never be published, she said, but she enclosed a draft of what she had written:

Great poetry has the power to capture your heart;
the greatest seizes us without revealing how it does
so. We may glimpse devices of craftsmanship, skilful
juxtapositions of words, onomatopoeia or rhymes that

tug at our emotions. These are the outward signs of the artist's grace. They are the jewels and adornments worn by a beautiful woman, but they are not the essence of her beauty. That lies within.

Though we may not know why we surrender to a poem's beauty, yet we can describe the effect it has on us. And the closer we come to understanding the emotions we experience while under its spell, the closer we feel to the noble mind behind it.

As in love, so in poetry.

Great poetry lifts us out of our workaday life. It excites and sharpens our faculties. We become more receptive to the world, perceive our fellows with greater understanding and deeper sympathy.

The whole adventure of life on earth gains in moment, precariousness and beauty. Living becomes sweeter, more vital than we had ever thought. We feel ourselves in the presence of extraordinary possibilities.

I experienced all these things last night when I heard Sergei Alexandrovich Yesenin recite his poetry at the Pegasus Stable on Tverskaya.

Z. N. Raikh, *Delo Naroda*, Moscow

Sergei turned over the page and his heart leapt – she had included her address.

Zinaida's review was a love letter. Sergei longed to respond in kind. He wanted to write about the feelings she had stirred in him, about his joy at discovering someone who felt things as deeply as he did – someone with a sensibility comparable to his own.

But his reply offered none of that. Something close to fear held him back.

Dear Zinaida Nikolaevna,

Thank you for your kind review. I agree with many of your views on poetry. Poetry is the highest form of human understanding. At its best, it illuminates the ferment of our inner life, redeems our sorrow and offers consolation to both poet and reader.

I was concerned to learn that your newspaper has ceased publication. Do you have other employment to fall back on? Please let me know if I may be of help. I live in central Moscow and my work leaves me free during the day.

Yours,

Sergei Yesenin

A reply came within hours.

Dear Poet,

If you are at such a loose end, we had better meet for tea. You can find me at Perlov's Tea Rooms on Myasnitskaya Street tomorrow afternoon at four o'clock.

Zinaida

Perlov's Tea Rooms were a Moscow institution. Everyone knew their glittering facade with its Chinese dragons and gilded pagodas. These had been added in 1896 to impress the Chinese High Ambassador, whom Sergei Perlov was courting in a bid to win the licence to import China tea. The ambassador had paid his compliments, enjoyed Perlov's hospitality and signed a deal with his main competitor.

Perlov's hard luck touched the hearts of Muscovites. They flocked to drink his tea. Having survived the privations of war and revolution, the tea rooms continued to thrive, a relic of the past overlooked by the new regime.

Perlov's Tea Rooms, Moscow

Sergei found her in the jade room. Its mirrored walls and steaming samovars, the noisy chatter of the customers and the uniformed waiters darting back and forth gave the place an air of imperviousness to time and the world. It eased the awkwardness between them.

'How are you?' he asked. 'I'm sorry to hear about your newspaper.'

Zinaida spoke about losing her job without bitterness. It was one of those things that life throws at us; worse things were happening in the world; we need to keep a sense of proportion.

'But don't you think life has changed?' he said. 'Life in general, I mean. When we were young, there were duties and obligations to people and institutions we regarded as permanent. We respected the monarchy, believed in the Church, honoured our parents and our country. Life had a solidity that made it easier to accept when bad things happened. Now everything seems to have been swept away. It's as if we were children led by grown-ups, but the grown-ups have turned tail and run.'

'Yes,' Zinaida said. 'And I can tell that all those changes have upset you. I can feel it in your poetry – that sense of being adrift in the world. But don't you think we can find meaning in ourselves? I mean, we can replace the outside certainties with certainties from within … I'm expressing it badly, but we need to decide things for ourselves now – now that others have stopped doing it for us. It seems to me that we can find guidance in our own hearts, in the natural decency we all have within us …'

She saw that Sergei was dubious.

'Look,' she said. 'We can't rely on others to tell us how to live our lives. But we can rely on human goodness – goodness that will triumph over the chaos and the disintegration, goodness that will make everything all right.'

They parted with a tentative kiss. Zinaida's kindness, her transparent integrity, and the evident interest she took in him and his concerns had moved him. She had faith in people. She sensed there was a way forward, a life beyond the doubts and the sorrow.

He couldn't work. He could think of nothing but the magnificent woman who had come so wonderfully into his life. He pictured her day and night – black hair, high cheekbones, tender brown eyes glowing with empathy.

He found himself on Pokrovka Street on a morning of sharp January cold, ice crystals flitting like fireflies in the reluctant sunshine. He was on Basmannaya, approaching the old German Quarter before he realised what he was doing.

In a rutted side street in the bakers' district, he stood at the door of her block. Children playing at ice battles were rolling snow into shapes that grew to Teutonic Knights and Russian princes, belligerent Father Frosts with birch-branch lances and pebble eyes.

A dog yelped in the yard, seeking attention. Sergei heard the longing in its bark. He heard things he hadn't heard before; saw life around him that years of introspection had hidden from his gaze.

A woman passed carrying firewood. He nodded good morning and she smiled.

The cold felt good on his skin. The morning sun, low in the sky, sent its rays into the cracks and broken bricks of the facades. A mouse, bloated with winter fat, peered from a gap at the base of the wall then scurried back in.

Standing in this street, on this morning, he felt a barely containable joy. It was fortune enough. He turned and ran.

On Nikolskaya Street he overtook a group of Red Guards. They were marching out of step. An officer was shouting orders, but the men went their own way.

At Varvarskaya Square, a building with foreign lettering on it was being requisitioned by the police. Sergei watched as an elderly gentleman in a black frock coat was pushed out of the front door into the street, remonstrating in a language that was not Russian, pleading to be allowed back in.

A crowd had gathered. Flustered and humiliated, the foreigner dropped his spectacles. He bent down to search for them and the crowd laughed. Someone shouted abuse.

The Red Guards, who had entered the square from Varvarka Street, halted to see what was going on. Sergei was close enough to catch the smell of tobacco and vodka on their breath.

The man beside him lifted his rifle and fired in a single, practised movement. Blood gushed from the foreigner's neck.

Sergei gasped. The Red Guard looked at him.

'What? What, comrade? He was resisting arrest. A bloodsucker.'

Red Guards in Nikolskaya Street

The world was frozen in darkness, but a fire had been lit with the power to thaw his heart.

'You have opened my eyes,' he wrote. 'You have illuminated my days and freed my dreams. I cannot describe what thoughts and hopes I have experienced since we met. May I see you, Zina? May I tell you honestly everything that is in my mind?'

A reply arrived. He tore open the envelope. He saw that it ran to several pages, but its tone puzzled him. She wrote of feelings, but not her own. Instead, she wrote of the emotions of a dead woman, now resurrected in a play.

'I shall be an actress,' Zina wrote:

> I believe I have a gift for it. I have been rehearsing a play, in which I play the role of Harriet Taylor. Do you know her?

Or her husband? He was an Englishman called John Stuart
Mill and he wrote about philosophy. The Bolsheviks like
him because he denounced autocracy and embraced a sort
of socialism. The play is about love.

John was remarkable, but Harriet was his equal – equal
in intelligence, equal in talent, equal in sensibility. When
they meet at the start of the play, she is twenty-three – our
age! – and a great beauty. She has 'large, dark eyes, not soft
or sleepy; with a look of quiet command in them'. They
fall in love, but Harriet is already married. She does not
wish to betray her husband, but her attraction to John is
so overwhelming that they begin an affair. And they truly
love each other. This is what she writes after their beautiful
night of lovemaking:

> I feel as though you have never loved me half so well
> as last night. I am glad you said those things to me. I
> am happy that you have. No one with any fineness and
> beauty of character but must feel compelled to say all to
> the being they really love. While there is any reservation,
> however little, their love is imperfect . . .

John's friends try to tear him away from her. They circulate
malicious gossip to ruin their relationship. But John prizes
Harriet so highly that he turns his back on society and
gives up his position in the world.

When Harriet's husband falls ill with cancer, the
prospect of his death opens the possibility of her and John
finally being able to marry. But Harriet suffers terribly
during her husband's illness, both from the horror of what
he is going through, and also – I think – from the guilt she
feels at the way she has deceived him. She writes some
bitter letters to John:

The sadness and horror of nature's doing exceed a million-fold all the attempts of the poets! There is nothing on earth I would not do for my husband and there is nothing on earth that can be done. Do not write to me!

When Harriet's husband dies, and she and John are free to live as man and wife, John's mother and sisters disown him. He accepts even that sorrow because of the strength of his love for Harriet, and she loves him in return.

'There has been so much more pain than I thought I was capable of,' she writes, 'but Oh! How much happiness now!'

They have seven years of bliss together, and when Harriet dies, John is overcome by inconsolable grief. 'The spring of my life is broken,' he writes.

On her grave – in Avignon in France, where she had died as they were travelling through Europe – he has an inscription carved.

Her great and loving heart, her noble soul, her clear, powerful, original and comprehensive intellect, made her the guide and support, the instructor in wisdom, the example in goodness, as she was the chief earthly delight, of those who had the happiness to belong to her. Were there even a few hearts like hers, this world would already become the hoped-for heaven.

For the next fourteen years, until his own death, he lived in Avignon close to her grave because he could not bear to be parted from the woman he loved ...

You may wonder, dear poet, why I have written of this at such length. It is because I am excited at the prospect of playing such a remarkable woman. And because I am in awe of the mark that love can make on our lives.

Your Zinaida

She asked him not to see her before the performance. She wanted him to come as an impartial spectator, she said, so he could give her an objective account of the play.

The production was in a converted basement. The audience shivered in the unheated space. The staging was awkward and it seemed as if the playwright had simply given the characters long extracts from diaries and letters to read to each other. The deficiencies made it hard for him to judge if Zinaida's performance were good or bad. He suspected she was a little amateurish.

But nothing of that mattered. He saw the beautiful, radiant being behind the costume. This was the woman who could haul him from his hell of despair.

She came to him afterwards, still in her make-up, with her hair held back under a scarf. The flawlessness of her beauty made him tremble.

'Now you have witnessed me performing,' she said, 'just as I witnessed you. Our spheres are different, but we are equals.'

He put his arm around her and she laid her head on his breast.

'Yes,' he said. 'We are. Equal in all things . . .'

Zinaida in costume

She had prepared a supper of cold meat. At the door to her apartment building, Sergei told her how he had stood there three weeks earlier with the intention of knocking, but had felt so happy that he had run away.

'So happy that you had to run away!' She laughed. 'Really? They say women are strange, but I think men are stranger – or perhaps it is poets!'

They sat across the table from each other, looking each other in the eye then looking away, trying to discern what the other might be thinking, trying to express and then to disguise the joy they were feeling.

Zinaida told him her story. She had been born in Odessa in 1894, one year earlier than him. Her father, Nikolai, an engineer of German descent, had been active in opposition circles in his youth. He had served time in exile and in tsarist jails, but had fallen in love with a Russian noblewoman.

Anna Viktorova came from a distinguished family, who insisted that her young suitor renounce his Roman Catholicism and convert to Orthodoxy. It was the 1880s, a decade of change, and they turned a blind eye to Nikolai's political views.

Zinaida grew up in a cheerful home with devoted parents,

whose love of music and art, respect for the life of the mind and liberal views helped imbue her with a contemplative outlook on life and a personality that remained for the most part level-headed and optimistic.

Nikolai had continued his political activism. After the 1905 revolution the family were exiled from Odessa to a town on the Moldavian border. Zinaida's oppositionist views, inherited from her father, got her expelled from school. She went to university in Kiev, where she joined the Socialist Revolutionary Party and in 1913 was sentenced to two months in prison. Unable to continue her studies in the south, she had moved to St Petersburg and enrolled in a free university similar to the one Sergei had attended. Her SR connections had helped her find work on the party's newspaper, *Delo Naroda*, which had sent her to interview the young poet everyone was talking about . . .

Sergei laughed. 'Talking about me, are they? So tell me – what are they saying?'

Zinaida smiled and shook her head. 'I shan't tell you. You are already far too proud of yourself. I don't want to make your head any bigger than it is!'

'You said I was strange,' he said, 'because I ran away from your door. Well, perhaps I am strange. I ran away because I sensed the intensity of the happiness that lay before me. Just standing there filled me with such joy that it made the prospect of being with you seem impossibly, overwhelmingly wonderful. And now that I am sitting with you, here at your table, I realise I was right . . .'

She took his hand.

'Seryozha,' she said. 'I have felt the same about you, since I came to see you at the Pegasus club. I had read so much of your poetry that it seemed I knew you already. But when I saw you there on stage, my heart filled with such emotion . . . You were such a mass of contradictions – handsome and strong, yet sad and alone; writing poems of such beauty, yet filled with self-loathing. I listened to you reading your verses about death and despair in the city, and I couldn't reconcile the self-hatred of the poetry with the physical and spiritual nobility of the poet. You seemed such a young boy, so irresistibly attractive in his unhappiness and pain that I wanted to hold you and love you forever!'

Outside, the bells of the Cathedral of the Epiphany, not yet silenced by the Bolsheviks, struck midnight. They spoke passionately; joked, laughed, surprised themselves with views shared or opinions divided. They were discovering each other, delighting in the other's responses. By the time the night lightened above the rooftops, they had known each other forever.

Each ached for the other's body, but neither wished to be the first to say it. Sergei slept on the couch. When Zinaida shook him awake, the room was filled with daylight. He stared at her with such puzzled wonder in his eyes that she laughed out loud. When he told her how beautiful she was, she covered her face with her hands.

'I'm tired and bleary-eyed, Seryozha, not beautiful!'

He shook his head.

'Infinitely, wonderfully beautiful! A beauty so deep and natural. Others have superficial beauty, but yours comes from within. It starts deep inside you and bubbles to the surface like the mineral spring of . . . Évian-les-bains . . . Well, no, that's wrong because Évian is flat . . . so let's say like Borzhomi, or—'

He broke off, amused by his own sleepy incoherence. Zinaida said she would make some tea. There was nothing for breakfast, but they could try later at the old market to see if any traders had turned up. When she returned with the tea, he had ordered his thoughts.

'You are beautiful now,' he said. 'And you were beautiful last evening when you came off stage in your costume and greasepaint. It was a different sort of beauty. You know what the poet Baudelaire said about women and make-up? "When a woman uses make-up to disguise the blemishes on her skin, she rises above nature, transforms nature, she becomes magical and surreal . . ."'

Zinaida laughed. 'And there was I thinking it was just to cover up a few freckles! If you like it, I'll be sure to use it . . . although, it isn't easy to get nowadays. The Bolsheviks have closed down the cosmetics firms and turned them into soap factories for the Red Army – not that you'd notice from the smell of them on the trams and buses! Brocard, Rallet and Coty have been sent packing back to France. I sometimes think it's unfair that women are expected to wear make-up, while men can appear however they want . . .'

'I make an effort,' Sergei said. 'And I wear make-up on stage . . .'

'Well, you don't need to, my dear,' she said. 'You have one of those faces that women always fall for. I think it's time for you to tell me about your history with women. Mine with men is hardly worth mentioning – a couple of boyfriends at university, but nothing serious. I suspect things are different with you . . .'

'I have had women,' he said. 'Never anyone who meant much to me. But I need to tell you something – when you asked if I were married, I said I wasn't. In fact, I married a woman five years ago. We were both young. I had a child with her. I haven't seen her for a long time . . .'

'Oh?' Zinaida said. 'And when did you get divorced?'

'That's what I was going to tell you: I haven't . . .'

'I don't want an affair,' she said. 'That's not enough for me. I want more than that.'

The winter had been cold. There had been little snow and what had fallen was ground into the streets in rutted furrows, as hard as marble, black with soot, littered with detritus. In the beleaguered, dispossessed city, the freeze had kept disease at bay, but temperatures rose in early March and the babushkas shook their heads. The mercury clambered to minus ten, minus five, then close to zero. The bacilli stirred as the snow fell. It came in sudden, blinding waves, smacking the ground with sodden flakes that lay, uncertain whether to live or die. Rain followed, grey sheets of tumbling water, turning the earth to a no man's land of rancid mud. The lice sensed the warmth. The first cases of typhus appeared.

Sergei went to the church where he and Anna were married. The facade had been defaced, statues and crosses smashed. A bell lay in pieces, flung from the tower where the barrel of a machine gun now kept watch. A sentry challenged him. Sergei asked if the church was still functioning.

'Yes, comrade,' the man replied. 'Functioning nicely. Horses in the nave, cavalrymen in the aisles. Anything else you wanted? Not a believer, are you?'

There was menace in the question. Sergei turned and left.

When Zinaida wrote to ask why she hadn't heard from him, he replied that he was 'trying to put things right'.

'I need to tell you that there have been bad things in my life,' he wrote. 'I have seen bad things, done bad things, and bad things have been done to me. I have seen men shot before my eyes; I have jostled the corpses of the drowned, drunk wine with the holy *starets* who thought he could save Russia, and broken bread with the royal daughters he helped send to their deaths. I have abandoned my home and my family. I want to put things right, Zina. Wait for me.'

Sergei went to the Kitai Gorod Registry. A red star had replaced the tsarist eagle. In the vestibule, a crowd of petitioners was waiting for identity papers or residence permits, one or more of the myriad documents the regime was constantly introducing to keep tabs on a sullen population it had reason to mistrust.

The faces ahead of him had the expression of disoriented hopelessness that had become Moscow's norm. Without the right papers and the right stamps, you could be shot by a patrol. The process of getting them fostered fear and a lucrative trade in bribes for the registry officials. Was this the Revolution's paradise?

It took him five hours to reach the front of the line. A registrar with a red armband beckoned him forward.

'I need a copy of my marriage certificate. My wife and I have been separated for years. We won't be getting back together. I need to talk to her about a divorce – it will free her ... and free me.'

The official laughed.

'You're way behind the times! Marriage certificates, divorce settlements – that's all gone out the window. Didn't you know? The Bolsheviks don't hold with bourgeois marriage. It's free love now, comrade.'

'Nonetheless,' Sergei hesitated. 'I want to do this properly. I want to do the right thing by Anna. And I want to reassure someone else, someone very close to me—'

It wasn't the first time the official had had such a case.

'Look,' he said. 'You don't need a certificate, like I told you. But I might be able to produce one for you – one that proves you're divorced good and proper; one that'll keep your new lady happy. I can do it, but it don't come cheap.'

'I don't have any money on me,' Sergei said. 'I can go and get it from the Pegasus . . . from my employment station . . .'

'That'd be well too late, comrade. The queue's out the doors and there'd be someone else on duty by the time you got back. Nah – I like the look of your jacket, though . . .'

'When you see a beautiful view, do you wonder if I would like it?' Sergei wrote to Zinaida. 'When you hear music, do you wonder what I would make of it? When you read a book, do you understand it through the prism of us? I do. I love your mind; I love your body; I love your soul. Come with me, Zina! Come with me, away from this dreadful city!'

CHAPTER 15

The train picked its way through deserted suburbs, where makeshift barricades of cobblestones and overturned vehicles still littered the streets. The fighting had moved south and the railway official assured them that the line north from Moscow to Vologda was safe. Sergei and Zinaida said little.

In northern Moscow, the factories were idle. The vast Mytishchi Industrial Complex, constructor of Russia's trams and trains, was silent, hangar doors thrown open, chimneys un-stoked. Catherine the Great's Millionny aqueduct, built in 1780 to provide the Kremlin with clean water, was damaged and leaking.

The city was dirt and dark, poverty and destruction. The dimly lit carriage crawled through blackness. Zina snuggled into Sergei's shoulder. The contact reassured them and they slept.

When they stirred, the window was lit with insistent brightness. Sergei threw up the blind and they blinked at the white, virgin snow that stretched to the horizon.

The train slowed; Vologda's cupolas appeared. Such beauty, Zinaida thought. Such beauty, and she there to see it. Such beauty, and she alive to feel it. A flock of rooks rose in unison from the birches.

The domes of Saint Sophia's Cathedral, built by Ivan the

Terrible when, in a fit of pique, he moved his capital here from Moscow, flicked the spring sunshine into the limpid air. The slope between the station and white-walled city was dotted with sledges and skiers.

'Oh!' Zinaida said. 'Straight out of Brueghel!'

Sergei looked puzzled. She laughed.

'You have much to teach me, Seryozha, but it seems there are things I can teach you, too.'

Vologda

Vologda was a way station; their destination was higher and more remote. For the next three days, as dawn broke and again when the sun set over the western plain, Sergei walked down to the railway, enquiring about the possibility of onward trains. On the morning of the third day, he returned at a run.

'That's it!' he said. 'Two o'clock. Guaranteed. Let's get our stuff and go wait at the station.'

Two o'clock became three, then four. The promised train arrived and they boarded it. They were travelling into the real north now, beyond the temperate region, towards the White Sea, whose very name promised absolution.

Four days of stops and starts, hours waiting for signals to

rise or the line to clear, brought them close. The terminus was the port of Onega, a centre for timber, from where icebreakers left year-round, delivering pines and spruces to Archangel and Murmansk.

'So beautiful,' Zinaida said as they sat on the quayside looking on to the still icy sea. 'How wonderful that one country – our country! – can contain so much. A week ago, we were in a great European metropolis, cribbed by conflict and suffering; and now here we are, at the edge of the world – almost on the roof of the world – surrounded by peace and beauty.'

'Onega is where Pushkin took the name of his hero, Yevgeny Onegin from,' Sergei said. 'Onegin has always puzzled me. He knows he loves Tatiana, and he knows she loves him. Yet he pushes her away. When he realises what a fool he has been, it is too late. The human heart is imponderable, Zina. We mustn't let it lead us into regrets . . .'

They waited in Onega, as they had waited in Vologda. Waiting to push north again, further into the unknown.

Sergei sat on the balcony while Zinaida showered and dressed. He heard her sing and her voice filled the night. He wrote of the moment:

> Is the sky above us really that depth of white?
> Or did they paint it with water steeped in salt?
> You sing, my love, and, hearing your beauty in
>   the night,
> The shore-bound waves pause, enraptured, halt.
> A celestial miller ground and threw
> Grains of water, grains of flour around us.
> By skies of gold, by heaven's endless blue,

The longing notes of unseen song have bound us.
Your sun-blessed arm caressed the horizon's arc
And revealed its covert promise of our eternity.
Come away, my love! Let's both of us embark
On the boat which sails for the holy realm of Solovki!

The Solovki archipelago, a string of islands in the north-western reaches of the White Sea, held a special position in Russians' imagination. Mysterious labyrinths from pre-Christian times spoke of the place's role as a frontier between this world and the underworld, the site of ancient rituals to help ease the souls of the dead into the beyond.

Orthodox monks arrived in the fifteenth century and founded what would become the remotest Christian centre of northern Europe. The islands' strategic location persuaded Ivan the Terrible to build granite churches and monasteries, surrounded by fortifications to keep Russia's enemies at bay.

In the disastrous Schism of the seventeenth century, the monks of Solovki resisted the Patriarch's reforms, expelled the tsar's ambassadors and suffered a siege that lasted seven years. In the centuries that followed, the island would see off attacks from Sweden, the Teutonic Knights and the British. Before the revolution, Nicholas II used Solovki as a political prison, an example that the Bolsheviks would later copy on a grander scale.

Sergei and Zinaida waited for the ship that would take them there. Spring had come, but there was still ice to negotiate. When the engines rumbled into life, they stood on the deck and watched Onega recede.

Zinaida told stories from her childhood, of ancient monasteries consumed by the waters and ghostly communities of monks that lived on even now in the depths beneath them. Sergei relished the élan of her imagination.

The sea, white and infinite, stretched in all directions. They were travelling through a timeless region to a destination they sensed would hold the key to their future.

The spires of the monastery appeared from the mist, ethereal at first, then gaining substance as the ship approached, threading its way through sounds and inlets, passing tiny islands dotted with tumbledown huts, coming all at once to the quayside hard up against Ivan's fortified walls with their green-capped bastions and beyond them the domes of cathedrals, churches and shrines.

The place's remoteness, a thousand miles from Moscow, and its reputation for independence, meant the Red zealots had not yet brought it to heel. Monks came to greet them, to receive the provisions the ship had brought and welcome the guests, increasingly rare since the revolution, who had come so far.

The senior cleric asked if they were married. Sergei hesitated; Zinaida said, 'No, *Batiushka*, we are not. But I believe we shall be,' then blushed and smiled.

The monk explained that only men were allowed inside the monastery. Sergei would be accommodated in a visitor's cell, but Zinaida would have to stay with the female cooks who had their dormitory outside the walls.

The spring weather eased their souls. Nature's untroubled beauty spoke of a rhythm and an order that their lives had lost in the chaos of events. The anxieties, the terror and despair seemed less unbearable, Russia's time of troubles less all-consuming.

Their week on Solovki, with its daily walks, sea air, simple meals in the refectory and evenings spent in contemplation was a time of affection. It brought them close, showed them the completeness of love between a man and a woman that is so rare in this world.

Father Zosima spoke to them. 'I have been watching you. I see that you love each other. Love in these difficult times is a gift. It will shield you from the harshness of life and provide solace when the world is dark and hostile. If you have love, then all the rest – all the problems, all the uncertainties, all the bitterness – is as nothing.'

On the day before the ship was due to take them back, Sergei showed Zinaida the certificate he had obtained from the Moscow registry.

'I am free to marry you,' he said. 'If you will have me, I am the happiest man in Russia. If you refuse, my life is over . . .'

The journey back to Vologda was a shimmer of excitement. Sergei jumped from the train at every station, running to the telegraph operator. When Zinaida asked who he was messaging and what he was arranging, he smiled his little boy smile.

'Wait, my love. Wait and you shall see!'

She asked him to send a telegram to her parents and wrote out the text for him:

```
Please send cash. Am to be married.
Loving daughter, Zina.
```

When the train arrived in Vologda, a group of men and women in traditional Russian dress stepped forward. With curtseys and bows, they proffered the tray of bread and salt, the symbol of hospitality.

A three-horse open sleigh was waiting, decked in ribbons and flowers. The driver showed them to their seats and cracked his whip. The troika pulled away, the horses tossing their heads, speeding them onward through forests, along riverbanks then out into the vast expanse of the Russian plain, where wheat fields had been ploughed and sown and green shoots were struggling upwards in the black earth. Under the furs and rugs that sheltered them, Zinaida squeezed Sergei's hand.

'I love you so much!' she said. 'I will go with you wherever you take me!'

The troika halted at the Church of Saint Cyricus and Julitta, a white-walled chapel in an isolated clearing on the banks of the River Shogrash. The welcoming party shook Sergei's hand and offered him a flask with vodka. The women beckoned Zinaida to the vestry.

'Well!' Zinaida said. 'It seems I am to be married. I have no wedding dress, only the clothes I stand up in.'

The women laughed. 'Such a beauty! Such a lovely girl! You have no need of decoration. The man who has you is the luckiest man in the world!'

They produced a traditional wedding headdress with its trailing veils and adjusted it on her head.

'The priest will be here shortly,' they said. 'You mustn't fret.'

'But I am fretting,' Zinaida said. 'Marriage is such a big thing.'

'Do you love him, dearie? That's the question.'

'Yes,' she said. 'I do love him. I love him more than I have ever loved anyone or anything. I love him with all my heart. But I am afraid.'

'Afraid of what, dearie? Afraid he won't love you as much as you love him? Or afraid of *the thing* ...? Have you ever ...?'

Zinaida knew what the women were referring to.

'Yes ... No ... I don't know. I suppose, yes – I am afraid of *the thing*. He has had many women. I haven't spoken to him about it ... I'm sure he thinks I am still a maiden, but ...'

Sensing her embarrassment, the women changed the subject. They told her the story of the church where she would be wed, of how the eighteenth-century general Ivan Musin wanted to give thanks to God for saving his life after he was wounded in battle against the Swedes and how he had caught sight of his horrifically disfigured face in the mirror and elected to build his chapel of thanks in the remotest spot of his estate, where he could praise the Almighty without being glimpsed by the rest of His creation.

A knock came at the door. It was the priest.

The Church of Saint Cyricus and Julitta

Sergei and Zinaida agreed later that the service was the most beautiful, the priest the most wonderful, the people the most hospitable and the singing the most glorious they had ever known.

A friend of Sergei's, a young poet named Alexei Ganin from a village outside Vologda, arrived to act as best man. Sergei had served with him in the hospital at Tsarskoe Selo during the war and they had remained close.

When they emerged from the chapel they found the clearing set with tables laden with local produce. The people chanted *Gorko! Gorko!* – 'Life is bitter; make it sweet!' – to signal that they must kiss and kiss and kiss again until the well-wishers were satisfied. Realising that Zinaida had no bouquet, Sergei ran to pick a bunch of winter jasmine. He drew laughter and applause when he offered it to her on one knee.

Ganin declared that he was in love with Zinaida himself and was jealous of his friend's good fortune. He read a poem he had composed, in which Zinaida is a beautiful mermaid who has turned her back on the poet to marry – unwisely, he says – a curly haired brigand from the fields.

Alexei Ganin

After the wedding dinner, Sergei and Zinaida were escorted to a hut in a forest glade. A fire burned in the stove; candles had been lit upstairs and down. There was food on the table, with wine and water. A bed with deep mattresses and goose feather pillows was piled with blankets of lambs' wool.

When their hosts had embraced them, embraced them again and finally departed, Sergei and Zinaida sat at the table.

'Seryozha, you are full of surprises!' Zinaida said. 'How did you arrange all those marvels? You told me you had no money with you.'

'Money isn't everything,' he said. 'I cabled them to say the great poet Sergei Yesenin was on his way.'

Zinaida laughed. 'You mean they know you, even out here, in the remotest provinces?'

'The countryside is where they love me the most,' Sergei said. 'They say I am the poet of the Russian soul.'

Their first night of married life flamed with a passion that neither would forget. The long postponement of the union, the weeks of spiritual closeness accompanied by physical abstinence had prepared them. They understood each other so well that now neither had to explain, request or demur.

Sergei, undressing, mumbled, 'I am not ashamed of my body,' and Zinaida laughed.

'Neither am I ashamed – of yours!' she said. 'As for mine, you must be the judge,' and she slipped off her dress.

She was as beautiful naked as she was lovely in thought and conversation.

'Be gentle, Seryozha,' she said. 'I have no experience . . .'

He caressed her skin, delighting in its softness, slipped his arm under her waist, let his fingers brush against her nipples, always putting off the moment, always stoking the warmth in her body that would make his entry into it a delight and not a trial. The moment hovered, like the first sip of the first glass of champagne. When it came, she sighed and gripped him tight. 'I love you, Seryozha,' she said. 'The first sip . . . The most beautiful moment in the world . . .'

They were woken by a knock at the door. The sun was high and one of the women who had attended Zinaida at the church was standing beneath their window with a pail of milk.

'Don't disturb yourselves, my dears,' she said. 'I just came to see if you need anything.'

Sergei pulled on his clothes. The woman gave him the milk, a loaf of fresh-baked bread and a bundle of papers.

'These are for you,' she said. 'Letters from the village girls, mainly; souvenir albums, poetry notebooks – they'd be thrilled if you would sign them. A couple of telegrams, too.'

Sergei sat down to open the letters. He was surprised by how well they were written – the grammar and the spelling were good – and by the detailed knowledge their authors had of his poetry. They quoted poems he himself had forgotten, asking insightful questions about their meaning and his intentions. Zinaida, who had washed and dressed, came to sit with him.

'Do you get these admirers' letters all the time?' she asked. 'Does it not make you proud to hear how many lives your work has touched?'

Sergei shrugged. 'It used to, when I was young. In recent years, nothing has been enough to silence the voice that tells me how worthless I am. But now,' – he took her hand – 'now I need the approbation of only one person.'

Zina moved closer. 'You have made me the proudest man in Russia,' he said. 'I am so blessed to have you.'

They opened the telegrams that the woman had left. One was from Zinaida's father, confirming that he had wired a hundred roubles to the state bank in Vologda. The other was from Marienhof.

'Many thanks your invitation. Unable attend. Celebratory poem follows.'

Sergei turned to Zinaida and read what Marienhof had written:

> Here's to the poet and his latest floozy;
> Hope your wedding night was boozy!
> But are you sure you're right to marry,
> Or is that a burden you'll be doomed to carry?
> Seryozha married just don't sound right;
> When she snared you, you must have been tight!

Zinaida laughed, but he could see she was hurt.

'Don't worry,' he said. 'Marienhof's like that. He's always making fun, always caustic . . .'

'He's the Carabosse at our wedding,' Zinaida said, and ran back upstairs.

Marienhof's message was an uncomfortable reminder of the embittered city from which they had fled. The time spent in Solovki, the magical days of their wedding and the kindness and respect they had encountered had filled them with hope, an earnest of the human goodness in which Zinaida had long placed her faith.

When they sat down to discuss their plans for the future, neither was enthused by the thought of returning to Moscow.

'I have the money from my father,' Zinaida said. 'I was intending to buy a wedding dress, but there was no need. We could go to see my parents in Oryol. They would be delighted to meet you. We could spend some time there while we think of what to do next.'

Sergei nodded. They went up to the bed with the goose feathers and the lambs' wool. He undressed her, pulled her close. That night as she lay beside him, the seeds of the future were planted within her.

For Russia, 1919 was the cruellest year; for Sergei and Zinaida, the happiest. The murderous utopians in the Kremlin woke each morning to new forests of white ribbons on the battlefield charts covering the walls of their offices, indicators of the noose tightening around them.

In Oryol, Sergei woke to the beauty of the woman whose hair flowed in waves over his pillow and the rapture of knowing that Fate had sent him a love that was everything he had ever dreamed of.

'I shall go to the market today,' she said when she awoke. 'I heard that the traders may come.'

Food was easier to come by than in Moscow. Oryol was a small city with the countryside on its doorstep, and peasants would ride into town with provisions. Patrols of soldiers and sailors ransacked the markets in the name of stamping out 'speculation', but traders still came. Zina would scour the streets and return in triumph with bags of cucumbers, cottage cheese, boiled beef and rye pancakes. Little victories were confirmation that the realm they inhabited, a universe unto itself, was meaning and validation enough. So long as they each believed in it, there was no need for bigger things beyond.

'Don't you think it paradoxical?' Sergei said. 'The world is in thrall, but we are free. Before I met you, I was tormented. I was a prisoner of the big questions. How must I live, when the world is dying? What must I do with my life, when life itself is crumbling? Is my existence worthy only if my poetry is praised and my name celebrated? My soul was at war with itself, Zina. But that torment has gone.'

'Yes,' she said, 'the world is the same – worse, perhaps – but we have changed. We see the world in a new way. I lived on my nerves, always expecting the worst – shall I be put to the test? – but no longer. Knowing that you love me has removed that. It is *enough* to be with you. Our love has made the world make sense.'

Zinaida's parents, literate and sensitive, admired Sergei as a poet but doubted him as a husband. They took their daughter aside and asked if she were sure he was the man for her. Did she not know of his bad reputation and his self-destructive behaviour?

She reassured them. Sergei's heart was good. Behind all the bluster, he was a little boy who had lost his way in the world. He had sunk into despair and that despair had led him to adopt the role of a hooligan. She had rescued him. Sergei had told her how grateful he was and how he would not slip back into the self-immolation. He was happy with life, and happy with her.

When her mother asked if she was pregnant, Zinaida smiled and nodded.

'Then it's good that you are here,' her mother said, 'where we can look after you. A husband is a husband, but parents are for life.'

Zinaida thanked her. She said how grateful she and Sergei were for the apartment they had found for them and the rent they were paying every month.

As she was leaving, her mother slipped a photograph into her hand. It was of Zinaida as a young girl, sitting with her father, Nikolai, looking protective and concerned.

Nikolai Raikh and young Zinaida

Sergei noticed changes in himself. Not all were easy to pin down, but one was clear – he was looking outwards. He realised with a shock that for months, perhaps years, he had spent his life peering into himself; and for the most part he had found only darkness. Now he was looking out into the world. Zinaida occupied the vast portion of this, but he was looking too at the people and things around him, as he hadn't done since his gaze was trained on the forests and rivers and animals of his childhood. He would walk down a street in Oryol and look at the passers-by now; he would wonder who they were and what their lives held in store.

There was another, even more subliminal change. In the past, his mind had been gripped by a pervasive dissatisfaction, a feeling that life was elsewhere and he must be forever chasing if he didn't want it to pass him by. It had to do with his need to prove himself, and he could prove himself only through his poetry. Time was running out, life was short; he could not enjoy life, because enjoying the moment meant he was not writing. The sense of unease never left him. If he didn't write for a week, he would go mad with fear.

He began to understand this only when he met Zinaida. He had been living a shadow-life. With Zinaida, life was truly here. When you are loved, he thought to himself, there's no need to worry about what is happening elsewhere, because everything that matters happens within oneself.

The troubles, the dilemmas, the anxieties and fears, the horror of the war, the pain of loneliness, the future of the country – even the deepest-seated anxiety, the worry about the value of his poetry – became manageable. The only thing that mattered was Zinaida; if she were to love him, nothing could impinge on his happiness. With Zinaida, *life made sense.*

'If she loves me,' he told himself, 'it doesn't matter what else happens. Her love fills the world with warmth and meaning. The purpose of my life is love. I could live in obscurity and no longer fret over what the world might think of me.'

CHAPTER 16

Denikin was coming; Denikin was advancing; Denikin the murderer, the Jew slayer, the tyrant who took no prisoners, slaughtered those who surrendered, hanged civilians ... Or Denikin the liberator, the avenging angel, restorer of truth and justice ...

South of Moscow and held by the Reds since the start of the civil war, Oryol had escaped the worst of the fighting. But now the Whites were moving north from Ukraine and the city was in their path.

Oryol trembled. But Sergei and Zina had each other, and their closeness shut out the horrors of the world. New life was swelling Zinaida's belly. The future would be with them and with their child.

Anton Denikin was a lucky general. He had led the tsarist army's successes and avoided the defeats. The Western allies gambled on his luck and supplied him with half a million rifles. The Bolsheviks sent the fearsome Leon Trotsky to counter his advance, but the Whites were in the ascendancy.

War rumbled and threatened; Sergei and Zinaida barely noticed. He wrote little, but felt no guilt. She grew larger. He looked after her, shared her joy.

'I was too young when I had my son, Yuri,' he said. 'I didn't appreciate what a thing it is to have children. I won't make the same mistake this time!'

They had been together for almost a year. Sergei said it was their Halcyon year, the happiest of his life, when Aeolus the god of wind had unleashed raging storms to batter the world but had cocooned the two of them in a magic space of peace and love.

Denikin's White Army

Marienhof continued to write. Letters that began affectionately but ended with caustic barbs.

'Are you sure you're happy out there in the sticks, Seryozha? Don't you miss the big time? How do you spend your days – dreaming your life away? Watching shadows on the wall?'

Sergei sent good-natured replies.

'I am doing fine, Anatoly. Don't worry about me. It's good to be off the merry-go-round.'

There was jealousy of Zinaida in Marienhof's messages. He reproached Sergei for abandoning the merry band of boys who were the Imagists. How could he love *a woman* more than he loved his friends? He made it clear that he thought Zinaida was to blame for their estrangement.

Sergei didn't rise to the bait. His letters remained cheery and affable. He was sad that his closest friend and mentor had taken against the woman he loved.

Vexed by Yesenin's insouciance, Marienhof sent him a shellac disk of the Russian bass Fyodor Chaliapin singing the folk ballad 'Stenka Razin'. Sergei listened to it on the gramophone at Zinaida's parents' house. The message was in the lyrics. He hid the thing away so Zinaida would not see it.

> From beyond the wooded island
> To the river wide and free
> Proudly sailed the arrow-breasted
> Ships of Cossack yeomanry.
> On the first is Stenka Razin,
> With his princess by his side;
> Drunk and proud in marriage revels
> With his beauteous young bride.
> But from his crew there comes a murmur:
> 'He has quit his sword to woo!
> One short night and Stenka Razin
> Has become a woman, too!'
> Stenka Razin hears the murmur
> Of his discontented band
> And his lovely Persian princess
> He wraps about with his firm hand.
> His dark brows are drawn together
> As the waves of anger rise
> And the blood comes rushing swiftly
> To his piercing deep black eyes.
> I will give you all you ask for,
> Head and heart and life and hand!

And his voice rolls out like thunder
Far across the distant land:
Volga, Volga, Mother Volga
Wide and deep beneath the sun,
You have ne'er seen such a present
From the Cossacks of the Don.
So that peace may reign forever
In our band so free and brave,
Volga, Volga, Mother Volga
Make this lovely girl a grave!
Now, with one swift mighty motion
He has raised his bride on high
And has cast her where the waters
Of the Volga roll and sigh.
Dance, you fools, and let's be merry
What is this that's in your eyes?
Let us thunder out a chorus
To the place where beauty lies ...

Tatiana Yesenin was born at midnight in the Oryol maternity home. A blackout imposed because of the advancing White forces meant there was no electric light, but there was no mistaking the blond curls that were the mark of the Yesenin family. Sergei hugged the woman who had brought him such joy.

The weeks after Tatiana's birth were difficult. Zinaida was young. The arrival of a child was an upheaval. The baby was pampered; Sergei spent much of the day peering fondly into her cradle. Zinaida felt disoriented and alone.

She spent more time at her parents, seeking the stability of a life in which she herself had been a child, unburdened by responsibilities.

Sergei spoke to Zinaida's father, who reassured him. It was a natural reaction, he said. His own wife had been through something similar when she gave birth.

Zinaida recovered her equilibrium. They resumed their life together and neither noticed – or at least, mentioned – the subtle changes in them. Sergei never said he had felt slighted by Zinaida's flight to her parents. She never said that his evident love for Tatiana seemed a dilution of his love for her.

No one spoke of it, but there was an undercurrent in their relationship that had not existed before. The threat of the Whites arriving in Oryol no longer felt quite so irrelevant. The hectoring of Marienhof no longer so easily dismissed, by either of them.

Zinaida found the record. She played it on her father's phonograph and knew at once what Marienhof had intended.

'You didn't show me this,' she said.

'I didn't want to upset you.'

'If you genuinely were paying no heed to what Marienhof tells you, I would have had no cause to be upset. The fact that you hid the record means you *are* tempted by what he says – part of you *does* want to go back!'

They made up. But as with all such arguments, a trace remained. And traces accumulate.

Sergei said, 'We ... I ... might have to go to Moscow ...'

'I wondered how long it would take you to say that,' Zinaida said. 'I'm surprised it has taken you so long ...'

'Don't be angry, Zina. It's for my poetry. I need to get back in touch with things ...'

'If you are returning to Moscow for the sake of your art, I won't stop you. You are a great poet. But if you are going because that man is mocking you and making you feel bad about the life you have chosen, that would be a mistake. We have our happiness. And now we have the baby. Don't sacrifice such a rare thing, Seryozha. Don't go back to a life that will torment you . . . and probably kill you!'

'You are right,' he said. 'If you don't want to go to Moscow – and if you don't want me to go – I shall stay.'

That night in bed, they heard the White artillery on the outskirts of the city.

Refugees from the White advance poured into Oryol. The Reds hesitated between manning the guns and packing their bags. The peasant traders who had kept the population supplied with food had not been seen for a week.

Zinaida's parents told her she should leave for Moscow while she still could, but she was reluctant.

'I hate Moscow. I am worried for Sergei if we go there. I don't want him slipping back into the brawling and the drinking. His so-called friends have taken against me. They're trying to turn him away from me. I fear they may succeed . . .'

They left two days before the fighting began. Sergei, Zinaida and Tatiana Yesenin caught the last train for Moscow before the White Army seized Oryol and Denikin announced that his next target would be the capital itself.

White victory parade, Oryol

Marienhof had said he would come to the station. They hadn't been in Moscow for a year and it would be the first time he and Zinaida would meet. Marienhof was charming.

'Where will you be staying?' he asked. 'You are welcome at Bogoslovsky Lane. Kusikov and Shershenevich will be delighted. And I'm sure our little collective can provide the communal crèche facilities the Bolsheviks are demanding everyone set up nowadays.'

Zina squeezed Sergei's hand.

'I think we need somewhere else,' he said to Marienhof. 'I have a family now, Anatoly. I'm not going back to my old life.'

'Then there are the rooms at the old Poets' Union,' Marienhof said. 'The Bolsheviks are "recasting the nature of art", or so they tell us. They're about to set up their own Soviet Writers' Union or some such thing, but in the meantime we still have the premises and possession is nine tenths of the law.'

The rooms were Spartan, without heating. Winter came early. When they threw their overcoats on the back of a chair, the snowflakes on them didn't melt. But Zinaida was adamant they must be independent. They would put up with the hardship; it was only temporary; they would find something better.

Marienhof invited them for dinner and Zinaida agreed it would be churlish to refuse.

'I can't tell you what to do or how to live your life, Seryozha,' she said. 'But I know that man is trouble. Will you keep your dealings with him to poetry and business matters?'

The evening was a pleasant surprise. Marienhof was a good host, the attic on Bogoslovsky Lane was heated now, and Kusikov and Shershenevich were delightful. All three were genuinely pleased to have Sergei back. He was the most successful and most widely read of all of them. His collected poems had drawn praise from Lunacharsky, the Bolshevik Commissar of Culture. Trotsky himself was said to be an admirer.

On the way home, they wrapped Tatiana in shawls and furs. Winter had bitten, temperatures dropped. On Myasnitskaya, outside Perlov's Tea Rooms, stray dogs were picking at a dead horse. Death had drawn back its lips to reveal a smile of white teeth. A Siberian Husky was tearing at its flesh. A passing cabbie lashed out at it with his whip and the dog pulled its snout out of the horse's belly with annoyance. Its white, handsome muzzle was covered in blood from ear to ear, like a red mask from a carnival.

Money was short. Zinaida's parents had kept them for a year and continued to send cash when they could. But Moscow prices had risen as the capital's food supplies dwindled. Sergei and Zinaida decided that one or both of them would need to start earning.

Sergei met Marienhof for lunch. The inexplicable mystery of the Russian soul, Marienhof said, was that even when Russians are starving, when their apartments are freezing and they have bartered their grandmother's silver for firewood, they will still set money aside for art.

'I don't understand it. Poetry won't save you from hunger; music doesn't heat the stove. Yet we Russians need it as much as we need food. It's to do with the way we view ourselves – we may be repressed and downtrodden, but the knowledge of art means we can look ourselves in the eye ... Which is great for us, of course!' he laughed. 'The authorisation we got from Lunacharsky to set up our own press has been a godsend. What have you got that we can print, Seryozha?'

Sergei ran through the poems he had written over the last year. There were love lyrics, poems of the city and the village, some political verse. 'And there are a couple of quite personal things,' he said. 'Regarding you and Klyuev.'

'Unlikely to be complimentary then,' Marienhof smiled. 'You'd better read them to me.'

'All right. I'll start with Klyuev:

> My love for you is gone;
> You grieve that we should part.
> The paintbrush of the moon
> No longer stirs the lyre-strings of my heart.
> You both love and hate the star
> That fell upon your brow.
> You spread your love too far;
> You are homeless now.
> The one you wait for in the night
> Has passed your door again.
> Your door keys, song-rubbed bright,
> Have rusted in the rain.
> You shall no longer sing the sun
> Or heaven in your window bound.

Like the windmill's sails you turn and turn
But stay, forever, shackled to the ground.'

Sergei sighed. 'Quite harsh, I suppose. But I'm a different person now. I'm not the man who lived with him. I needed to draw a line. And he has written terrible things about me. Did you see his poem comparing my verse to the burnt-out ashes of a plague fire in the steppe? He blames you for debauching me; says you have stained my gift with coffee and nicotine. Yet he still refers to me and him as a couple, with poetic offspring whose voices will echo down the years. He curses me and I curse him. But there is always a sort of love that remains.'

Marienhof nodded. 'Relationships are like that. What have you written about me?'

'Not *about* you; it's a poem I've dedicated *to* you. Something dear to me. It's called "Forty Days Mourning", an elegy for the Russia we loved that is dying:

'It sounds, it sounds, the fateful trumpet!
What are we to do? How then should we live
On the highway's muddy haunches?
Soon the hoarfrost will bleach
The village and the meadows with its quicklime.
Nowhere can you hide from death,
Nowhere escape the clutches of your foe.
There he is! There he is with his iron belly,
Stretching out his fingers
To squeeze the throat of the steppe!
The old windmill pricks up its ears.
The silent bull, scenting trouble in the fields,
Wears out its tongue against the iron ring.
On, on, on rides the frightful herald,
Smashing through thicket after thicket.

All of us long for the chirping of the frogs
Under the hay; but oh! electric sunrise,
Blind grasp of belts and smoke-stacks,
Behold how the steel fever shakes
The wooden belly of our peasant huts!
Did you not see
How, across the steppe
Vanishing in the lake fogs
With iron nostrils snorting
On cast-iron hooves the train now thunders?
And behind it
Through the endless grass
In a carnival of despairing haste
With thin legs tossing up to its head
Gallops a red-maned colt?
Dear, dear, ridiculous foal!
Where does he think he's dashing?
Does he not know the steel beast
Has crushed the living horse?
Does he not know that
All his racing through the fields
Will not bring back the time
When a nomad tribe would trade a pair of
          Russian beauties
For a stallion?
Now, a thousand pounds of horsemeat
Buys a locomotive.
Devil take you, stinking guest!
My song will not make its peace with you.
When folk stand and gawp,
Their mouths set in tin-plate kisses,
I, like an ancient sexton, will sing
An alleluia for my native land.'

Sergei had promised Zinaida he would not drink. He reached across the table and poured himself a glass of wine.

'It is my greatest work, Anatoly. I dedicate it to you, because you are my greatest friend.'

The adrenalin of reciting and the rush of the wine loosened Sergei's tongue. He couldn't stop himself. He spoke of Zinaida's beauty, her emotional wisdom, the marvellous gift of love she had bestowed on him, the profound changes she had made in his life. Far from discouraging him, Marienhof smiled and poured more wine. By late afternoon, they were drunk and elated.

It was only as he walked home that Sergei began to worry he might have talked too much. The shared intimacy of the conversation had led him to touch on things about his life with Zinaida that should have remained unspoken. Marienhof was a fine fellow, but he didn't know how to keep a secret.

Chapter 17

Things happened quickly in those years. Every day brought news of such events that in normal times would have sufficed for a month. History was a whirlwind and the centre of the storm was Russia. Sergei and Zinaida had been together for less than two years, but, so close had they become, so completely did they share their thoughts, that it seemed they had known each other forever. They understood each other without words, their minds tuned to the same wavelength.

Sergei found an apartment on Petrovka Street and the three of them moved in. Tatiana grew pretty, intelligent, drawing admiration from all who saw her. She had a doting father, which didn't matter, and a good mother, which did. Zinaida fed her daughter better than she fed herself, scoured the markets and street vendors for clothes that would keep her baby warm.

Zinaida and Tatiana

'But am I still beautiful?' she asked Sergei. 'Sometimes I feel that life is passing, that we are losing our youth in struggles.'

Sergei hugged her. 'Beautiful, beautiful, beautiful,' he said. 'You will always be. All men will love you, but never one as much as I do ... and always shall.'

Sergei boasted about his wife. He couldn't help himself. He loved her youth, her beauty and the air of calm she had brought to his life, a serenity he had never known and would scarcely know again.

She cared for him as she cared for their child. She knew success was important to him and she wanted him to succeed.

'You know, Zina,' he said, 'readers of poetry expect their poets to live the life they describe in their poems. Otherwise it's all just words.'

'Well, that's worrying,' Zinaida said with a smile. 'Because your poems are full of self-destruction. I hope you're not planning to act all that out!'

'No,' he said. 'It's just such a contrast between the life I am living with you and the inner world of the poems ...'

'You funny old thing,' she said. 'I shall save you from the poet's doom!'

The revolution had inverted society. The powerful were cast down, former slaves now the masters. Dispossessed aristocrats hawked their possessions on street corners, to feed their families and rid themselves of belongings that betrayed their shameful past. Beautiful ball gowns were sold for a pittance. Stylish suits and shoes, silk shirts and French overcoats were ten a penny.

No one wanted to be seen in such incriminating garb. Only a poet, otherworldly and fantastical, could get away with it. Sergei asked Zinaida to buy him the most elegant outfits – smartly cut jackets, fine flannel trousers, dress shirts, spats – and he wore them in the street.

Yesenin had what the nineteenth-century writer Mikhail Lermontov had diagnosed as the Russian's inborn passion for contradiction. When the ideal had been sophistication, he had dressed as a peasant. Now, when everyone strove to look like peasants, he dressed as Beau Brummel.

The Imagists were in business. They had their own printing press, but they wanted more. Marienhof, Yesenin, Kusikov and Shershenevich spent hours in the offices of the Moscow City Soviet, lobbying for a licence to open a bookshop. The Bolsheviks had understood the importance of the written word; control the distribution of information and you are half way to controlling the country. Moscow had only two independent bookstores, run by surviving members of the old Writers' Union. Lev Kamenev, Chairman of the Moscow Soviet, was reluctant to give permission for more.

Worn down by the Imagists' persistence, Kamenev granted them an audience. Marienhof set out the case, but it was Yesenin whose charm won the old Bolshevik round. He spoke of how

Kamenev had edited the party's newspaper in exile, praised his commitment to the ideals of socialism and mentioned the feats of Kamenev's brother-in-law, Leon Trotsky, in protecting Russia from the White menace. The Imagists, he said, had been permitted to print and publish books because of their true understanding of the spirit of the revolution. Allowing them to open their own bookshop would redouble their enthusiasm. Kamenev signed.

Afterwards, Kusikov and Marienhof wondered at the bravura of Yesenin's performance. Since his marriage to Zinaida, he had become more manly, more self-assured. His grey suit, white collar and blue tie gave him the sophisticated elegance of an intellectual, his graceful figure full of confidence and strength, pink youthfulness shining in his face, straw-blond hair vigorous and thick. His speech was light and easy, flitting from one subject to another, entertaining and – where appropriate – ingratiating. When he listened, he seemed to speak without words. Everything about him played a part – the slightest nod of the head, the expressive gestures of his slender hands, a sudden knitting of his brows or the screwing up of his blue eyes. When he replied to a question, he seemed to weigh every word, modulating his intonation so that a person listening would come away convinced that he was expressing his innermost being. In fact, very few could see to the bottom of Yesenin's mind.

The revolution was a Manichean affair. Everything had to be black or white. It was the result of fear; the revolutionaries' fear of failure and the dreadful retribution that failure would bring down upon them. If you weren't vociferously with us, it meant you must be against us. Foes must be smitten with such dreadful force that they could no longer pose a threat. And friends must be embraced, clasped close with gifts and rewards, so that they might be kept from the lures and enticements of the enemy.

Zinaida got a job with them.

The revolutionary connections of her youth and the time she served in a tsarist jail were credentials that appealed to a regime determined to enlist its own. She began work at the Narkompros – the People's Commissariat of Enlightenment – as an administrator in the embryonic, still amateurish, propaganda department.

The pay was low, but it was paid. The benefits included a communal crèche for employees' children, which solved the problem of Tatiana, and a communal canteen from which Zinaida was able to secrete the odd piece of food to take home in her handbag. The Bolsheviks were committed to liberating women from drudgery at home. In its place, they instituted drudgery at work.

'Down with housework! Use communal kitchens and crèches!'

The document signed by Kamenev gave the Imagists permission to open a bookshop in the unused south wing of the

Moscow Conservatoire on Bolshaya Nikitskaya Street. The vacant rooms were administered by a sitting caretaker and the Imagists would have to negotiate with him to get the key.

Marienhof and Yesenin showed the caretaker the authorisation from the Moscow Soviet. He took them round the premises, but made it clear he expected a bribe. Yesenin, who had noticed that the key was still in the lock, whispered to Marienhof that he should distract the fellow's attention while Yesenin slipped the key into his pocket. Times were tough and all methods were fair.

Signs were painted, shelves installed, the shop stocked with books. The Poets' Bookstore opened with a fanfare. Sergei took his turn serving there with Kusikov and Shershenevich. Marienhof oversaw the operation, dropping in with sandwiches and, at times, vodka.

Sergei enjoyed the company, the excitement and the larks. They rifled through the books, mocked the customers, treated it as an adventure. It was a taste of the old life he thought he had left behind.

Nineteen-twenty. Zinaida was pregnant again.

'It should be a boy this time!' Sergei said. 'Let's have a boy and make our family complete!'

Zinaida smiled, but she was troubled. 'Are we right, though?' she said. 'Are we right to bring children into this frightful world?'

The tide of the war was turning in favour of the Bolsheviks. The Whites were ousted from Oryol and driven south towards Ukraine. Denikin pledged he would return and renew the assault on Moscow, but the loss of Oryol was a critical blow. Trotsky, putting aside ideological considerations, concluded a pact with the Black Army of the Ukrainian anarchist, Nestor Makhno. It meant that the Whites were battling the Bolsheviks in the north, while their supply lines were harried from the south. From now on they would be in retreat, pursued by the vengeful Reds, driven back ever further towards Crimea and the sea.

Having murdered the tsar, the revolutionaries were tracking down and eliminating his relatives. Britain had failed to rescue Nicholas and Alexandra, but now London acted. Lloyd George dispatched the destroyer HMS *Marlborough* to the Crimean port of Yalta, where it embarked four generations of the tsar's family, including his mother, Marie Fyodorovna, the Grand Dukes Peter and Nicholas, their children and their children's children. Prince Felix Yusupov, the killer of Rasputin, and his wife Irina, who had been used as bait, were among the refugees.

Ordinary Russians, who thought they were inured to suffering, discovered that the unbearable could get worse. The 1920 grain harvest was half what it had been in 1913. Coal production declined from 27 million tons to 7 million. Factory output was down tenfold. Famine loomed, deadlier than anything Russia had seen.

In Moscow, Sergei's poems were a success. The Pegasus Press made more money from his work than from its other titles combined. Marienhof, founder and leader of the Imagists, smiled and congratulated him.

The Pegasus Stable thrived. Marienhof pressed Sergei to appear more often, to resume the scandalous late-night recitals that had won the place its reputation. Sergei was reluctant. He performed from time to time, but didn't drink, didn't brawl and didn't provoke.

His poetry hovered between a world torn by horror and a home blessed by the promise of new life.

Evacuation of the Russian royal family on HMS Marlborough

Zinaida's first assignment was to work on the Commissariat's anti-illiteracy drive. Her job, an irony that wasn't lost on her, was to root out the spelling mistakes in the posters and information sheets.

The Commissar for Enlightenment kept a benevolent eye. Anatoly Lunacharsky was a gentle, cultivated presence, committed to knowledge and education, eager to undo the backwardness of centuries. Zinaida liked him.

'It's an exciting time to be an artist,' Lunacharsky said, 'an exciting time to be alive. The state has recognised how important the arts are. We're according them the respect they are due and the role in public life they deserve. We have all sorts of geniuses who've been energised by the revolution. Mayakovsky, of course; the Futurists – they're at the heart of our project. And people like Vasily Kandinsky, who's helping us ensure we sponsor the right artists with the right opinions. And Marc Chagall – the head of our committee in Vitebsk, where they've literally taken art on to the streets. He's got artists like Kazimir Malevich and El Lissitzky signed up to transform the whole of Vitebsk into an outdoor gallery, with all the buildings and squares covered in Soviet agitprop!'

'Can I show you something we're working on?' Zinaida said. 'Slightly less elevated, but still important. The first one's a woodcut of a young girl showing her mother her homework and saying rather despairingly, "Oh, Mummy – if only you weren't illiterate, you'd be able to help me!" I find that one quite touching. Then there's something a bit more light-hearted. We've engaged the artists Rotov and Yeliseev and the poet Agnivtsev to produce a simple guide to all the People's Commissariats, so that folk can understand what the government is doing on their behalf. I hope you'll like the one for Narkompros – it's got a cartoon of you holding a globe and saying to a young lad, "Narkompros, our aim is famous, To stop you being an ignoramus!"'

The People's Commissariat of Enlightenment anti-illiteracy drive

Narkompros was the epicentre of a cultural earthquake. Zinaida was swept along by the energy of it, introduced to painters, writers, directors and musicians whose work was transforming the face of art, building the new culture that the new world demanded. Before the revolution, artists such as Lyubov Popova, Natalia Goncharova and Alexander Rodchenko had flirted with the avant-garde, as had Kandinsky, Malevich and Chagall. Distracted by war and unrest, the tsarist regime had allowed culture to slip the leash. But it was 1917, with its promise of liberation from the past, that set all the arts aflame.

The poets Blok, Bely, Akhmatova and Mandelstam produced their most important work. Mikhail Zoshchenko and Mikhail Bulgakov pushed at the bounds of satire and fantasy. The Futurists embraced the revolution while proclaiming the renewal of art. The Fellow Travellers, sympathetic to Bolshevism but nervous about commitment, clashed with the self-proclaimed Proletarian writers who brashly claimed the right to speak for the Party.

Musical experimentalism broke through the barriers of harmony, overflowed into jazz and created orchestras without conductors. The watchword was novelty and invention, with pre-revolutionary forms raucously jettisoned from the steamship of modernity. 'The streets are our brushes,' said Mayakovsky, 'and the squares our palettes.'

Malevich and his Suprematist followers took painting into new regions of abstract geometric purity. 'By Suprematism, I mean the supremacy of pure feeling,' he wrote. 'Objective representation is pointless; emotion is the crucial thing.' Painting was alive with rhythmic form and space, dynamic shapes flying precipitously towards the viewer, full of the energy of the age of flight.

Lenin at first was tolerant, preoccupied with more pressing matters. But from 1920, as the civil war turned in their favour, the leadership started to look disapprovingly at the radicalism and the abstraction. They were shaping the doctrine that would subjugate all art to the aims of socialism.

Zinaida was sure it was a boy. The bulge in her belly sat so much lower than when she was carrying Tatiana and, even if it were an old wives' tale, she felt in her heart that it was true. Her girlfriends said the same. The women from the Commissariat admired her bump and envied her her husband. Sergei Yesenin was the second most famous poet in Russia. The first was Vladimir Mayakovsky, but his poems could be austere and forbidding. Women preferred the tender, doubt-filled lyrics of the boy from Ryazan. His verses were what young girls copied out in their private diaries, not the Futurists' increasingly bombastic socialist jingoism.

Zinaida knew how much Sergei wanted a son, but she promised nothing. If she were wrong, she didn't want to add to his disappointment. And she was worried about his future: her work at Narkompros gave her an insight into the way the regime was thinking.

The Bolsheviks were tightening their grip on the flow of information. It was partly to bring education – enlightenment, as the department's title called it – to the people. But there was an aspiration to mould the thoughts of a population that was showing insufficient enthusiasm for casting off the ways of the past. Culture would be a tool of social policy. Poets were tasked with producing snappy, easy to understand slogans that would encapsulate the regime's messages. The Futurists, always regarded as the heralds of the revolution, leapt at the opportunity. Mayakovsky, Burliuk and others wrote everything the regime demanded – from revolutionary epics to advertising jingles, from heroic propaganda to jokey cartoons.

Zinaida saw where it was leading. The artists and writers that Narkompros sponsored were the ones who had the rosiest futures. She worried that Sergei was not signing up for the new way of doing things.

Other matters were upsetting her, too. Some of the girls at work were regular visitors to the Pegasus Stable and they were quick to tell her the gossip. Some of the things she heard from them were disturbing.

'Seryozha, can I ask you a question? Did I give you reason to be disappointed on our wedding night?'

Her face was serious.

'No,' he said. 'That was the most wonderful night of my life – that one and all the others since.'

Zinaida did not smile.

'It's just something that Masha said. Masha at the Commissariat. She heard a rumour – or she heard someone say – that you were angry with me, because ... well, because you thought I wasn't all I should have been; that I wasn't ... inexperienced.'

The Red Army pushed into southern Russia then into Ukraine, driving back the Whites. Fighting was fierce. The frontline moved south, then north, then south again. Villages were captured and recaptured, pillaged and re-pillaged, bled dry.

A British journalist with a taste for adventure followed the Red advance. Philip Gibbs had been a war correspondent with British forces on the Somme and at Passchendaele. What he saw now was even more distressing.

'The harvest has been annihilated by two terrible droughts,' he cabled to London:

The reserves of grain which had always been kept by the peasants have been used up to feed the Red Army. There are twenty-five million people threatened by starvation and many of them are dead and dying. I went into cottages where a whole family would be lying down to die. I saw some terrible sights which filled my heart with pity. The children looked like fairy-tale children. It was most pitiful to see them dying of hunger with their stomachs swollen out.

The Bolshevik advance could not disguise problems in the army. Defections were rife. Around forty thousand Red Army men, most of them Ukrainians, had switched sides to join Makhno's nationalist forces in Crimea.

Leon Trotsky, Commissar of War and architect of world revolution, saw the Marxist explanation, understood the dialectical cause. The working class had not yet realised that national identities were a thing of the past. Workers and peasants must be taught to fight for class identity – the people against the bosses – and not for national allegiance. A campaign of political education was necessary. Political commissars, attached to every division of the fighting forces, would be provided with clear, simple pamphlets to convince even the least educated soldier.

On a visit to Anatoly Lunacharsky's Narkompros, Trotsky explained what was required and was introduced to the workers who would produce it. In the graphic design room, he asked the attractive girl with the black hair and dark eyes what her name was.

'Raikh . . . Raikh-Yesenina,' Zinaida said.

'Related to the poet? I have things to say about him. A great writer. A potential asset. On the wrong path.'

Trotsky turned to his adjutant. 'Make a note. Arrange a meeting with the poet, Yesenin.'

Leon Trotsky, Bolshevik Commissar of War

CHAPTER 18

Zinaida overheard a conversation in the canteen.

'He just can't stand her. You know what he calls her? A crummy Jewish broad with a fat arse and flabby lips on a face like a dinner plate.'

She knew the women were talking about her. When she challenged them, they didn't deny it.

'Who says that about me?'

'Oh, no one. Just—'

'Who says it?'

'Well, if you must know – your husband's best pal, Anatoly Marienhof!'

Crimea was the Whites' Calvary. The Western powers had withdrawn their support. The last monarchist general, Peter Wrangel, led the flight south, pursued by the Red Army.

Hundreds of thousands of White soldiers, with their wives, children and belongings, were trapped in the ports of Sevastopol and Yevpatoria, hoping to be evacuated by the remnants of the Imperial Navy. Being left behind meant certain death. The writer Konstantin Paustovsky described the panic:

Gaping mouths, torn open by cries for help, eyes bulging from their sockets, faces livid and deeply etched by fear of death, of people who could see nothing but the one, blinding, terrible sight: rickety ships' gangplanks with handrails snapping under the weight of human bodies, soldiers' rifle-butts crashing down overhead, mothers stretching up their arms to lift their children above the demented human herd. The moment anyone gained a hold on the plank or the rail, hands grabbed and clutched at him, clusters of bodies hung on him. Ships listed under the weight of people clinging to the deck rails. Some sailed away without stowing the gangplanks, which slid into the sea, with people still clinging to them.

Fifty thousand men, women and children who were left behind were rounded up and shot.

White Army forces evacuated from Crimea, 1920

Sergei had promised Zinaida he would not fall back into his old life of drinking and brawling. For the most part, he had kept his word. He avoided the controversies and scandals, rebuffed the advances of female admirers, drank in moderation.

Marienhof said little. In the month before Zinaida was due

to give birth, he noticed that Sergei was leaving the Pegasus early in the evening.

'Poor Seryozha,' Marienhof joshed him. 'Got to scurry back to the boss?'

'What's it got to do with you?'

'It's got to do with us,' Marienhof said, 'because that woman has driven a wedge between us. She's torn apart our band of comrades. She's stolen the fire from your belly. You've gone soft since you met her. Why have you let a woman turn you against your friends?'

Trotsky had accomplished his task. His elimination of the Whites established the template for the next seven decades of Soviet rule. Opposition would be crushed and its supporters repressed.

It was Trotsky's image that appeared on posters celebrating the prowess of the Soviet state. It was he who emerged as favourite in the hugger-mugger battle for the future leadership of the party, daily more pressing as Lenin, his health wrecked by Fanny Kaplan's bullets, slid into decline.

Two years at the head of the Red Army had taught Trotsky the importance of maintaining morale. He was an advocate of agitprop and mass information, the harnessing of culture to the message of the state. For men who murdered millions with little compunction, the Bolsheviks took a strangely obsessive interest in the fate of writers and artists. The self-styled poet Josef Stalin had artistic pretensions and personal tastes that he would seek to impose on Russian culture. Lenin the pragmatist saw culture as merely a tool.

'I'm no good at art,' he said. 'Art for me is a just an appendage, and when its use as propaganda – which we need at the moment – is over, we'll cut it out as useless: snip, snip!'

When he heard that Yesenin had been summoned to Trotsky's office, Marienhof told people how terrified Sergei had been. 'He had to change his trousers three times! Then he ran away in a fit of excitement to wash his hair, which he always does when he wants to look more handsome and poetic.'

Trotsky was to the point.

'I admire your poetry,' he said. 'But it's out of date. Feelings, nature, love – it's trivial and personal. It belongs to yesterday. Russia has changed. We need poetry on a new scale – poetry that deals with the destiny of all men, not just an individual.'

Yesenin wanted to speak, but Trotsky was in full flow.

'We are developing a new policy for the arts. We recognise how vital culture is to social progress, and writers like you are important for us. Socialism taps into man's natural goodness, the wellsprings of altruism that are in all of us. Capitalism relies on greed and the desire to do down one's fellow man. But mankind's true instincts are to work for the common good, for collective success – cooperation and love, instead of hatred and mistrust. Won't you join our effort to change the world? Won't you put your gift at the service of humanity?'

Sergei understood the argument. But there were things in

the old Russia he still loved, the old world of village values and human warmth that he was not yet ready to renounce.

'The Bolsheviks are conducting the greatest operation in history,' Yesenin said. 'You are excising the cancer that took hold of Russia. You are cutting deep into her flesh, and you have sacrificed yourselves and your own lives to do so. You have no time for love or emotions. But are you to sacrifice the lives of the people you set out to save? I am only a poet, but shouldn't someone keep the patient alive ... by continuing to live?'

Trotsky wrote something in his notebook.

'You are Russia's second greatest poet,' he said. 'Mayakovsky has won immortality by celebrating the future of mankind. You can, too. But if you use your gift for other purposes, you will be forgotten.'

A flotilla of battleships, cruisers and destroyers, merchant vessels, barges, fishing boats and private yachts carried the remnants of the White Army into exile. The holds, decks, passageways and gratings were crammed with people. Possessions had been left behind. Food was short. Sailing time to Constantinople was five days; supplies of drinking water ran out after one.

Physical conditions were hard, but the mental torment was worse. Those on board had fought for a cause they believed in, a final, despairing attempt to save their Russia from the hands of savages. A White lament captured the anguish of their departure:

> So many days now the farmsteads ablaze;
> The wind blows hard through the lands of the Don.
> Don't lose heart, Lieutenant Golitsyn!

Captain Obolensky, pour out the wine!
Dry your tears, gentlemen, officers;
We'll not regain that which is gone.
Lost is our land, our family, our faith;
The path behind is soaked in our blood.
In the harbour the ships glint in the sun;
But what is our fault? Wherein lies our guilt?
Lieutenant Golitsyn, shall we never return?
Shall we never know our homeland again?

With no country willing to grant them asylum, the ships of the Imperial Navy were interned first in Turkey then for the next four years in Tunisia. The White officers were left in limbo, helpless bystanders as the enemy tightened his grip on Russia.

Тов. Ленин ОЧИЩАЕТ
землю от нечисти.

'Comrade Lenin sweeps the human filth from the face of the earth'

Writers and artists had suffered under the tsars. Maxim Gorky had been exiled, Fyodor Dostoevsky transported to Siberia. But they had survived. Pressure on the arts had for the most part been gentlemanly or inept.

The new Soviet state was going to do better. It made stars of its favourites. Gorky and Mayakovsky were worshipped, lesser writers elevated for their willingness to do what the regime demanded. The Bolshevik poet Demyan Bedny was summoned to witness the execution of Fanny Kaplan, because seeing an anorexic, half-blind girl shot and burned would stiffen his socialist inspiration. The regime compared him to Shakespeare; in reality, he was McGonagall.

The Bolsheviks prized obedience over talent. The rewards were substantial and many grasped them. But there were also penalties, harsher than those of the tsars. Writers with a tender conscience, dubious about the revolutionary cause, the bloodshed and the violence, faced stark choices.

A new *codex artis* was being formulated, to be known as socialist realism. It decreed that all art should depict man's struggle for progress towards a communist society. The creative community would serve the proletariat by being realistic, optimistic and heroic. Other forms were degenerate.

Going against the regime was fraught with danger. The poet Osip Mandelstam wrote that 'Russia is the place where poetry really matters – they shoot you for it.' Nikolai Gumilev, husband of Anna Akhmatova, wrote poems of childlike wonder, trams that lose their way, dreamlike adventures of hippos, crocodiles and white giraffes. But he made no secret of his contempt for the Bolsheviks, crossed himself in public and in 1920 founded the independent All-Russia Union of Writers. He was arrested and charged with fomenting a monarchist plot. Gorky appealed in vain against his death sentence. The fanatical head of the Cheka secret police, Felix Dzerzhinsky, said, 'Are we entitled to make an exception for a poet and still shoot the rest?'

Nikolai Gumilev: prison photo

When Zinaida went into labour, Sergei couldn't find a cab. He ran the length of Petrovka Street as far as Neglinnaya then back again. In a panic, he flagged down a delivery van. The driver, at first suspicious, laughed. 'I've got four of my own,' he said. 'Don't take no brains to make that happen!'

They drove over cobbles and potholes. Sergei held Zinaida's hand and counted the blocks to the hospital. The place was dirty and cold, but the staff were efficient. Two nurses took Zinaida to the delivery room and told Sergei to wait. In the corridor, he heard them giggle. '*That* Yesenin – yes, the poet . . .'

The birth was a long one. When he was invited in, Zinaida was smiling. It was a boy.

Sergei was gazing at her. She pretended not to notice.

'Your face,' he said.

'What about my face?'

'You are so beautiful. So wonderful! I cannot tell you how much you mean to me. You have saved me from damnation.'

By some miracle of fate, he had stumbled upon a treasure

that other men spend lifetimes seeking. Happiness had fallen into his lap from the white of the sky.

Konstantin Yesenin was underweight and yellow. He cried pitifully then slept for hours. The hospital agreed to discharge him only because Sergei said their apartment had heating and there would be help on hand.

Zinaida, exhausted, fell asleep as soon as they got home. Sergei nursed his son until the boy closed his eyes then placed him in the cot beside the bed. He scribbled a note to say he was going out 'to wet the baby's head'.

It was morning when he returned. Konstantin was screaming. Zinaida was walking him up and down but he refused to be comforted. Tatiana was pulling at her mother's skirts.

'Where have you been?' Zinaida said. 'How could you go out and leave me here with no one to help?'

Sergei, buoyed by the birth of a son and tipsy from the night's drinking, put his arm around her. She pushed him away.

'You know how hard this is for me! You know the problems we had when Tanya was born, yet you think it's just fine to get drunk with your pals!'

'But that's what fathers do,' Sergei said. 'They go out and celebrate . . .'

He tried to help by nursing the baby, brewing tea, going out to the market in search of food.

Zinaida saw he was trying. She smiled when he served her overcooked meat and burnt toast. But she was finding the baby difficult. Konstantin was not well and his crying set her on edge. Tatiana's demands for attention tried her patience. She took it out on Sergei.

'You don't love me!' she said. 'You don't care for me! I bet you went to Marienhof and Kusikov. I bet you were all talking about me and saying how stupid and ugly I am. Seryozha, how could you treat me so badly?'

'That's nonsense, Zina. You know it's nonsense. How many times have I told you I love you! I don't know what else I can do!'

He slammed the door as he left.

CHAPTER 19

Marienhof had been expecting him.

'Come on, Seryozha,' he said. 'Let's get you a drink and cheer you up. I don't blame you for wanting out of that screaming madhouse!'

Kusikov and Shershenevich joined them in the basement of the Pegasus Stable. Moscow's literary circles were buzzing with the news of Nikolai Gumilev's execution. He had been a close friend of Sergei Gorodetsky, with whom Sergei had stayed when he first arrived in Petrograd.

'Surely they must have had reasons to do it?' Sergei said. 'He was an anti-Bolshevik plotter. He wanted to overthrow the regime ...'

Marienhof laughed.

'Don't be naïve. That's nonsense. There was no plot. They just didn't like him calling them illiterate peasants. They didn't like him crossing himself in public. They didn't like him mocking their socialist realism and refusing to write what they told him to write.'

The realities of art under the Bolsheviks were becoming starker.

'The ivory tower is no longer an option,' Marienhof said. 'All of us will have to make decisions about what we write and what we do with our lives. I have to say, the choices are not very appealing.'

The Pegasus closed for the night, but the four of them sat on. Long silences, during which they stared intently at the vodka glasses in their hands, were broken by bursts of argument.

'You're not going back to that woman, are you?' Marienhof said. 'We're all staying here tonight. Tomorrow you can move into your old room at Bogoslovsky Lane.'

Sergei didn't quite know why he had walked out. His pride was hurt; the responsibilities of a new baby and an unhappy wife made his old life alluring. But he knew that his happiness lay with Zinaida. He knew it, yet he didn't go back.

Marienhof reassured him that he was right to feel resentful.

'Don't be in thrall to a woman, Seryozha!' Marienhof said. 'Come back to your friends. You know that's what you want!'

Moving in with Marienhof seemed too provocative and too cruel. Sergei hesitated. When Kusikov said he could come to stay at his apartment on Afanasievsky Lane, Sergei agreed.

No.30 Afanasievsky Lane

The meeting with Trotsky and the death of Gumilev preyed on him. In Kusikov's spare bedroom, his suitcase half-unpacked on the floor, he sat down to write. Draft followed draft, but form and content would not gel. He gave up polishing – the key thing was to get the politics right.

Song of the Great Crusade

The Whites they came a stealing,
Stealing our cattle,
Drinking our vodka,
Fingering our wives,
Pawing our daughters.
'You bastards!' they called us.
'You animals! We'll hang you high!
We'll flog you sideways
And fuck your mothers!'
But cheer up, o Russian folk!
Today we have new strength,
For Soviet power is with us!
Who can forget the speech
Comrade Zinoviev made?
To all he said, 'Brothers!
Better to fight and die,
Better here lay down our lives
Than give up our Russia to the Whites
And return once more to bondage!'
O, great commanders!
Great leaders, great chiefs!
We communists have comrade Trotsky!
No tears he pours, no empty words;
Just the promise brave and true
That we shall battle on to the Don
That our steeds may drink of its waters.

From all sides our men attack.
A cry comes from the Whites,
A moan, a groan.
The Whites are struck by panic;
They're praying to their tsar,
To their old Holy Russia,
While getting drunk on wine
And tumbling their whores.
Our boys greet the dawn
With a whistle in the wind,
Eyes raised in hope,
Hands poised to strike.
The commander says,
'Brothers! If here we fail,
If the enemy defeat us,
The dawn of October
Shall be forever crushed . . .'

He read through the draft, folded it in half and stuffed it in the bottom of his suitcase. It lay there for days. Days in which Zinaida sent him messages, pleading with him to return.

He neither replied to her nor reopened the suitcase.

Gumilev's widow, Anna Akhmatova, transmuted her grief into a series of anguished poems. They could not be published, but they circulated in furtive, handwritten copies. Sergei read them and crumpled his 'Great Crusade' into the waste basket.

Terror, rummaging through the apartment
        in the dark,
Glints like a moonbeam on an axe.
A thud from behind the wall –
What's there? Rats? A ghost? A thief?
Terror drips like water in the narrow kitchen,

Scraping the creaky floorboards,
Flashing past the window,
Dark and hooded with a gleaming, glossy beard,
Then falls silent. How evil, how crafty he is.
Terror hides the matches then blows out the candle.
Much better to have the daylight
And rifles aimed at my heart . . .
A.A.

Anna Akhmatova

Word of Zinaida's plight circulated among her colleagues at Narkompros. Girlfriends came to offer their condolences.

Zinaida asked if they had news of Sergei. Two of the women, habituées of the Pegasus Stable, were delighted to tell her.

'He's there every night,' they said. 'Back reciting on stage. We all missed him so much when he dropped out of sight. And he looks terrific – really back on form.'

'Does he say anything about me?' Zinaida asked.

The women shook their heads.

'No, dear. Not a word. Marienhof has plenty to say, though. He says it was the sight of young Konstantin that upset Sergei. The baby's got black hair and the Yesenins have always been blond. Don't take it to heart, but Marienhof says Sergei walked out because he thinks his son is a bastard!'

It was late and the knock on the door was peremptory. They had been drinking – Kusikov's brother Rueben had come to stay at the apartment and the three of them had hit the vodka.

Yesenin laughed, 'Probably some drunkard come home and lost his keys . . .' But Rueben looked concerned. Kusikov got up to unlock the door. It burst open. Four uniformed men pushed past him.

'Cheka! Don't move!'

The unit's commander waved his pistol. The others chose a target. Kusikov, Yesenin and Rueben were handcuffed before they realised what was happening.

The commander was reading aloud from a piece of paper, listing paragraphs from the criminal code.

'Wait! Comrade!' Sergei said. 'There's been a mistake! I am Yesenin – the poet—'

'Shut it! I'm not your comrade, you White shit! And the only mistake is yours. You're off to the Lubyanka!'

Zinaida was notified of Yesenin's arrest. In later years people would disappear into the state's maw with no acknowledgement of their fate, but this was early and some of the old protocols still seemed to apply.

She went to the Lubyanka to join the ashen-faced women seeking news of husbands, sons and daughters. It was a queue of trembling fear, lowered eyes and submissive smiles. It was her first brush with the terror that would stalk Russia. It was disconcerting, grotesque.

The clerk at the desk looked at Zinaida's papers then consulted a register.

'No. Nothing. Sorry.'

He was about to call the next in line, but Zinaida stopped him.

'Wait!' she said. 'Sergei Yesenin. Yesenin, the poet. Please – look again!'

Something flickered in the man's face. Poetry is a force in Russia. He disappeared into a back office and returned with more papers.

'Yes. We've got him. Consorting with treasonous elements. Could be bad.'

Zinaida had questions, but the man's goodwill was exhausted.

'Write. You'll have to write, like all the rest. Get someone to help you, if you can. Send the form in. That's the best I can do. Next!'

The civil war had ended, but the wounds were monstrous, bloody, the towns crippled by strikes, the countryside in revolt.

The Bolsheviks were a paramilitary fraternity, uninterested in debate, surrounded by an untrustworthy population. They were austere zealots, denying themselves sympathy or pity. 'I can't listen to music,' Lenin said, 'because it makes me want to say sweet, silly things and pat people on the head ... but you have to beat people's heads, beat them mercilessly!'

The revolution was far from secure. Its leaders gathered for the Party Congress of March 1921 in a climate of menace. Workers who had supported the October coup were on the streets again, marching now against the Bolsheviks. On the day the Congress opened, the sailors of the Kronstadt island fortress in the Gulf of Finland outside Petrograd rose up in rebellion. Four years earlier they had murdered their tsarist officers, stormed the Winter Palace and fought with ferocious zeal as the revolution's shock troops. Now they were tearing up their Party cards. Their manifesto demanded that Lenin step down and call new elections.

> The working class expected the Revolution to bring freedom, but it has brought enslavement whose horrors exceed those of tsarism. The Communists threaten us constantly with fear of arrest, torture and murder by the Cheka. They are even forcing the people to *think* the way they want them to!

Lenin dispatched Trotsky from the Congress directly to Kronstadt with orders to crush the revolt. Trotsky's artillery bombarded the fortress from the shore. His troops set out to march five miles across the frozen sea but, exposed on the ice with nowhere to hide, were mowed down in their thousands. The Kronstadt rebellion looked as if it would succeed. And if Kronstadt were allowed to rebel, the rest of Russia would follow. The Bolsheviks faced annihilation.

Trotsky gathered forty-five thousand fresh troops and lined up machine gunners to fire on any who refused to advance. Thousands more died, but Kronstadt was taken. Fifteen thousand rebels were executed or sent to the Gulag.

Kronstadt was a warning. The Bolsheviks, Lenin admitted, were 'barely hanging on'. It would lead to a rethink of the Party's priorities and economic strategy. But the immediate response was terror. The Cheka was given new powers. A so-called troika of three secret policemen or party officials could now have prisoners executed without trial.

Zinaida left the children with a neighbour. She spent days searching for information, trying to discover what charges

Sergei was facing, if and when he might be put on trial. The longer it took, the more desperate she grew.

She asked to speak to Lunacharsky, but was told he was unavailable. She sat in his ante-room and refused to leave. When he appeared, he was non-committal.

'It seems Sergei Alexandrovich has been consorting with undesirable elements. Rueben Kusikov is accused of involvement in anti-revolutionary activities and of having served in White units suspected of war crimes. His brother, the poet, is charged with harbouring White fugitives. Your husband was present when the security organs discovered the two suspects and was arrested accordingly.'

'Then he's not personally accused of being involved?' Zinaida said. 'He was simply in the wrong place?'

Lunacharsky raised his hand.

'That is for the investigating authorities to decide. The fact that he was colluding with presumed traitors may be proof enough.'

'But he was there by accident,' Zinaida said. 'He is my man. He lives with me and our children. He should never even have been at Kusikov's flat.'

Lunacharsky softened.

'Yes, perhaps . . .'

'Please, Anatoly Vasilyevich!' she said. 'I beg you – please write and explain things. I fear I may never see my husband again . . . I love him . . . I miss him so much!'

The Kronstadt revolt deepened the Bolsheviks' siege mentality. They would soon close Russia's borders. But in the early 1920s, flight was still possible and millions fled.

The cultural exodus was startling. The painters Chagall

and Kandinsky quit their state positions and left for the West; writers including Nabokov, Bunin, Tsvetaeva and Khodasevich went too, as did the composers Stravinsky, Prokofiev and Rachmaninov.

The émigrés exiled themselves to limbo, cut off from their past, hoping the separation from their homeland would be only temporary, unable or unwilling to put down new roots.

'When I left Russia,' wrote Rachmaninov, 'I lost my desire to create. Devoid of my homeland I have lost myself.'

The country they loved had ceased to exist in 1917. They saw themselves now as custodians of the true Russia. It was their duty to keep the flame alive until the barbarians were driven out.

The jailer shouted.

'Yesenin, Sergei Alexandrovich! Kusikov, Alexander Borisovich!'

They stood.

'You two, follow me!'

Sergei stepped forward, but Kusikov remained.

'What about my brother?' he said. 'Rueben Borisovich?'

The jailer looked at his list.

'No. No call for him. Come on; quick now!'

As a girl, Zinaida had been calm. Her serenity flowed from inner confidence and a Germanic fortitude inherited from her father.

Now she was under pressure from the constant necessity of finding the material means to survive in a world fallen apart, from the responsibility and fear she felt for the children she had brought into it, from the daily uncertainties of a violent, capricious state.

She was tormented by a job serving a regime she had come to mistrust, helping to keep in power men who had revealed themselves as murderers. By Marienhof's endless needling. By his attempts to lure Sergei away from her. By the supposed friends who delighted in telling her how much her husband despised her. And now by his dreadful, numbing absence.

'Poets!'

It was said with a smile, part-mocking, part-admiring.

'Lucky poets at that!'

The prison governor brandished a sheet of paper.

'People's Commissar, Anatoly Lunacharsky, no less. He's getting you out of here.'

The governor read the investigators' conclusions:

> In the case of Yesenin, Sergei, it has been established through interrogation that the subject's involvement in the Kusikov affair is not proven. Decision: release the subject on the surety of Comrade Blumkin, Yakov Grigorevich, who will answer for subject's future attendance in court, if this be so required.

He handed Sergei a copy of the decision and turned to Kusikov.

> In the case of Kusikov, Alexander. Subject's involvement in the affair of Rueben Kusikov, subject's brother, is not established. Investigation, followed by interrogation of the subject (duration seven hours), have not proven subject's guilt in the

matter of harbouring White fugitives. The prisoner is one of our most famous revolutionary poets. Decision: release subject and terminate investigation.

Lunacharsky's intervention had evidently been wholehearted. The governor proffered his hand. Sergei shook it, but Kusikov held back.

'What about my brother? Why is there no word on him?'

The governor shook his head.

'Investigations are continuing.'

After three weeks in the cells, Moscow's smoke-filled air smelled of freedom. Walking through Lubyanka Square to the tram stop, Kusikov asked what Sergei was intending to do.

'A drink! That's the first thing,' Sergei said. 'We'd better get Marienhof to come!'

ЗАКЛЮЧЕНИЕ ПО ДЕЛУ ЕСЕНИНА

Произведенным допросом выяснено, что причастность Есенина к делу Кусиковых не достаточно установлена, и посему полагаю гр. Есенина Сергея Александровича из-под ареста освободить под поручительство тов. Блюмкина.

Я, нижеподписавшийся Блюмкин Яков Григорьевич, проживающий в гостинице «Савой», № 136, беру на поруки гр. Есенина и под личной ответственностью ручаюсь в том, что он от суда и следствия не скроется и явится по первому требованию следственных и судебных властей. Подпись поручителя, Яков Блюмкин.

Conclusion in the case of Sergei Alexandrovich Yesenin

No one told Zinaida that Sergei was free. Neither could he be certain that his release was thanks to her, although he might have deduced as much from the evidence of Lunacharsky's involvement. He chose to celebrate his freedom not with his wife but at the Pegasus club.

Marienhof and Shershenevich produced a case of French champagne, secretly stored since 1917, and launched into the complex ritual of Russian toasts, opening with the matter in hand – 'Freedom!' 'Brotherhood!' – meandering through standard topics – 'Womankind!' 'Beauty!' – and ending with the traditional, 'Drink up; we'll meet under the table!'

The Imagists were reunited. The old days were back. Kusikov was hesitant – his brother's detention and the seriousness of the charges against him were disquieting – but alcohol helped. By the time Blumkin arrived and announced with a grin that he had come to supervise the criminals who had been released into his charge, they all were drunk.

Yakov Blumkin was a remarkable study in self-reinvention. Like Fanny Kaplan, he had been a Left Socialist Revolutionary when the party fell out with the Bolsheviks in 1918. It was Blumkin who had carried out the murder that sparked the Left SRs' shelling of the Kremlin. But when the SR rebellion failed, he had switched sides. He had become so close to Trotsky that he was trusted to edit the great man's memoirs, with Trotsky remarking wryly that Blumkin had persuaded him to let an SR conspirator write the official account of the SR conspiracy.

Trotsky had assigned Blumkin to duties with the Cheka, where his skill as an assassin did not go unutilised. But Blumkin also aspired to culture. He was close to the leading poets, including the Imagists. He was a familiar figure at their drinking sessions, striding through the bar with a glass in one hand and a revolver in the other. When Trotsky was thinking of opening a Bolshevik literary journal, Blumkin proposed Yesenin as its editor.

That closeness to Trotsky would later cost Blumkin his life, but at the time of Sergei's arrest he was an influential figure. The release papers from the Lubyanka had enjoined Yesenin and Kusikov to heed Blumkin's moral tutelage in matters of drink and personal conduct. The two of them did so with such enthusiasm that for the next week they were never sober.

Yakov Blumkin

'My God!'

Zinaida steadied herself on the doorframe.

'I thought you were dead!'

She reeled. Sergei caught her. Her cheek brushed his.

'Reports of my demise are ... what did he say? ... exaggerated.'

Her closeness stirred him; feelings, sudden, deep, unexpected. Her arms around his neck were a memory of tenderness.

'When did you get out? Seryozha, I've been frantic!'

'The other day. I went to get some clothes ... from Kusikov's—'

'The other day?'

'It was terrible, Zina. And poor Rueben Kusikov – he's still in that hellhole. God knows what they're doing to him.'

'Was it a hellhole, Seryozha? Was it terrible for you?'

He described the interrogations, the uncertainty, the threats.

'But why did they arrest you?' she said. 'None of you has done anything.'

'I'd say it was a denunciation. There's a lot of that now.' He shrugged. 'Neighbours doing down neighbours; professional grudges; people after someone else's flat. If it was done maliciously, that's frightening. If it was someone playing a prank on us, they didn't realise the danger of it. In the old days, it might have been amusing to get your friends pulled in for a bit of third degree – things usually ended without too much damage. But nowadays, they put people in front of a firing squad without a second thought. There were times when I thought it might be me.'

Zinaida pulled him close, stroked his cheek, solicitous, gentle.

'Sit down,' she said. 'I've been sleeping with the children since you went, but I'll make up our bed.'

Zinaida seemed recovered from the troubles that overtook her after Konstantin's birth. The baby was still not well, but she was coping and she loved her son. Having Sergei back made everything easier; they had missed each other more than either had realised. Life together was not always smooth – reproaches smouldered – but there was a bond between them, an understanding and affection that outweighed the rest. His time of going away seemed unreal now, as if an illness had clouded his brain.

> The evening knits its brows; horses
> Stand in the yard; can it be true
> That yesterday I walked away?
> Fell out of love with you?
> Ah, troika, peace; you're late; so what?
> Our lives may pass without a trace,
> Maybe tomorrow a hospital cot
> Will be my final resting place.
> I may sink beneath the powers
> That harrow me and lay me waste.

But you always shall I remember,
And only you, sweet tender face.
And if I fell in love again,
E'en with that new love, with her,
I'd talk of you, my dearest girl,
My love, my sweet, the girl I still call dear.
I'd talk of life that flowed away,
I'd say I had no past.
But you, my headstrong heart, oh say –
Where will you lead me at the last?

He had begun it as a love song, but the poem's momentum was a wilful voice and it led to an equivocal ending.

Happiness was on offer. If he chose not to take it, he would do so knowing the heartbreak it would bring.

CHAPTER 20

The Kronstadt rebellion had brought the Bolsheviks close to disaster. Lenin called it a threat more dangerous than the Whites. A regime claiming to rule on behalf of the people had come perilously close to being deposed by the people.

Russia in 1921 was sick of the Bolsheviks' War Communism, weary of hunger and economic meltdown, no longer willing to suffer in the name of some future Utopia. Mass terror could no longer contain rebellion.

Lenin made concessions. His New Economic Policy offered to soften the state's dictatorship and reintroduce some elements of capitalism. The hated practice of grain seizures was abandoned. If peasants handed over a portion of their produce, they would be allowed to sell the rest. In industry, small private cooperatives would be permitted. And the black market trade in food that had been stigmatised and banned would now be tolerated.

It was the only way to placate the people, but hard-line Bolsheviks were appalled. The NEP seemed a betrayal of Communist ideals, a capitulation to capital. Even Mayakovsky lampooned it:

> They asked me if I love the NEP.
> I said I do,

If it weren't so darned absurd.
Come on, comrades!
Get out there
And slug it out with the businessmen and merchants!
Lenin says it's 'here for good':
But who knows?
Another revolution could be along soon!

The New Economic Policy halted the decline in agriculture and industry and averted the threat of counter-revolution. But Lenin feared the ferocity of opposition in the Party and he moved to crush it. His decree 'On Party Unity' demanded the dissolution of dissenting groups. Debate was throttled. Divergent views were denounced as 'factionalist' treachery. Show trials of political opponents began. The way was paved for the intolerant, monolithic Communist Party that would rule for seventy years.

'From the NEP, a socialist Russia will grow'

The NEP did wonders for the Pegasus café. The black market spivs who previously hid their wealth for fear of having their collars felt now spent with abandon, drank more, ate more, dressed even more garishly and showered their floozies with ever more expensive gifts. The new class of NEP-men exploited the economic freedoms. The people hated them and needed them.

Tables at the Pegasus were rarely empty. Demand for the poets grew. Sergei spent the days writing, evenings reciting and nights with Zinaida. She noticed he was returning home later and smelling of alcohol, but she said nothing.

For the public, the NEP was a brief mirage of tolerance. It seemed an indication that the Bolsheviks were willing to heed the people's wishes. In reality, it was a ploy to keep themselves in power until circumstances allowed them to ditch it.

For Sergei, it was a period of acclaim. The themes of his poetry – love, doubt, sorrow, loneliness – resonated with a population weary of official jollity and vacuous socialist cheerleading. A review in the *Narodny Uchitel* – 'People's Teacher' – magazine pinpointed the reasons for his appeal.

No living poet evokes the reader's sympathies as much as Sergei Yesenin. Yesenin lacks the sweep and strength of Mayakovsky, the cultural resonance of Mandelstam or the lyrical intensity of Pasternak. But he has the quality that is most important of all – the ability to reach the reader's heart, to move us and touch us. That is something quite rare in the times we live in. Yesenin has no agenda to push, no -ism to promote. He does not seek to convince us of anything, addresses no issues. He tells us only about himself. But when a Yesenin poem says 'I', it sounds almost always like 'we'. He has understood the heart of the Russian people. He shares our emotions, our fears and our need for love.

Sergei was enjoying his recitals again, the applause, the respect and the lines of admirers. His lust for fame, the thirst for personal validation he had harboured since childhood, drove him on. But the more it was assuaged, the more he needed. If his pre-eminence was questioned, he felt belittled.

When Boris Pasternak recited two of his poems and was well received, Yesenin sought him out, pretending not to know who he was.

'Your poems are like tongue-twisters,' he said. 'No one will ever understand them. The people will never admire you.'

Pasternak replied with feigned courtesy that one should be cautious when invoking 'the people'; but Yesenin would not back off.

'I know the people,' he said. 'And I know that in future they will say, "Pasternak? A poet? Never heard of him . . . although we do like vegetables!"' referring to the word *pasternak*, which in Russian means parsnip.

Later he went after the man whose status as Russia's number one irked him the most. Yesenin and Mayakovsky were performance poets in an age when poets were stars, equal in fame to any actor or singer. Mayakovsky, too, was a provocateur, given to scandalous acts and shocking outbursts. His verse, noisily celebrating modernity and the march of Soviet industrialisation was the antithesis of Sergei's gentle laments for the disappearing world of the old Russian village.

At a poetry evening chaired by the venerable Symbolist Valery Bryusov, Yesenin and Mayakovsky came to blows. Mayakovsky began by decrying the decadent backwardness of poets who praise the past and lack the vision to understand the communist future.

Yesenin, who had been drinking, responded with a volley of abuse, to which Mayakovsky made an insulting reply.

'Attention!' he boomed to the audience. 'News of a crime! Some children have killed their mother. They said she was a no good, dissolute whore. The mother was Poetry. The murderers are Yesenin and his Imagist cronies!'

Yesenin tore off his jacket and tie and leapt on to the chairman's table.

'We are not the murderers of poetry!' he yelled. 'You are! You don't write poems! You write stupid jingles and whorish propaganda!'

The auditorium erupted. Punches were thrown. Marienhof pulled Sergei away, but not before he had been hit in the face.

When Zinaida saw his injuries, he shrugged.

'It's an act,' he said. 'Poetry. It's about being noticed. About being heard.'

Yesenin   Mayakovsky

It was true that the Bolsheviks were changing the way people thought. They claimed they were creating a new breed of men, with socialist minds that thought in socialist ways. But there were other changes. In the old days, a knock at the door meant a friend or a neighbour. Now it filled people with terror. The fear that agents of the state might at any moment appear moulded the thoughts of every Russian.

When Zinaida opened the door, a man with a revolver staggered in. She screamed. He waved the gun in a theatrical sweep. It flashed through her mind that he was drunk.

'Calm yourself, madam,' the man said. 'No need for alarm ... I have come ... I have come ...'

His words were slurred.

'I have come to visit the criminal, Seryozha! . . . The criminal Seryozha, who is under my charge . . . ! Yakov Blumkin, at your service. I shall enter your apartment . . .'

She tried to push him out, but he was already past her.

'So this is the residence of the criminal Seryozha!' he said, gesturing with his revolver.

Zinaida had experience dealing with drunks. She took the gun from him.

'Yes, madam. Good precaution. That gun has killed and shall kill again! Not you, of course . . . Not such a beauty as yourself . . .'

She offered him tea. He was walking unsteadily towards the kitchen.

'Not tea, madam! Something stronger . . . something such as this!'

He glanced at the bottle, pulled the cork with his teeth and poured a glass of vodka. It seemed to calm him.

'Ah!' he said. 'Better. Now to business. I have, as you know, been empowered to supervise . . . to oversee . . . you know, Seryozha and I are good friends, drinking partners, even . . . and I am also his moral guardian while he remains subject to the . . . I am unsure of his crime . . . but I do know he must comply with my demands – and my demand is that you produce him at once to have a drink with me!'

'He's not here,' Zinaida said.

'Then where is he?' Blumkin's tone was immediately suspicious. 'You are not attempting to conceal the subject from me, are you? . . . Are you concealing a criminal from the duly empowered agents of the . . . ?'

'Of course not,' Zinaida said. 'He isn't here. I'm surprised *you* don't know where he is. He seems to spend more time drinking with you and Marienhof than he spends with his wife and children.'

Blumkin picked up the nuance.

'Ah, madam's husband deserting her? Neglecting madam's needs ...'

He was advancing towards her. 'We can remedy that!'

He had his arm around her waist, pulling her towards him. She screamed, but he clamped her mouth.

'No need for resistance,' he said. 'Blumkin at your service ... to satisfy, as they say, your every ...'

He was strong, pushing her towards the bedroom.

'Not in there!' Zinaida managed to say. 'The children are sleeping!'

Mention of the children chastened him. He released her.

Zinaida ran to the window, but Blumkin raised his hand.

'No need for that, madam. No need to shout ... I see how things ... I am Jewish ...'

The incongruity of it made her pause.

'I know you are Jewish. Why are you telling me?'

'Because you are also Jewish. I thought that you ...'

'I'm not Jewish,' Zinaida said.

'Then whence cometh this *Raikh* of yours?'

'My father's family were from Germany.'

'Aha!' Blumkin leapt to his feet, suddenly alert. 'Then you are the enemy! ... the enemy that we fought for so—'

'Don't be absurd,' Zinaida said. 'My father's as Russian as they come. And you Bolsheviks keep telling us to forget national identities and concentrate on class warfare, workers of all nations united against the ruling class. My father did plenty of that.'

Blumkin seemed exhausted, his arguments defeated.

'Oh well,' he mumbled. 'There's nothing more to say.'

He was at the door on his way out when he remembered why he had come.

'Before I go,' he said. 'This is for Seryozha.'

After he left, she read what he had handed her.

DECISION IN THE CASE OF KUSIKOV,
RUEBEN BORISOVICH

Rueben Kusikov stands accused of counter-revolutionary activities under Article 58 of the Soviet Criminal Code, a charge carrying the death penalty.

The subject was questioned in regard to his service in the Circassian Regiment of the White Army's Savage Division, suspected of the perpetration of war crimes.

The charges of counter-revolution against him were investigated by the State Political Directorate of the Cheka.

Having carried out our inquiries, we conclude that the charges against the subject remain unproven. Decision: release the subject on the surety of Comrade Yakov G Blumkin.

She realised her hands were shaking. It wasn't just the brush with Blumkin. Her nerves were shot.

Poetry has always been Russia's secret garden of liberty, defying censorship, keeping freedom alive when autocracy strove to crush it. The Bolsheviks recognised its power. They bullied it and courted it, trying to buy off its censure.

Osip Mandelstam, Marina Tsvetaeva, Anna Akhmatova, Nikolai Gumilev, Nikolai Klyuev and others would resist the regime's blandishments. They would use poetry's currency against the autocrats. All would suffer for it. Others hesitated.

Mikhail Kuzmin, the playwright who had long ago been Klyuev's lover, wrote enthusiastically in praise of the revolution.

We're building us a brand-new home.
Tomorrow we'll find space for all.
Laugh now, don't be dour;
Heed the revolution's call!
The Soviets' giddy, shining promise
Of food and freedom for all men,
The word we heard and heard again,
Proud and mighty, 'Soviet citizen'!
Our Revolution's youthful, chaste and good.
Not like the French; more than its equal,
An angel of deliverance in workers'
        clothes,
A promise written in our blood.

Sergei sniffed when he read it. Alexander Blok's assessment of the revolution was more subtle, an ambiguous, equivocal epic titled, 'The Twelve'.

Black night,
White snow.
The wind, the wind!
It all but lays you low.
The wind, the wind,
Across God's earth it blows!
Stumbling and tumbling,
Folk slip and fall.
God pity all!
Oh, what bitter sorrow!
A sweet life we have won!
Now we vow we'll set the world on fire,
Flaming, flaming amidst blood –
Bless us, Lord God!
March to the revolution's pace:

We've an enemy to face!
On and on, the steady beat
Of the workers' marching feet!
... And The Twelve, unblessed, unhallowed,
Still go marching on.
Ready for what chance may offer,
Pitying none.
On, with rifles lifted,
Through dead alleys where sleet has sifted,
Where the blizzard tosses free.
Onward, where the snow has drifted
Clutching at the marcher's knee.
The red flag
Whips their faces.
Creaking snow,
Measured paces.
The grim foe
Marks their traces.
Crrack-crack-crack!
Crrack-crack-crack!
... Forward as a haughty host they tread.
A starving mongrel shambles in the rear.
Above them flies the banner, bloody red,
That He holds in hands no bullets sear;
Hidden as the flying snow veils veer.
Lightly walking on the wind, as though
He Himself were diamond snow,
With mist-white roses garlanded:
Jesus Christ is marching at their head!

The poem moved Sergei. He sat down to write, fired with
determination to love the revolution. Great historical events,
the social, political upheaval engulfing Russia demanded

to be addressed. It wasn't his natural subject matter, but he had to do it.

> I know a thing about talent; poetry's a simple
>   game.
> But when the subject is my love for Russia,
> That tortured, burned-out love of my land,
> It's not so easy to write it all the same.
> Turn out a couplet, dash off a rhyme –
> Anyone can do it: *the moon and girls and love and bed* –
> But that's not the tenor of the time,
> Not the thing that fills my head.
> I want to be a poet and a citizen now,
> A shining son of the mighty Soviet state!
> Someone she can be proud of,
> Not a bastard come too late.

He showed Marienhof the first three stanzas of what he planned to be a celebration of Russia's redemption, a paean to the men leading her to the fulfilment of communism.

'Poor little Seryozha,' Marienhof laughed. 'Always scurrying to do what the big boys tell him. You don't believe any of this socialist nonsense! You're making yourself write doggerel for the sake of keeping them happy.'

'It's not doggerel,' Sergei said. 'And I do admire what they are doing for Russia. But it's hard. I still love the world they are destroying – the old world of the village, rural backwardness, old-fashioned affection . . .'

'So write what you feel,' Marienhof said. 'Write the rest of it sincerely. Then come back and show me.'

Zinaida forced herself to be calm. It helped that the children were behaving well – she wondered if Tanya and Kostya could sense that their mother was struggling and were trying to help her.

She decided she would tell Sergei. Then decided she wouldn't. Then decided she needed to tell him or she would go mad.

When he came in she hugged him, but she didn't mention Blumkin. She didn't know why not. She told herself it was because Sergei needed protecting. He would go and confront the man, put himself in danger. Perhaps she had another fear – that Sergei would make light of her ordeal, say it was nothing, laugh at her distress.

She resolved to say nothing. Then in bed he was so tender, his lovemaking so kind and patient, so affectionate, that she told him everything.

Sergei cursed the man who had tormented his wife. He leapt out of bed, pulled on his clothes. He would find Blumkin, beat him to pulp. Zinaida took his arm. He was going to shoot the bastard. Zinaida embraced him, laid her head on his shoulder. He hugged her. He was in tears.

They huddled together under the bedclothes and held each other close in the consolation of love.

In the morning, Sergei asked Marienhof if he had seen Blumkin.

'No,' he said. 'We were expecting him last night, but he didn't come. I think something might have happened to him.'

'Something has!' Sergei said. 'And something worse is about to!'

He explained. Marienhof shook his head.

'You can't go against Blumkin,' he said. 'The man's too powerful, too close to Trotsky and the Cheka. He would crush you and all of us with you. They'd close down the Pegasus; the bookshop, too. These people are vengeful, Seryozha.'

Sergei didn't listen. He found Blumkin in a bar on Tverskaya. He threw himself at him with animal ferocity. He was landing punches on the man's face and neck, kicking him, yelling obscenities.

Blumkin was taken by surprise. When he roused himself, he was more than a match. He held Sergei at arm's length.

'What the hell is this about?'

'You know what it's about!'

Sergei had laid the charge and Blumkin nodded his acceptance.

'I'm sorry,' he said. 'I wasn't going to do anything. She stopped me, anyway.'

'Goddam lucky for you that she did!'

They sat in silence.

'All right,' Sergei said. 'It may seem a trifle to you. But it comes on top of everything else. It's all got too much for her . . . and for me . . .'

When he told Zinaida what had happened, she cried.

'It's not just Blumkin,' she said. 'It's the children, the violence, the times we live in . . .'

He comforted her; she was shaking.

'I'm under pressure to go back to work,' Zinaida said. 'I've had extra maternity leave because Kostya's been ill, but it's run out now. If I don't go back, they won't keep the job for me. Have you seen the new slogan they've come up with? "*He who does not work shall not eat!*" We thought it was aimed at the aristos – they don't give them jobs anyway, so they starve to death – but it's aimed at us, too!'

Sergei took her hand.

'Don't worry, Zina. I won't let you starve. Everything will be all right. You'll see.'

'Blumkin molesting me just made me realise how defenceless we are,' she said. 'We live in a country where things happen and people can do what they like to us. We don't have the right to defend ourselves. It's like a dog sitting waiting for someone to kick you or stroke you. It robs you of certainty; it torments your mind.'

In the morning, Zinaida was calmer. She spoke more encouragingly about the prospect of going back to work. There was an opening in the Commissariat's Theatre Directorate.

'I've always loved the theatre,' she said. 'I don't want to spend my life working on propaganda. I want to be an actress.'

'I know,' Sergei said. 'And you've got a boss who will do what he can to help you. Lunacharsky's on your side – look how he helped get me and the Kusikov brothers released.'

'He who does not work shall not eat!'

Kusikov brought his brother to the Pegasus Stable. Rueben was celebrating his release then planning to leave town. The weeks in the Lubyanka, the shadow of the death penalty had taken their toll. Moscow was a jungle, filled with threats and lurking danger.

Marienhof opened champagne. Shershenevich arrived. The four of them began the toasts. Midnight struck and Sergei had still not appeared.

'Looks like Seryozha's decided he loves his wife more than us,' Kusikov said with a laugh.

'He's besotted,' said Marienhof. 'He picked a fight with Blumkin to defend her, even though I told him it would put every one of us in danger. We need to do something before he loses all sense of proportion.'

Sergei appeared the following day with a sheaf of poems, eager to show Marienhof what he had written. Marienhof had laughed at the opening stanzas of his planned epic in praise of the Revolution. The poet's desire to be a good citizen of the Soviet state had rung hollow. The continuation of the poem suggested why.

> I'm not a canary! I'm a poet!
> Not one of your tame and sorry hacks!
> Sure, I'm drunk; and at times I blow it,
> But my mind's wild genius seldom lacks.
> I see through it all; I understand!
> You reckon your New Era's pretty grand,
> That the name of Lenin, like the wind,
> Must whistle thunder through the land.
> OK then, I'm with you! Yesenin, make an effort!

Start reading Marx – read, digest, take note!
Start guessing at the depth and wisdom
Of all that boring stuff he wrote!
For so long I hated Moscow,
Where, drunk and bridling, they'd hold me in a cell.
I can't deal with a policeman's greeting
When vodka dumps me in my hell.
A prisoner on a prison bench
Yelling poems in my drunken voice
Of sad canaries in a cage
Is not my scenario of choice.

The rest of the poem dealt with canonical subjects of socialist realism, industrial power and the electrification of the country. But it was shot through with mockery – who would believe the poet's contention that he would rather sing of streetlights than the stars?

He showed Marienhof other poems that were more direct in their criticism. 'The Stern October has Deceived Me' was a barely coded lament for Yesenin's disappointment with the October Revolution. Another, unfinished draft seethed with Hieronymus Bosch-like images of the revolution's cruelty.

If the wolf bays at a star,
Cloud has eaten the sky.
The ripped open bowels of mares
And crows' black sails slide by.
The azure thrusts no rays
Through the snows' red coughing stench.
A garden of skulls, goldly glowing,
Circles beneath the whinnying storm.
You heard the cheerful knocking?
Sunset rakes the groves.

With chopped-off arms for oars
They are rowing us to the Promised Land.
My Russia, can this be you? Whose bucket
Plumbs the scum of your snows?
Along the roads, voracious hounds
Of a dead dawn devour the land.
Who's then to sing? O who,
In this mad radiance of corpses?
I sang the Wondrous Guest, it's clear now,
Only in self-derision.
Evil October strews from the brown
Birch-hands its rings.
You beasts, come near, weep out
Your grief in my cupped hands.

He had tried to love the revolution; this was the result. Marienhof advised him against publishing any of what he had written.

'I'll publish the one that describes my efforts to understand Karl Marx,' Sergei said. 'It's called "Stanzas". At least it'll convince them I'm trying!'

CHAPTER 21

After the trauma of Sergei's arrest, the brawl with Mayakovsky and Blumkin's assault on Zinaida, there was a lull.

Sergei took Marienhof's advice not to publish those poems that were openly critical of the revolution, but went ahead and published 'Stanzas', with its slighting references to 'boring' Karl Marx and its mockery of socialist realism.

Zinaida returned to work. She got the job she wanted in the Ministry's Theatre and Drama Division, headed by the famous director, Vsevolod Meyerhold. It brought her into contact with Moscow's actors and directors. It was satisfying. It revived her ambitions to make a career in acting.

The children were well cared for in the People's Crèche, although Zinaida continued to worry about Konstantin's health. He was cheerful but weak, and he had recurring bouts of jaundice.

Sergei seemed to be balancing his life at the Pegasus with his commitments at home. He and Zinaida were close.

It wasn't easy for them to go out together. Sergei had recitals. Zinaida had the children. But Trofim Lysenko was coming to give a lecture, so they asked the neighbours if they would look after Tanya and Kostya.

Lysenko was a biologist who had been making headlines in the Soviet press. He was a remarkable man with a remarkable gift. People were flocking to hear his plans to save Russia from starvation.

The famine that began in 1921 had continued well into the following year. Six million people had died, although the Bolsheviks kept the figure secret. Russia could no longer feed herself. If nothing was done, hunger would return more terrible and more deadly.

Lysenko shuffled on to the stage. He wore peasant clothes; an autodidact, 'the barefoot scientist'. It was clear why the authorities loved him. A modesty of manner amplified his charisma. Piercing blue eyes radiated a burning sense of mission.

He explained that bourgeois Western theories of crop genetics were to blame for Russia's problems. Darwin had instilled the belief that species compete for dominance, that was because competition was the essence of capitalism. Socialism believed in cooperation. He, Lysenko, had discovered that nature was governed by mutual *assistance*, not only within species, but between species as well.

It was a momentous breakthrough. It had enabled him to grow crops in places where they had never grown before, to fertilise fields without using fertilisers. In the future, it would turn Russia's barren lands green, save cattle from starvation and furnish the nation with boundless supplies of grain and vegetables.

Sergei and Zinaida listened intently. Lysenko had another ground-breaking discovery to announce. He had succeeded in making summer-wheat seedlings grow in winter. He had reprogrammed their genetic make-up by treating them over a prolonged period with moisture and carefully controlled temperatures. The audience gasped. But Lysenko was not finished.

'Bourgeois science maintains that qualities acquired by one generation cannot be passed on to the next,' he said. 'They say this because capitalism cannot countenance the possibility that mankind can change and be changed. Socialism believes that all men are open to change; that generations can be moulded for the better, just as plants can be reprogrammed for the better. And that these genetic improvements – in man and in nature – can be cascaded down generations for the benefit of the world. It is a discovery that confirms the whole basis of the glorious mission we Soviets have embarked upon – the moulding and improvement of humankind until we reach the Nirvana we all believe in; the Nirvana of communism!'

Such was the enthusiasm generated by his discoveries that Lysenko's closing words were barely audible under the applause that shook the auditorium.

Trofim Lysenko

Marienhof was in a foul mood. When Kusikov asked the reason, Marienhof said, 'Sergei! He's so naïve!'

Kusikov raised a questioning eyebrow.

'He was here this morning,' Marienhof said, 'telling me all about a lecture by that Lysenko fellow.'

'Ah,' Kusikov said. 'You mean he believed the guff about re-educating plants into being good socialist saplings ...'

'Not just that,' Marienhof said. 'He was going on about how lovely it was to go out with that wife of his. He's too blind to understand that she's the reason he's lost his inspiration, that he's neglecting his friends. We need to get him away from Zinaida. I think I know how to do it.'

The critical response to his 'Stanzas' poem, with its references to Marx and half-hearted attempts to tackle socialist themes, was not slow in coming. Those who envied Yesenin's popularity were quick to pour scorn. But there was a feeling, too, that Sergei had asked for it. His conscience, his pride – his self-destructive cussedness – had led him to write lines that he knew would court denunciation.

'Yesenin's poem, "Stanzas", is a patently false pretence at revolutionary fervour,' wrote the Marxist critic, Alexander Voronsky.

> He says he wants to be a worthy citizen of the mighty Soviet state. He says he wants to read and learn from Marx. But it is obvious that he has never done so! He is profoundly indifferent. He writes, sneeringly, 'you reckon your New Era's pretty grand', meaning that it is not *his* Era. It's as if he is saying, 'You want some revolutionary verse? Sure, I can write about Marx and Lenin. I've written rubbish? Well, who cares? Just get on and publish it!'

For the influential journal *Red Virgin Soil*, Yesenin was the ringleader of a deplorable tendency in Russian literature.

> There are a lot of poems like this being written. And they represent a real danger. On the face of it, they seem

fine – they address proper socialist themes, such as industrialisation and so forth. But the writer deliberately makes
it clear that he's just going through the motions. He doesn't
have the slightest interest or belief in the things he is writing
about. It is a mockery!

Such criticism of a nationally renowned poet could not have
been printed without the approval of the authorities. It was a
warning to Yesenin from the very top. The onus was on him
to make amends.

Sergei made light. Marienhof was tempted to say that he had
warned him not to publish, but held his tongue. Instead, he
offered advice.

'First of all, don't make things worse. Don't get into a con-
frontation with the regime. You can't win. Don't think you can
take them on, because you can't.'

He looked at Sergei.

'Second, concentrate on your poetry. Don't get distracted by
trivia. Your gift is more important than some bourgeois wife
and family. You should be a poet of all countries and all nations.
You need to be read all over the globe, not just here.'

Sergei was listening.

'Seryozha,' Marienhof said, 'I can introduce you to someone
who will bring your poetry to the attention of the world.'

Contrariness defined Sergei.

In the barroom brawls that were a feature of his life, he
never backed off. A bigger, stronger opponent might beat

him mercilessly – his friends would be yelling, 'Leave it, Seryozha!' – but he would keep on punching until he was bloodied and broken.

It spoke of the belief imbibed in childhood that he was unworthy; of the need to prove himself at every turn.

He felt the criticism of his 'Stanzas' poem belittled him. Without telling Marienhof, he wrote and sent for publication a new poem, 'The First of May', in which the poet-narrator celebrates the workers' holiday with toasts to the proletariat, to the Soviet government, to the peasants and, finally, 'to myself'.

> For the holiday there's music, poetry and dances.
> Then there's lying and deceit.
> Let them curse me for my 'Stanzas',
> But all the same, what I said was right!

Lola Kinel was a young woman of Polish-Russian extraction. She spoke several languages, including English, and had been a friend of Arthur Ransome, the British journalist and future author of *Swallows and Amazons*, during his five-year posting as a correspondent in Russia.

Lola had introduced Ransome to Yevgenia Shelepina, the personal secretary of Leon Trotsky, and the two had fallen in love. Ransome conducted an affair with Shelepina and would later marry her. The British were grateful to him for the intelligence he was able to glean about the Bolsheviks – MI6 gave him the codename S[py].76 – and the Bolsheviks were equally grateful for the intelligence he passed the other way.

Lola was looking for work and Marienhof had the perfect role for her. He introduced her to Sergei.

Kusikov laughed when Marienhof told him what he had done.

'You mean, translating his poems into English was just a pretext—'

'Of course! Have you ever known Seryozha refuse anything that might further his reputation?'

'... and you think this Lola will really turn his head?'

'I could see him looking at her with that animal desire in his eyes. I'm willing to bet a month's royalties they'll hit it off.'

They spoke about poetry. Lola had read all his poems. She knew many by heart.

They spoke about translation. She was dubious.

'Your work depends on Russian rhymes, Russian rhythms and Russian assonance,' she said. 'The puns, the playing with words; it sounds so brilliant in Russian. A lot of that will be lost if I put it into English.'

'No! Let's do it!' Sergei said. 'This is important for me. And I can help you with the translations. I'll hold your hand ...'

Zinaida had thought about Lysenko's ideas, now so popular that newspapers referred to them, approvingly, as 'the science of Lysenkoism'.

'I just don't see how things we learn during our lifetime can alter our genes,' she said. 'This "inheritability of acquired characteristics" is like cutting off a cat's tail and expecting it to give birth to tailless kittens. It's useful for the Bolsheviks, because they claim to be constructing a new human being – the noble Homo Sovieticus we keep hearing about – but it's not true. I've inherited my father's genes – steady, Germanic and robust. It's the only thing that has kept me sane this past year.'

Her mental state had improved since the near-breakdown she had suffered. She was calmer now, enjoying her work.

'The theatre is such a magical place,' she told Sergei. 'Partly because it's all about make-believe – an escape from the real world we have to live in – but also because of the people. I've met so many fascinating actors and actresses – Olga Knipper, Chekhov's widow; Maria Babanova; Mikhail Zharkov; Igor Ilyinsky. Today I was introduced to Meyerhold himself – what an amazing director!'

Sergei smiled, but his thoughts were elsewhere.

Lola pored over Sergei's tender lyrics, trying to fit his sumptuous Russian into English. She produced literal translations that captured all the words (although not the poem's meaning, such were the unlikely concatenations of clashing nouns and verbs, often based on sound and suggestion rather than semantic substance). She dabbled in more impressionistic versions that sounded pleasing, but could never be sure if her English conjectures corresponded with the poet's intentions. She tried with rhymes and without rhymes, then free verse.

Yesenin himself spoke only Russian and was no help in choosing between versions. She tried to tell him how frustrating the task of translation was.

'Just take your poem about the bitch and her drowned puppies. When you describe her lying in the hayshed, you write, *Utrom v rzhanom zakutie* ... which literally means, *Of a morning, in a rye shelter.* I know you chose the word *zakuta*, rather than *konura*, because it fits the Russian cadence, and because you can use the assonance it has with the word *suka*, a bitch. In English, it makes no sense. I could choose a quite different set of English words that would make a beautiful line and even fit your cadence. But it would be very different, because the law of phonetic beauty varies between languages. I would end up changing each or nearly each word, and the result would be that I had changed the entire poem.'

'But, Lola, can't you just write down what I have written? I draw beautiful pictures, don't I? I have ideas. I describe feelings. They are worth something, aren't they?'

'Yes, they are,' Lola said. 'They are worth a great deal ... to me, and millions of others.'

Sergei looked forward to his sessions with Lola. Her feeling for his artistic vision was studiously sensitive. She valued what he wrote and was determined to do the best for it.

He was demanding. A poem was his child that was to be sent out alone into a hostile world. He feared for its welfare and could be overly protective.

After one fraught session, Lola asked why it was so important to have his poems translated into English. He looked surprised that she should ask.

'Don't you see?' he said. 'How many people will read me in Russia? Twenty million, perhaps thirty – all our peasants are illiterate. But in English ... !'

He spread his arms and his eyes shone.

His 'First of May' poem, with its defiant reaffirmation of the doubts he had been criticised for in 'Stanzas', attracted little attention.

Being ignored was worse than being attacked. He remembered Stavrogin's confession in 'The Devils': 'Because thou art neither hot nor cold,' said the Ruler of creation, 'so shall I spue thee from my mouth.'

'The Dove of Jordan' was one more punch by the runner-up in the barroom brawl.

> The sky's a bell,
> The moon a tongue-lick.
> My mother's my country;
> I'm a Bolshevik!
> Brothers of all races,
> My song is sung for you.
> Wrapped in the mist of history,
> I proclaim the joyful news.
> Ah, brothers, brothers; people!
> Will we not all someday
> Rise to that blessed region
> Where shines the Milky Way?
> Down here, love's chaperone's a sinner,
> All our days begot by sorrow,
> And love's discontented winner
> Shall be a beggar tomorrow.

This time the reaction was prompt and unforgiving.

'Yesenin has finally and completely committed himself

to the camp of the reactionaries,' fulminated the journal *Proletarian Culture.* 'Now he says it straight out: the "world beyond the stars" touted by the church's conmen-clerics is better than the world we are building here and now. Comrades, this is impermissible!'

Pavel Bessalko, a friend of Lunacharsky's, writing in *The Future,* was outraged:

> Yesenin says he's a Bolshevik, but goddammit! his poetry saps our will to fight. What's the point of building socialism if things are better in some imaginary heaven than here on earth? Yesenin and poets like him must be brought to book!

'The critics are like sheep,' Sergei told Zinaida. 'They wait for a lead from the top. Now it's open season on Yesenin.'

'But why do you do it, Seryozha? Why do you insist on provoking them?' She was annoyed. 'Wasn't it enough when they attacked you for the other two poems?'

'I don't know,' he said. 'I hate the critics. I get upset when someone says bad things about my work.'

'So much more reason not to give them the chance—'

'You don't understand,' he said. 'I hate the critics because they have never created anything, yet they presume to judge someone who has sacrificed his life to it. How can they even begin—'

'Yes,' Zinaida said, 'but don't you—'

'I provoke them because I hate them. I hate them because I define myself through what I create. A slight on my poetry cuts me. I can't let them get away with that!'

Lola was more understanding. She told Sergei that he was right to fight back. The people attacking him were pygmies.

She asked if *she* might recite something. It was Pushkin's 'Exegi monumentum'.

> A monument of mine did I erect with pride,
> Not wrought by work of hands; the pathway
>   to its site,
> Trodden by the people, weeds will never hide,
> And Alexander's column will pale before its height.
> Death shall not wipe me out; within my lyre's shrine
> Decay and rot my spirit shall survive,
> And underneath the moon this fame of mine
> Shall endure, so long as one lone poet stays alive.
> The Lord's command obey, my sweet, my
>   dearest Muse!
> For you need fear no hurt, you need
>   demand no crown.
> Accept both praise and slander, smile at their abuse,
> Dismiss the fool and do not quarrel with the clown.

'He's smitten with his translator,' Kusikov told Marienhof. 'He told me, and you can see it in his eyes.'

'Then why doesn't he do something about it?' Marienhof said. 'In the old days, he was happy to jump into bed with any girl that crossed his path.'

'He's been resisting,' Kusikov said. 'It's because he loves

Zinaida. And the children. He got quite emotional talking about them. At the end he said, "I almost suspected Marienhof threw me and Lola together deliberately, as a sort of test. But of course, that's ridiculous . . ."'

Lola produced a first draft of translations. Sergei, unable to assess what she had written, asked her for her honest assessment.

'I think they are good,' she said. 'They aren't your originals, of course – they're in a different language, with different rhymes, different rhythms, different assonances. All the same, I think they do you justice. It hasn't been an easy task. I managed it only because I know you. Because I feel so close to what you have written . . . and so close to you.'

Sergei, in a voice that was little more than a murmur, began to speak about his childhood. He spoke of the days when he was a barelegged peasant boy, running through the long grass of the meadow to the river, of the horses that drank the moon and the puppies that were drowned. He spoke of the day he wrote his first poem, at the age of nine; of the many poems he had written since; of how, at seventeen, he chose but a few and burned the rest; of how his family wanted him to become a priest, and how he had been flogged because he ran away from school; of his grandfather and the beatings he had administered; of beautiful faces and the most beautiful face he had ever seen, that of a young nun in a Russian convent, a face that was absolutely guileless and pure; of his rise to fame and his life in Petrograd; of his running away from the army; of women and of words, words that were alive and others that were dead; of the language of the peasants, pilgrims and thieves, which was always alive . . .

He fell silent. His hand lay on the table. Lola reached out and pressed it.

A regime which claimed control of culture, which demanded that the arts unite behind its socialist message, could not afford to tolerate dissent. Even one divergent voice could be fatal; others would see that independence was permitted and the monolith would crumble. Yesenin had to be dealt with.

The journal *Communist Revolution* was the first to take aim.

Comrades, is it not strange as we look around us in the country we have built, and indeed at the global state of the proletarian Revolution, that we may discover what can only be termed a wave of defeatist emotions?

How is it possible that such depressive feelings exist not among the vanquished enemies of our Revolution, but among its supporters, among the youth of our nation? Hooliganism and anti-social behaviour are increasing among our socialist youth. How can this be?

When we examine the other side of the coin – defeatism – by far the most frequent reason given by young people for wishing to leave the Komsomol is that they 'have become disillusioned' or that they are 'dissatisfied'.

Where does this stem from? Where are the societal roots of this dual phenomenon of hooliganism and defeatism?

The word Yeseninism is a new one in our socialist vocabulary, but it encapsulates some of the influences being exerted on the youth of our country. Yesenin is the voice of the hooligan. Yesenin is the voice of the alienated, the depressive and the defeatist.

We may identify all these stages in his poetry.

The first, his so-called rural or peasant poems, reek of incense. They are full of church bells and holy claptrap, which he expounds with reverence and awe. This is no example to set for our society.

His second period is an unconvincing pretence of revolutionary commitment, which simply cannot be taken seriously. His so-called revolutionary feelings were swept away as the poet failed miserably to comprehend the essence of the Revolution.

He lapsed into cynicism, depravity and self-loathing, a fetid wave of alcohol and debauchery. This was his so-called period of Moscow taverns. He set out to prove that he could out-drink, out-swindle, out-hooliganise the whole world. The face of his Muse was smeared with excrement.

Now his head spins. He is a drunkard and a pessimist, an individualist who does not feel part of the collective, a superfluous man in a society that needs no superfluous people.

Millions of our young people read Yesenin's poetry; too many of them take their example from him. We need a campaign of cultural re-education to combat Yeseninism. We must do everything in our power to ensure that this debilitating phenomenon does not weaken our socialist resolve!

'Yeseninism: decadent feelings among our youth'

Sergei had picked up the journal from the newsstand on his way to meet Lola. Waiting for her in the café on Tverskaya, he leafed through the article and turned pale. When she arrived, he was close to tears. He told her what had happened. She put her arm around him.

'Come home with me, Seryozha. Come now and let me look after you.'

CHAPTER 22

Zinaida knocked on the door. Normally, she would never have come. She disliked and mistrusted Marienhof.

He was, as always, polite. Excessively so.

'Ah, Zinaida Nikolaevna! To what do I owe this unexpected pleasure?'

He showed her in, offered her tea. She had not been to Marienhof's apartment since she and Sergei came for dinner when they first arrived from Oryol. He could see she was looking around.

'If I may ask, what is it that you are seeking?' he said.

'I . . . Have you seen Seryozha?'

He had been missing for four days.

Marienhof had read the attack on Yesenin in the press. He was surprised that Sergei had not come seeking advice. Zinaida's visit had explained why.

Marienhof was preparing to call on Lola Kinel when Sergei himself appeared. He looked as if he had not slept.

'You look dreadful,' Marienhof said.

Yesenin went to the cupboard and poured himself some vodka.

'I don't know what's been happening,' he said. 'I don't know what to do. I don't—'

Marienhof calmed him.

'Sit down,' he said. 'We can fix this.'

The vodka knocked him out. He fell asleep in the armchair. Marienhof heard him prowling round the apartment during the night.

In the morning, he was ready to talk. He had been dismayed by the attack on him. He had felt helpless. Lola had offered him comfort and he took it.

Marienhof understood. Lola had provided the validation Sergei was seeking – 'She loves me, so I must be worth something . . .' He asked him if he had been happy in the short time he had spent with her and Sergei nodded.

'You trust me, don't you, Seryozha?' Marienhof said. 'Let me sort this out.'

He did not mention that Zinaida had come looking for him.

Literary denunciations rarely came single spies; the regime marshalled battalions.

The word was that the leadership were preparing an official pronouncement on Yeseninism.

When things reached such a pitch, they almost always ended badly.

Marienhof called on Zinaida at work. He began to explain what had happened, but she motioned him outside.

In the corridor, he said that Sergei wished to apologise for not coming himself. He, Marienhof, was charged with bringing her some unfortunate news. Sergei had met someone and would not be returning home.

Zinaida said, 'What?'

Marienhof repeated the message.

'That's nonsense,' she said. 'He wouldn't do that. Who is this person you say he's met?'

'I am not liberty to say.'

'Where is Seryozha now?'

'I am not at liberty . . .'

It felt like a slap.

'I don't believe you,' she said. 'Tell me what Seryozha said to you!'

Marienhof bowed. He had been expecting the question.

'I can tell you exactly what he said. He put his arm around my shoulder. He fixed his blue eyes on mine and said, "*Do you love me, Anatoly? Are you a true friend of mine? The fact is, I cannot live with Zinaida. I have tried to tell her, but she doesn't understand. She just says, 'You love me, Sergei. I know it, so don't tell me you don't.' Anatoly, you go and tell her! – I can't beg any harder – you tell her!*" I objected, of course, but Sergei was insistent. "*Are you my friend or not?*" he said. "*Zinaida's love is a noose for me . . . Tolya, sweet Tolya! Go and tell her! She will quiz you, for sure – just tell her that I am at the other woman's, that I've been seeing her since spring and that I'm crazy about her. Let me kiss you!*" and he did.'

It was a speech Marienhof had rehearsed. He would remember it and include it word-for-word, many years later, when he came to write his memoirs.

When he got home, he took Sergei aside.

'A word of advice, Seryozha. Best to keep a low profile for the moment. Stay at Lola's. Don't tell anyone where you are.'

It was the Culture Commissar, Lunacharsky, who marshalled the battalions. He gave the opening speech at a remarkable meeting of politicians and writers, called to heap derision on the poet whose verse was undermining socialist optimism.

> Yeseninism is the single most influential factor in the attempts we have been witnessing to create an ideology of defeatism and despair in this country. Comrades, it must be resisted with all our strength!

Nikolai Bukharin, the man whom Lenin referred to as 'the darling of the party' and hoped would succeed him as leader, went further.

> Is Yesenin talented? Yes, he is. There is no disputing that. But other writers can be said to be talented, and all of them enemies of the people.
> Yes, Yesenin's poetry flows like a stream of purest silver. But the content of his verse is a disgusting mass of foulness, brazenly painted over with rouge and face powder, copiously smeared by drunken tears and all the more vile and repulsive for it.

On behalf of Soviet poets, Vladimir Mayakovsky took the floor with a withering assessment of Yesenin's work.

> Does Yesenin know how to write poetry? No. It's absolute trash. Drivel. Nowadays everyone thinks they can write

poems. But who among them has the talent to make poetry a weapon of the working class, a weapon of the revolution! We have heard our political leaders speak out against Yesenin and Yeseninism, but let me ask you this: why then do our journals continue to print his work? Why are his poems still being published, sometimes in millions of copies? Is no one aware that a large percentage of even our most proletarian poets are subject to his malign influence, in danger of being corrupted by his malevolent shadow? Why is Yesenin still being published?

Sergei had walked out on the woman he loved and done so of his own free will. He had fallen out of love with the revolution and the revolution had fallen out with him. He was desperate for consolation. He found it in his friendship with Marienhof.

Sergei was not unaware. Marienhof was a complicated man with selfish interests and desires. Sergei knew he had taken against Zinaida and that he was jealous of her.

But for all that, Marienhof was his friend. At heart, he was a good person. He cared for Sergei, looked out for him, perhaps even loved him.

Zinaida searched for him, but he didn't want to be found.

Marienhof had assumed the role of protecting angel. From the journalists desperate to interview the poet at the centre of such political controversy. From the officials who wanted to talk to him about what he might do to rehabilitate himself. From the outraged admirers who wanted to offer him their support. And, most immediately, from the woman who wanted him back.

Zinaida went to Marienhof's flat on Bogoslovsky, to Kusikov's on Afanasievsky, to the Pegasus Stable on Tverskaya. Sergei was at none of them. She stood outside waiting to see if he would appear, but he didn't. No one was able, or willing, to say where he might be.

She secured a promise from Marienhof that he would pass on her letters. She had no way of knowing if he would keep his word, but she wrote anyway, pleading messages urging her lover to return.

> My dear love,
>
> Do you remember the first night we ever spent together? Do you remember what you asked me that night as we lay in each other's arms? You asked me if we would love each other and cherish each other forever, and I said we would. I said we would care for each other 'til the end of our days.
>
> I have always done that, ever since that moment, and I want us to do it now.
>
> I was sincere when I said those things and I think you were, too. Even now, after everything that has happened, I do not doubt that you love me. And I know that I love you.
>
> I am sorry this has been such a bruising time for you, Seryozha. I am sorry to have been in part the cause of your pain. I hope you have at least reached the state of calm that you'd hoped for.

Then, in a scribbled appendix.

> Please, my love – please come back to me.
>
> The fact is that I am completely heartbroken. I don't know how I am getting from one day to the next . . .

The Bolsheviks understood the importance of the moving image. Cinema for the masses was as young as the Soviet state. A vigorous symbiosis had developed between them.

Directors such as Sergei Eisenstein, Vsevolod Pudovkin and Alexander Dovzhenko put their art at the service of socialism, deploying innovative techniques to create powerful, politically charged films.

Even more potent were the silent newsreels that invited viewers into the public and private lives of the Soviet leadership. For the first time, the Russian people were shown politicians at work on their behalf. It both humanised them and made them superhuman – in the case of Lenin, almost saintly.

Footage of Lenin was everywhere. Audiences saw him haranguing crowds, addressing congresses, chatting self-consciously in the Kremlin, stroking his pet cat, signing letters at his desk.

Marienhof kept his word. He passed on Zinaida's letters. Sergei read them at the breakfast table, concealing their contents from Lola.

He was haunted by guilt and foreboding. Lola tried to reassure him. The politicians were attacking him because they feared him, she said; because he was an important poet. It was he who had the power – history would judge.

When Zinaida discovered whom Sergei was living with, she gave in to rage.

'Who is this nobody?' she wrote to him. 'This absurd little woman whose only aspiration is to bed a famous writer? This unknown interpreter so gratified by the condescending attention of such a great man?'

She could not bring herself to call Lola by her name. In her letters, she referred to her as *your Grateful Little Translator.*

In early 1922, Lenin vanished from the cinemas. The founder of the USSR had suffered a stroke, the belated legacy of Fanny Kaplan's bullets fired at him in 1918 and never removed from his body. For the two years of life left to him, Lenin would be paralysed and barely able to speak, only one hemisphere of his brain still alive.

At his dacha outside Moscow, he struggled to express his instructions for the country's future. In a document that became known as 'Lenin's Testament', he ran the rule over his possible successors. There were warm words for the young Nikolai Bukharin, but doubts about Trotsky who, although 'distinguished by outstanding ability', had 'displayed excessive self-assurance'. Lenin's strongest reservations were about Josef Stalin.

Comrade Stalin has too much power in his hands and I am not sure that he knows how to use it with sufficient caution. I propose that we remove Stalin from the post of General

Secretary and give it to someone more patient, more loyal, more polite and more attentive to his comrades.

Lenin's warning was never presented to the Party. The man it warned against ensured it was buried. In the imminent expectation of Lenin's death, 1922 and 1923 would be years of jockeying for position.

Marienhof visited the House of Writers to ask if they would intervene on Sergei's behalf. The officials he spoke to offered no help.

'It's political now,' they said, 'beyond our control. Part of the problem is that Yesenin has been too close to Trotsky and Blumkin. The big boys are jostling for position and Trotsky isn't winning. So for them, attacking Yesenin is like attacking Trotsky.'

Sergei was living from day to day, waiting for the next blow to fall. Marienhof's friendship and Lola's devotion were a comfort, but he was drinking heavily again.

When Zinaida asked if they could meet, he was surprised by the shudder of happiness he felt.

He suggested Perlov's and Zinaida replied immediately.

'My heart is like a singing bird!' she wrote. 'How shall I live till I see you?'

Kusikov was drunk and the drink made him talk.

In language Sergei had never heard him use, Kusikov cursed the country that had locked him up, threatened him, executed fellow poets and nearly sent his brother to a firing squad.

'I've had enough of this bastard place,' he said. 'How can anyone live in a society that so demeans and despises its people, that rules by terror and cruelty, where ordinary folk are proclaimed as heroes but have no rights, where the individual is nothing and the state a monster? I am going, boys! I am going and don't try to stop me!'

Kusikov pulled a document from his pocket. It was an exit visa. It gave him permission to travel abroad for a period of one month on official cultural business. He had had to beg and promise, but Lunacharsky had endorsed his application and papers had been issued for him and several other writers, including Boris Pilnyak.

Kusikov made no secret of the fact that he would not be coming back. But, at the same time, the sorrow of emigration, the sacrifice of a life that will never return, the ache of regret that Russians call *toska*, hung over him.

Alexander Kusikov

He saw her at the table in Perlov's Tea Rooms where they had met all that time ago and was engulfed by her beauty as if seeing her for the first time.

'Oh, Zina!' he said. 'How lovely ... How – splendid ...'

Zinaida smiled, torn between anger and tenderness, between joy at seeing him and perplexity at his behaviour. She resented Lola.

'You are wasting yourself, Seryozha,' she said. 'And people say she is stupid, too.'

She wanted to know more about the woman who had taken her place, but feared to ask. Sergei didn't object when she said Lola was a nobody; but neither did he say he was leaving her.

Zinaida wanted to say he should come back, but was waiting for Sergei to say it. She heard him say how beautiful she was; they spoke of how happy they had been; she could see the love in his eyes. So why didn't he say it?

In the end, she couldn't stop herself. 'Seryozha,' she said. 'Are you coming back to me?'

He hesitated. In that moment she knew she had been fooling herself.

'We can be friends,' he said. 'We can see each other. We can love each other—'

'But you're not coming back to live with me?'

He was silent.

'Then go to hell!' she said, rising to her feet. 'Go to hell, Sergei!'

She lifted the table, tipping the cups on to the floor as she walked out.

Later she wrote to him.

> Should I apologise for smashing the plates? An overreaction on my part? You said you love me. You said how beautiful I am. It's good to hear you say these things. But I am finding it unbearable, and inconsistent with the feelings we are each expressing, that your life carries on as before. How can we live like this? When you are away from me, I will always imagine you are doing something lovely – listening to music, drinking champagne, going out – with *your Grateful Little Translator*. You live with her; you wake up together; it's a perfect Sunday morning to do something à deux. It is there that my imagination takes me. That is how I picture you together – because that's how things would be if you and I were together.
>
> I can't bear to be on the outside of your life, love. I don't want to be your friend or your occasional lover. I love you too much to share you. I don't want to be destroyed by this. I have had no sign from you that anything has changed. It breaks my heart.

Kusikov's departure was on hold. He had to wait for the Commissariat to assemble the delegation on which he would be travelling. He spent his days at the Pegasus, drinking, talking, storing up memories. He told Marienhof he would stay in touch once he was 'on the other side', but both suspected it would be impossible.

'What about Seryozha?' Kusikov said. 'Has he not thought of leaving? He's got more problems with the Bolsheviks than any of us.'

'I'm not sure Seryozha is capable of any logical thought right now,' Marienhof said. 'He seems bent on making his life as complicated as possible.'

'Certainly his emotional life,' Kusikov agreed. 'Why does he persist in driving away the woman he loves? Is he some sort of Onegin, determined to hurt those who care for him?'

'It's not that,' Marienhof said. 'Sergei isn't naïve. And I don't think he is cynical. He fears being abandoned. He has told me more than once how hurt he was by his mother leaving him. He shrinks from being hurt again. When a relationship becomes meaningful, he leaves before he can be left. It's nonsensical and I'm sure he has never thought of it like that, but that's what's at the root of it . . .'

Zinaida wrote again.

My dearest Seryozha,
    I went to Meyerhold's theatre today. He is proposing
to use some Bach arias as incidental music in a new
play and the Ministry is worried it might amount to
religious propaganda. The singing moved me profoundly,
in particular one aria titled, *Bist du bei mir.* These are
the words:

If thou art near, I'll go with joy
To death's eternal rest.
O how happy would my ending be,
If only thy fair hands
Might close my faithful eyes.

Are you not moved by that blurring of human love with the redemptive love of the Creator? It is more than just cleverness on the part of the poet. It's an assertion that love between a man and a woman is an echo of the love divine that allows us to transcend this material world. It's an affirmation of the only two things – physical love and spiritual love – that can make our life a full one.

But now I shall not have your fair hands to close my faithful eyes.

What shall I do, Seryozha? What shall I become?

CHAPTER 23

Djugashvili was a thug, but useful – it was he who planned and executed the bank robberies that funded the early days of the Party. The others looked down on him. Or at least, he felt they looked down on him. Lenin, Trotsky, Kamenev, Bukharin, Lunacharsky; they were all intellectuals, educated; either Jewish or petty aristocracy. Djugashvili was sure they mocked him behind his back; sneered at his seminary education and his artistic pretensions, at the poetry he had written and continued, secretly, to write.

He adopted the *nom de guerre* of Koba to disguise his Georgian origins. When it came to a Party name, he called himself 'Man of Steel'. The assonance of Stalin and Lenin planted the seed, the merest hint, of a line of succession.

Zinaida received no reply to either of her letters. She decided she would not write again.

A week later, she wrote again.

I am sorry I was distraught at our meeting. I was
distraught at the thought of our apartness. Do you still love
me? Do you want to see me? I can't bear not to see you,

to touch you and reconnect; to leave behind sorrow and tribulation.

Don't renounce our happiness, Seryozha! Don't give up this woman who loves you. Come to the flat. The children are with my parents. We can talk properly.

The Party gave the important ministries to its stars. Stalin was not one of them. He got the irksome jobs – integrating the recalcitrant national territories into the new empire; compiling personnel files, tabulating the qualifications, skills, foibles and transgressions of the Party's cadres. It was thankless work, but Stalin did it willingly. He was gathering the knowledge of the buried skeletons and tender underbellies that would serve him well.

Sergei wrote to say that he would be coming. Zinaida replied at once.

The passion of love bursting into flame is more powerful than death, stronger than the grave. Love cannot be drowned by oceans or floods. Hurry to me, my darling; run faster than a deer to the mountain of spices!

They met at the flat they had lived in. The familiarity drew him back. To the days of happiness, of love that had conferred meaning on his life.

It was easier to talk than it had been in the restaurant.

Conversation oscillated between the sweetness of rekindled tenderness and the bitter threads of reproach and incomprehension. She told him how much she missed him, how much the children missed him. She opened a bottle of Georgian wine. The more they spoke, the more Zinaida struggled to grasp with her reason something that was beyond reason's grasp.

'But *why*,' she said. 'Why do you not do what your heart is telling you?'

Sergei couldn't explain things that he himself did not understand. Reason gave way to desire. The muscle memory of hands held and knees brushed led them to bed. To the shared sip of joy that consumes us in the moment then fades from our senses, effaces itself from our comprehension until next we experience it. Sergei had missed the joy. Missed Zinaida. He loved her and wanted her.

In the morning, he left. With a mumbled explanation that made no sense.

He wasn't being published. The Union of Writers assured him it was a temporary hiatus; he remained their most demanded poet; when the politics had calmed down, his work would appear again.

In the meantime, he wrote for the drawer. Bleak, self-accusatory lyrics, in which drunkenness and wild behaviour were no longer a role to be adopted and thrown off at will; no longer a poetic affectation, but an addiction that the poet struggled to control. He began the first sketches for an epic poem, to be called 'The Dark Man'.

My friend, my friend
I'm ill; so very ill.

Nor do I know
Whence came this sickness.
Either the wind whistles
Over the desolate unpeopled field;
Or, as September strips a copse,
Alcohol strips my brain.
The black man
The black, black man
Sits by me on the bed all night,
And will not let me sleep.
The black man
Runs his fingers over a vile book,
And, leaning over me,
Like a sleepy monk over a corpse,
Reads a life
Of some drunken wretch,
Filling my heart with longing and despair.

'The Dark Man' was a poem that would be with him for the remaining years of his life, developing, expanding, changing its form as his troubles mutated and grew.

My darling Seryozha,

We are both articulate people. We can both make clever remarks, we can both flirt and we can both be amusing. But, love, I don't want to play these games with you. I invited you to the flat because I so wanted to find out how you are, how you feel, what is happening to you in this new and separate life. I loved our physical intimacy – I still tremble at the thought of it – but you deferred all serious conversation, you refused to answer my questions and you left with no explanation. I know that if we met again, you would continue to avoid talking to me about what matters. I think you are afraid.

I feel it is completely and utterly over between us. So why are you so cruel as to play with my feelings?

I don't want to be angry and bitter. And I also don't want to be toyed with. I gave you all of me. You broke all your promises. You left me, and now you want to see me as a casual friend or as your mistress.

Can you really not see how cruel this is? If you can't, then you are monumentally unfeeling. It feels as if you are punishing me for something and I genuinely cannot imagine what that might be.

You have made your decision; you are not proposing to reverse it, it seems, and therefore I ask you to leave me alone.

Where on earth are you going, love? Do you think you will find happiness with your grateful little translator and others like her? These are sad, hollow women. For you it will feel increasingly empty and humiliating. Perhaps you envisage your life becoming all work – writing, publishing, reciting – but that life, for which you will have traded in so much, will not be enough on its own.

I do not understand how you could have given up the love we had. It is so unnecessary and so tragic. But I am not the one who can change things. I love you, and I assume you must once have felt something for me; so please honour that love and don't hurt me any more.

The note of resignation in Zinaida's letter shook Sergei. He had not given her a proper explanation; her reproaches were justified, and he felt guilt for that. But sharper than guilt was the fear that gripped him at her suggestion that their relationship might be over. He had treated her badly, but he had never contemplated the possibility that she would wash her hands of him. Losing Zinaida would be the amputation of half of himself. He went to the flat.

She did not seem surprised. There was affection in her greeting. He stayed for two days and two nights. In long conversations over the dinner table, over bottles of wine, then entwined in bed, he explained why he loved her and needed her.

'We have always shared,' he said. 'You tell me your thoughts and I tell you mine. You try to impress me; I show off to you. You are my reason for trying. Hearing you say you love me is my life's validation.' He paused. 'I have been reading our letters from when we first met. They are such an outpouring of fresh, happy tenderness. But when harsh things are said, from sorrow or from anger, it is hard to escape that shadow. I don't want to lose touch with you, my love.'

'I understand that you love me,' Zinaida said. 'What I don't understand is why you left me.'

Sergei talked of the sadness that had dogged him since his childhood, of his mother leaving and his grandfather's severity. Zinaida was unmoved.

'Human beings are unhappy,' she said. 'And it's natural to feel that there must be someone to blame for it. We reach for the person or people closest to us, because they are the easiest candidates. Too many of us blame our parents . . .'

Sergei laughed. 'Then when our parents are gone, I suppose we reach for our lovers—'

'I am serious,' Zinaida said. 'And I am puzzled by your attitude to your mother. You never speak of her except to say how she abandoned you. Yet, in your poems, she is kind and loving. How do you explain that?'

'Because that is what poetry is for,' he said. 'To take the pain of life and turn it into something finer.'

'But do you never think that it might be your fault, Seryozha? That it might be you who is to blame?'

'Yes,' he said. 'All the time. I sit at night and I turn over in my mind all the moments of ignominy and guilt, the humiliation and the vile, loathsome behaviour. It makes me curl in shame . . .'

The Commissariat for Enlightenment wrote to Kusikov with a departure date. The People's Cultural Delegation would travel initially to Tallinn in the newly independent Estonia and from there to Berlin. It would be made up of writers and poets considered trustworthy supporters of the Revolution, tasked with the dissemination of socialist culture to the proletariat of the West.

Kusikov's exit was to be a civilised one. But 1922 was a year of other, less willing departures. A report to the politburo from the head of the Comintern, Grigory Zinoviev, had identified growing evidence of anti-Bolshevik plotting among the Russian intelligentsia. 'Different groups of intellectuals are launching journals and societies,' he wrote. 'For the moment, they are independent of each other, but it is only a matter of time before they unite into a powerful and dangerous source of opposition.'

Lenin demanded a purge. The teaching staff of all Soviet universities were to be investigated; 'reactionary' professors replaced by new 'red' ones. History and philosophy faculties were decimated; the heads of charitable, cultural and social organisations removed without explanation.

The politburo debated what to do with them. It identified

three potential solutions – shoot them, exile them to Siberia or deport them from the country. Trotsky announced that the Party had chosen the humanitarian option.

> These elements that we send away, and will send away in future, are a potential weapon in the hands of our foes. In the event of new international conflicts, these irreconcilable dissidents would become military-political agents of the enemy. We would have to shoot them in accordance with the rules of war. This is why we prefer to deport them now, while peace prevails. I trust the world will recognise our prudence and our humanity.

The cream of the Russian intelligentsia, including many of her best philosophers, historians and thinkers were imprisoned, forced to sign documents acknowledging that they were being deported and that any attempt to return would be punished by execution.

The Soviet government hired two German steamships, the *Oberbürgermeister Haken* and the *Preussen*, to take the unwanted intellectuals to Stettin on the north German coast. Each of them was permitted to take one summer coat and one winter coat, two pairs of trousers, or two short skirts and two long skirts, together with the equivalent of around $20 in currency.

Among the 160 or more on the first steamship were the leading representatives of the school of Russian idealistic philosophy, condemned because their quasi-religious beliefs conflicted with the materialistic Marxism that was now de rigueur. The operation became known as the Philosophers' Steamships. It was overseen by Josef Stalin, urged on by Lenin from his sickbed:

Comrade Stalin, In my opinion we need to expel all such 'gentlemen'. Pay particular attention to writers and private publishers. The House of Writers must be ransacked; we have no idea what is going on in there. We must clean up quickly. They are cunning and dangerous; relentless enemies. They must be driven out without mercy. We must cleanse Russia once and for all. Chuck them all out. All at once. With no delay and no explanation of motives. We must just say: Get out!

The 'Philosophers' Steamship', Bürgermeister Haken

Sergei and Zinaida fell into the life that she had sworn to avoid. They would meet for a day, a night, a weekend together. Then he would leave.

When he was with her, he was her Seryozha; she could block out the thoughts of his other life. The joy of touch, of warmth, comfort and support; the joy of understanding each other with a word, a gesture, a nod. It was fulfilling and beautiful.

When he went, her imagination darkened. She knew for her sanity, for her dignity, she should cast him off. But she didn't.

She was spending more time at the Meyerhold Theatre. At first, she had come on official business, observing for the

Ministry. She struck up friendships with the actors, then with Meyerhold himself. Her comments on rehearsals were astute and helpful. The troupe accepted her. When Meyerhold asked if she was interested in acting, she nodded.

At the end of a stolen weekend in the country – neither Lola nor the children knew about it – she told him that Meyerhold had asked her to try out for a role in a new production of Ostrovsky's *The Forest*. She saw Sergei's frown and realised he was jealous. She felt an unexpected spike of gratification.

Vsevolod Meyerhold

Vsevolod Meyerhold was forty-eight years old and Russia's most famous director. He had learned his trade in the Moscow Arts Theatre under Stanislavsky and Nemirovich-Danchenko. When he outgrew the company's naturalist acting style, he formed his own troupe. The Meyerhold Theatre, on the corner of Tverskaya and the Garden Ring, had become the first port of call for the dramatists of the Revolution. Highly stylised productions of plays by Mayakovsky and other socialist modernists alternated with witty reimaginings of the classics.

Meyerhold's relations with the Bolsheviks were cordial. His penchant for experimentalism tested the dictates of socialist realism, but his revolutionary commitment bought him credit. When he needed extras and equipment from the Red Army for a production about the war, he was able to call on his personal friendship with Trotsky to secure them.

He took a liking to Zinaida. Like her, he came from a family of German origin. They were Lutherans, but their name, Maiergold, sounded Jewish. On his twenty-first birthday, weary of Russian anti-Semitism, he changed it to Meyerhold.

Zinaida told Sergei how much she admired her new boss. She had auditioned and Meyerhold had given her the part. She had quit her job at the Commissariat and was going to be an actress.

Kusikov left. He had waited months, but the day came and his friends took him to the station.

He made them promise they would not get emotional. It wasn't just that he himself was feeling close to tears; there would be officials accompanying the delegation and he needed to keep up the pretence that he was simply taking a short trip, from which he would return.

The train was at the platform. Kusikov located his minders, thickset, muscle-bound men who pored over his papers, lips moving as they read. When they allowed him through, he turned, waved goodbye and imitated an orangutan.

Other writers were on the train. Few knew what lay ahead; all knew what they were leaving behind. The poet Vladislav Khodasevich, travelling with his wife, the novelist and memoirist Nina Berberova, scribbled some lines to give them courage:

> Russia's stepson, what am I to Europe?
> What do I know of her; how shall I understand?
> All I take are my eight slim tomes of Pushkin,
> But they contain my native land.
> For those who stay, the neck beneath the yoke;
> For those in exile, bitterness and woe.
> But I have packed my Russia in my suitcase,
> And she will comfort me – wherever I go!

Sergei continued to write; the state continued to turn him down. With independent presses closed on Lenin's orders, the newly formed state publisher, Goslitizdat, had a stranglehold. He submitted three collections of poetry; all were rejected. He sent some poems to a publisher in Berlin, but publishing abroad smacked of collaboration with the capitalist West, an increasingly perilous business.

Zinaida, by contrast, was finding success. She was a competent actress and she enjoyed the patronage of the boss. Meyerhold was beginning to offer her leading roles, to the chagrin of some of her fellow actors.

When she told Sergei about the close interest Meyerhold was taking in her, he bridled.

'So what are his intentions?' he asked. 'Why have you been keeping this secret from me?'

Meyerhold

CHAPTER 24

One thing the new Soviet state excelled in was acronyms – Cheka, OGPU, Narkompros, Gulag … In 1922 the acronyms spread to literature.

Goslitizdat – the State Literary Publishing Committee – already decided who could be published and who not. Now a new authority, Glavlit, would examine the content of writers' work in search of treason or sedition. Yet another body – Goskomizdat, the State Committee on Publishing, Reproduction and the Book Trade – would be added later, to control printing plants and booksellers and to ensure that literature and poetry supported the ideological goals of the regime.

Censorship under the tsars had been short of draconian. When Pushkin wrote poems supporting an uprising against Alexander I, he was sent to his mother's country estate. The Bolsheviks were more resolute. Writing pejoratively about, or revealing information that might harm the state carried serious penalties under Article 58 of the criminal code. They would range from twelve years in a labour camp to death.

Sergei's time with Lola had run its course. He asked Marienhof if he could move back in with him at the apartment on Bogoslovsky Lane.

Marienhof was delighted. He asked what had happened between him and Lola.

'Nothing,' Sergei said. 'We didn't quarrel, didn't fall out. It was just time to say goodbye; time to change things – for me, at least.'

'And what about Zinaida?' Marienhof asked.

Sergei was on the point of telling him how worried he was about his relationship with Zinaida, about his fear that she was losing patience with him and the jealousy he felt about her friendship with Meyerhold.

Telling a story changes it. However much we try to see with another's person's eyes, we tell it with our own. Anatoly Marienhof would recall the period in which he and Yesenin lived together as a time of fun. In his memoirs, the two of them were carefree and happy.

We shared everything, including a bed. It would get so cold that we had to curl up in a ball together. One night we had a brainwave. There were some poplar trees in our courtyard with a nice wooden picket-fence. But in times like these, who needs picket-fences! We purloined a few planks to put on the fire and our room got warmer. If the other neighbours hadn't spotted us and copied our example, we'd have been warm for a year.

When the fence ran out, we enlisted the holy icons. A venerable St Nicholas that hung in the corner of our room boiled the samovar nicely for our tea. Only our friend Molabukh wouldn't drink the holy beverage. His grandfather had been an Old Believer and the sacrilege might offend his memory, so Molabukh went thirsty.

When it got even colder, Yesenin and I moved into the tiny

bathroom. We made ourselves a bed with a mattress on top of the bathtub and a writing desk with planks on the washstand. We kept the water heater fuelled with pages ripped from our books and its warmth fuelled our muse.

We were poets, stars, adored by women. Yesenin, though, was jealous. One night I went out and didn't come home until the morning. I found Yesenin asleep in the bathroom and an empty vodka bottle on the washstand.

I shook Yesenin awake and he looked at me through heavy eyes.

'What's this, Seryozha,' I said. 'You drank all that on your own?'

'Yeah, that's right,' he said. 'And I'll do it again if you're going to start spending the night away from home ... Look – you can fool around with whoever you want to, but just come home to sleep!'

We laughed ourselves crazy.

The fundamental thing about Yesenin was his tremendous, all-consuming fear of being alone. It never left him for as long as he lived.

The days that Marienhof remembered as larks and laughter weighed on Yesenin with the anguish of a disquieting future. He could have bowed to the cultural watchdogs, written some panegyric to the revolution and tried to mend his relationship with the state. It would have allayed the persecution and eased the way for him to be published again.

He could have apologised to Zinaida and told her he was coming back. It would have ended the torment – his and hers – and rekindled the happiness they both regretted.

He did neither. He drank, brawled and tortured himself.

Marienhof's memoirs document the drinking, but in a jocular way. They were drunk because they were lads together, sharing secrets, jokes and beds.

> Yesenin and I slept in the same bed. We'd pile a mountain of blankets and coats on top of us. On the odd dates of the month, I would be the first to get in, warming up the ice-cold bed with my breath and my body heat. On the even dates, Yesenin did it.
>
> Then an aspiring young poetess asked him if he could help her get a job. She had rosy cheeks, shapely hips and nice shoulders.
>
> Yesenin said he would help her if she would come round to our place every night at midnight, undress and crawl in between our freezing sheets. It would take her about fifteen minutes to warm our bed. Then she could crawl out, get dressed and go home. He promised we would keep our backs to her and our eyes glued on our books.
>
> For the next three days, we kept our promises and we lay down to sleep each night in a bed warmed by a poetess.
>
> On the fourth day, our poetess handed in her notice. Her voice was indignant, her eyes round with rage.
>
> 'What's wrong?' we said. 'We kept to all the conditions we'd agreed.'
>
> 'Precisely!' she said. 'I didn't hire myself out to warm the beds of saints!'
>
> She walked out and slammed the door. We tried to call her back, but it was too late . . .
>
> The thing is that Sergei understood the emotional secrets of people's souls. That was the source of his charm. He

knew how to make everybody love him, to turn hearts and win minds.

In the normal course of things, I would say we love those who love us.

But the truth about Yesenin is that he loved no one.

Zinaida was the least mendacious of women. When she wrote to say Meyerhold was taking a romantic interest in her, Sergei was hurt and resentful; but he believed her. At their next meeting, he pressed her for details. He both wanted and feared the truth.

She told him how Meyerhold had promised her new roles and offered her private coaching. He was developing an innovatory style of acting, employing elements of Stanislavsky's 'System' or' 'Method of Physical Action', but constructing more rigorous correlations between an actor's physical and psychological states. He was exploring specific movements that would capture the essence of moods and emotions. He wanted his actors to learn the links between internal motivation and posture, to unleash feelings through poses, bodily expressions and gestures. Meyerhold was looking for a name for his revolutionary method and Zinaida had suggested 'Physical Theatre' or 'Biomechanics'.

Sergei's reaction took her aback. He leapt to his feet in a combination of gestures that she involuntarily noted as the perfect representation of extreme jealousy.

'Goddammit, Zina!' he said. 'Why are you letting this man come near you! He's twenty years older than you. He's married with grown-up children. I can't bear the thought of him touching you . . .'

Zinaida and Meyerhold rehearsing

Zinaida had been flattered by Meyerhold's attention. She knew that his interest in her acting career was not unconnected with his interest in her body. She neither encouraged nor discouraged him. It was far from clear, even to herself, where she wanted it to lead.

Sergei's extravagant expression of envy gave the situation added piquancy. The man she had been trying to entice back to her, who had steadfastly kept her hanging on his capricious indecision, impervious to her arguments and urgings, had been stung by something over which she *had control*. It gave her a power she had previously lacked.

Zinaida was not driven by passionate desire for Meyerhold. Neither was she consciously using Meyerhold's interest as a lever to get Sergei back. She was in a muddle.

Sergei had put off speaking to Marienhof. The divergence of their views about Zinaida was unlikely to be bridged. But he needed advice.

'Anatoly,' he said, 'you know I have been seeing Zinaida. You know she has been asking me to come back to her. I have spent so long without making a decision that I think she is losing patience—'

'Ha! Don't believe it, Seryozha. Don't let her—'

'No, wait. She has met someone—'

'Oh, for God's sake! Women always say that!'

'Not Zinaida. She is the most truthful person—'

'Then if she has met someone else, let her go with him—'

The conversation was becoming heated.

'Anatoly,' Sergei said, 'you are my friend. I need you to listen to what I am saying. I can't bear the thought that she will be with someone else. My time with her was the happiest of my life. We loved each other so completely that our beings converged. I don't know how to explain it. Our souls were bared to each other. Her heart and my heart locked in a single pulse. I saw with her eyes and she saw with mine . . .'

'Oh God, Seryozha. The way you tell it is so—'

'The way I tell it is the truth! I love her and I can't live without her—'

'Maybe!' said Marienhof. 'But neither, it seems, can you live with her!'

Vsevolod Meyerhold had been married for twenty-five years. He and his wife, the actress Olga Munt, had three daughters in their twenties.

But he was in love with Zinaida Raikh. He told her so. If she would have him, he would leave Olga. They would marry as soon as his divorce came through.

Olga Munt

Sergei wrote to Zinaida. Fear and jealousy vied in his note.

> Zina, my love!
>
> I beg you – do not accept or encourage him. He does not love you. I do!
>
> Turn him down. I will come back.
>
> Your one love. True. Eternal.
>
> Yesenin

A week went by and Zinaida heard no more.

> Seryozha,
>
> You said in your note that you would come back to me. Where are you?
>
> You said in your note that Meyerhold does not love me. I believe he does.
>
> You have been promising for so long to act, yet have done nothing.
>
> Meyerhold offered to leave his wife for me; he has filed for divorce.

Mikhail Zoshchenko, the future creator of some of the wittiest works of Russian literature, had just been demobbed from the Red Army. He had been wounded, decorated, wounded and decorated again. But his heroism did not produce the freedoms he had fought for and his wickedly childish satires would mock the disappointments of Bolshevik society. The Bolsheviks would denounce him. He would die in poverty. But that was the future.

In 1922, Zoshchenko was a habitué of Moscow's drinking dens.

A man comes towards our table, walking uncertainly. He is wearing a black velvet blouse, with a silk cravat trailing from his neck. His face is smeared with powder, his lips made-up and his eyes pencilled. On his face is a smile – a drunken, embarrassed smile. I see it is Yesenin.

'Don't be alone, Seryozha. Sit with us.'

'All of us are alone,' he says. 'In the hour of our death. I fear loneliness. The fear is with me always.'

'But what can we do about it?'

'Love might save us from emptiness. One person with whom we share everything – affection, trouble, conscience, fear – it may lessen the horror ... But love is gone. It is gone because I willed it ...'

Mikhail Zoshchenko

Anger and jealousy, despair and regret fed on themselves. They consumed Sergei. He wrote bitter letters then threw them in the trash. The note he sent her rose from muddied, alcoholic depths.

> I'm happy for you, love. I hope Meyerhold is giving you the emotional, physical, intellectual, spiritual fulfilment you've been looking for. That he can give you everything I have given you.

Zinaida replied:

> No, he doesn't give me all that you once gave me – I don't think anyone could – but he does give me some of the things that you don't give me any more. And, unlike you, he wants to be with me.
>
> You have never fought for me, as a man who loved me would (and as I did for you), and you never will. Your reaction to my news is telling. You could still have done something to hold on to me. But you just don't care enough.

Alexander Blok died. He was the last great figure of Russian poetry's Silver Age, read and admired by millions. In a nation where poetry matters, the nation mourned his passing. Blok had recanted his initial welcome for the revolution. His muse had fallen silent. His funeral was a poignant, shared catharsis of national grief.

Funeral of Alexander Blok

To mock a poet held in such universal affection was to invite contempt. Yesenin, self-destructing, did so. Appearing at the Pegasus Stable, he rambled through a speech titled 'Time to Speak Frankly about the Whorehouse Mystic', disparaging the memory of the man who had guided his first steps in the literary world. The audience booed. Drunk and depressed, Sergei ended the evening slumped at a table in tears.

'It is hard to imagine anything more abhorrent than what occurred at the Pegasus club,' wrote the *Literary Herald*. 'No one can be unmoved by this despicable attempt to defile the memory of a great Russian poet. With sneers and loathsome insults, the vilest of speakers has trampled with swinish feet on the grave of a saint.'

Attacking Mayakovsky had been pardonable; the socialist poets were fair game. Attacking Blok, still fresh in his grave, was petty and shameful.

Sergei had spat on everything. On the regime. On love. And now on poetry.

It was a self-abasement born of despair, close to a death wish.

Half a century later, with the benefit of hindsight and her mother's reflections, Tatiana Yesenina, the daughter of Zinaida and Sergei, would write:

> My mother was willing to listen to Meyerhold's proposal because he loved her enough to leave his family and commit himself, heart and soul, to being with her. It had been difficult with my father. There had been terrible scenes between them. But my mother was in love with Sergei Yesenin and he was in love with my mother – as they would be all their lives.

Sergei, lost in an alcohol-fuelled fog, thickened by years of terror, stumbled through a blackened world, incapable of feeling his way or making lucid decisions.

There were times when the fog lifted, moments of clarity. In one of them, he wrote 'My Russia Cast Adrift':

> I am not a Soviet Man! Why pretend? I'm not.
> I lagged behind, one foot in the past.
> When I tried to catch up with the revolution's troops,
> I slipped and fell – and I never got up.

Marienhof's memoirs are relentlessly denigrating of Zinaida and scathing about Sergei's love for her. But there is honesty in them.

> I said Yesenin never loved anybody. Perhaps with one exception . . . Who did Yesenin love? Most of all, he hated Zinaida Raikh. And this woman, this woman whom he hated more than anyone else in his life – her, her alone, did he love.
>
> She, too, loved only him and, after him, could never love again. If Yesenin had beckoned to her with his little finger, she would have run away from Meyerhold without an umbrella in storm and hail to be with him forever.

Her letter informing him that she intended to accept Meyerhold's proposal burned with the anger of hope dangled then dashed.

> My dear love,
>
> What do you want from me? Do you think I should just wait and wait and wait for you?
>
> Well, how dare you! How dare you! Do you really think that is all I deserve? Do you really think I value myself so little?
>
> I am baffled about how you feel and how that relates to the decisions you have made. You appear more concerned to please others, to the point of making yourself abject, than to do what your heart knows to be right. For some reason it is more acceptable for you to leave me torn apart – and to tear us apart – than to give up your empty freedom. How is this rational, love? It seems to me driven by cowardice, not your heart.

I am sorry for you. I am sorry that you are so helplessly
lacking in courage. You must be out of your mind to think
that I would be willing to stick with you when you are
unwilling to do anything at all to act on the great love you
ostensibly feel for me. How dare you, Sergei!

I know you miss me and want to see me. But then
you leave. We spend lovely days and nights. And then
you leave!

I know you care about me – just not enough to commit
yourself. And that is very hard. You have hurt me so much.

Take care, my love, and know that I love you and miss
you and am in pieces.

I refuse to be either manipulative or self-demeaning.
And I have to guard my heart. I ask you to respect that. I
think we both need to learn acceptance. I can't have you –
and you can't have me.

Zinaida

An hour later, another letter came.

My love, I don't want that to be the last I write to you. I
want to say one more thing. If you will come back to me, I
shall refuse Meyerhold.

You are the man I love. Come back. Let us cherish each
other for as long as we shall live.

The fog lifted. He knew it was his last chance. He wrote to
Zinaida to say he was coming back.

At a party that evening in the studio of the artist Georgy
Yakulov, he told his friends.

'I have spent too long living in darkness. I must have been

blind. I have been torturing myself, when the answer was in front of me. Zinaida is all that matters, the only thing to give my life meaning. When it seemed I would lose her, my heart filled with such horror – all the old memories of being left; the awful, terrible pain. I can't live with that. I have told her that I love her and we will be together forever!'

Yakulov, the artist who had painted the frescoes on the walls of the Pegasus Stable, knew Yesenin. He knew the contradictions at the heart of the man.

'Then you should go at once,' he said. 'Go before you lose your way.'

The partygoers drank to Sergei's happiness. Even Marienhof raised a glass. Yakulov's studio filled with artists and writers. More drink appeared. The place grew rowdy.

It was late when he saw her. She had been watching from the other side of the room. Suave and elegant; in clothes that marked her out as a foreigner, a Westerner.

'Golden hair,' she said, with her hand on his neck. 'My angel; my demon.'

She kissed him on the mouth. He kissed her back. She bit him on the lip. He put his hand to his face and felt the blood.

CHAPTER 25

Yakulov's party was attended by poets and other inventors; a hundred versions circulated . . .

. . . Yesenin had fallen madly in love. She had seduced him. It was a moment of passion. It was a charade. An irresistible attraction. Ridiculous self-promotion. A betrayal. A prelude to tragedy.

What they all agreed on was that Isadora had taken him by the hand and led him to Yakulov's bedroom. Within hours, the story was being told across the city.

Sergei woke up in a bed that was not his, a room he did not recognise and a building that was not Yakulov's. The elegant Western clothes she had worn at the party were on the floor. She was beside him, naked, demanding more sex.

He pushed her away and looked around the room. Isadora Duncan was everywhere. On dressing tables, on desks, on walls; paintings and photographs of the world's most famous dancer, head thrown back in the ecstasy of movement, sensuous, flowing poses, gossamer costumes artfully slipped to reveal legs and shapely breasts.

He glanced from art to life. The real Isadora was attractive;

her eyes dark, her body voluptuous. But she was a woman in her mid-forties, no longer the lissom Venus of the icons. His gaze lingered on soft arms and plump shoulders, fleshy waist and buttocks. She was desirable – and he desired her, in a comforting, maternal sort of way – but Isadora in 1922 was not the goddess of the flesh that the world held her to be.

Young Isadora

For twenty years the world had gasped in admiration and delighted in indignation. Isadora Duncan was the progenitor of modern dance. Everyone had their opinion of her. She was adored by fans, excoriated by defenders of morality.

Growing up in San Francisco, she had rebelled against the conventions of classical ballet. She declared her intention to return dance to its roots as the sacred art of Ancient Greece. Since few knew what that art might be, Isadora could experiment with free, natural movement. She melded elements of folklore and pagan ritual with skipping, jumping, running, leaping and tossing. Dance was not mere entertainment, but the means to encompass all human experience.

I sought that dance which might be the divine expression of the human spirit through the medium of the body's movement ... the source of the spirit flowing into the body, filling it with vibrating light. The rays and vibrations of music streamed into the fount of light within me and reflected themselves in the Spiritual Vision – not the brain's vision, but the soul's.

Like Stanislavsky on the other side of the globe, she felt that emotions might be expressed through physicality, that the apotheosis of dance emerges from the deepest inner springs of joy and sorrow.

She performed in a loose-fitting Greek tunic and bare feet. It gave her greater freedom than conventional tutus and pointe shoes. Inadvertent costume slips in *fin de siècle* America caused such outrage – and such publicity – that she incorporated them into her act.

Sergei Yesenin and Isadora Duncan began to be seen together. They were spotted at Moscow parties and restaurants, in concert halls, strolling in the park. It made the newspapers.

They were stars; glamorous, attractive, the stuff of gossip. And they were from different worlds, emblems of political systems at odds – potentially at war – with each other. The paparazzi snapped them, the editors splashed their photos.

More than one person told Zinaida what had happened. Some were concerned for her; others came to gloat. Marienhof did not appear.

In any event, she could read all about it. The Kremlin's vendetta against Yesenin had been put on hold to allow the press to celebrate the romantic tale of the Soviet poet and the brave, beautiful American who had quit her bourgeois homeland to seek freedom in the workers' paradise.

At a time when Russians were fleeing the USSR, any Westerner coming to live in Moscow was a hero. A star such as Isadora, willing to spout pro-Soviet views, was a coup. Lenin numbered her among his 'useful idiots', along with other prominent sympathisers such as George Bernard Shaw, H.G. Wells, the Webbs and André Gide.

Sergei Yesenin spoke not a word of English. Since she'd arrived in Moscow, Isadora Duncan had picked up the odd Russian expression, but far from enough to conduct a conversation.

That she had been able to declaim the Russian for 'golden hair', 'my angel' and 'my demon' on their first meeting made more than one observer suspect she must have crammed in advance.

In their early weeks together, they communicated with gestures, smiles and tender touches. If Sergei treated her roughly, Isadora would laugh and repeat the words she felt explained everything – *'Akh, russkaya lyubov,'* she would say, 'Russian love!'

When eventually they acknowledged that they needed an interpreter, Sergei said he would take care of it.

Zinaida cried until she could cry no more.

The Bolsheviks, contemptuous of bourgeois codes of morality, had simplified the process of divorce. Meyerhold was freed in an afternoon from the union to Olga that had lasted a quarter of a century. The theatre world was abuzz with talk of the great director and his actress bride-to-be.

Sergei presented Lola Kinel. Isadora could tell him her story now, and Sergei could tell her his. He glossed over the provenance of their young interpreter.

Sergei wanted to hear the tales of Isadora's scandalous youth. Lola, translating, wondered if he was trying to convince himself he hadn't made a mistake; that the woman with whom he had thrown in his lot was indeed the sensuous siren of legend, and not the slightly faded lady of a certain age.

Ten years earlier, living in Paris, Isadora had been the pin-up of the beau monde and the voodoo doll of *bien-pensant*

society. Her male admirers were legion. She was generous
to them. When the fashion designer, Paul Poiret, recreated
the bacchanalian revels of Louis XIV at his mansion in Saint-
Cloud, she had danced on the tables for three hundred guests.
She had begun the night wearing a Greek-style evening dress
that Poiret had designed for her. A thousand bottles of champagne had been drunk. Isadora's gown had slipped from her
shoulders.

The year before the Poiret bacchanalia, Isadora had met
the English Satanist and bisexual libertine, Aleister Crowley.
Crowley was a poet and drug addict whose occult powers
lured young men and women into his coven. Hashish and
Sex Magick were Crowley's recipe for the penetration of the
spirit world. Isadora, together with her friend Mary Desti, had
become part of it. Crowley had made her perform for him,
crediting her dancing with opening the doors of perception.

> Isadora has the gift ... Let the reader study her dancing, if
> possible in private, and learn the superb unconsciousness,
> which is magical consciousness ...

Sergei smiled. 'Was she naked?'
Lola nodded.
'Were she and this Mary Desti lesbians?'
Lola said she did not know.
'Ask her what year she was born.'
Lola asked; Isadora demurred.
Sergei insisted; Isadora said 1877.
'Old enough to be my mother,' he laughed.
Lola translated as, 'Still very beautiful.'

Isadora had given Sergei the scandal he asked for. Now she told him about her real life and the travails that had brought her to Moscow.

Puritan America had denounced her performances as immoral. She felt she would never be appreciated in her homeland. In 1898, at the age of twenty-one, she had moved to London.

Gazing at Greek vases and friezes in the British Museum helped her refine her vision of the dancer. She performed in private drawing rooms for wealthy patrons, who provided money for her to open a studio and appear on the London stage.

Visiting Paris, she met the lesbian American burlesque dancer, Loie Fuller. They began a close friendship. They would perform together for several years, touring in Europe, Russia and America. The fiery, unbridled movement of their performances inspired artists and poets, including Rodin, Mallarmé and Toulouse-Lautrec.

It was the height of Isadora's career. She moved to Berlin, where her fame brought disciples, eager to learn her philosophy and techniques. She opened a school for young girls, six of whom became so devoted that she legally adopted them. To the public, they were known as The Isadorables.

In 1906, Isadora gave birth to a daughter, Deirdre. The father was Gordon Craig, the dashing English theatre director and son of the actress Ellen Terry. Their liaison was passionate. Their letters overflow with love and joy. He introduced her to Konstantin Stanislavsky when the great Russian director came to Paris.

Gordon Craig and Isadora

Craig and Isadora would continue to write for many years, but he was the son of an absent father and he became one himself. Isadora was left to bring up Deirdre as best she could.

In 1910, she had a son, Patrick, with Paris Singer, the heir to the Singer Sewing Machine empire. Singer was one of Europe's richest men. He did not leave his wife, but he cared for Isadora and she settled in the French capital to be near him.

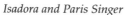

Isadora and Paris Singer   *With Deirdre and Patrick*

In April 1913, the Singer family chauffeur was bringing Deirdre and Patrick home from a birthday party. They stopped briefly by the side of the Seine at Neuilly, while the driver went to collect some things from a shop. With the children still in the car, the driver turned the crank handle to restart the engine. He had left it in gear. The car shot backwards over the edge of the quay and sank to the bottom of the river. Deirdre and Patrick, along with their Scottish nanny, Annie Sim, were drowned.

Isadora was finding it hard to continue speaking.

'Tell her I understand,' Sergei said to Lola. 'Tell her I understand a mother's grief.'

Isadora thanked him. He said he wished to recite a poem.

> ... lifting her eyes
> To the moon above the trees,
> She saw her children's souls
> Glide darkly through the sky.
> Keening at the deep-blue void,
> She watched them – the moon, the souls –
> All shimmer, slide and vanish
> To a place unseen, beyond the hill.
> And now, when men mock her,
> Throwing not meat but stones
> In her face, her dull eyes flow
> With tears that are wrought from stars ...

When Lola had read her English translation, they held hands. All three were in tears.

Isadora never came to terms with the loss of her children. She parted from Paris Singer and threw herself back into her stage career. She was desperate for another child. She begged a young stranger to make her pregnant, but she lost the baby.

She was getting older. She had put on weight; her dancing was less accomplished. She struggled with the fading of fame and the loss of youth. Her decision to move to Moscow in 1921 was born of all these things. She wanted to escape the past and find a future.

She had made no secret of her scorn for the American philistines who mocked her dancing and her supposed immorality. She had denounced their bourgeois chauvinism and outraged public opinion by declaring her support for socialism.

Words were one thing; moving to communist Russia was much more daring. She announced that in Moscow she would found a new school of socialist dance. It would resurrect her career. It was also guaranteed to get her name in the newspapers. Isadora courted controversy. She was showing her contempt for Western society, avenging herself on the ignoramuses who had once condemned her and now – much worse! – ignored her.

When she met Yesenin at the party, they were damaged people, each of them looking for something that had eluded them in life. Isadora wanted sex, reassurance and help to rekindle her fame. Yesenin was desperate to make his name in the West.

Isadora was past her prime, eighteen years older than he was, but she was his passport to success. Abruptly, he agreed to marry her.

CHAPTER 26

Yevgeny Onegin, the title character of Pushkin's 1833 masterpiece, is the prototype of the 'superfluous man', a literary figure that would haunt Russian literature. These are sensitive individuals who agonise over the problems of life – the emotional dilemmas of the individual, the evils of society – but are superfluous because they are gripped by Hamlet-like catatonia. Their frustration finds expression in gratuitous cruelty towards those they love and actions they know will bring ruin on themselves.

Pushkin's Onegin, a bored Petersburg dandy, attracts the love of Tatiana Larina. Young, impressionable and romantic, she bares her soul to him in a passionate letter, but Onegin turns her down. A fateful duel forces him to flee from Russia. He travels abroad to deaden his anguish.

When he returns, Onegin sees Tatiana at a ball. She is beautiful. He is overwhelmed by love for her. He writes burning, passionate letters, but she does not reply. While he was away, Tatiana has married an aged general. Onegin curses himself for having spurned her love. He is obsessed with winning her back. Tatiana recalls the days when they might have been happy. She admits she still loves him; but she must respect the duty that binds her to her husband. Onegin's actions have brought sorrow on her and despair upon himself.

When Zinaida Raikh married Vsevolod Meyerhold in the spring of 1922, those versed in the new conventions of Soviet-speak followed the press coverage with interest. Meyerhold, previously described as 'the great director', was now elevated to 'the great socialist director'. Zinaida, formerly 'the actress Raikh', became 'the socialist actress' (but did not gain the final accolade). Nuanced adjectives in the Soviet era would become an official codification of the recipients' standing in the Bolshevik cosmology.

The theatre world turned out for the wedding. Leading actors lent their voices to the speeches. Meyerhold's political connections ensured a Bolshevik presence. Lunacharsky was there. Trotsky accepted, but was unable to attend. Meyerhold had wanted to invite Stalin, but Zinaida objected.

'Stalin is a peasant,' she said, 'with dirty boots. We can't have him soiling the carpets. Trotsky would never forgive us if we invited the little upstart.'

Meyerhold fretted. Had they repeated the error of Sleeping Beauty's father?

Picking up the paper with news of the wedding, Sergei's throat tightened. For an agonised moment he could not breathe. He sat down to write to Zinaida. He had the poem's title – 'Letter to a Woman' – and the opening lines.

> You remember
> – for you remember everything –
> How I stood there leaning on the doorframe
> As you strode, angry, back and forth,
> Hurling barbs in my direction.
> My love!
> I tortured you.
> I saw the suffering in your eyes,
> As I destroyed myself in wild deeds before you.
> What you did not know
> Was that I was adrift, lost in the storm ...

He could get no further. He wanted to voice the anguish and bewilderment, the self-inflicted loss; but the words would not come. Onegin had felt it a hundred years before him. He settled for Pushkin's version of what he was feeling.

> I loved you; even now I must confess,
> The embers of my love still smoulder here.
> But do not let it cause you more distress,
> I have no wish to sadden you, my dear.
> Silently, hopelessly I loved you,
> At times too jealous, at times too shy.
> God grant you find another who will love you
> As tenderly and truthfully as I.

He sent it to Zinaida, with a note that struggled to be serene.

'The greatest test of love,' he wrote, 'is the ability to wish the other person well, even if you lose her. Tatiana and Onegin's story is the choice between cynicism and love. Sooner or later, everyone must make it.'

Like Isadora, Meyerhold was older. Twenty years Zinaida's senior, he appeared staid. Beside Sergei, he was dull.

But he cared for her and he cared for her children. He obtained a formal adoption order for Tanya and Kostya and looked after them as his own. He gave them the paternal presence that Sergei had never offered. He gave Zinaida the steady, reliable affection she had never had.

Tatiana and Konstantin, Yesenin's children with Zinaida

'Letter to a Woman', the poem to Zinaida that he had failed to complete, was stuffed in the drawer. He would return to it endlessly, extending, amending and polishing.

Just as 'The Dark Man' would become the lyric diary of the poet's struggle with his demons, so 'Letter to a Woman' would be the evolving record of his feelings for Zinaida; feelings that would alter, but never fade.

He married Isadora Duncan on 2 May 1922 at the Registry Office of Moscow's Khamovnichesky District Soviet. The wedding certificate tactfully deducted eight years from her age.

The two weddings took place within days of each other, in the same city, with the parted lovers each marrying partners two decades older than themselves.

Sergei and Zinaida pledged their future to people they didn't really love, for reasons involving desperation, rage and revenge. The consequences would be as intense as any Greek drama.

Isadora's relationship with the revolution never wavered. To love an ideal was easier than to love a person; and loving a foreign ideal far less complicated than having one foisted upon you.

Sergei, like most Russians, did waver. A generation of artists and writers had greeted the perception of freedom bestowed by the Bolsheviks with exhilaration. In the years that followed, the youthful passion that overwhelms caution had given way to suspicions, the dawn of mistrust. When doubts surfaced about the purity of the regime's motives, they suppressed them. When the regime's faults became manifest, they looked away. The revolution would turn against them. Some it would consume in the killing machine of the Gulag; others would renounce their art. More than one would succumb to despair. Some would conclude their life was no longer worth living.

He found Isadora's unqualified enthusiasm irritating. In 1917, in New York, she had declared her unconditional devotion to the ideals of the Red October.

'In my red tunic,' she wrote – in words swiftly communicated to the Kremlin – 'I have constantly danced the Revolution and the call to arms of the oppressed. On the night of the Russian Revolution I danced with a terrible fierce joy. My heart was bursting within me at the release of all those who had suffered, been tortured or died in the cause of humanity.'

Four years later, in the spring of 1921, the Bolsheviks invited her to Moscow. Her dance school had been struggling in the West; they guaranteed her success. 'The Russian government alone can understand you,' they wrote – or, at least, that is what she told Sergei they wrote. 'Come to us! We will make your school. We will give you a building and a thousand children. You may carry out your idea on a grand scale.'

She showed him the reply she had sent to Lunacharsky:

> I do not wish money in exchange for my work. I want a studio-workshop, a house for myself and my pupils and the opportunity to give our best work. I am sick of bourgeois commercialism. I want to dance for the masses, for the working people who need my art. I will come and work for the future of the Russian Republic and its children!

Sergei told Lola to explain that not everything was as simple or as sunny as Isadora thought. Isadora was not dissuaded:

'On the way here to Russia, I was a soul ascending to a higher sphere. I was travelling to the ideal state. When the boat arrived, my heart gave a great throb of joy. I was entering the domain of communism, the beautiful new world of comrades. A great force had given capitalism, with its monstrous greed and villainy, one great blow. It was the dream that resounded through all the words of Christ, the ultimate hope of all great artists. It was a dream that Lenin has turned into reality. I have been called upon to assist it in its first steps. I am part of this great dream, and my work and my life will be a part of its glorious future!'

The Bolsheviks rewarded her with a studio at 20 Prechistenka Street in central Moscow. It had been the property of the tsar's favourite ballerina, Alexandra Balashova, and – before that – the mansion of Pyotr Smirnov, the vodka distiller. There was a ballroom and a dance studio, with marble columns and high mahogany doors, and accommodation for Isadora and her staff. Lunacharsky ensured that the Duncan State School of Dance received, if not a thousand, then a good hundred or so willing students.

At the age of forty-five, Isadora was a skilful teacher. Her pupils found her warm and encouraging. But she was no longer the lithe dancer of her youth. When the Kremlin, eager to exploit her propaganda value, invited her to perform at the Bolshoi, she should probably have declined. She didn't.

In her trademark bare feet and Greek tunic she danced her most revolutionary programme. In those passages where Tchaikovsky's *Marche Slave* quotes the tsarist national anthem she gave her interpretation of the suffering masses, followed by the downtrodden people rising up to throw off their chains. The *'Internationale'*, played fast and loud, was a stirring, whirling finale of revolutionary fervour, designed to unleash a storm of applause.

The audience did applaud, but half-heartedly. They seemed bemused. There was a moment of hesitation and the theatre emptied almost at once.

In the morning, with Lola's help, Isadora scanned the press. The political commentators spoke of her Bolshevik commitment. *Izvestiya* praised her 'inimitable mime'.

> Against the background of Tchaikovsky, Duncan depicted in moving gestures a bent, oppressed, fettered slave who falls exhausted to his knees. But at the first notes of the accursed tsarist hymn, he lifts his tormented head in an awful grimace of hatred. Then with all his force he straightens himself and breaks his chains. His arms rise in triumph and he walks onwards to a new and joyful life. Everyone understood the allegory. This was Duncan's revolutionary interpretation of the oppressed Russian people who break the chains of tsarism and triumph in the revolution.

But the arts correspondents – those who knew about dance – were scathing. The critic, Denis Leshkov, compared the Isadora of 1922 with the young dancer he had first seen fifteen years earlier.

Pitiless time has wrought great changes in Duncan. Not a trace of her former lightness now remains. Her interpretation of Tchaikovsky is so subjective, so like random improvisation, that one begins to feel sorry for the composer. His music has been reduced to an incidental accompaniment for inexpressive poses and slightly absurd arm waving. Can, for instance, any purpose be discerned in her protracted and monotonous sweeping of the floor with her hair? The audience's response was unambiguous – faint applause, mingled with boos and catcalls. The overall impression was one of monotonous boredom and exceptional feebleness.

The ballet dancer, Igor Schwezoff, was merciless.

I saw a woman who looked over fifty, wearing a transparent *giton* over a naked, flabby body, massive and shapeless, hopping and tripping with rudimentary movements whose range was limited in the extreme. Now and then some of the audience tittered. Her dances called forth half-hearted applause. She walked about the stage for an interminable time, paying no attention to the music. Isadora Duncan's body was quite expressionless and gave me a feeling of embarrassment at its helpless clumsiness. When her *giton* slipped and left her bosom more than generously exposed, she was in such an ecstasy that she made no attempt to correct it. Those who wanted to giggle at this tragi-comic spectacle had to keep a straight face, for the music was the national anthem. This was the great Duncan! An artist of such prestige, reduced to using such cheap devices, wringing applause from her audience by a kind of flattery that I found particularly nauseating. I saw a mediocre danseuse taking refuge behind a lot of sham philosophy and spurious classicism.

Isadora put the reviews in the trash and opened a bottle. By evening, she was incoherent. She insisted on going out to a restaurant, where she was so disorderly that the police were called to arrest her.

On the evening that Isadora was being escorted to a police cell, Zinaida had her first breakdown.

She had not slept for four days; she was unable to stop the crying that convulsed her body. When Meyerhold tried to calm her, she screamed and threw herself to the floor. He called a doctor.

The medic gave her an injection. 'In times like ours,' he said, 'many are suffering. I have seen even the strongest laid low. The trials of our heartless century have ground us down. Madame Raikh is far from the worst case. Will you allow me to take her into our care for a few days? I can observe her and decide what is best for the future.'

In his colourful, sometimes truthful, sometimes mendacious memoirs, Marienhof describes a scene in which Vsevolod Meyerhold, still married to his wife Olga, supposedly speaks to Yesenin, still married to Zinaida.

'You know, Seryozha,' said Meyerhold. 'I am really in love with your wife. Would you mind terribly if we were to get married?'

'Not at all,' said Yesenin, with an effusive bow. 'Be my guest. Take her. You'll be doing me a favour. I'll be grateful to you until my dying day.'

Then Yesenin lifted up his lip to show Meyerhold a sore on his gum and smiled. 'Do you think I've got syphilis?'

The account is typical Marienhof – waspish, amusing and spiteful. Yesenin's mischievous hint that he has syphilis (he didn't) suggests a warning to the man who is taking his wife. His purported eagerness to give her away suggests he has tired of her or knows already that she is mentally disturbed. Neither was true. Her troubles would begin only after – perhaps because of – her split from the man she loved.

That Zinaida was admitted to the psychiatric clinic as Isadora was sitting in the police cell was a coincidence. Neither woman – neither couple – knew what was happening to the other.

Sergei did not know what was happening to Zinaida because she had ceased to write to him. He had heard nothing from her since the weddings that disunited them as man and wife. When she fell ill, she instructed Meyerhold not to tell anyone, least of all Sergei.

Isadora's arrest was hushed up by a Bolshevik leadership that did not want its supporters discredited. The police officer who had her in custody was instructed to apologise then release her in the morning.

Those who knew both Sergei and Zinaida did not inform either of them of the other's life. Had they done so, Sergei might have run to Zinaida that morning, rather than going to collect his wife from the police.

CHAPTER 27

Zinaida was excluded from Sergei's private life, but she could not avoid the public side of it. It was in all the newspapers. Photographs of him and Isadora smiling, looking into each other's eyes, were hard to avoid. It was the constant reminders of the man she had lost – and of his being with another woman – that helped tip her over the edge.

The breakdown had been coming. The births of the two children had upset her balance. Konstantin's ill health was a worry. Life in Moscow was dirty and difficult. But it was the constant criticism of her by Marienhof and Sergei's other friends, followed by his cooling towards her, that had done the damage. Paranoia had wormed its way into her soul.

Meyerhold was lovingly supportive. He visited her in the clinic, reassured her that all would be well. When the doctors said she would benefit from time in a sanatorium, away from the stress of Moscow, he said at once that he would look after the children so she could go.

Isadora was an alcoholic. Her addiction had grown over the years. By the time she met and married Sergei Yesenin, she could not go a day, sometimes even an hour, without a drink.

Yesenin had brought his drinking under control for part of the time he was with Zinaida, but it was always a struggle. Now, in the company of a woman who was not interested in restraint, he matched her glass for glass then carried on when she had stopped. The two of them would drink until they fell. Or until they lashed out in anger.

On a visit to Petrograd, they spent three nights at the Hotel Angleterre on St Isaac's Square. Sergei asked for room number 5, where he had stayed in the past. The central heating was not working. The radiator was cold. He placed a chair on top of the writing desk and climbed up to feel the heating pipe that ran up to the ceiling.

He ordered wine, then vodka, then more wine. In the evening, the hotel staff found him in the corridor, naked and roaring obscenities. Two porters returned him to his room. Isadora, upset and anxious, gave him another drink.

The Hotel Angleterre, St Petersburg

Isadora's friend Mary Desti came to stay. The two of them had been close since their involvement with the Satanist Aleister Crowley a decade earlier. They confided in each other about everything. Isadora was eager to show Mary the beautiful Russian poet who had miraculously become her husband.

Mary was a fabulist. Born in an Irish-American family, she had jettisoned her real name, Dempsey, to become Mary d'Este. Her face cream and cosmetics company, Maison d'Este, made her famous, but attracted the attention of the real d'Este family, Italian aristocrats, who objected. By the time she met Isadora she was Mary Desti, married and separated from a wealthy tycoon and mother of young Preston, the future movie director, Preston Sturges. She liked the company of men. Where Isadora had baulked at Crowley's sexual demands, Mary had enjoyed them.

She was not easily shocked, but in slightly incredulous letters to friends back home she described the goings-on at Isadora's mansion on Prechistenka Street.

Day after day, night after night, the house fills up with a wild, mad band of writers, painters and artists. They are the spoiled darlings of the Bolsheviks, yet they roundly abuse the government on every occasion. They carry on as if we were in Montmartre. They call themselves the Imagists, or the Scandalists – and my goodness, they live up to their name! They are drunk every night. They never dream of going to sleep until daylight. In fact, they keep up their wild parties for two, three, four days at a time, roaming from one house to another, defying everyone and everything, the law included. For some reason, the police don't lay a hand on them. Yesenin is the ring-leader. He and another poet, Marienhof, own some sort of a nightclub where only the intelligentsia are allowed in and where everything is always smashed to pieces before the end of the evening.

Knowing that the men would continue drinking, Isadora and Mary left them to it. In Isadora's bedroom they huddled under the blankets, giggling, sharing secrets, talking about relationships. Isadora pointed to the painting over her bed and said, 'That's Sergei! The beautiful Cherub! Him to a T!'

William-Adolphe Bouguereau, Cupid and Psyche, 1890

At a party in the Prechistenka studio, the men demanded that Isadora dance for them. They were drunk. The type of dance they had in mind had little to do with classical ballet.

Isadora demurred, but Sergei told her she must do what they asked. Yakulov, at the piano, made an attempt at 'Salome's Dance', a favourite number of Isadora's former friend, Loie Fuller.

Reluctant at first, Isadora entered into the spirit. The rhythms snared her feet, the tempo quickened, she threw back her head. The men were shouting, calling for her to remove her tunic. Caught up in the dance, she ignored them. There was discontent in the room. Sergei pushed her out of the way.

'I can do better than that!' he shouted, to laughter and applause. 'Let me show you how to do it!'

With Yakulov at the piano, Yesenin danced wildly, running, twisting and leaping in a cruel parody of Isadora. Wolf whistles from the audience encouraged him. He slid off his tie, unbuttoned his shirt.

When the music stopped, he found Isadora in tears. He held out his hand, half apologising, half mocking. She pushed him away. He swore.

'Then go to the devil!' he said, in Russian that she understood.

'Your dance is nothing!' he shouted, in words incomprehensible. 'It's trash! Dance is nothing. Dance does not endure. You dance tonight and tomorrow it's gone. Only poetry endures. My art will be here when you are not!'

Yakulov saw the rage on Sergei's face and tried to intervene. Isadora gave a half smile.

'*Russkaya lyubov . . .*' she muttered, with a shrug towards Sergei.

'*Russkaya lyubov?* Russian love? I'll show you Russian love!' he yelled, and hit her face.

Mary treated Isadora's black eye with a raw steak. Isadora marvelled that her friend had found such a thing in a Moscow still suffering from shortages.

'Never mind about the steak,' Mary said. 'What are we going to do about that brute of a husband of yours? It's no good to keep on saying "Russian love". Sure, the Russkies are tough guys, but one of these days he's gonna do you some serious harm!'

Isadora shook her head.

'No, Mary. Not Sergei. He's hot-headed and passionate, but it's because he's a poet. He feels everything more keenly than ordinary folk. He gets angry, but he loves me. And, God knows, I love him. You've seen how beautiful he is. And he's a genius. Genius has always had a fatal attraction for me. I knew from the very start that he's an angel and a demon. But he is the love I waited for for so long, the love that will resurrect the autumn of my life.'

Mary was not convinced.

'Well, I say someone needs to knock some sense into that genius of yours!'

'No, Mary,' Isadora said. 'I couldn't bear to hurt a hair of his golden head. Do you not see the resemblance? He's the image of little Patrick. Patrick would have looked like that one day. Do you think I could allow *him* to be hurt?'

Mary Desti

Marienhof disliked Isadora almost as much as he disliked Zinaida. Another woman had stolen Seryozha away from him. He wrote to friends to say that Yesenin had made a mistake.

> He didn't fall in love with Isadora Duncan, but with her fame. He didn't marry an overweight woman with dyed hair, he married her fame. He loves to walk hand-in-hand with this global celebrity on the streets of Moscow; he loves to appear with her at the Poets' Café, at concerts, at theatre premieres and to hear people whispering, 'Duncan-Yesenin' ... 'Yesenin-Duncan'. That's all.

Like all who knew them, Marienhof recognised the love and the hatred at the heart of their relationship.

> There is mutual tenderness between them. Affection, even. But Seryozha is tyrannical and coarse towards her. He beats her and calls her foul names. She puts up with it because he is young and virile. He has become her master. Like a dog, she kisses the hand he has raised to strike her and the eyes in which hatred for her burns more frequently than love.

Flipping through Isadora's notebooks, in which she was noting down Russian words she wanted to learn, Marienhof claims to have discovered the phrases, 'My last love!' and 'I worship the ground you walk on', whereas – he told friends – Yesenin taught the unsuspecting Isadora a string of Russian obscenities.

Ignoring Isadora, Mary Desti went to him, with Lola in tow.

'What the hell do you think you are doing?' she told Lola to ask him. 'You are a bully and a fool. When you strike a woman, you hurt her physically, but you damage yourself much more, because you damage yourself morally and spiritually.'

Lola made no effort to soften the severity of the words.

'But . . . but she likes it . . .' Sergei said.

'You fool!' Mary said. 'She loves you and you return that love with violence. How can a man and a woman live that way?'

'*Bit' znachit lyubit'*,' Sergei said, quoting one of Russia's most famous proverbs – 'If you hit her, you love her.'

Mary snorted. 'Then you understand absolutely nothing! Isadora's life has been smashed by tragedy. Since her children died, she has been crying out for someone to rescue her. Her whole existence has been a flight from the horror of it; her only desire to escape the memory and forget the pain. At times she finds relief in the triumph of her work. At times in the oblivion of drink or sex. But what she wants is love. And she thought she had found it in you!'

Goslitizdat agreed to print Yesenin's narrative poem, *Pugachov,* about the leader of an eighteenth-century peasant revolt. Convinced of its revolutionary content, the publisher put it out as a slim paperback with brick-red covers.

Sergei was delighted. When the first copy arrived, he presented it to Isadora with a scrawled dedication: 'For everything, for everything, for everything I thank you. My dear one, my good one, my beautiful one.'

Marienhof thought Yesenin's brutality could be explained.

The problem with Yesenin is that he would sacrifice any-thing for this wonderful, this terrible, this stupid *fame*. For Yesenin, fame is more precious than life. Because of it, he lost everything. He lost the money from his pocket. He lost the shame from his soul. He lost the hat from his head and he lost his head in a bottle. He lost his friends. He lost the woman he loved. The only thing he did not lose was his poems. His poems are the beating of his heart; his poems are his very breath.

But poetry did not bring him peace. Sergei may have chained himself to Isadora in the hope of finding celebrity, but it left him frustrated and violent. Worst of all, he knew he had sacrificed the love that might have brought him ease – the love of Zinaida.

Chapter 28

Zinaida was in the Clinic for Nervous Illnesses in the spa town of Kislovodsk. In the Northern Caucasus, between the Black Sea and the Caspian, it had the sunshine and mountain air that doctors prescribed to soothe the nerves of human beings shattered by the strains of their angry century.

Kislovodsk was beautiful. Built in 1803 as a garrison post during Alexander I's subjugation of the wild Caucasian tribes, it took its name – literally, Oxygen Water – from the mineral springs in the mountains that bubble up in the town. For a century, artists and writers had mingled with the aristocracy in its shady avenues. It was the setting for the first great Russian novel, *A Hero of Our Time*, written in 1840 while its author, Mikhail Lermontov, was serving there in the tsar's dragoons.

'When there is a storm,' Lermontov wrote, 'it comes right down to the roof of the house. To the west is Mount Beshtau, blue as the last cloud in a dispersing storm. Mashuk, like a shaggy Persian cap, covers the entire northern horizon. Farther away, the mountains are darker, mistier ... and at the very limit of sight, a silver chain of snowy peaks runs from Kazbek to mighty Elbrus with its towering summits. What joy it is to live in such a land!'

Kislovodsk sanatorium

Alcohol was not Isadora's only addiction. Early in their friendship, she had written to Mary Desti about her experience of physical love.

> My breasts begin to swell and astonish me with charming but embarrassing sensations. My hips take on a new undulation and through my whole being I feel one great surging, longing, irresistible urge ... I have learnt the desire, the gradual approach to the ultimate madness, leading me to the crucial and furious abandon of the final moment. Let those judge me who can, but rather blame Nature or God that He has made this one moment so powerful and worth so much more than all else in the universe.

Sergei, used to taking the lead in bed, was surprised; Isadora's demands were knowing and specific. It took him a while to adapt, but he did so. She was needy and insistent, then flatteringly grateful. She was controlling; he had the power to satisfy her.

When Marienhof asked what 'La Duncan' was like between the sheets, Sergei hesitated.

'She tells me to get into bed,' he said. 'Then she performs a sort of dance of the seven veils. I enjoy it and I think she does, too. When she is wearing nothing but her brassiere, she glides towards me and flings herself upon me.'

Sergei stopped. He saw the jealousy in Marienhof's face.

Zinaida was far from the worst case. Her diagnosis was nervous exhaustion. There were other patients on the ward, seriously ill, leering, pulling at their hair and cheeks.

She and the other 'good cases' were allowed to spend the afternoons in town. With the end of the Civil War, the south of Russia was returning to normality. The spas and hotels of Kislovodsk were getting back to business.

On the main street she saw a sign for the Princess Mary Café and looked twice – princesses were rare in the Bolshevik state. Sitting at a table by the window, she thought of *The Lady with the Lapdog*; Kislovodsk had something of Yalta about it. She ordered a tea. How did the story go? Chekhov's heroine is alone, away from her husband. She sees a stranger. He comes to talk to her. He is handsome. Zinaida caught herself looking towards the door and laughed.

She couldn't even remember how Chekhov ends the story. Does the lady with the dog find love? Is she jilted and disappointed? Zinaida stopped herself. Her husband would be in Kislovodsk in a few days.

'How old is Meyerhold?' she found herself thinking. 'Forty-eight ... so, how long left? Twenty years? Have I sentenced myself to twenty years of boredom?'

The waitress asked if she would like the bill, but Zinaida said, 'No, I am waiting for someone.'

Sergei had questions he wanted to put to Isadora, intimate questions that men and women ask each other in quiet moments after making love. The language barrier frustrated him. Getting Lola to interpret would be freighted with memories of their own past relationship, still hidden from Isadora, and with the embarrassment of airing personal concerns in a shared forum.

He asked Lola to speak to Isadora in private.

'Tell her you want to know what she thinks about sex,' he said. 'If she asks, you can say that I want to know. Find out everything you can.'

Lola was surprised by Isadora's eagerness to talk.

'I have loved many men,' she told her. 'If I have parted from so many, I can blame only the fickleness of men or the cruelty of fate, for I have always been faithful. I would never have left any of them if they had been faithful to me.'

Sergei had told her to ask about Isadora's libido. Lola took a deep breath and did so. Isadora smiled.

'What nonsense women speak about that,' she said. 'I hear so often that a woman's love life should end at forty. What nonsense! The joys of autumn are a thousand-fold more powerful, terrible, beautiful than those of spring. I was once the timid prey, then the aggressive bacchante. Now I close over my lover as the sea over a bold swimmer, enclosing, swirling, encircling him in waves of cloud and fire.'

Lola, embarrassed and thinking of her own time with Yesenin, made to leave, but Isadora hadn't finished.

'Please tell Seryozha that I understand why he has sent you to ask me these questions. I know my approach to love is uncommon, and it has tormented me over the years. I am a pagan puritan; my soul is a battleground between Christ and Dionysus, between chastity and desire. Ever since my children died, I have carried a poison in my blood. The yearning pain, the haunted remorse, the sorrowful sacrifice. Sex is the means to soar above anguish, to soar above the world. But, just as the flight is high, so the crash of awakening is terrible.'

Zinaida realised with a jolt that it was Sergei she was waiting for.

And she realised why it was called the Princess Mary Café. It had nothing to do with the Romanovs; Princess Mary was the love interest in Lermontov's novel, *A Hero of Our Time*. The Regional Soviet had alighted on a clever way to capitalise on Kislovodsk's literary heritage. Now that she understood what was going on, she began to spot other references to the book's characters. There was the Pechorin Casino, the Lermontov Reading Rooms, the Grushnitsky Tea Shop. The book was on sale everywhere.

She spent the afternoon trying to remember the plot. She knew that someone argued with someone – about a woman? – and that someone shot someone else. On the way back to the sanatorium, she bought a copy and read it after lights-out with a flashlight. Grigory Pechorin, Lermontov's cynical anti-hero, was even more horrible than she remembered him. He deliberately seduces his best friend's fiancée, Princess Mary, just to sow trouble in the world. When his friend challenges him to a duel, Pechorin shoots him dead.

Zinaida lay awake for a long time. Asking if Pechorin deserves our pity was like asking if the devil might be saved. Yet Lermontov allows us to see through Pechorin's eyes and as Lermontov said, don't we tend to excuse that which we understand? We learn that Pechorin's nihilism stems from an inner sadness, an awareness of the hopelessness of the human condition that nothing can sweeten. Women are a game for him, a divertissement; he seems incapable of love. His old flame, Vera, says, 'All you ever gave me is pain.' And yet . . . Vera loves him.

Zinaida found the end of the book disturbing. Pechorin appears to realise, too late, that he too loves Vera. His unfeelingness was a device to protect himself, but it has made him repress his true emotions. He races to tell her, but Vera has gone forever. Pechorin dies of a broken heart.

His final words ran through her dream.

Afraid of decision, I buried my finer feelings in the depths of my heart and they died there. I saw how futile and senseless it was to pursue lost happiness. Tomorrow, my friends will forget me; and women, in the embrace of another man, will laugh at me so that he does not feel jealous of the departed.

Mount Elbrus, from Kislovodsk

Isadora suffered Sergei's cruelty with patient determination. Perhaps she was desperate. Perhaps marriage to a Russian was useful for her career. Perhaps she loved him.

The loss of her children undoubtedly sharpened her lifelong need for drink and sex. She would write movingly about the effect their deaths had on her.

> The most terrible part of a great sorrow is not the beginning, but afterwards, long afterwards, when people say, 'Oh, she has got over it' – or, 'She is all right now, she outlived it'; when one is, perhaps, at what might be considered a merry dinner party, to feel Grief with one icy hand oppressing the heart, or clutching at one's throat with the other burning claw – Ice and Fire, Hell and Despair, overcoming all – and, lifting the glass of champagne, one endeavours to stifle this misery in whatever forgetfulness – possible or impossible.
>
> The sight of any little child who enters the room suddenly, calling 'Mother', stabs my heart and twists my whole being with such anguish that the brain can only cry out for Lethe, for Oblivion, in one form or another . . .
>
> I envy the resignation of those nuns who pray with pale lips, murmuring incessant prayers all through the night before the coffins of strangers. Such temperaments are the envy of the artist who Revolts and cries, 'I will love, love; create joy, joy.'
>
> What a Hell!

The tension between Yesenin and Marienhof did not go unnoticed. The two friends, long inseparable, grew cool. Their bickering became public. The literary wit, Sashka Sakharov, composed a ditty that did the rounds of Moscow society.

> Now unwashed Anatoly scarcely cheeps,
> But Sergei's looking friskier.
> That's because Yesenin sleeps
> With lovely Duncan on Prechistenka.

Marienhof's response was to announce that he, too, was in a relationship. The actress Anna Nikritina moved into the bed in Bogoslovsky Lane that had previously been shared with Yesenin. Yesenin gave her the nickname of *Martyshon*, 'little monkey'.

The two men started to avoid each other. When they met by chance in the Pegasus Stable, both were angry and Yesenin was drunk. Marienhof's version survives.

> I was sitting there listening to the doleful wail of a double bass. The place was deserted apart from a couple of waitresses, one with a toothache and the other who hadn't even bothered to put on make-up. The weather outside was dismal – sleet falling through the jaundiced yellow of a feeble street lamp. I was wallowing in autumnal misery, when Yesenin walked in.
>
> The waitresses recoiled from him. His eyes were dull and porous, like a sugar cube dunked in coffee. His clothes were a mess. His hat was stained and crushed, his collar limp and his tie askew. His golden hair was dishevelled and discoloured. It was starting to look like the dirty water left in a washtub after a load of laundry.
>
> Without saying hello, Yesenin strode up to me. His thrust his hands into his pockets and, without a word, fixed me with a stare that was glazed and hostile.

I carried on stirring my coffee and stared back at him in silence. He had some nonentity of a Petersburg poet with him who was fussing all over him. A woman with him started tugging at his sleeve. Yesenin pushed her away.

'Fuck off!' he said. 'Can't you see I'm busy!'

He stank of alcohol. The stench was acrid, vile.

'Well?' I said.

He slammed his hands down on my table. He leaned forward and jammed his face into mine.

'I will demolish you,' he said, spitting out every syllable. 'I will gobble you up and chew you out.'

'Well, you're not the Big Bad Wolf,' I said. 'And I'm not Little Red Riding Hood, so maybe you won't.'

I forced myself to smile. I raised my cup and swallowed some scalding coffee.

'No! I will!' he said, brandishing his fist.

The Petersburg scribbler, puny and morose with a snub nose, and the unknown woman were trying to calm him down. They were whispering in his ear and gesturing to me.

Yesenin straightened up and turned away. He staggered off, with the poet and the woman each supporting an elbow, but at the door he spun around.

'That's it then. Adieu . . .'

His jaws were working but no sound was coming. He forced the words out.

'Remember! I've warned you!'

And that was it. They edged him out of the door. From then on, if we saw each other in the street, we'd turn away.

Isadora was returning from an appointment in a taxi. The driver smelled of alcohol. He took no notice when Isadora told him he was driving too fast. Turning a corner, they came upon a group of children playing in a dusty lane. The children scattered, but one of them, taken by surprise, first stopped dead then rushed across in front of the car, which hit him. Isadora was paralysed with horror. She got out of the taxi with the anguished certainty that nothing could be done to save the boy, when suddenly she saw him get up from the ground, dash across the road and disappear through a gap in a fence into the yard of a house.

Women on the pavement who had seen the incident, screamed, 'He's alive! Alive!'

Isadora ordered the driver to take her to a confectionery shop. She could hardly bear to look at the man. How could he drive so fast in a street where children were playing?

From the confectioner's she bought boxes of chocolates and sweets. Back at the gate where the little boy had disappeared, a young girl took her to the basement room where they lived. It had almost no furniture, but there were five or six children in it. A baby with sallow eyes stretched out its arms to the girl who had brought Isadora in. The little boy who had been knocked down was there, still shaking. His older sister had dressed a wound on his forehead with cotton wool and pieces of linen.

Isadora opened the boxes. The children fell on the chocolates. The baby took a boiled sweet.

'A miracle!' exclaimed Isadora.

The girl explained that their mother was away and knew nothing of what had happened. Turning to her young brother, she said severely, 'Just let me catch you running about in the road again!'

As she was leaving, Isadora looked back at the baby with the sallow eyes.

'To come to this country for the sake of the children and nearly kill one! If that had happened, I would wish myself dead on the spot.'

Isadora's dance school was in trouble. With the Soviet economy still recovering from years of catastrophe, the politburo reneged on Lunacharsky's promises of continuing financial support. He wrote to her apologetically to suggest she give paying performances or take fees from her pupils.

Isadora could neither accept such an arrangement nor publicly express her disenchantment with the Bolsheviks. Her solution was to go West.

She spoke to her American agent, Sol Hurok, about a comeback tour that would take her and Sergei to Europe and North America. Hurok replied that the time was right. Isadora's escapades in Moscow had not gone unnoticed in the Western media; her marriage to a 'Red' and her outspoken support for Soviet socialism had thrust her back into the headlines. She had a notoriety – heroine of the left; bogeywoman of the right – that would fill the theatres.

Sergei was enthusiastic. Moscow held little charm for him now. He had cut his links with Marienhof and quarrelled with former friends. Alcohol had made him unpredictable and violent. People avoided him.

Isadora hoped a year away might calm her husband and help steady their marriage. Sergei wanted his poetry to reach a new public in the English-speaking world. He told her they must take Lola with them.

The exit visas came. Having failed to assist the ever-supportive Duncan and happy to rid itself of the troublesome Yesenin, the Kremlin seemed content to see them go.

Sergei reeled between elation and despair. He told Shershenevich that he would become the world's most famous poet.

'I'm not going there to loaf around,' he said. 'And I'm not going just as the husband of Isadora Duncan. I'm going to conquer Europe, then I'm going to conquer America. I'm going to show them in the West what a real Russian genius is like!'

He cabled Alexander Kusikov, who was now living in Berlin, to inform him of his imminent arrival and to ask him to arrange recital dates, with the maximum publicity.

He told the world he was travelling in hope, in search of fame, but his diary told another story. He had scribbled down Shershenevich's translation of Baudelaire's 'Voyage' – *This fire burns our brains so fierce, we plunge into the abyss; Heaven or Hell, what matter? To the Unknown depths in search of something new!* – and, on the facing page, an acknowledgement that he, too, was fleeing from his own existence.

> So many idle no-goods have attached themselves to me in Moscow. They disturb me. They insist on getting me drunk. I don't know how to get out of the mess I'm in. I lead a rootless life, homeless, without refuge. I burn with shame and pity. I want to flee from everything – or retire to a monastery. But there is nowhere to flee to . . . *nowhere in the world I can escape from myself.*

Two cables arrived. Sol Hurok's confirmed the details of Isadora's tour – fifty performances in Europe and the United

States, for a fee of forty thousand dollars plus expenses. The other, from Paris, informed her that her mother, Mary Dora Gray, had died in the French capital at the age of seventy-three. There was an estate to settle and a property on the Rue de la Pompe that belonged to Isadora.

A week before they were due to fly, Sergei wrote to Zinaida. He could not bear the thought that he had become nothing for her, that she never pined for him as he did for her. He needed her acknowledgement – a nod of her head, a glance from her eye – that he was still in the world. Without it, he might as well not be.

CHAPTER 29

Of all the Western countries, only the Baltic States had by 1922 established diplomatic relations with the new Soviet Republic. Britain and Germany would not do so for another year, and the USA not until 1933. But the Red victory in the Civil War had made Bolshevik power a reality, and economic ties were being renewed. Sergei and Isadora left on one of the first scheduled flights between Moscow and the West, a small six-seat Fokker F.III to the northern German city of Konigsberg. Pupils from Isadora's dance school came to see them off, but Sergei had few friends. Only Yakulov and Shershenevich were there, convinced he intended never to return.

From Konigsberg, they travelled by train to Berlin. They were met by Kusikov and stayed at the luxurious Hotel Adlon. The advance on Isadora's fee had arrived; their trip would be financed by her comfortable expense account.

Berlin was the refuge of many of the Russians who had fled after 1917. The émigré community was a microcosm of pre-revolutionary Moscow. Supporters of all ideologies – left, right; Red, White; monarchist, socialist, communist; democrats and dictators – continued to fight Russian quarrels on German streets.

Sergei found the place intimidating. The soldiers on every corner, the incomprehensible language, the tension and resentment of a defeated nation, the unspoken violence that hung in the air.

Isadora knew the city well. She sought out old haunts. She wanted to visit the site of the dance school she had run for ten years in Grunewald, ten miles from the centre, but Sergei told her he wasn't coming. He spent the day in a bar. By evening, he was drunk and lost. Zinaida had not replied to the letter he wrote before leaving Moscow. Her absence grew like an abscess in his soul.

Berlin, 1922

They went with Kusikov to parties hosted by Berlin's Russians and were struck by the melancholia that haunted them. Sad-faced men and women spoke longingly of the old days, before their homeland was taken from them, exchanging nostalgic tales of how delightful it would be to be in Moscow. Sergei was tempted to disabuse them but remembered that, even abroad, the Kremlin monitored the opinions of its subjects.

At their enforced distance from the real Russia, the exiles created an imaginary land, a Russia that never changed, in which they could live. Their salons and drawing rooms became a closed world where Russian was spoken and contemporary life excluded. Kusikov took them to see the poets, Marina Tsvetaeva and Vladislav Khodasevich, and the essayist Vladimir Nabokov, all of whom had made Berlin their home.

Nabokov seemed distant. When he spoke, he insisted on talking about his father, also called Vladimir, who had been a minister in the Provisional Government.

'My father said it would have been easy to eliminate Lenin and his gang,' Nabokov said, 'but the Provisional Government were too honourable. They played by the rules of democracy, while the Bolsheviks were fanatics. Lenin just said, "When you chop down a forest, chips must fly." That was their justification for the lies and the repression and murder.'

Afterwards, Sergei asked why Nabokov had been so obsessed with his father. Kusikov said it was because he was in mourning. In exile from Russia, Nabokov senior had continued to campaign for democratic socialism. At a Berlin conference a few months earlier, he had hosted the former Constitutional Democrat leader, Pavel Milyukov. As Milyukov was speaking, two White officers had run towards the stage and shot at him. Nabokov senior was in his fifties, unfit and overweight, but he jumped off the stage and wrestled them to the floor. His action saved Milyukov's life. Nabokov himself was shot in the chest and died in minutes.

Vladimir Nabokov Snr, 1870–1922

Yesenin read as much as he could of the young Nabokov's writings, nostalgic tales about the pain of being cut off from one's past, of émigrés who never unpacked their suitcases, 'imitating in foreign cities a dead civilisation, now remote, almost legendary'.

Nabokov's characters long to return, but fear the reality might not match the dream. A sketch for an unfinished story had the unnamed narrator enter a foreign art gallery in search of an old Russian painting. In a dreamlike passage, he wanders through endless, ever-expanding corridors until he opens a door and emerges not in exile but in the snowy streets of his hometown, St Petersburg. To his horror, his past has been transformed by the Bolsheviks into an inimical, alien realm.

It was not the Russia I remembered, but the factual Russia of today, forbidden to me, hopelessly slavish – and hopelessly my native land.

Vladimir Nabokov Jnr

Isadora's first performance was to take place in three days' time. The Berlin press were eager to hear from the celebrity who had sacrificed American affluence for the privations of Russian socialism.

'I love Russia,' she said. 'So much so that I have married a Russian and taken his nationality.'

She brandished her red Soviet passport.

'I love the Russian people and I intend to go back there next year, when my tour is over. Nevertheless, I will say that it is comforting to come to a place where one can have warm water, napkins and central heating. One has other things in Russia, but, poor weak humans that we are, we become accustomed to luxuries and it is hard to give them up. Not that the Russians believe in giving up luxuries. On the contrary – they believe in luxuries for all, not just a privileged few. So, at times when there is not enough to go round, everyone must be content with a little less.'

Isadora made a point of presenting Sergei, but the journalists showed no interest. It was Isadora they wanted to talk to.

Sergei left without saying a word. When Isadora told him she had reserved him the best seat in the theatre for her performance, he said, 'I'm not coming.' He was going to give a recital of his own.

Sergei appeared at the Berlin House of Arts. A last-minute publicity drive by Kusikov attracted two hundred members of the city's White Russian community, expecting to hear anti-Bolshevik poems from a poet who had fallen foul of the regime.

Sergei had had a couple of drinks, but he wasn't drunk. He walked on stage and stood in silence. He looked around. The audience grew impatient. There were shouts of, 'Get on with it!'

Well-fed faces stared at him expectantly. He knew what they wanted, but he was damned if he was going to give it to them.

'Ladies and gentlemen,' he said. 'I propose that we begin by singing the *"Internationale"* – in the spirit of universal socialist brotherhood!'

The audience looked at each other. Sergei began singing.

> Arise, you victims of oppression!
> Arise, you wretched of the earth!
> For justice thunders condemnation –
> A better world's in birth!

A few voices joined in but were drowned by cries of indignation. Sergei sang louder.

> No, comrades! Come together!
> Now's the time and this the place!
> For the Internationale shall
> Unite the human race!

He scarcely knew why he was doing it. The scandal gave him a thrill – the furious, outraged faces were a spectacle. But he wasn't helping himself. He called for calm. The crowd grumbled then settled down.

'Thank you! Thank you! And now for poetry!'

He began with his early lyrics, hymns to nature's beauty and the poet's love of his native land. They had been published abroad, so the audience knew them. The Russia they celebrated was pre-revolutionary; there was a murmur of appreciation.

But Yesenin was possessed by contrariness. In the sweetest

of voices, he read the fiercest of his revolutionary verses, from 'Russia of the Soviets' to 'I am a Bolshevik'. Anger spread; voices were raised, a book of his poems was torn up.

There was something elemental about the passion of it that Sergei didn't want to stop. Isadora had told him about the speech she was planning to give after her performance and he decided to give it himself.

'Dear Comrades!'

There were shouts of, 'We are not your comrades!' and 'Go home, you scoundrel!'

'Comrades! I have come to tell you of the miracle that is taking place in Russia! One of the greatest miracles in the history of mankind; a miracle that happens only once in two thousand years. We are too close to see anything other than its material consequences, but those who come after us – those who will live in the next century – will realise that communism is a leap forward for mankind greater than any that has gone before! Only the brotherhood of the workers of the whole world, only the Socialist Internationale can save humanity!'

His words were lost as the hall erupted. Bottles and glasses, sticks and seats were hurled. In a frenzy of nervous elation, Sergei ran from the stage and Kusikov dragged him outside to a waiting taxi.

Isadora arrived at the House of Arts to find indignant knots of Russians discussing the scandal.

Her own performance had gone well. She was applauded by a full house. She had decided not to spoil the evening by giving political speeches but to enjoy the acclaim and the flowers. No one could tell her where Yesenin had gone.

When Kusikov had bundled him into the taxi, Sergei could

hardly speak. His voice was choked with excitement, overcome by the drama and the triumph.

'Goddamit,' he said. 'I did something! God knows what I did, but I *did* something at last! I've spent so long not knowing, not deciding, not acting. Tonight I did something real!'

Kusikov wanted him to go back to the hotel, but Sergei was too agitated.

'I'm not ready to go back,' he said. 'Tell the driver we're going to one of those special clubs . . . the ones that people talk about – you know, the ones with the homosexuals.'

The driver dropped them on Mulackstrasse in the Mitte district. Music from the gay cabarets spilled into the street. Inside, in the twilight of the club, heavily mascaraed, rouged transvestites in short skirts and white aprons, with pink ribbons in their wigs, circulated with trays, waiting on tables. Yesenin swilled champagne and vodka and leered at the acts on stage. He was drunk and unruly, noisily enthusiastic.

'When are they going to bugger each other?' he shouted in Russian.

When Graf Heinrich Kessler, sitting at a neighbouring table, peered at him, Yesenin jumped to his feet.

'Tell that fucking queer to stop ogling me! Tell him to fuck off or I'll smash his fucking face!'

He had an appointment for breakfast with Maxim Gorky. Gorky had been the teenage Yesenin's hero; he and Anna had cheered him when he gave a speech at Sytin's publishing house before the war. Gorky's courage in opposing tsarist repression had earned him prison and exile and would eventually see him sanctified as the Grand Old Man of Bolshevik literature.

Sergei was bleary eyed. His thoughts were slow. Gorky found him irritating. He would write dismissively of the young drunkard and his dancer wife.

> Yesenin seemed uneasy, alarmed, unfriendly towards people. It was abundantly evident that he was a drinker. His eyelids were swollen, the whites of his eyes inflamed. The skin on his face and neck was grey and faded, like that of a man who is seldom in the open air and sleeps badly. His gaze slid over people's faces, at times challenging and disdainful, then suddenly embarrassed and mistrustful. His hands were restless, endlessly drumming on the table. There was a haunted, hunted look about him – like a man who has forgotten some crucial, life-changing secret and cannot even remember that he has forgotten.

Gorky's presence in Berlin was an anomaly. In the years after 1917, it was not only irreconcilable opponents of the revolution who went to live abroad, but many who tentatively supported it. Gorky had reservations about the ruthlessness of Lenin's methods, but maintained cordial relations with the Kremlin. In Berlin, he and Alexei Tolstoy, the writer of children's stories and science fiction books, edited a pro-Bolshevik magazine. Both of them would later return to Stalin's USSR and a hero's welcome. Tolstoy would be known as the 'comrade-count'; Gorky would preside over the imposition of socialist realism in all branches of literature.

Sergei and Isadora were introduced to Tolstoy's wife, the poetess Natalia Krandievskaya. When Isadora saw the couple's five-year-old son, she fell to her knees. She caressed the boy. Tears appeared in her eyes. When she walked away, unseeing and lost in grief, Natalia understood the reason.

'She is a figure from a tragedy of Sophocles,' she said to Sergei. 'Her son was the same age. How can you not pity a woman whom the gods torture for their sport?'

Natalia and Alexei Tolstoy invited them to dinner. Gorky was a guest. His young mistress, Moura Budberg, acted as interpreter.

Buoyed by her stage success and happy to be in Berlin, Isadora was voluble. She told them how Sergei had marvelled at the wealth and luxury of the West, 'like a young boy in a magic sweetshop'. Every day, he would insist on the hotel's beauty spa giving him a shampoo and private bath, with eau de cologne, powder and perfume. She had set up an expense account for him at Berlin's best tailor and was amazed to discover that he had ordered more clothes than any one person could wear in a lifetime.

'But he's such a child,' she said. 'And he has never had anything in his life. I couldn't bear to chide him.'

Isadora's stories were told from elation and affection. Sergei listened to Moura's translations and said nothing.

Later in the meal, he told his own stories.

'My wife is famous,' he said. 'The toast of all Germany. I, on the other hand, just sit here and do nothing. I married her for her fame, of course; but did you know why she married me? She married me for this—'

He looked around the table and made the sign of copulation.

By the end of the meal, when much wine had been consumed,

it was suggested – perhaps by Isadora – that Isadora should dance for them. A gramophone was cranked and she obliged.

Midnight brought the extremes of emotion that Russian parties engender. Pledges of eternal friendship were followed by an argument that no one quite remembered beginning. It ended with Yesenin grabbing the wine glasses and smashing them against the wall.

Maxim Gorky and Moura Budberg

Gorky and Moura discussed the events of the evening. Moura thought Yesenin and Isadora were ill-assorted. The age gap of nearly twenty years was too apparent; Isadora's undisguised greed for a last, great romance in her life was pathetic.

Gorky smiled. He was twenty-three years older than Moura and he knew she was not impartial to the charms of young men. He asked her what she thought of Yesenin.

'He is a brute,' she said. 'He treats his wife abominably, yet she makes excuses for him. It seems abhorrent, but I can understand it. Yesenin is wild and out of control; he is a Russian peasant, coarse and violent. But he has another side to him that is vulnerable and very beautiful. He has the soul of a poet; he feels everything so deeply and suffers so much from the sensitivity of his nature that it is hard not to love him ... at least, it must be hard for Isadora not to love him.'

Gorky remembered the dinner with unease.

This famous woman, Isadora Duncan, sitting next to the boyish Ryazan poet, was the embodiment of everything Yesenin did not need. She ate copiously and drank too much. Then she danced. Ageing, grown heavy and with a red, ugly face, she wheeled and writhed in the cramped room, a meaningless smile frozen on her lips. While she danced, Yesenin sat at the table, drinking wine and frowning as he looked at her out of the corner of his eye. One could feel that he regarded his wife as a nightmare that had become so familiar it was no longer frightening, but which oppressed him nonetheless.

Isadora and Sergei in 1922

CHAPTER 30

Isadora's next performances were scheduled for Paris. The French authorities were wary. News of Yesenin's exploits in Berlin and Isadora's Soviet propagandising led to questions at the highest level. The Foreign Ministry delayed their visas, then issued them only on condition that neither must engage in any political activity. Fear of the socialist menace was acute.

Arriving in Paris, they went to the house on the Rue de la Pompe, between the Bois de Boulogne and Trocadéro in the west of the city. Isadora was attached to the French capital by memories of love and death. Now she had to deal with her mother's estate and decide what to do with the house. For the first part of their stay, she would be occupied and Sergei would be dangerously idle.

Paris was crowded with Russians. They had colonised the streets around the Orthodox cathedral on the Rue Daru and taken over the western suburb of Boulogne-Billancourt. The workforce of the Renault factories at Billancourt and the Ile Seguin spoke with the accents of the East.

Emigration was a leveller. Princes and tsarist generals swept streets, waited on tables and drove taxis. The acrimony that had riven Russian society at home bubbled and boiled in the pressure cooker of Paris. Neighbours mistrusted neighbours.

Everyone feared the hand of Moscow. Rumours of Red agents carrying out murders and kidnaps circulated constantly.

Sergei frequented Russian bookshops and Russian bars, ate and drank on Isadora's account. At a restaurant late in the evening, he was served by two former guardsmen of the tsarist army. He baited them.

'You're the aristocrats, you sons-of-bitches, but now you're serving me, a Russian peasant. Well, get used to it! And ask me nicely for a tip!'

The man who reviled the Bolsheviks in his poetry and once kowtowed to the tsarina, delighted in playing the Red card, waving the socialist banner in a charade of provocation.

The waiters were waiting when he emerged into the night. They followed him for three blocks until the street darkened. They removed his jacket, his shoes and his shirt and beat him with their fists. They took his wallet and left him lying in the gutter.

Isadora settled the probate on her mother's estate and put the house up for sale. She gave her first two performances and received respectable reviews. She and Sergei were public figures, invited to social events in the French and Russian communities.

They were taken to dinner with the poet Dmitry Merezhkovsky and his poet wife, Zinaida Gippius. These were the doyens of Russian Paris, Petersburg aristocrats who had shone in the tsarist world and were excoriated in the Bolsheviks'. Sergei had not seen them since 1916, when he was a young peasant poet ingratiating himself in the Petrograd salons.

Sergei's brawl with the tsarist officers had been reported

in *Le Figaro* and Merezhkovsky had read it. He proffered an indolent hand.

'So how fares the workers' paradise?' he asked in a drawl of exaggerated boredom.

Sergei leapt to the defence of the Soviet state. Merezhkovsky stiffened.

'The whole question,' Merezhkovsky said, 'of Russia's existence as such – and it is *non*-existent at the moment, as far as I am concerned – depends on Europe's recognising at last the true nature of Bolshevism. Europe has to open its eyes to the fact that Bolshevism uses the socialist banner only as a camouflage; that it is a global threat, not just a local Russian disease . . . There is not a trace in Russia of either socialism or even the much-vaunted dictatorship of the proletariat. In my view, there is a dictatorship of just two men – Lenin and Trotsky.'

Sergei laughed. Merezhkovsky, used to being treated with more respect, turned away. Yesenin was marked for future reckoning.

Zinaida Gippius (left) and Dmitry Merezhkovsky (right)

Sergei called Lola into his room. She found him in bed.

'I'm naked beneath the sheets,' he said.

'You shouldn't be talking like that.'

'Aren't you even tempted?'

'That's beside the point.' Lola fastened the top button of her blouse. 'You tired of me long ago. And, anyway, Isadora is getting worried. She keeps coming into my room without knocking. And she's been asking about you and Jeanne, the maid.'

Sergei laughed.

'It's true I've been idle – and you know what they say about idle hands. But I've turned into an Oblomov. I don't do anything. I haven't written a line of poetry for weeks.'

'Why are you telling me this, Seryozha? I'm not your wife. It's Isadora you should be telling.'

'What's the point? She understands nothing. She wouldn't even know who Oblomov is. Or how a man can spend five-hundred pages deciding if he should get out of bed. How can she understand the centuries of Russian entropy that weigh on us and make us incapable of deciding or doing? That's what I am battling against!'

'Then you should do something about it, Seryozha, instead of just lying there and talking. Act rationally for a change!'

'Ha!' he said with a flourish. 'I've written a letter to the newspapers. Let me read it to you:

I am a Russian poet and your French newspapers report that I drink. This is true. I drink because of an all-consuming melancholy that has come over me since I arrived here in the West.

To us, in Moscow, it seemed that Europe was the greatest forum for the appreciation of our ideas about poetry, but now I see this is nonsense and I say, My God! what a rich and beautiful country Russia is! There has never been such a country and there never will be.

It may be true that in the West everything is better, bigger, grander. Yet I do not want this. Everything here oppresses me.

The trees are all clipped, there's nowhere for birds to hide; the streets are all scrubbed, there's nowhere you can spit.

And what a realm of philistinism, bordering on idiocy! Apart from the foxtrot, the West has nothing. People gorge themselves and drink, and then the foxtrot once more. Money is king. No one gives a damn for art. Such vileness, such spiritual poverty make one feel like vomiting.

Even if we Russians are poor, even if we do have famine and cold and cannibalism, yet we also have a soul, which people here hire out to others as something unwanted. Even if we are Asiatics, even if we are foul-smelling and scratch our backsides in public, yet we do not stink as much as it stinks here. The only thing that can save the West is an invasion of barbarians such as ourselves. Russia should prepare itself for an invasion of Europe!

'I want to send this to *Le Figaro*,' he said. 'Only I can't speak French. But you do, Lolichka. Would you translate it for me and get it published?'

Lola laughed.

'You *are* mad! The idea that a newspaper would print something as rabid as that! And that's without mentioning the harm it would do to Isadora. And the harm it would do to you. You should be more circumspect. You keep making all these political scandals. And now you're picking fights with Whites and Reds and goodness knows who else . . .'

Sergei beckoned her to him. He put his arm around her neck and pulled her close.

'I will tell you a secret, Lola. Something very few people know. We no longer need to worry about the Bolsheviks.' He adopted a conspiratorial whisper. 'Lenin is dead, you know. He's been dead for a year, but they can't let the news get out or Bolshevism would collapse in an hour.'

'How could they conceal such news?' Lola said. 'It would be known in no time.'

'Well, they have done. Only a few trusted people know the truth. Once in a great while, if someone insists, the doctors let him in just for a minute and show him that Lenin is asleep. But he isn't asleep! He's embalmed! Dead! Marvellously embalmed. German specialists did it; it took them weeks. In the meantime, they keep putting out bulletins saying Lenin is poorly or Lenin is feeling better. Haven't you noticed it? Haven't you noticed how few people are admitted to the Kremlin? That there are no interviews?'

Yesenin appeared deadly serious. 'Only, mind you remember – if you squeal one word about this, you will not live. There are ways and means. We have spies everywhere.'

Yesenin sat with a satisfied, secretive smile. Lola thought he looked slightly insane.

Instead of Yesenin's letter, it was one from Merezhkovsky that appeared; and not in *Le Figaro*, but in the Parisian evening paper, *L'Éclair*.

From Monsieur Dimitri Merejkovski, poet:

Sirs,

One of our so-called Soviet poets has been making himself heard in France. Sergei Yesenin is a noisy young man, who has already found himself well served by the defenders of the true Russia, ending up shoeless and shirtless in a Parisian gutter. But before the reader evince pity for this person, he would be well advised to know that Yesenin is a drunken brawler and a wife-beater, whose

alleged Bolshevism takes the form of perpetual inebriation
and scandal. He has been known to smash crockery
and foment riots in honour of his socialist credentials.
Meanwhile, his faithful Isadora, regularly beaten black
and blue by her young husband, continues to deploy her
failing legs to rouse the Parisian public with something
resembling dancing, together with a hefty helping of crude
socialist propaganda. From the lofty stage of the Trocadéro,
and despite the French government's interdiction, she
invites Frenchmen and women to place their hands on
their chests while repeating after her, 'Vladimir Ilyich
Lenin is an angel.'

Isadora was furious. She, too, wrote to *L'Éclair*.

Sirs,
　　Sergei Yesenin and I wish to protest against the
slanderous lies of Mr Dmitry Merezhkovsky, published in
your newspaper.
　　Mr Merezhkovsky says that I am beaten by my 'young
husband'. This is a lie. Mr Merezhkovsky is fortunate that
he is protected by his great age, for otherwise Yesenin
would come and make him eat those words.
　　Mr Merezhkovsky alleges that during a performance at
the Trocadéro, I called Lenin an angel. Again he is wrong.
I did not speak of Lenin. It was Yesenin that I called an
angel and I call him that now, for Yesenin is the man
I love.
　　Yesenin is a writer of genius, Russia's greatest poet
since the death of Alexander Blok. This is the man
that Mr Merezhkovsky seeks to stigmatise by calling a
'drunken muzhik'.
　　I quite understand that Mr Merezhkovsky finds it hard

to live in the proximity of such beings, for talent is always resentful of genius.

I wish Mr Merezhkovsky continuing peace in his bourgeois old age and a respectable funeral with black plumes and plenty of hired mourners in black gloves.

As for myself, I should prefer to be burned at the stake in Moscow, while thousands of children in red tunics dance around me singing the 'Internationale'.

Yours,

Isadora Duncan

Isadora and Sergei in Paris

Yesenin overcame his writer's block. He began work on a poem that would address the criticism levelled against him. Yes, he drank; yes, he brawled; yes, he misbehaved. But it was the act of a poet sacrificing his personal happiness, his life, in the cause of his art. He thought he might give it the title, 'A Hooligan's Plea for Forgiveness':

One joy alone is left to me
And that's my dirty, quarrelsome fame.
I stick my fingers in my mouth

And whistle out my scandalous name.
I laugh at what I've lost,
For life brings legion losses.
I blush to think I once believed in God,
And now I long for His bitter crosses.
Oh, you endless, golden, Russian land,
Our life must end in fog and night.
You know I played the brawler's hand
So in my verse I might burn more bright.
The poet's gift – to love, to scorch, to harry –
Weighs down my heart with its cursed load.
On earth I strove in vain to marry
A lucent rose and a vile black toad.
So what if I fall, my dreams untold?
So what if the devil makes my hopes congeal?
Still somewhere in my deepest soul
I know the angels set their seal.
For all this joyful pain and torment,
For all this anguish and all the love,
I ask of you whose time, like mine, is spent
To pray for me to saints and stars above,
For all the weight of all my sins,
For my loss of faith in the power of grace,
That I might die beneath the icons,
And Holy Russia caress my face.

He asked Lola to translate the poem for Isadora. He wanted her to understand. He had hurt those close to him, brought shame upon himself.

The poem didn't minimise the darkness in his soul.

But its prayer was clear: that the beauty of the poetry he

created from the ugliness of his life might count for something on the day when souls are judged.

There was something else, something he didn't speak about. He was losing confidence in the power of his gift. The poems no longer flowed.

He had sacrificed happiness, love and affection for the sake of poetry, but poetry was beginning to leave him.

They sailed from Le Havre on the SS *Paris*. Sergei wrote that the ship's dining room alone was larger than Moscow's Bolshoi Theatre.

Arriving in America, they found their reputation had arrived before them. The Red dancer and the Red poet were put in quarantine, like dogs with a virus, denied permission to disembark until they could be interrogated by the US immigration authorities.

Under the headline, 'Isadora Duncan held at Ellis Island' the *New York Tribune* wrote:

America has a habit of putting her worst foot forward when an alien or a citizen arrives at her shore. She knew not why she had been detained and neither did the immigration officials, apparently. Painful as the experience was to Miss Duncan, it can hardly have brought tears to the eyes of her press agent.

Isadora and Yesenin revelled. They had a photograph taken, pointing to the Statue of Liberty with sceptical smiles on their faces. The newspapers published it, with a quote from Isadora:

'"This is the American goddess of liberty," said Miss Duncan yesterday. "In her name, they have detained us on the Island of Tears."'

The publicity delighted Isadora's manager, Sol Hurok. The clumsiness of the Immigration Authority bolstered her invective against America. Her trophy husband was a poke in the eye for a country that had condemned her amorality and disrespected her art. When the press reports were delivered, Sergei made Lola translate them. The *New York Herald* wrote:

> Miss Duncan's husband is a superblond young Russian poet. Sergei Yesenin, who is of athletic build, broad-shouldered and slim-waisted, spoke to Isadora chiefly through an interpreter. Unable to understand English, he hung over his wife and smiled approval at everything she said. With her left arm thrown gracefully round his neck, she patted his boyish face and told him in French to be 'tranquil'. Drawing her husband's curly head down on her shoulder, Miss Duncan said he was the greatest Russian poet since Pushkin. The young Yesenin, though down as 27 years old on the ship's manifest, does not look more than 17. Miss Duncan dusted the powder from the poet's hair before the photographers posed them together. Both appeared to be genuinely in love and took no pains to conceal their mutual adoration.

Sergei liked the descriptions of his physique. He got Lola to repeat the report in the *New York World*:

Mme Duncan's husband is a boyish chap. He looks as if he might be an excellent half-back for any football team. About 5 feet 10 inches, with a blond clean-cut head set on a pair of broad shoulders, with narrow hips and feet that might do a hundred yards in about ten seconds. Mr Yesenin grinned like a sophomore when he was asked to pose with his arm around his wife. Mme Duncan kissed him for a picture. Her husband smiled and smoked an American cigarette with critical inhalations. His press notices call him melancholy, but he seems the most cheerful Bolshevist that ever crossed the Atlantic.

They were interrogated by an official from the Immigration Department, sternly moustached, with a regulation Homberg and mackintosh. His first words were, 'You've got to go back.' Isadora charmed him.

'I am not a communist,' she said. 'I am simply a woman in love. Call me a mystic, but I know that my soul ascended into the world where souls meet, and there I met the soul of my beautiful Serge. We fell in love in the world of souls, so when we met in the flesh we loved again and were married. Not only was it a union of love, it was also a marriage that united Russia and the United States.'

The man in the mackintosh phoned his boss. Assistant Commissioner for Immigration H.R. Landis told him to let them go.

Released by immigration officials

The press followed them on the ferry from Ellis Island to Manhattan. Disembarking at Battery Park, Isadora waved away the taxicabs and beckoned Sergei to follow her. In red leather boots and Russian karakul hat, with red hair and cape flying, accompanied by crowds of curious New Yorkers, she marched up Broadway and Fifth Avenue until they reached the Waldorf-Astoria.

It was exhilarating. The world was paying attention and everything seemed possible. Isadora would win over her critics. Sergei would be acclaimed in America. Together, they would use their fame to change the world. They issued a statement.

We come to America with only one idea, to tell the world of the Russian conscience and to work for the rapprochement of our two great countries. No politics, no propaganda. There are only two countries that matter, and we believe the soul of

Russia and the soul of America can understand each other. On the journey here, we crossed all of Europe and found nothing but museums, death and disillusionment. America – our last, but our greatest hope! We extend our greetings and our thanks to the American people!

They were world celebrities, calling for peace. They discussed how they might use their status to make people listen. Sergei suggested a happening, the sort of scandalous performance art that the Imagists were good at. Isadora said they should hold it in their bed. They would invite journalists to their room in the Waldorf and be interviewed about their message for the world. They would say they were naked beneath the bedclothes. The media frenzy would create a storm of publicity.

Sol Hurok, the impresario behind Isadora's tour, was astute, of Russian origin himself. He understood Yesenin's Slavic elation and he would witness its collapse.

Yesenin responded to the capitalist world like a child, a spirited, unstable child of poverty who has been pushed into a monstrous toyshop and told he can do what he likes. He could not get enough at first of beautiful clothes, beautiful luggage, shaving lotions, hair tonics, luxurious masculine accessories. Or liquor. Or women. And then, surfeited, guilty, his inner hunger still unsatisfied by this superficial banquet, he became unruly and downright destructive.

Sol Hurok

Hurok was paraphrasing Mikhail Lermontov's novel, *A Hero of Our Time*, with its ambiguous anti-hero Pechorin.

> People have been surfeited with sweetmeats, and their digestion has been ruined . . . Pechorin was open to both good and evil; no one caressed him and he grew vindictive. He was prepared to love the world; no one understood him and he learned to hate.

Yesenin himself compared his travels to those of Pushkin's Yevgeny Onegin, wandering the globe in an attempt to escape the anguish of lost happiness, to dull his guilt and regret.

CHAPTER 31

The bed-in never happened. They were under surveillance, followed by men in mackintoshes. Sol Hurok didn't want his clients deported.

Sergei decided not to call his poem 'A Hooligan's Plea for Forgiveness'. Forgiveness is hard when the offence continues.

And, just like Onegin, his travels failed to bring him peace.

Under surveillance in New York

The publicity from her detention on Ellis Island filled the theatres. Three thousand people came to Carnegie Hall for Duncan's first appearance, an all Tchaikovsky programme with music from his Symphonie 'Pathétique' and *Marche Slave*.

Isadora danced with a red scarf round her neck, a welcome-home present from Mary Desti that she treasured both for its elegance and for its colour.

The show went well. Isadora waved to quiet the applause. She was under instructions from the Immigration Department not to engage in political activities, but the opportunity was too good.

'This is red!' she proclaimed, waving her scarf above her head. 'And so am I! It is the colour of life and vigour! You once were wild in America. Don't let them tame you!'

Sol Hurok took her in a limousine from Carnegie Hall to a reception at the Plaza Hotel. Isadora was jubilant. She spent the three-block journey persuading Hurok to book more dates in bigger halls in every state. Sergei sat in silence.

At the reception, Isadora was surrounded by well-wishers. Mary Desti, at her elbow, shared in the adulation. Sergei felt ignored. He had a drink. He was being slighted. He had another. As Isadora was making a speech of thanks, he crumpled to the floor, knocking over a table laden with glasses.

Isadora's second Carnegie Hall appearance, four days later, was an all-Wagner programme. The critics thought it 'less heroic' than her first.

Next she gave what was billed as a 'Classical Programme' and received tepid notices.

For her fourth appearance, the Hall was no longer full. The shock value of the Red Dancer seemed to have faded.

'Thank God the critics don't like me!' she told a bemused

audience. 'If they did, I should feel I was hopeless. They like the bogus dancers who imitate me. But I give you something from the heart. I bring you something real!'

There was polite applause.

'You all should read Maxim Gorky, the great Soviet writer. He says there are three kinds of people – the Black, the Red and the Grey. The Black are the tyrants, like the former Kaiser and the former tsar, who bring terror and suffering. The Red are those who rejoice in freedom, in the untrammelled progress of the soul. The Grey, I am sorry to say, are people like you – lukewarm, half-hearted and afraid. Neither hot nor cold; afraid to take risks, afraid stand up for anything!'

There was a murmur of discontent and some boos.

'Don't boo!' Isadora replied. 'Listen to what I am saying! America needs my dancing. The Americans are Grey. Children here are apathetic, nervous. I know the American nervous child, for I was one myself. But then I discovered idealism and belief and commitment. Bring my husband up here!'

There was a pause as people stood aside to let Yesenin on to the stage.

'Look at him!' Isadora shouted. 'Look at this beautiful boy. He is a poet and a Bolshevik – and he is my husband! Serge Yesenin is to Russia what Walt Whitman once was to America – the symbol of faith and beauty; of genius and passion.'

There was discontent in the hall. The booing was noisier.

'No! I said don't boo!' Isadora was struggling to make herself heard. 'Reach out your hand! Why will America not reach out its hand to Russia as I have reached out my hand to this beautiful boy!'

The moment hung between sympathy and indignation. Then a deep voice from the back of the stalls yelled, 'Judas! You're a traitor to your country!' and the hall erupted in an outpouring of anger.

Sergei didn't mind the boos or the insults. They meant people were taking notice of him. It was the neglect and having to live in Isadora's shadow that hurt him.

He wrote to a friend, the poet Vsevolod Rozhdestvensky.

You ask what I am doing and seeing abroad. Nothing except bars and streets. I don't even remember people's faces. I see some mug smiling at me, but I've no idea who it is or what he wants. New York is so cramped and dark. You can't even see the sky. People are rushing about the whole time, but nobody cares a fig for you. That really hurt me.

I saw a newspaper-seller on the corner and my face was in every paper. I thought, 'There's fame for you!' So I bought a dozen copies and rushed home thinking, 'I must send this to so-and-so and what's-his-name.' But when I got someone to translate the words beneath my picture, it said, 'Sergei Yesenin, the Russian peasant, husband of the famous, incomparable, enchanting dancer, Isadora Duncan, whose immortal talent etc. etc.' I was so upset that I tore the newspapers to shreds and went out and got drunk. I just sat there and drank and drank and started crying. I wanted to go home *so much*.

The *New York Times* acknowledged Isadora's influence on the world of dance. It was less complimentary about her political views.

An article headlined 'Incorrigibly Dramatic Dancing' asked:

> How does it happen that one untrained American woman has been able to inspire sculptors and painters, famous actors and technically trained dancers to accept as authentic and to champion a virtual amateur? Is she yet a prophet without honor in her own country? She remains a sphinx whose riddle remains unanswered.

Sol Hurok understood that America in 1922 was the wrong place for Isadora's socialism.

> The wave of reaction to the war, to Wilson, to liberalism was rolling up in a fearful tide. It was a year when Red was the colour of all evil, and to call a man a Bolshevik was to damn his eternal soul as well as send his earthly body to jail. Suspicion and mistrust of the Soviet Union are a force to be reckoned with in this country. In 1922 it was more than suspicion; it was sheer, unreasoning terror.

Things came to a head in Boston. At Symphony Hall, Isadora danced the same Tchaikovsky and Wagner programmes that she had given in New York. The reaction was scathing.

'Isadora Duncan in Flaming Scarf says She's a Red. Many

Spectators Leave Performance Shocked at her Undress,' head-lined the *Boston Globe*.

Angered by the audience's antipathy, Isadora had gone out of her way to provoke them. She waved her red scarf and harangued them for their philistinism.

'You grey people are like the walls of this hall. Look at those statues overhead! They are not real. Knock them down! They are not the statues of real Greek gods. Life is not real here! I cannot dance here!'

Someone in the audience shouted, 'So go back to Russia, then!'

'I have given my hand to Russia!' Isadora replied. 'And I tell you to do the same! I tell you to love Russia, for Russia has everything that America lacks. The day when Russia and America understand each other will mark the dawn of a new epoch for humanity!'

In a parting jibe at New England prudery, she had pulled down her tunic and bared one of her breasts.

'This – this is beauty!' she yelled. 'Take a good look, for there is no other beauty in this city!'

Boston's mayor saw votes in banishing the lewd dancer.

'This city has seen the last of Isadora Duncan, if Mayor Curley lives up to his present intentions,' wrote the *Boston*

Globe. 'Aroused by the widespread criticism of her appearance in Symphony Hall, the Mayor is determined that the dancer shall not appear again on any Boston stage. Boston is still talking of her two performances, at which many audience members, shocked by her scanty costumes and radical addresses, left the hall.'

The controversy thrust her back into the public eye. In the foyer of Boston's Copley-Plaza Hotel, Isadora was mobbed by reporters, whom she obliged with a statement.

'Nudity is truth,' she told the crowd. 'It is beauty. It is art. My body is the temple of my art. I expose it as a shrine for the worship of beauty. I wanted to free the Boston audience from the chains of Puritanism!'

The journalists recognised good copy when they heard it.

'They say I tore off my dress and waved it above my head. That is a lie. They say I mismanaged my garments. But why should I care what part of my body I reveal? Is not all of my body and all of my soul the instrument through which I express the message of inner beauty? You Puritans have an instinct for concealed lust. That is the disease that infects Puritans. They want to satisfy their baseness without admitting it. A nude body terrifies them. A suggestively clothed body delights them. They are afraid of the truth!'

Yesenin watched the melee from a table in the foyer. Prohibition was in its second year, but liquor was available to those with cash and Sergei had drunk his way through a pint of bourbon. He was smarting from being ignored.

'What were they saying about me?' he asked Lola. She said no one had been talking about him. It angered him even more.

'Don't lie!' he said. 'I know they were laughing at me in their stupid foreign language. Tell her' – he gestured to Isadora – 'tell her that I know she was saying things about me.'

Isadora protested that nobody was mocking him, that the Americans spoke well of him, that she always praised him. He rose unsteadily to his feet and grabbed her by the neck.

'Don't lie! Tell me the truth!'

Two security guards pulled him away. They took him to his room and locked the door.

Sol Hurok began to receive cancellation notices from venues that had booked Isadora. The events in Boston had alerted city authorities and alarmed theatre managers. The celebrity honeymoon had become the hooligan tour, a troubled odyssey through America, overshadowed by disappointment and mis-adventure. Mary Desti, who travelled with the couple, put the blame on Yesenin.

America did not receive him as he had hoped. And he held it as a grudge against Isadora, insulting her and her country on every occasion. It was during the tour in America that Sergei's madness began to show itself.

Yesenin was mistrustful by nature. He dreaded being patronised or regarded as an appendage to a famous wife. Her dancing spoke an international language; his poetry was untranslatable. He was jealous of his wife's fame and contemptuous of what he declared to be America's lack of culture.

They spent Christmas and New Year with Sol Hurok in New York. Without informing Hurok, Isadora told the press that she would dance on Christmas Eve in the Episcopal Church of St Mark's-in-the-Bouwerie and that she intended to deliver a sermon on 'The moralising effect of dancing on the human soul'. The announcement prompted complaints from parishioners and a statement by New York's Episcopal Bishop, William T. Manning.

> The Bishop has received letters of earnest protest from many parts of the country that a dancer whose exhibitions have aroused great criticism in many of our cities would appear and speak at St Mark's-in-the-Bouwerie. Bishop Manning wishes to state that the dancer referred to will not appear at St Mark's or professionally in any connection with the Church.

Hurok came to Isadora's defence. 'It's in the nature of a great artist to be temperamental,' he told the press. 'If they're not temperamental, I don't want them.' Asked about the falling attendances for Isadora's performances, he spread his hands. 'When people don't want to come, nothing will stop them! … If I would be in this business for business, I wouldn't be in this business!'

Hurok cared for all his artists. He liked Isadora and was sympathetic towards Yesenin. Remembering his own arrival from Russia twenty years earlier, he understood what the young poet was feeling. He tolerated the drinking, the rowdiness and the gracelessness of his behaviour.

> In Moscow, he was the great Yesenin, the young genius, the new Pushkin. Isadora bowed to his immortal gift. But in America, who had ever heard of Yesenin? It was Isadora, Isadora, Isadora. He missed the nectar of public adoration and was the more bitter because Isadora had become the more important of the two. He was violently jealous of her; so jealous that he denied she was an artist at all.

With the big cities shunning the Duncan tour, and needing to recoup his advance, Hurok booked her into the provinces.

Isadora and Sergei took the railroad to Indianapolis. Stepping on to the station platform, they found police waiting. When Isadora tried to speak to journalists, the lawmen hustled her away.

The city's mayor, Lew Shank, saw a chance for good publicity. He made a long statement that friendly correspondents printed verbatim:

> 'Isadora ain't fooling me any,' said Mayor Shank last evening. 'She talks about art. Huh! I've seen a lot of these twisters and I know as much about art as any person in America, but I never went to see these sorts of dances for the sake of art. No sir! I'll bet 90 per cent of the men who go to see these so-called classical dances pretend they think it's artistic just to fool their wives! Remove a woman's clothing and that's her modesty gone. You only have vulgarity left and that's what these men all go to see. No sir! These nude dancers don't get by me!'

Asked what he would do if the Boston scandal were to be repeated, Mayor Shank was resolute.

> If she goes to pulling off her clothes and throwing them up in the air, like as she is said to have done in Boston, then there's going to be someone getting a ride in a police wagon. Yes sir! If she pulls anything rough, we'll be right on her!

Isadora mocked the Mayor – 'Disgustingly vulgar! Not even in English! Thank God he is only Mayor of Indianapolis! The savages of darkest Africa have more artistic sense!' – but she didn't disrobe and she didn't make any speeches.

To celebrate the evening, Isadora, Sergei and the local press agent drove out to a roadhouse beyond the city limits, where they had supper and a generous quantity of Prohibition liquor. Yesenin picked a fight with some of the customers. Unable to tear him away, Isadora and the agent took the only taxi back to town. Sergei was left by the roadside in his dinner jacket in the pouring rain. He walked back through the darkness and crawled into the hotel with mud up to his ankles.

Yesenin was now swigging bootleg liquor that Isadora described as 'thick enough to kill an elephant'. His physical and mental health suffered. He knew that in the West he could attract attention only by creating scandals. The Imagists' escapades had been high-spirited, but Yesenin's outbursts in America were fuelled by desperation.

'Yes, I cause scandals,' he wrote to a Russian friend. 'I need to, in order to make myself known and be remembered. Do you think I could recite my verse to them? Verse for the Americans! I'd be a laughing stock. But when I pull a tablecloth with all the plates and dishes on to the floor, they can understand that.'

January 1923 was a low point for Isadora. Few bookings remained and those that did were not sold out. Her last scheduled performance, at Carnegie Hall on Monday, 15 January, should have been a triumphant farewell. According to the *New York Herald*, it was anything but.

The emotional Russophile dancer, who has had many unhappy experiences since she returned to America, made her farewell appearance before an audience that did not more than half fill the hall. Miss Duncan said that she and her poet husband, Sergei Yesenin, shortly will go back to Moscow, and she added that they will never return to America.

At the end of the month, Yesenin recited his poems to a gathering of Russian-Jewish poets in the Bronx, chaired by the Yiddish-language writer, Mani Leib. He drank moonshine, insulted his hosts with remarks bordering on the anti-Semitic and had to be held down by force.

His letter of apology, written to Leib the following morning, was full of remorse.

> Dear, good Mani!
> I beg for your indulgence. I plead for your pity. My reason has reawakened and makes me shed the bitterest of tears. I have fits that I am unable to control. It is the same illness that afflicted both Poe and Musset. Edgar Poe used to smash up whole houses when in the grip of it. I had another attack after I left your party. Today I lie crushed, morally and physically. A nurse kept watch over me all night. A doctor came and gave me a morphine injection. Good Mani, please believe that my soul is innocent. The sickness from which I suffer is an inherited one. My grandfather once was whipped in the stables and contracted the falling sickness. It has been transmitted to his grandson . . .

Yesenin had begun to suffer from manic outbursts – often directed to destructive ends – followed by fits and blackouts. He told friends that he had a form of epilepsy, an explanation that smacked of a desire to evince pity or, perhaps, admiration. Dostoevsky, among others, had imbued the disease with an aura of creative transcendence.

In early February, he told Sol Hurok he would throw himself from the viewing platform of New York's Woolworth Building, with the manuscript of his final poem in his hand. Mary Desti found him brandishing a revolver and threatening to kill someone – perhaps his wife, more likely himself.

CHAPTER 32

Isadora decided it was time to leave. Russia alone could save her husband.

When she went to take the boat fare from her bank account, the cashier told her it was empty. Isadora was profligate; she paid little attention to money, but this time it was Yesenin who had spent it. He had withdrawn every cent and could hardly say where it had gone.

Sol Hurok was angry on her behalf, but Isadora made excuses. Sergei was a child. He was naïve. He had never known what it was like to have money or how to use it.

She cabled Paris Singer, her former lover and father of her dead son, Patrick. Singer was living in Florida now, constructing the Spanish Revival buildings that would leave his mark on Palm Beach and Boca Raton. His affection for Isadora was undiminished. He wired the funds by return.

Their departure, from Hoboken on board the SS *George Washington*, was accompanied by a media scrum as lively as the one that greeted their arrival.

'Isadora and Russian Husband Vow Never to Return!' headlined the *New York Sun*. 'Better Freedom, Black Bread and Vodka in Russia, Says Dancer, than Life in Capitalistic USA!'

It was a most unfriendly farewell that the dancer gave reporters to transmit to the American public.

'No interview!' she snapped. And then: 'You newspapermen have wrecked my career. I've been constantly misrepresented. Instead of asking me about dancing, you keep asking me what I think of free love and common ownership of property. I'm going back to Russia. I'd rather live on black bread and vodka than have the best you've got in the United States. We've got freedom in Russia. You people don't know what that is!'

She appeared equally annoyed with the Prohibitionists and the bootleggers who, she said, had forced her to drink liquor of inferior quality that had nearly killed her.

'Pah! When I got up the other morning, I read a story in a newspaper that my beloved Serge' (here she patted the blond poet's head affectionately) 'had given me a black eye. It's a darned lie!'

America, said Miss Duncan, was founded by 'a bunch of bandits, adventurers and puritans – and now the bandits hold the upper hand ... Americans would do anything for money. They would sell their souls, their mothers or their fathers. America is no longer my country!'

Turning away, she said to her husband, 'Come, Serge. We shall go to our cabin. Someone is probably watching us even now.'

Paris Singer's money that had rescued Isadora financed Sergei's drinking. On board the *George Washington*, freed from the constraints of Prohibition, he was rarely sober. He was drunk when they arrived in Paris and drunk when Isadora checked them into the city's finest hotel. The manager of the Crillon, who came to welcome his guests, found them fractious and inebriated.

They had dinner in the Crillon's chic restaurant, Les Ambassadeurs. Mary Desti, who ate with them, sensed that Sergei was on a knife edge, quivering between exultation and fury.

> He recited some of his poems. He looked beautiful, like a young god from Olympus. But he was never still. He was bounding here and there in a sort of ecstasy, now throwing himself on his knees before Isadora, now laying his curly head in her lap like a tired child.

Sergei drank until it tipped him over the edge. He ran from the restaurant and did not return. Isadora, anxious and upset, confided in Mary.

'When he drinks, he becomes mad. Quite, quite mad. He gets to thinking that I am his greatest enemy. He can be violent ...'

Mary asked her why she put up with it. Isadora said, 'I can't explain. It would take much too long. There's something about it that I like, something deep, deep in my life ...'

It was after midnight when Sergei came back. Isadora was in their third-floor suite with Mary. He seized a chair and threw it through the glass door of the balcony on to the street below. He picked up a gilt-covered standard lamp and used it to smash windows and a mirror, then clambered on a dressing table and swung it at the chandelier.

The women ran into the corridor. They called the hotel's management, who called the police.

The gendarmes found Yesenin standing in the centre of the room, covered in glass from the mirror he had smashed. He was peering at his reflection in a fragment that had survived, weeping, laughing and talking to himself.

A night in a police cell failed to calm him. Doctor Jules Marcus, called to inject him with a sedative, diagnosed alcoholic psychosis and delirium tremens. He asked Isadora if she would sign the papers for her husband to be committed to a clinic. She agreed.

The police recognised the newsworthiness of the story. Reporters from the news agencies were tipped off.

'Isadora's Poet Stirs Riot in Paris Hotel' cabled a correspondent of the *New York Times*.

PARIS, Feb. 15, 1923

The unfettered soul of Serge Yesenin has proven too much for Isadora Duncan, who has had him committed to a psychiatric asylum.

The details are somewhat obscure, but it appears that at a fête given by Isadora in her suite at the Hotel Crillon last night in celebration of her return to France, Serge was seized with a sudden craving for self-expression. In the moments that followed, he broke several conventions and most of the furniture.

A hurry call was sent for gendarmes, and under this escort of honor, the acrobatic poet was removed to the local commissariat.

The International News Service splashed the headline, 'HE'S CRACKED! POET SMASHES UP FURNITURE. Dancer Declares Marriage Between Artists Impossible.'

PARIS, Feb. 16

Isadora Duncan, premiere danseuse, is through with marriage. The bloom is off the rose and Serge Yesenin, the dancer's unthrottled genius hubby has been confined, at her suggestion, after one final outburst of temperament that wrecked their suite at the Hotel Crillon and shocked its fashionable clientele.

Isadora, through a maze of excited gestures, unburdened herself to the International News Service.

'I never believed in marriage and now I believe in it less than ever,' she declared. 'Serge is a genius and marriage between artists is impossible.'

'Serge loves the ground I walk on,' she went on, rather defiantly. 'When he goes mad, he could kill me – he loves me so much. He is the loveliest boy in the world, but a victim of fate – like all geniuses, he's cracked. I've given up hope of ever curing him of this occasional madness. Yesterday, I saw an attack coming on and went to get a doctor. When I returned, the room was wrecked.'

The authorities, though, give a different story. They say that gendarmes summoned by guests at the hotel arrived too late to halt Serge in his abandonment to the primal urge, but in time to carry him off to the police station after he smashed most of the furniture, curtains and bric-a-brac in the Crillon suite. Here he was held overnight and has now been detained as 'suffering from epileptic attacks and alcohol poisoning.'

The Crillon asked Isadora to pay for the damage and leave. With Yesenin confined in the Bicêtre asylum, she and Mary Desti found rooms at the Hotel Réservoir in Versailles. She spent the day writing to the press.

To the *New York Herald* and the *Chicago Tribune*
PARIS, Feb. 17

Dear Sirs,

In the course of the last week there have appeared front-page articles in which my name has been used in large, disrespectful headlines and in which my character has been put before the public in an extremely false light.

You state that my husband, Sergei Alexandrovich Yesenin, having broken up everything in our apartment at the Hotel Crillon, threw articles of toilet at me. This is not true.

The crisis of madness which Yesenin was suffering was not due to alcohol alone, but results from his shocking experiences during the war, terrible privations and sufferings during the Revolution, and also blood poisoning caused by the drinking of Prohibition whiskey in America.

The exact truth is that Sergei Yesenin is the unfortunate victim of momentary fits of madness, during which he is no longer responsible for his actions.

I know it is the practice of American journalism to make a joke of grief and disaster, but truly this young poet, who from his eighteenth year has known only the horror of war, revolution and famine, is more deserving of tears than of laughter. Sergei Yesenin is a great poet and a beautiful spirit, whom all his friends adore. Alas, the Fate of Poets is marked with tragedy.

What has happened has left me grieving and desolate.

Isadora gave an interview to a Paris-based American correspondent, Lorimer Hammond, who concocted a maliciously mocking piece about her and her husband. She wrote despairingly to Hammond's editor:

Mr Hammond was pleased to make a huge joke of our tragedy. If this sort of journalism continues, we will have your reporters coming into every house of misfortune and grief and making a joke at the tears of the mourners.

No one will be safe. They will be opening the coffin lids and describing in humorous fashion the expressions on the faces of the dead.

Sergei's refuge was poetry, the art that justified his life. He clung to it. 'The Dark Man', the chronicle of his struggle with alcohol, conscience and psychosis, grew:

> My friend, my friend
> I'm ill; so very ill.
> Nor do I know
> Whence came this sickness.
> Either the wind whistles
> Over the desolate unpeopled field;
> Or, as September strips a copse,
> Alcohol strips my brain.
> The black man,

The black, black,
Black man
Sits by me on the bed all night,
And will not let me sleep.
The black man
Runs his fingers over a vile book,
And, leaning over me,
Like a sleepy monk over a corpse,
Reads a life
Of some drunken wretch,
Filling my heart with longing and despair.

'Listen!' he whispers,
'This book contains the key
To exquisite plans,
Seductive visions.
For this man lived out his life
In repulsive vice,
In deceptions and derision.
His December fields
Were dressed by snow,
Masked in the devil's white.
The winter storms would help him spin
His verse of artifice and sleight.
Sure he was handsome,
A poet, a boy;
But his gifts were facile,
His genius faded.
He went with a woman
Of forty, or more;
She called him her sweetheart,
He called her a whore.
He thought to be happy

You had to be smart,
That the world would love him
For the sheen of his art.
He didn't know
That lies and pretence
Are the things that leave
All human hearts rent.
In storms and tempests,
In life's sad routine,
When losses are heavy
And the soul is dejected,
The art of appearing blithe and serene
Is the one of the skills
Our poet perfected.'

I yelled back at the man in black:
'Do not dare to be so cruel!
It's none of your business to dig in such dirt.
Don't slander me behind my back;
The poet is not me that you take for a fool!'
The man in black
Stares in my face.
His blue eyes are clouded
With the grey sheen of vomit.
Calmly he tells me
I'm a thief, a disgrace,
Who's knifed a good friend
And slept soundly upon it.

My friend, my friend
I'm ill; so very ill.
Nor do I know
Whence came this sickness.

Either the wind whistles
Over the desolate unpeopled field;
Or, as September strips a copse,
Alcohol strips my brain.

The night is calm;
I am at the window.
The frost lies like balm
On the trees and the grass.
I'm expecting no one;
My heart is at rest;
My thoughts have been freed
From the sins of the past.
Then the bird of night stirs,
An ill-starred cry on frosty air.
From an unseen hoof, a sharp wooden note,
And the black man takes his place in my chair;
Lifts his top hat, doffs his coat.
'Listen to me!' he croaks in my face.
'I have never seen a man so base
Whose conscience plagues him as he sleeps.
Were you expecting me, or was it her,
Thirsting for your cynical, doggerel verse,
For your bleeding heart that makes her weep?
You poets make me laugh,
With your tales of sorrow and damnation
That lure the girls between your sheets
Then leave them panting in frustration.
Am I wrong? Have I forgotten?
Was there not once in some village or other
– Perhaps Ryazan; once I knew –
A shy young boy and his grandmother?
His hair was yellow, his eyes pale-blue . . .

What happened to that child?
Did he grow so evil and so wild?
Why did he throw away the heart
Of the woman he loved, who took his part?
She loved him; she was his happiness.
Yet he sacrificed her with all the rest.'

'Black man!' I curse my loathsome guest,
But recognise the truth of what he's said.
My throat is choked with wormwood and disgrace;
Angered, distressed, *I hurl my stick at his face* . . .
. . . the moon has died.
It's dawn. The dark blue sky
Of awful night.
Night and day and dreams are dashed.
I stand alone, no soul nearby.
Alone forever . . .
And the mirror smashed.

The French authorities declared Yesenin a danger to himself and to others. They agreed he could be released from custody, but only on condition that he leave the country.

Isadora booked them on the Paris Simplon-Orient-Express from the Gare de l'Est. Sergei was sedated, and she, Lola and Jeanne, the maid, took turns watching over him. The train sped south towards the Alps and the Simplon Tunnel. Emerging into Italian sunshine, Isadora squeezed his hand. In a day they would be in Venice, with the privacy and tranquillity that would restore his sanity.

Chapter 33

They checked into the Excelsior-Palace at the Lido di Venezia. The season was young and the hotel not busy. The staff were attentive; the air was warm. Isadora and Sergei had a room with a balcony overlooking the beach. Cooler evenings brought a refreshing end to the day and the desire to wake in the morning.

Excelsior-Palace Hotel

Sergei lay on a sun lounger under the hotel's beachside awning. Isadora made sure that he drank only lemonade and seltzer water. The place was calm. It eased his soul.

Sergei at the Venice Lido

He swam. The Adriatic restored him. Isadora found a bookshop with a selection of second-hand Russian paperbacks. When she showed them to Sergei, he laughed. They were children's stories, but he read them. She hid the newspapers and shielded him from other sources of anxiety. His appetite returned; they ate well.

There was some talk on the Lido about the *'danzatrice americana'* and the *'poeta russo'*, but the Italians gave them space. Sergei was surprised when a young man approached him.

'Scusi, signore. Mi dispiace disturbarla ...'

'*Russki!*' Sergei said. '*Tol'ko po-russki!*'

To his astonishment, the young man understood. He looked in his early twenties, slender, with a delicate face and a bearing that Sergei thought aristocratic.

'Yes, I know,' the young man said. 'I didn't want to disturb you, so do please say if you would rather I left you in peace.'

His Russian was fluent, the accent hard to pin down. It wasn't Italian and it wasn't English. There was something melodic about it.

'I understand you and Madame Duncan are spending some time in Venice.'

'How do you know about us?' Sergei was wary of being drawn into conversation.

'I have read the newspapers. I understand you are a Bolshevist . . .'

'I hate the Bolsheviks!' Sergei said sharply. 'If it's all that Red nonsense you want, you'll have to talk to Isadora. She'll be down in a moment. In fact, she rarely leaves me in peace . . .'

'I'm sorry to hear that.' The young man picked up on the nuance. 'But no, it isn't Madame Duncan I am interested in – it's you.'

Sergei looked at him. The boy was handsome. And he was interested in Sergei Yesenin, not Isadora Duncan.

'I asked if you were a Bolshevist for a reason,' the stranger was saying. 'An odd reason, I admit. I have just returned from fighting your armies – that is, the Bolshevik armies. I was a soldier in the 24th Polish Uhlans. I saw action at Radzymin and the Battle of Warsaw.'

He lifted up his shirt to show a sabre slash across his stomach. Sergei gave a whistle.

'It was the Reds who gave me this, Tukhachevsky's boys. But that's not what I want to talk to you about—'

Isadora called from the veranda, 'Seryozha! Come along – it's time for tea!'

Sergei stood up.

'I'm sorry; we'll have to talk later,' he said. 'You evidently know my name, so what is yours?'

'Władysław Moes,' said the young man with a slight bow. 'But everyone calls me Adzio.'

Władysław Moes

The following morning, Sergei returned from swimming and was drying himself when the young man from the previous day appeared.

'Forgive me,' he said. 'May I . . . ?'

He sat down beside Sergei on the sun lounger.

'I am an admirer of your poetry. Russian is not my native tongue, but I have a grasp of the language sufficient to appreciate the beauty of what you write. I understand you are on your way back to your homeland.'

'Yes,' Sergei said. 'You seem to know a lot about me, but you have told me nothing about yourself.'

'Well, I am Polish, as you know. My father is Count Juliusz Moes and my mother Countess Janina. Our estate is at Wierbka, fifty kilometres from Kattowitz. My father owns factories. But I am a poet . . .'

Sergei understood. He was used to young poets approaching him for advice.

'A poet's life is one of hardship,' he said. 'However great your talent, you will be forced to sell yourself if you want to succeed – I mean literally, sell yourself to people you despise, your soul and your body. The Muse can bring great rewards, but happiness is not among them.'

Adzio nodded.

'Thank you,' he said. 'I shall not forget your advice. But that is not what I wanted to talk to you about. I have come to Venice because something happened to me here. It is, in part, a literary matter, which is why I thought you might be able to help.'

Sergei gestured for him to continue.

'When I was last here, I was ten years old,' Adzio said. 'It was 1911 – a different time, a different world from the one we now inhabit, but it is forever in my memory. My mother was here, my sisters and my cousin, Janusz. He and I used to play on this beach.'

He waved an arm towards the deckchairs on the sand.

'I was considered a very beautiful child. Women admired me and kissed me when I walked along the promenade. Some of them sketched and painted me. But I remember, at the time, this all seemed inconsequential; it was just how things were. I was a pampered child. I had that childish negligence about the world.'

Sergei smiled. His own childhood was filled with such memories.

'What I do remember,' Adzio said, 'is that an older man was staying at our hotel. I can picture him quite clearly. He was German. His name was Thomas. I could see that he, too, admired me. When I came into the dining room in the evening he would be waiting, watching me from his table where he sat with his wife. It must have pleased me, because I remember showing off for him. I would parade across the floor in my favourite clothes, looking to see if he had noticed. I had a striped linen sailor suit and a red bow tie, with my favourite blue jacket with gold buttons.'

Adzio hesitated.

'The reason I remember him is that he kissed me. It was in the lift, as we were going up to our rooms . . .'

'Really?' Sergei said. 'You remember that – you remember him – all these years later, after all that has happened and all that has changed in the world?'

'Yes. I know it sounds odd. There was something . . .'

'Did you fuck him?' Sergei said. 'I mean, did you love him?'

'The answer to the first question is, No. As for the second, I am unsure. I felt something for him. And I am certain he loved me.'

'What happened to him?'

'I don't know,' Adzio said. 'There was cholera in Venice. People were dying from it. My mother took us away, but Thomas stayed behind. The last time I last saw him, he was sitting in a deckchair, right here on the beach.'

'And you're worried what became of him?'

'Worried? I don't know . . . Concerned, perhaps. How can I put it? I feel that without knowing, there will be a void I am unable to fill. I'm sure this sounds like nonsense and you have no idea what I am talking about . . .'

'I do know what you are talking about,' Sergei said. 'Many of us have that void ... Why did you think I might be able to help you?'

'Because you are a writer. My cousin Janusz says that Thomas was a writer; that he was going to write about Janusz and me playing – wrestling – here on the beach. I wondered if you might know who he is or what he wrote ...'

Sergei shook his head.

'Never mind,' Adzio said. 'I shall wait here in case he comes back. I feel like those primitive tribesmen who believe that if a white man photographs them, their soul will be imprisoned in his camera. If Thomas has captured my soul in his book, I want to see myself in its amber.'

Lola was fired the next day. Isadora gave little in the way of explanation. Lola was still hurting when she wrote about it a decade and a half later, now a wife and mother, living a different life in a different world.

I remember that the morning was hot, the hotel room stuffy. Yesenin announced he was going out for a walk. When Isadora said she would come with him, he said, 'I am going alone. I want to be alone.'

Isadora insisted on coming and Yesenin's eyes grew angry. He hated being dictated to. Isadora's love for him was tender, but it was smothering and devouring.

I turned to Isadora and said, 'Oh, do let him go out. It must be terrible being cooped up with us. Everyone wants to be alone sometimes.'

Isadora said, 'I won't let him go alone! You don't know him. He may run away. And – there are women ...'

Yesenin watched us with tightly compressed lips. We were conversing in English, but he needed no translation. Isadora saw he was determined and ran out on to the balcony. She was crying like a child, sobbing hysterically, muttering something about her love in between gulps.

We found Yesenin a couple of hours later, in the hotel garden with an empty champagne bottle. He lifted his eyes slowly. His face was grey. I had the sensation that at any moment he might go berserk.

'Those scum,' he said, waving an eloquent hand. 'Aristos, bourgeois – someone should throw them into the sea!'

The blue of his eyes was framed by reddened lids. He looked around warily, like a bull on the point of charging. He leaned forward. His neck seemed swollen.

Isadora and I led him away, supporting him between us. Yesenin was unsteady, muttering incoherent imprecations, but we got him upstairs to the room.

Isadora ordered two more bottles of champagne then took me aside and told me to ask the hotel doctor to put a strong sleeping potion in one of them. A waiter brought the two bottles and showed me discreetly which one contained the medicine. Yesenin took a tremendous swig and immediately grimaced.

'So that's your game, is it? You think I can't taste the stuff! Put me to sleep? Poison me?'

He got up heavily and lurched towards me, then slumped into a chair. Isadora, meanwhile, had been drinking from the other bottle. I was stunned by the change in her. She had gone from a middle-aged woman on the verge of hysterics to a carefree girl. The drink made her dreamy. She rambled on about her former lovers, about the strange fate that seemed to bring her only eccentric men, about the nicest way to commit suicide, then said, 'Oh, but I oughtn't to die without writing my biography. It's quite amazing – you could help me write it . . .'

Isadora's eyes began to droop. The last thing she said before falling asleep was, 'I don't think I shall commit suicide just yet; my legs are still very beautiful.'

Yesenin woke up. He paced around the room. He was restless, trying to change his clothes, or at least take off the white cotton pyjama-style outfit he had been wearing. His hands trembled and he struggled with a knot in the cord.

Jeanne, the maid, and I helped him dress. With joint effort, we got him into one of his beautiful linen suits. He sat down at the dresser and began to comb his hair. He was very vain and proud of his blond locks. Then he splashed himself generously with Isadora's perfume, covered his cheeks in powder and sat there contemplating the face that looked at him from the mirror.

It was impossible to tell what thoughts were swirling in his head. His deep-set eyes had turned a bleary grey; dark, heavy eyebrows, like wings; pale, dry skin and flaxen curls whose youthfulness seemed out of place on a visage so prematurely aged. The powder, which, in his drunken clumsiness, he had applied much too thickly, gave him the masklike air of a pantomime dame.

Moved by a sudden impulse, he took some of Isadora's lipstick and applied it in a red slash across his lips. It completed the picture. He looked half gigolo, half clown. He stood up and said, 'Well, I'm going.'

We discovered him much, much later. He was slumped in a deckchair on the beach, facing out towards the Lagoon. Sweat had smudged his make-up and left runnels in the powder on his cheeks. His eyes were closed; there was a fleeting expression of mockery and embarrassment on his face. His lips, improved by cosmetic artifice, were forming occasional words from the dreamlike logic of his half-sleeping brain. He looked like a living corpse.

Isadora asked him where he had been and with whom he had spent the day. He pretended not to understand. Lola was no longer there to translate; Isadora had sent her packing. She said it was because the girl's English was deficient, but Sergei knew the reason was jealousy.

Venice had failed to reconcile them; the last hope was Russia. They drove north in an open-topped car. It was cold, but Isadora refused to enter a closed vehicle. It conjured visions of her children struggling for breath in the water-filled cell of their automobile. And besides, she said, how marvellous to feel your hair swept by the wind, how dramatic the scarf that trails behind like a turbulent plume of red air!

They parted company. Isadora returned to Paris to finalise the sale of the house at Rue de la Pompe. Sergei, barred from French soil, went to stay with Kusikov in Berlin. The press followed them both, eager for the story of their separation.

Isadora repeated her belief that marriage between artists is impossible. Yesenin went further. In a drunken interview with the Berlin evening newspaper *Acht-Uhr-Abendblatt*, he was reported as saying, 'I'd rather be sent to Siberia than stay married to Isadora Duncan.'

Thin and pale and no despiser of alcohol, Sergei Yesenin gave way to a startling outburst of Russian frankness. He was distinctly unenthusiastic about the great Isadora.

'If she follows me to Moscow,' he exclaimed, 'I shall flee to Siberia. Russia is vast and I will always find a place where this terrible woman cannot reach me.'

It seems that even during their honeymoon they quarrelled incessantly.

'I married her for her money and the chance to travel. But I got no pleasure from it. America is a country that doesn't appreciate art. It is full of crass materialism. Americans think they are wonderful people because they are so rich, but give me poverty in Russia any day.'

As for Isadora, the young poet says he never wishes to see her again.

'She was never willing to let me be myself,' says Yesenin. 'She wanted always to dominate me. She was jealous and demanding; she wanted me to be her slave. She wore me out so much that I began to look as if I'd been raped. For the first time since my wedding day I feel a free man again, beholden to no one.'

Agitated and quite beside himself, his young Dorian-Gray-face darkens ominously.

From Paris, Isadora sent a plaintive telegram to Kusikov's address:

```
To: Kusikov, Alexander
Martin Luther Strasse 8, Berlin

Essential Yesenin write to newspapers
to refute interview stating he never
loved me but stayed with me for status.
Such an article shows him in bad light.
Wire news.

Isadora Duncan,
103 Rue de la Pompe, Paris
```

Yesenin wrote no letter. In a cycle of poems completed in Berlin, he adumbrated the depths of his disillusionment.

> In this woman I looked for happiness,
> But by accident I found my doom.
> I'd not realised that love's an infection,
> I'd not realised that love is the plague.

Yet he lingered. He told the world he was fleeing from Isadora, but sat in Berlin waiting for her. At a recital for Russian students, he staggered on to the stage with a glass of wine, splashed it in all directions, laughed, cursed the audience, resisted attempts to lead him away.

The journalist and writer Roman Gul sat with him afterwards.

> He was deathly pale, in a dinner jacket and patent leather shoes, his eyes staring out into drunken space, his elbows resting on a table amid the flowers and bottles. His once handsome face was sickly, deathly, with a hollow blue glow. Seen close up, his features were terrible, covered in violet powder. His golden hair and blue eyes were from another time, from a youthful face that had been left behind in the past. He took his wine and drained it in one draught, as if it were water. In everything – in the way he took it, the way he drank it then slammed down the glass – there was something doomed about him.

Gul took him back to Kusikov's. He felt there was no hope; and if there were, it was not in Berlin.

When Yesenin and I left at five in the morning, he walked as if perplexed, as if he were hurrying somewhere without himself knowing where to, or why.

He said, 'You know, I love nothing. Nothing at all.'

Then he corrected himself. 'Perhaps I love my children.'

He thought for a moment.

'And Zinaida, my one true wife ... My daughter, Tatiana, who's as beautiful as her beautiful mother ... Tatiana who stamps her foot and shouts, *My name is Yesenin!*'

He smiled and was silent.

'I need to be back in Russia,' he said. 'I need to be with the woman who loves me. I've spent too long rushing around trying to find something ... trying to escape from something.'

Isadora sold her house in Paris. She came to Berlin with plans for their future, determined to correct mistakes of the past. She was sorry for the things she had said. She wanted a fresh start and hoped Sergei did, too.

Sergei had resolved to tell her it was over, but the intensity of her hope checked him. He couldn't bring himself to say it.

Isadora took a room at the Hotel Adlon and asked him to join her. Sergei said he was fine at Kusikov's.

They met for dinner. Afterwards, when he hailed a cab, she climbed in with him and insisted on coming to the apartment. Kusikov served them drinks. Conversation was awkward. They skirted around intimacy, talked instead about politics and art.

Kusikov had read that the Bolsheviks, in their anti-religious fervour, had forbidden the use of the word 'God' in print.

In broken Russian, Isadora said, 'Bolsheviki right. No God. Old. Stupid.'

Yesenin replied as if talking to a child, '*Ekh, Isadora! Vyed' vse ot Boga. Poeziya, i dazhe tvoyi tantsy.*' – 'Oh, Isadora! Everything comes from God. All poetry, and even your dancing.'

'No, you're wrong!' Isadora said in English and turned to Kusikov. 'Please tell Sergei that there is no God. People invent gods for their consolation. There is nothing beyond what we know and see. All heaven and all hell are right here on earth. The only gods are Beauty and Love.' Raising her arm and pointing through the open door to the bedroom, she said, 'Please tell him that God is here!'

Yesenin looked and nodded. 'Sex . . . love . . . Yes. But it is for a moment. It lifts us and it lets us fall. However beautiful, can it really rescue us from all the rest?'

Kusikov struggled to translate.

'Like dance . . .' Yesenin was saying. 'Dance is with us and then it's gone. A dancer can never be great, because her art is gone the moment she dies—'

'No!' said Isadora. 'A great dancer gives people something they carry forever. She has changed them, though they may not know it.'

'But what about when those people are gone?' Sergei said. 'Dancers are like actors: one generation remembers them, the next reads about them and the third knows nothing.'

Isadora tried to speak, but there was cruelty in Yesenin and he was determined to express it.

'People may come and admire you, even cry. But after you are dead, no one will remember you. Within a few years all your fame will be gone – no more dance . . . no more Isadora!'

She burst into tears. Still he had not finished.

'Only poets live. I shall leave my poems behind me. Poems live, but you leave nothing!'

'It is men who leave nothing!' Isadora said through her tears. 'Women are the ones who recreate the world, who produce the children who become the future—'

'For fuck's sake!' Yesenin had lost control. 'Stop talking about your fucking children! They're dead! And you keep on using them as an excuse for every fucking thing that's wrong with your life.'

CHAPTER 34

The train journey from Berlin to Moscow passed in brooding silence. Both of them knew it was over. Neither of them knew why they were sitting in the same compartment. Isadora stared out of the window. Yesenin leaned over a sheaf of paper, shielding the letter he was writing to Kusikov.

Oh, Sandro, Sandro!

I am filled with such unbearable longing. I felt so foreign and so superfluous in the West, but now, as I remember Russia and think what awaits me there, I have no desire to return! I am a stranger abroad and an outcast in my own land.

I hate the condescending attitude of the Bolsheviks and the fawning reverence of our fellow writers towards them. I can't stand it. There's no point shouting for help. You may as well grab a knife and stick it to them on the highway.

Do you remember the old days, when we used to come to the Party bosses and they wouldn't even give us a chair to sit on? Back then, we used to laugh about it; but now, it makes me sick. I no longer know what revolution I can belong to. I am full of despondency.

History is living through a terrible epoch of the destruction of the individual. The socialism that is

emerging is not at all what I hoped for. It is a deliberate,
confining creed without glory and without dreams,
with no room for the living personality, no scope for the
imagination, for a person to build a bridge into the world
of the soul, for these bridges are hacked down and blown
up beneath our feet.

The only thing I cling to now – the only hope for
meaning in my life – is that Zinaida will take me back.
That I can rescue the happiness I so stupidly threw away.

He was about to seal the envelope when another thought came.
He added a postscript.

The problem is that I believe the words of Griboyedov.
'Where is happiness?' he asks, then answers his own
question. 'The only happiness is *where we are not.*'

The train sped eastwards, turning day to fitful night and back
to day. Sergei slept badly, woke often. The lights through the
window rose and fell, lulling him back to dreams. In them, he
saw Zinaida and she had not aged. She was the magnificent
woman he remembered, but always beyond his reach. He
would call to her on the far bank of a river, but she was oblivious. He would spot her in the window of a crowded restaurant,
knock on the glass and wave his arms, but she could not see
him. She was at a table with a companion – was it a man? Oh,
God! Let it not be a man! When he woke, he was burdened by
loss and self-disgust.

They pulled into Moscow's Belorussky station. Sergei had written to Zinaida to tell her when he was arriving and had spent the journey from Berlin hoping to see her on the platform.

There was no sign of her. Isadora had a welcoming party. Tutors and pupils from her Prechistenka Academy were crowding round, offering greetings and kisses. They looked in his direction then took Isadora by the arm and led her away.

The platform cleared. He was alone. The porters who loaded his trunks on to donkey carts were impatient. He told them to drive to Kusikov's old apartment on Afanasievsky Lane. Shershenevich was living there now. It was the only place he would find shelter.

Vadim Shershenevich was eager to hear at first-hand what he had read about in the newspapers, fascinated by the passion and scandal of his friend's noisy odyssey. They had a common past and shared fears for the future. The Bolsheviks had tightened their grip. Independent thought was barely tolerated. Russia was waiting for Lenin to die, anxious about what would come next.

When Yesenin spoke of his travels, Shershenevich found him petulant and aggrieved.

'God died and the tsar was murdered,' Sergei said. 'The old order went. I couldn't love the new one. I had to make my own decisions and I made bad ones. Sex, fame, scandals; poetry, drink, danger – it's all nonsense!'

'Then what's the solution?' Shershenevich asked. 'Man cannot live by wormwood.'

'Precisely,' Sergei said. 'The Japanese have a special knife, long, with a curved blade, and a smaller one, sharp and thin, like a stiletto. They cut open their stomach with the large knife and when the bowels fall out, they cut off the last gut with the little dagger . . .'

'Good God, Seryozha!' Shershenevich exclaimed. 'You're talking like an idiot. There's always hope. There's always something. Love . . .'

'I had love!' Sergei said. 'But I threw it away. I was my own Mephistopheles. That's what makes it so awful. I wrote to Zinaida, but she didn't reply.'

'I'm not surprised,' Shershenevich said. 'After the way you treated her. You've been away over a year. She's married. And things have changed. Zinaida's famous now. Meyerhold gives her the leading roles. She isn't just going to leave him just because you ask her to . . .'

'I think she is!' Sergei jumped to his feet. 'She married Meyerhold to get back at me. He's a good man, but he's boring. She can't be happy with him. She can't love him! I was cruel, I hurt her, but I was never dull. Women don't love good men – they love bastards, and I'm the greatest of all of them . . . I want to write to her, Vadim; but I'm scared. If she refuses, there will be nothing left for me.'

Vadim Shershenevich

Shershenevich heard Sergei prowling at night, already dressed when he rose, agitated at lunchtime, drunk by evening.

They avoided the subjects that tormented him. Shershenevich

talked instead about old friends, about Marienhof. Sergei seemed interested, perhaps open to a reconciliation.

Marienhof had married Anna Nikritina, Shershenevich said. She had rescued him from the striving, the yearning, the need to justify himself; he had found fulfilment through love. A look of jealousy flitted over Yesenin's face.

'I don't want to see him.'

They drank most days. Late in the evening, Sergei announced that he was going to Meyerhold's 'to rescue my wife and my children'.

Shershenevich restrained him, calmed him.

'I need to do something, though,' Yesenin said. 'I have so many things eating at me, so many fears that give me no rest. Only Zina can help me. Not knowing where she is or what she's doing, what she's thinking ... it's driving me crazy. I'm nearly an old man, Vadim. I need to do something before it's too late.'

Shershenevich laughed.

'That's nonsense, Seryozha! How old are you?'

'I'm twenty-seven; twenty-eight in October. Hamlet was dead long before then. And Romeo. And Chatterton ...'

Henry Wallis, The Death of Thomas Chatterton, 1856

Shershenevich said he should write a brief, sensible letter, explaining that he was back in Moscow, that he was sorry for the past and that he would like to see her to talk about the children.

He wrote, but Zinaida did not reply.

He left it a week, then rang Meyerhold's number.

Meyerhold answered; Sergei put the phone down.

The next time he rang, it was Zinaida who picked up.

Hearing her voice loosened emotions that he had kept in check; his eyes filled.

'Zinochka ... Zinochka, it's me ...'

He sensed – hoped – that she wavered before she hung up.

Shershenevich warned him not to knock at her door. He didn't listen.

'If she opens the door,' Sergei said, 'she can do one of three things. She can hug me. She can tell me to go away. Or she can call Meyerhold and say that I am harassing her. Only the last would mean there is no hope.'

He knocked. Zinaida answered. He struggled to decipher the look on her face.

Meyerhold called from inside the apartment, 'Who's at the door?'

She hesitated, then called back, 'No one. Just the block committee about next week's meeting.'

'She didn't tell Meyerhold it was me,' he said to Shershenevich. 'It *must* mean she's still thinking of me!'

Shershenevich was doubtful. Sergei insisted, desperate to believe.

Lenin died on 21 January 1924. Communism's patron saint was gone. Arthur Ransome, the British journalist whom Lola Kinel had introduced into Trotsky's entourage, was present when the Party leadership heard the news.

When Congress met this morning, Kalinin, who was hardly able to speak, announced Lenin's death in a few broken sentences. Almost everybody burst into tears. Tears were running down the faces of the members of the Presidium. The funeral march of the Revolutionaries was played by a weeping orchestra.

Lenin lay in the Hall of the Unions. Queues formed. For three days and three nights, two abreast and hurried forward at marching speed, people filed past his corpse.

The body of Lenin lay on a crimson catafalque guarded by his comrades. Stalin stood with arms folded, iron like his name. Bukharin, beside him, was a figure carved in wax. The hall filled with Communists. Floodlights for the kinematograph operators lit up the white faces of bearded peasants and leather-jacketed workmen. There was absolute silence: then funeral music, while soldiers stood at attention. I had the feeling that I was present at the founding of a new religion.

Behind the tears, a power struggle was building. The kinematograph footage that Arthur Ransome saw being shot shows corpse and mourners eerily lit; the staging is Wagnerian, and barely a frame goes by without the brooding figure of Josef

Stalin coming into view. He unloads the coffin from the train; stands guard over the bier; steps forward as chief pallbearer.

Stalin was not of the first rank, but he was in charge of the funeral arrangements and he gave himself the leading role. In the film, he looks like Lenin's anointed successor. Trotsky is glaringly absent. He didn't make it to the funeral, because Stalin lied to him about the date.

Zinaida paid little attention to the public drama. She had her own.

When she received Sergei's first letter, written from Berlin to tell her of his imminent arrival, she had recognised his handwriting on the envelope and her hands had trembled as she stuffed it into her handbag then glanced at her husband.

Meyerhold asked her to pass the butter, eyes on his newspaper. Such a relief that he hadn't noticed!

But surely he must read it in my face? She felt an inexplicable disappointment when he didn't.

Josef Stalin had done little in the revolutions of 1917. By 1924 he was rewriting history to magnify his role and belittle his rivals.

In the weeks after Lenin's death, the Bolshevik bosses battled for the leadership. Stalin controlled the Party's bureaucracy and he slipped his supporters into key posts. His years compiling the *Nomenklatura's* personnel files meant he knew the blemishes on everyone's record. He could blacken his opponents. Trotsky was attacked for his historical support of the Mensheviks; Zinoviev and Kamenev denounced for hesitating over the start of the October rising.

Debate gave way to hysteria. When Trotsky published a memoir suggesting that he and Lenin were the architects of the revolution, he was hounded out of his ministerial post. Deviation from Bolshevik orthodoxy had become a deadly sin, and the man who defined that orthodoxy was, increasingly, Josef Stalin.

Sergei running off to the West with his fat, stupid, ugly American bitch had undermined Zinaida. It had shaken her, hurt her, demoralised her. It was the reason for her hasty remarriage and, yes – she made no secret of it – one of the causes of her breakdown.

She had done her time in the asylum in Kislovodsk. She had had no choice. She couldn't say she'd enjoyed it – she hadn't – but it had probably helped her.

Meyerhold, God bless him, had been a saint. He was such a good father to her children; such a generous supporter of her career. She was so grateful to him. She could never thank him enough. There was no doubt about it, he was a good man.

Zinaida and Meyerhold

The children liked him. Prevented by his former wife from seeing their daughters, Meyerhold directed his affection to Tatiana and Konstantin.

Young Tanya found him a calming presence, so different from the rowdiness and the noise her biological father used to bring to the family.

Meyerhold taught them music. Kostya learned the piano. He was a shy, rather sad boy, painfully short-sighted and fearful of the world. Being able to make beautiful sounds comforted him. Meyerhold pulled strings to get Tanya into the Bolshoi ballet school. It gave her poise and confidence.

He was proud of the transformation he wrought in the children. Zinaida was highly strung and at times hysterical. It made it all the more important for him to stay calm.

He engaged a photographer to take a series of family portraits. Zinaida chose the best of them to frame in their apartment on Bryusov Lane. She loved the ones of her husband putting a protective arm around a coquettish young Tatiana and an anxious-looking Konstantin.

Meyerhold was so reliable, so stable and predictable. He was a good man. She owed him a lot.

Bryusov Lane was a quiet side street, five minutes from Red Square. A monumental arch between two of Tverskaya's gothic blocks led from the city's bustle to a peaceful backwater. Whole buildings were reserved for representatives of the cultural world, writers, artists and musicians. Meyerhold, a Bolshevik favourite, had an eight-room apartment in the first block on the left, set behind low railings and a garden.

Apartment 11 had two front doors. One led to the part of the flat that was used for theatrical business – a large open-plan room with a Bechstein piano, where rehearsals could be held – and the other to the remaining rooms, which were for the family. There was central heating, two balconies and large windows. The kitchen was equipped with mains gas. A cook and a maid were provided by the state, in acknowledgement of Meyerhold's loyal service.

Zinaida's parents moved in with them. They had their own rooms and spent much of their time caring for the children. There was a family dacha outside Moscow and in the summer, they would decamp there with Tatiana and Konstantin, leaving Meyerhold and Zinaida to have time on their own.

A large dining room hosted frequent parties. Guests included Lunacharsky, Mayakovsky and Andrei Bely. Dmitry Shostakovich's dry, deadpan humour made young Tanya scream with laughter.

Politics were rarely discussed. When they were, it led to arguments. Meyerhold was a member of the Communist Party – he had to be, for the sake of his job – but Zinaida would tease him by declaring herself a Trotskyist or a Right Deviationist. Meyerhold did not rise to the bait. Zinaida was fragile. She needed peace, quiet and tender care. Irritations or too much excitement triggered crises.

Meyerhold was so kind in the way he looked after her and the children. He was such a good, dependable husband.

Meyerhold and Zinaida's flat at 12 Bryusov Lane

Years later, Tatiana would say the only thing her mother salvaged from her first marriage was a set of Pushkin. She had battled with the trauma of Russia's savage times, with her illness and with the unthinking cruelty of her first husband. Marrying Meyerhold, Tatiana said, was not an act of desperation, but it *was* one of necessity.

In the time Sergei was away from Russia, Zinaida's reputation had grown. She had taken leading roles in plays by Gogol,

Griboyedov and Mayakovsky. Meyerhold fostered her career, to the point of choosing productions that would highlight her talents. It made for jealousy. Other actors, other leading ladies, whispered about Meyerhold's nepotism. His enemies, of whom there were many, spread gossip about his use of state funds to promote his wife's career.

Meyerhold refused to bend. When he told the troupe that he would be staging Shakespeare's *Hamlet*, the actor Nikolai Okhlopkov muttered, 'And I suppose Raikh will play the prince.' Meyerhold fired him.

Zinaida's reviews were mostly good, but some critics took against her. She found their personal attacks on her hurtful. In addition to her mental fragility, she was prone to physical illness – childhood bouts of typhus had weakened her system. A bad review could trigger weeks of fatigue.

At a rehearsal of a Mayakovsky play, Zinaida exchanged some banter with the author. When the tall, rugged Mayakovsky went out for a cigarette, Zinaida followed him. Meyerhold called a break in the rehearsal and hurried to join them.

At home with her husband, she told him he needn't worry. She had every reason to be happy with him; every reason to respect him; every reason to be faithful to such a good man.

Zinaida in costume

She wasn't happy, though. Admirers like Mayakovsky she could turn away with equanimity. Only one man troubled her, and now he was back.

Sergei wrote again, this time a long, heartfelt letter.

Dearest Zina,

I just want to say that I am sad without you. I suspect this is how you felt two years ago. Leaving you then was wrong and I regret it very much. I hope things are going well for you. I am finding ways to cope. I want you to know that my feelings for you are as strong as ever. I never stopped loving you; life just swept me away.

You do not need to reply, but I want you to know that I am completely serious about us being together. If you have even the slightest doubt that your new man can satisfy you and fulfil you for the rest of your life, tell me and I will be yours. Forever.

Our love is the true metal, Zina. Shall we try not to end up as Tatiana and Onegin?

He had appended the manuscript of the poem he had been working on for months. The title had been written then scored out, so it was unclear if it read, 'Letter to a Woman' or, 'Letter to My Wife'. It would become one of the most famous works of Russian literature.

You remember
– for you remember everything –
How I stood there leaning on the doorframe
As you strode, angry, back and forth,

Hurling barbs in my face.
My love!
I tortured you.
I saw the suffering in your eyes,
As I destroyed myself in wild deeds before you.
What you did not know
Was that I was adrift, lost in the storm,
Suffering in my incomprehension
Of where the stars might lead us.
I drank, I brawled,
I misbehaved.
But the years have passed;
Things are no longer what they were.
The tenderness I felt for you
Still fills my heart.
I recall your sadness
And I hurry to tell you
What I have become.
My love!
I escaped the shipwreck on the rocks.
I've changed.
I would not torment you now
As once I used to.
I wouldn't hurt you now
The way I did.
... But, oh – forgive me:
I know that you're not staying.
You're leaving
With a good and serious husband.
You don't need our passion,
And you no longer need me.
Live! Live the way
The stars beckon,

Under the shade of a new protector.
With greetings, I remain forever
He who loves you and remembers you always,

Sergei Yesenin
Moscow, 1924

She had kept his earlier letters in a jewellery box locked with a key that she hid under the wardrobe. She had wanted to reply, but had not done so. The equation connecting him to her had been stable: he was back, he was remorseful, he yearned for her; not replying would upset nothing. But this new letter and the poem changed things. Sergei seemed to be contemplating a renunciation, an acceptance that she might stay with Meyerhold. Yesenin demanding her love was one thing; Yesenin resigned to losing her was another, and she didn't like it.

Dear Sergei,

Thank you for your letter. You have not lost your gift; the poem is beautiful.

You say we should not end up like Onegin and Tatiana, but you know very well that Onegin was the architect of his own tragedy. Tatiana was guiltless. She was wronged, but behaved with dignity.

You know, too, that Tatiana was torn. I suppose you know me well enough to understand that I might be. No woman can renounce the love of her life and hope to avoid regret. No couple can love each other with such passion as we did, then walk away without sorrow for the loss.

I loved you, Seryozha. I loved you truly and fully. I

loved you honestly, with no reservations and no pretence.
But you trifled with our love. You thought you could
play with me. You thought I would wait forever – that I'd
always be there for you, whatever happened or whatever
you did. But I couldn't, Seryozha. You hurt me too much.
For my own self-respect, I couldn't.

He read her letter with foreboding in his heart. In the afternoon, another arrived.

Seryozha,
   I meant everything I wrote to you. I will be in Perlov's
Tea Rooms tomorrow morning.

CHAPTER 35

Nineteen twenty-four was the year the Pegasus Café folded. It had struggled since Yesenin and Marienhof fell out. Sergei's absence abroad meant the club lost one of its biggest attractions. Customer numbers dropped.

The death of Lenin marked a change in society. Lenin had pushed through the New Economic Plan, relaxing the state's dictatorship, reintroducing elements of capitalism. It was the NEP that had created the new entrepreneurs, the garish, self-advertising spivs whose spending power had kept the Pegasus going.

With Lenin gone, only Bukharin championed the NEP. Stalin, Trotsky, Kalinin and Kamenev were against it. Communist orthodoxy reasserted itself. Things got tougher, private enterprise harder. Stalin would wait a few years before he formally abolished the NEP, but the speculators felt the wind blowing and drew in their horns.

Marienhof invited Yesenin to a meeting to sort out the accounts. Yesenin refused to go. Shershenevich thought he was jealous of the happiness Marienhof had found with his new wife. The problem with Yesenin, he said, was that he had built himself a fantasy world, pinned to the narrative of his poetry's lyric hero. It had become more real for him than the real world. He lived in it, drawn along by its logic.

'All of Yesenin's poems are so closely connected with his life,' Shershenevich wrote, 'and his life is so connected with his poetry that I cannot say *which* results from *which*; whether because *something* happened to him in his life he has affixed it in a poem or, because he has written lines in such a way, *he adjusts his life to fit his verse*. My fear is that Yesenin will sacrifice himself to the role his poetry has marked out for him.'

Sergei arrived first, anxious, excited. Perlov's had been nationalised. The upper floors were now communal flats; a single room for a family, regardless of numbers; shared kitchen and toilet. Lenin said communal living was a principled rejection of private property, a repudiation of the bourgeois nuclear family. In practice, it was a nightmare. Feuds broke out, possessions were stolen, murders committed. Neighbour spied on neighbour. Mistrust was rife.

Perlov himself had died. His family had gone abroad. Their descendants would get the building back only seventy years later. In 1924, the Chinese mouldings and statues were crumbling; windows were taped over; the waiters no longer wore waistcoats. But there *were* waiters! Tea drinking had seen off war, revolution and years of upheaval. Only the ground floor still operated, but it held a special magic for Sergei. He sat at the table, looked around, got up again, went to comb his hair in the bathroom.

Perlov's Tea Rooms, 1924

The last time they were here, Zinaida had cursed and stormed out. How he wished they could be back in those years of passion, of jealousy and affection, love and desire. He saw her walk in and stood up.

'No smashing the teacups!' he said.

A shadow of a smile warmed him. 'She loves me . . . She loves me still . . .'

'So?' she said. Half enquiring, half challenging.

'So – hello . . .'

'Yes, hello . . .'

Across the table. Her eyes. The hours they had sat like this, hours that had entwined their souls, such that no separation could undo them.

'Sergei Alexandrovich . . .' The prim form of his name; trying to be distant. 'Sergei . . .' Softening.

'Yes? – Zinochka?'

She shook herself.

'Really! Your sense of entitlement knows no bounds!'

'Zina . . . Zinaida . . .'

Her name on his lips sounded like a poem.

'You want to tell me something?'

'I want to tell you a lot of things.' He lowered his eyes. 'I want to tell you that I never realised until now, when I am feeling it myself, the extent of the hurt I caused you. I hurt you; I miss you. It has made me understand how much I love you ...'

She was not a calculating woman. But he was handing her all the cards.

'I don't know how you can say that, Seryozha. You left me in the most brutal and callous way imaginable. You broke all your promises. And now you want to meet me for a cup of tea, probably so that you can tell me about your travels round the world with another woman ... with a hateful, stupid American who should have no part in our lives ... whom you should never have let come between us ... Can you not see how cruel it is?'

'No, Zina. You're wrong—'

'I'm not wrong, Sergei! You're indulging your own feelings, without thinking about the effect it might be having on me. It's time you stopped thinking about yourself and thought a bit more about those you are hurting! You gave up the love we had. *That* was wrong; so stupidly wrong!'

He reached for her hand, but she pulled away.

'Zina! My Zina—'

'I *was* your Zina—'

'Don't say it! Say you love me! Tell me you still love me!'

'What do you think?'

'I think you love me! I couldn't bear it if you say you don't! I think you love me still!'

She looked at him.

'I love you,' she said quietly. 'But I love Meyerhold, too.'

Emotions collided. Immeasurable relief that Zina still cared for him. Immeasurable jealousy that another man should have a claim on her.

'Come and see me, Zina! Come to me! We can be together. I want it ... and you want it. I know you do!'

'How can I see you without losing my self-respect ... what little of it I have left? After all you've done to me, all the pain you have caused me!'

She stood up. He leapt to his feet after her.

'Don't close everything off, love! At least say you'll see me again ... for tea ... Just as we have today ...'

She turned. Looked at him. Nodded.

Their lovemaking was like coming home from a long absence in frozen foreign lands. The contours of her body were in his memory; he knew how to caress, how to elicit that unthinking, immersive confluence of flesh and thought known only to lovers of the truest metal; 1924 was their summer of hope.

Shershenevich laughed when Yesenin told him he needed the flat. He asked if it was for a woman and Sergei nodded. Shershenevich moved back to Marienhof's apartment on Bogoslovsky Lane.

At first, Zinaida would come for an hour. Later, she would stay a morning, an afternoon. She thirsted for him. And he was attentive, infinitely responsive to the signals in her eyes, her lips, her limbs. Afterwards, when they lay in each other's arms, she tried to put it into words. 'It's as if you know in advance what I want from you. It's as if you feel it from the inside.'

Sergei felt the same, but didn't say it. When Zina spoke of bliss and beauty, Sergei would grunt and smile. His reticence made her laugh.

'I have never felt so close to another person,' she said.

'I am the luckiest man,' he replied. 'I threw my life away. But you have rescued me.'

He celebrated the joy of happiness regained in a cycle of poems,
'A Hooligan's Love'. It grew into a narrative of closely worked
lyrics, alive with redemption and autumnal passion.

> You lit a pale blue fire, and I forgot the world.
> I sang of love, and for the first time knew its truth;
> No longer sought the madness, drink and brawls,
> The headlong flight in which I sank my youth.
> God's meadow in me grew to shameful seed,
> I swallowed women, booze and poisons.
> God grant that with you now to take my part,
> I'll break the hold of old soul-strangling notions.
> Let me gaze into your face,
> Drown in the vortex of your golden-hazel eyes.
> And tell me you no longer love the past,
> That you renounce the other who for your
> > presence sighs.
> ...
> For your beauty, for your touch, for your blessing,
> This hooligan gives his thanks and praise.
> Forever bows his head, swears love, obedience,
> And writes your glory on the page.
> If thou art near, I'll leave all behind,
> Renounce the world, the call of fame.
> All I need is to kiss your hand, your lips,
> And hear you call me by my name.
> I shall be with you when the trumpets call,
> I'll sing your love, I'll glory in its truth;
> And curse the madness, drink and brawls,
> The headlong flight in which I drowned my youth.
> ...
> As all life fades, then so fades mine;
> I'll die, if die we must.

But kiss me to the end of time,
Cradle me in your lust,
So that in our pale blue dreams,
Sincere and free and shorn of shame,
You may say, 'I am forever yours
Till death calls us by our names.'
Life's joy is the froth on my champagne,
It flattens, then it's gone.
So drink, my love, and sing the truth,
That on this earth we live just once.

Zinaida timed her visits to avoid being seen, made sure she gave her husband plausible explanations. Sergei hated caution. He wanted to tell the world of their love, wanted her to have it out with Meyerhold.

'I can't stand it that you are going back to another man,' he said each time she left.

'He is my husband.' Zinaida said. 'Now you see what I had to endure – the jealousy, the loneliness – while you were with your American bitch.'

The sun rose early, picking out the curls of dust from the street sweepers' birch-twig brooms, glancing off the Kremlin domes, anointing the bends of the Moskva River with its haze of silver incense. Sergei rose with the sun. He loved that hour in which the city shakes itself, idly preparing the day, setting out its stalls, raising its blinds, dropping off its bundles of newspapers, thinking how to spend God's summer.

His days were ruled by Zinaida's schedule – when she could see him, when she had to be back at the theatre or accompany Meyerhold. He hungered for her presence. He wanted her always, resented those who kept her from him.

Meyerhold's theatre was preparing for its autumn tour, two months travelling, first to Minsk and Kiev, then east as far as Vladivostok before returning through the Central Asian republics. Sergei tried not to think about it. Two months without her. Did she not realise it was impossible? She spoke offhandedly about the itinerary, the hotels, the repertoire. Some of the plays they were taking were standard pieces. Zinaida had performed them many times. But there were new works to try out on the provinces before bringing them to the capital. She disliked them. They made her nervous. She had told Meyerhold as much ...

'Don't go, Zina! I beg you, don't go!' Sergei couldn't bear to hear her talk of being away from him.

'But, love, this is what you put me through when you went off with Isadora.' She felt a tremor of satisfaction. 'Just wait for me, Seryozha. Two months – it will be a proof of our love ...'

The thought of Zinaida leaving kept him awake at night, tormented him by day.

He said he would kill himself if she went. She told him not to be so silly.

'Of course you won't kill yourself. It's only for two months.'

He said he couldn't bear her being with another man.

'But I have to go. Meyerhold is my husband. He'd be suspicious if I refused. Not going would be a betrayal.'

'But you're betraying him already!' Sergei said. 'You're betraying him just by being here with me!'

'That's different . . .'

'And anyway,' he said, 'how can you even speak of betrayal? *I* am the man you love, not Meyerhold! The only betrayal is not to be with the man you love. It's a betrayal of yourself!'

The departure of Meyerhold and his troupe was a public event. Sergei couldn't even see her off; there would be journalists at the station. Zinaida had told him it would be better if he stayed away.

The next day, he read the newspapers, looking for photographs of Zinaida, but found none. The headlines were about Meyerhold, full of praise for the genius who had revolutionised the revolution's art. He stuffed them in the bin. The flat was cold, his day unsweetened by the anticipation of love. There would be weeks of this. It was barely lunchtime, but he opened a bottle.

There was a knock at the door. He couldn't stand the thought of Shershenevich offering him consolation. He didn't answer.

The knock came again. He rose unsteadily and unfastened the latch. It was Zinaida!

CHAPTER 36

Meyerhold had been understanding; she said that was what troubled her the most. He was a good man; she felt bad lying to him. He knew her health was unsettled, so when she told him she was suffering from one of her bouts of fatigue, he was unsurprised. He said she should stay in Moscow, recuperate at home; it would help her be ready for the winter season. He had suspected she didn't like the new repertoire they were taking on tour, so she was probably right to cry off. She told him he would be in her thoughts as he travelled far and wide.

'And I wasn't lying, Seryozha. He *will* be in my thoughts. Even now, I'm not sure I've done the right thing. I told him my parents would look after me, but I've just told *them* that I'm fine, that they can take the children to the dacha, as they'd been planning.'

The constraints were gone. Meyerhold was hundreds of miles away, the children with Zina's parents. For the first time since Sergei had been tricked away from her by the Grateful Little Translator then gobbled up by the American Bitch, they could be properly together. It felt like being married again. It was exhilarating.

They lived in the apartment on Afanasievsky Lane. Sergei arranged weekends away, in the cities of the Golden Ring – Yaroslavl, Suzdal, Vladimir and Kostroma. They stayed at country inns, walked the Russian land, watched the leaves turn to reds and russet brown.

Sergei asked her to show him Meyerhold's apartment. She was reluctant. He said he wanted to see where she lived when she was not with him. She asked why he insisted on torturing himself. He said he was curious; and anyway, once they were officially back together, all the rest would mean nothing. Hearing him say it made her thrill. That night, their lovemaking took them to realms neither had dreamt possible.

'Do you remember my story of the creatures that Zeus split in two?'

It was September and they were in bed. Zinaida looked at the sun on his hair. How much healthier, how much happier he looked.

'Yes, love,' he said. 'I remember how they spent their lives searching for one another, desperate to be reunited. How fulfilment was possible only for those who found their other half.'

She kissed his forehead, his eyes, his lips.

She asked him about Isadora. Had she really been everything the newspapers said she was – drunken, scandalous, talented, wanton? Had he loved her?

He said Isadora was a remarkable woman. She had single-handedly changed the world's perception of dance. She had taken a stand for political opinions that were unpopular in her homeland, suffered for her espousal of socialism. But, he said, she was old. She had drunk herself into such a decline that her talent had been lost. She was no longer the luminous star she once had been. No, he didn't love her. And no, he never wished to see her again.

The conversation stalled.

'Zina?' he said, taking her hand. 'Forgive me. You asked me about Isadora—'

'And you want to ask me about Meyerhold.'

'Yes. It's all very well for me to pretend I am unconcerned . . . that I'm not jealous. But I can't help thinking about it – I mean, thinking about what it's like between you and him . . .'

Zinaida had expected the question.

'Meyerhold is a good man,' she said. 'I owe him a lot. Don't forget that when you abandoned me, I had nothing. He left his wife for me. He took me in. He adopted Tanya and Kostya. That's no trifle for a man his age.'

'Yes,' Sergei said. 'But what I mean is . . . do you find love . . . do you find the same love in bed with him that you find with me?'

Zinaida started to laugh, but checked herself.

'You're serious, Seryozha? I mean, that's the question you've been trying to ask me all this time?'

He nodded. 'Yes. And please tell me the truth. It's important.'

She answered softly.

'Meyerhold is old, Seryozha. He belongs to a different generation. For them – for him – I would say sex is something practical, something you do in order to get it over with. He thinks it is all right to make love once, quickly, and then go to sleep.' She turned her head to look at him. 'You are the only man I have known who understands that a woman needs time and understanding. You are patient and loving. Time slows down when we make love; the world slows down and life becomes so much sharper, so much clearer. You give me so much joy. I love you for it.'

Meyerhold's tour, reported in the Moscow newspapers, was progressing, the reviews adulatory and frequent. Another theatre, another city. The remaining dates were shrinking and, with them, the days until his return.

Zinaida said little. Sergei was a condemned man, watching the calendar on the wall of his cell. He wanted to ask her what she was thinking, wanted her to say that she would break with her husband. Fear held him back; fear of pushing her into a decision and discovering it was the wrong one. For as long as he didn't force a resolution, he could continue to hope.

A couple of weeks before Meyerhold was due back, Zinaida received a letter from Anatoly Marienhof.

Dear Zinaida Nikolaevna,

I understand you are living with Sergei Alexandrovich in the apartment on Afanasievsky Lane. Your husband is away on tour and I suspect you would not welcome him discovering what you are doing. But this is not my business. It is your choice.

I am sure it seems to you that your love is pure. Sergei is good at bouquets of white roses. But I need to tell you something. For Seryozha, it is all contrived. All cooked up for the sake of a new lyrical theme for his poetry. That is Yesenin's paradox: contrived love, contrived biography. One might ask, why? The answer is: in order to have material for his writing; in order that his verse should *not* be contrived. Everything in his life is for the sake of his art.

If you believe in it, Zinaida, if you believe what he tells you, you are a schoolgirl. Perhaps you imagine you can change him or save him. But he doesn't need that! Come what may, he'll run away from you to the nearest tart.

Zinaida did not mention Marienhof's letter. Sergei was already on the edge. She was anxious enough about the phone calls from Meyerhold.

Twice a week, at a prearranged time, she would go to the apartment on Bryusov Lane and wait for her husband to ring. The phone system was a nightmare – calls from the provinces had to be booked days in advance – and sometimes she would have to wait an hour or more. It made Sergei nervous. When he was nervous he could express his fear in anger. He became the little boy trembling before the school bullies, refusing to cry when he was hurt, forcing himself to fight back.

A week before the end of Meyerhold's tour, he phoned to tell her when he would be arriving. He asked her to meet him at the station. Sergei could no longer avoid the discussion.

'Are you going? To the station, I mean. Wouldn't it be easier for you to tell him on the phone, or even write to say you aren't coming back?'

'It's not that easy,' she said. 'I am married to him. It isn't like cancelling a subscription to a magazine.'

'But you're not going back, are you? You will stay with me?' She was silent.

'Zina . . . Zinochka!' His voice trembled. 'You know you love me. We can be together. With *our* children.'

'Don't push me, Seryozha. I have to think about things. It's my future, my life that we're talking about.'

'But I am the man you love . . .'

She took his hand.

'It's true, Seryozha. I do love you. It's true that Meyerhold is a lesser man than you – that he cannot give me the satisfaction, the excitement, the fulfilment you give me. But he is a good man who has committed himself to me . . .'

'I, too, Zina – I, too! I am committed to you. Body and soul. Forever!'

'But, love, you said that in the past. Then you left me. You hurt me so much. Was I just going to spend my whole life waiting? I am worth more than that, love.'

'But it's in the past!' Sergei said. 'That was wrong, but it's in the past!'

His words were charged with pleas for forgiveness, with yearning for a past that he had thrown away. He loved her; he hated himself.

Late at night, words faded. Their bodies took over. The tenderness of abiding affection, the eternity of love between them flooded their souls.

Zinaida went to the station. The struggle with her conscience had been lonely. She could discuss her decision with no one, least of all Sergei, who continued to press her to stay. She needed to assure herself she was making a choice based on reason, not the emotional urgings of his overpowering presence.

She weighed things up. She made herself repeat what a good person Meyerhold was and how kind he had been to her. But Sergei Yesenin, for all his inconstancy, for all his faults and cruelty, was the man she loved. She would love him for the rest of her days. Wouldn't it be perverse to renounce her own happiness, simply because Seryozha had behaved badly and Meyerhold behaved well?

Her parents had brought the children from the dacha. They wanted to accompany her to the station. Zinaida nodded her agreement. She had resolved to tell Meyerhold immediately, the moment he stepped off the train, that she was leaving him. It would be too cruel to delay; it would give him hope and then she would have to dash it. But she didn't want the others there when she spoke to him. She asked her parents to sit with the children in the station waiting room.

The platform was occupied by cheering crowds, eager to catch a glimpse of favourite actors and actresses, and by journalists come to interview Soviet Russia's famous director. Meyerhold and his troupe were surrounded. Zinaida waited. Meyerhold was craning his neck, looking about him, trying to shake off the journalists and admirers. She knew it was her he was looking for.

'Zinaida! Zina!' He spotted her, made the last round of handshakes and ran to her. His face filled with joy; he was telling her excitedly about his adventures on the road, elated at seeing her.

'Vsevolod . . .' she said. 'Seva . . . I have something I need to say to you—'

'Yes. Yes, of course, my dear. And I have so much I need to tell you—'

'No. Seva, you don't understand. It's something important—'

'Wait. Zinochka. First things first! Let me kiss you! I missed you so much. I know it was the right decision for you not to come – it wouldn't have been any fun for you on the road – but I missed you every day. It has been so long – too long! We mustn't ever be apart like this again. If you are ill, it is I who shall cancel engagements – performances, tours, whatever it takes. Nothing is as important to me as you are; you and the children—'

His enthusiasm swamped her.

'Vsevolod. I need you to listen to me. This is hard for me to say; it will be hard for you to hear, but I have to say it. For your sake and for mine. I have decided—'

'Oh, Zina – look!' Meyerhold grabbed her arm and spun her around. Coming through the crowd, almost upon them, were her parents. They were carrying the children, lifting them aloft so that their heads rose above all the others. The children were beaming, waving, radiant in the obvious joy they felt at seeing Meyerhold – Meyerhold, their *papa* – coming back to them.

Lenin's embalmed body was put on public display. Under the Kremlin wall on Red Square, gangs of men worked around the clock to construct first a wooden, then a permanent mausoleum in red and black marble.

The Bolsheviks had destroyed religion in a deeply Christian country. They needed to replace it in the minds of the people and Lenin was their choice. Just as the Church had displayed the relics of its martyrs, so Communism would display the miraculously preserved body of its patron saint. Pilgrims came in their millions from all over the Soviet Union to descend the steps into the reverential silence of the mausoleum's subterranean shrine.

When Arthur Ransome spoke of a new religion springing from the coffin of the dead leader, he could barely have known how true his words would prove. Christian Russia had believed for centuries in its God-given mission to bring truth and enlightenment to mankind. Now Communist Russia declared its own holy destiny to change, educate and perfect the human species. Lenin's mausoleum would become the epicentre of a messianic force, spreading its tentacles throughout the world.

At home, the Christian icons that had hung for centuries in the *krasny ugol* – the 'beautiful corner' – of peasants' huts and workers' apartments were replaced by icons of Lenin.

The Party had pledged to the people that it would lead them from the grim, corrupted present to the cleansed, harmonious future. But in return, it demanded unquestioning obedience from its followers: any deviation or dissent would be mercilessly punished.

Zinaida had told Sergei before she left for the station that it would be hard. The thought that she was about to walk out on the man who had rescued her and her children was a torment.

'But you *are* going to do it, aren't you? You *are* going to leave Meyerhold? You *are* going to come back?'

'Yes. I am resolved,' she said. 'But I have to be fair to him. I have to explain things properly. I have to listen to what he has to say. And I have to discuss with him what happens to the children.'

He had asked how long she thought it would take. She shrugged.

'I could be back tomorrow. It could take a week.'

A day passed. Two days. Zinaida did not appear. Fear overcame him. He convinced himself that his love was gone. He opened a bottle and emptied it.

Late at night, there was a knock at the door. Hope revived, galvanised his heart.

He opened the door to a party of uniformed men.

'Yesenin, Sergei Alexandrovich?'

He nodded.

'Date of birth, 21 October 1895?'

'Yes.'

Had something happened to Zinaida?

'Get your things. One suitcase. Small. Fifteen minutes.'

The door slammed and an OGPU operative pointed a rifle at

him, watching impassively as he struggled to stuff shirts and underwear into a bag.

The Soviet Union – the Union of Soviet Socialist Republics – had been formally constituted in December 1922. It was a chance for a new start, or at least some new names. The Cheka secret police had gained a reputation for unwarranted savagery. Lenin had no interest in curbing it, but he did recognise that it wasn't popular. Renaming it as the OGPU – the Joint State Political Directorate – might at least make it sound better.

After Lenin's death, Stalin instructed the OGPU's director, Felix Dzerzhinsky, to be even more brutal. Treachery and subversion were threatening the very survival of the USSR. All methods should be deployed against traitors to the motherland, at home and abroad.

Dzerzhinsky convinced himself that there were tens, perhaps hundreds of thousands of dangerous individuals in Russia, forming networks of sedition, dedicated to undoing the will of the people and overthrowing the communist state. It stood to reason that traitors at home were being supported by enemies abroad, by the hostile Western governments who had so recently sent troops and guns to destroy Bolshevism.

Dzerzhinsky launched Operation Trust to unmask the links between domestic treason and foreign powers. The OGPU sent secret agents to approach émigrés in Western Europe, pretending to represent the underground opposition in Russia. The émigrés offered them large sums of money and supplies, as did foreign intelligence agencies. Red agents succeeded in luring several of their representatives – including the British operative, Sidney Reilly, later known as the Ace of Spies – onto Soviet territory, where they were tortured and shot.

The OGPU extracted from them the names of thousands of other traitors living in Russia. All would be rounded up and dealt with.

Sergei was handcuffed and escorted to a van, a 'Black Raven', waiting outside. A guard shoved him on to a wooden bench in back. Half a dozen men were already there. It was dark, but he recognised one of them as Alexei Ganin, the young poet from Vologda who had acted as best man at Sergei and Zinaida's wedding.

'Good God, Alexei!' he said. 'What the hell are you doing here? What the hell am *I* doing here!'

A guard prodded him with the butt of his rifle.

'You – silence! Prisoners do not have the right of conversation.'

'What do you mean, The right of conversation? That's ridicu—'

The guard hit him. Blood spurted from his nose.

CHAPTER 37

It had taken an hour to unload the luggage and say goodbye to the actors, stagehands and technicians. Meyerhold had been caught up in the back-slapping and handshakes. For Zinaida, waiting with her parents and children, it had been agonising. Her resolution, so strong when she arrived at the station, had weakened with each glance, each smile Meyerhold had given her. The children's joy at seeing him had persuaded her to wait until they got home.

The six of them had taken a cab to the apartment on Bryusov Lane. Meyerhold had paid the driver to carry up the trunks and suitcases.

'This one here, comrade,' he said, pointing to a large leather bag. 'That's the important one.'

Meyerhold called for silence.

'And now, comrades, citizens, Madame, boys and girls, we have the official distribution of presents, gathered, I may say, with no regard to expense or effort, from every corner of our fine and fabled land!'

The children squealed with delight. They threw themselves on Meyerhold with hugs and kisses.

Meyerhold with Konstantin and Tatiana

Sergei had been arrested before. The pranks and scandals of the Imagists had stirred up public indignation. But the times were different now. The political climate was harsher; the regime was smiting its enemies.

Sergei Yesenin, Alexei Ganin and twelve others were charged with belonging to an illegal organisation dedicated to the overthrow of the legitimate government of the Soviet Union. Like them, nearly all the accused were poets or artists.

Pyotr Chekrygin, age 23, poet
Nikolai Chekrygin, 22, poet
Viktor Dvoryashin, 27, artist
Vladimir Galanov, 29, poet
Grigory Nikitin, 30, poet
Alexander Kudryavtsev, 39, typesetter
Alexander Poteryakhin, 32, writer
Mikhail Krotkov, 44, lawyer

Sergei Golovin, 58, doctor
Boris Glubokovsky, 30, theatre director
Ivan Kolobov, 37, profession unknown
Timofei Sakhno, 31, doctor

Sergei Yesenin and Alexei Ganin as young men

They were held in a cell of the Butyrskaya Prison. Sergei had sobered up. He asked Alexei if he had any idea why they had been arrested.

'Maybe,' Ganin said. 'In your case, I'd say it's pretty simple. You've been abroad. Abroad is full of enemies. If you've been there, you must have been consorting with them. And the fact that you've been writing such anti-Soviet poetry, well QED.'

'God Almighty, Alex! That is such horse shit!'

Sergei was exasperated and frightened. He knew that Soviet prisons were full of informers.

'Sure I went abroad,' he said loudly. 'But I spent the whole time defending the revolution and attacking the émigré scumbags. Didn't you read the newspapers? I sang the *Internationale*. I picked fights with White officers. I insulted Merezhkovsky and the other lousy traitors.'

Ganin laughed. 'OK, Seryozha. That's your defence. I'd say you have a better chance than most of us of getting out of here. As for me and the others, I'm not so sure.'

'What do you mean?' Sergei looked horrified.

'The trouble is that not all of us are prepared to let the Bolsheviks rape and pillage the Russia we love. Some of us have been standing up for what we believe in. You probably haven't read anything I've written, but I wrote a novel called *Tomorrow*. It was all in code, of course, but it's a real indictment of the bastards who've brought Russia to her knees.'

'A novel! For Christ's sake! They can't lock you up for a novel!' Ganin looked at him.

'Where have you been, Seryozha? They can lock you up for anything nowadays. Anyway, the novel isn't the whole of it. I've been working with a bunch of other guys – patriots, Russian nationalists; we all hate the Bolsheviks. We decided we had to offer an alternative to the dead-end the communists are taking us down. We wrote a couple of pamphlets; a manifesto, really. It's called "Theses for Russian National Rebirth" and it really gives the lie to Lenin and Stalin and co. Well, it seems they got wind of it and they've been arresting us all, one by one. They've been charging us with belonging to some stupid organisation they've invented themselves, called the Order of Russian Fascists. As if we'd use such an idiotic title. It doesn't matter what the truth is, though; if they want to crush you, they'll do it.'

Zinaida helped Meyerhold unpack his bags. He could not contain his joy at seeing her. He was so lucky to have her as his wife.

He had booked a table for a celebratory dinner in the Grand Hall of the Metropol Hotel. When they arrived, the Maître D showed them to their table and invited Zinaida to be seated. He apologised to her, said he would need to borrow her husband for a few moments and led Meyerhold through a mirrored door into a side room.

Meyerhold came back twenty minutes later with two bottles of vintage Georgian wine. He was flustered.

'A present from Josef Vissarionovich,' he said. 'From Stalin. He's in the private room with Molotov and Kalinin. He wanted to say how much he admires our work. But he says we need to make our heroes more heroic – Onegin, Chatsky, Pechorin – they all need to be heroes. It's madness, of course. But I was terrified. I just said fine, and agreed with him. I need a drink!'

They ate. They drank a bottle of Stalin's wine. Meyerhold regained his composure.

'Thank God I have you, Zina,' he said. 'God knows what I'd do without you. We must make sure we are never parted as we were these last months.'

Some of the other prisoners in the cell, long-term residents, spent the days arguing. It made the time pass. The arguments were heated. But there was a tacit convention that violence would not be used and grudges would not be borne.

Conversation turned to a discussion of the worst things about being in jail. The sound of rats scurrying around in the night topped the poll. Then the maggots in the food, the endless diarrhoea and vomiting, the shared lavatory pail. One man said the worst thing was the waiting, but a voice from a bunk in the corner said, 'You won't say that when you discover what you've been waiting for. Once the interrogators are beating your face to a pulp, you'll be wishing you could be back here, waiting forever.'

Butyrskaya Prison

The Order of Fascists was clearly a tricky case, the investigations long and complex. By the time the suspects were called for interrogation, their nerves were frayed.

Alexei Ganin went first. On 2 November 1924, he came before Senior OGPU Investigator Abram Slavatinsky. Slavatinsky produced documents that he said were found in the pocket of Ganin's raincoat at the time of his arrest. They were vile tracts, full of anti-Bolshevik, anti-Russian propaganda. There was a nasty streak of Fascism and anti-Semitism in them. Slavatinsky threw them on the table with an air of triumph.

Ganin looked at the documents and shook his head; he had never seen them before.

Slavatinsky made a sign with his hand and two guards stepped forward. One pinned Ganin's arms behind his back, while the other punched him repeatedly in the face.

'That's what they all say,' Slavatinsky said. 'They all deny the truth – at first. None of them keeps it up for long.'

Sergei was released without explanation. He was woken by a guard and told to collect his possessions from the desk. There was no time to say goodbye to Ganin or anyone else.

Back in the flat on Afanasievsky Lane, he scoured the newspapers. He could find no reference anywhere to Alexei Ganin and no mention of any organisation by the name of the Order of Russian Fascists.

A single news item on an inside page of *Evening Moscow* stated that the poet Sergei Yesenin had again been arrested – charges unknown – and subsequently released. There was a quote from Vladimir Mayakovsky to the effect that Yesenin was now appearing more frequently in newspaper crime columns than in poetry.

Sergei went looking for Zinaida. He had hoped she would be waiting for him at the flat. His unexplained disappearance and the lack of news about him must have alarmed her. He needed to find her and tell her he was safe.

He went to Shershenevich, who was relieved to see him. But no, he had heard nothing from Zinaida.

Zinaida was finding life in Bryusov Lane stressful. She felt guilty about breaking her promise to Sergei, sure he must have taken it badly. The fact that he hadn't come looking for her must mean he had started drinking again. He was probably lying in some gutter. She wanted to go and look for him, but she knew that would make things unbearably complicated. The longer Sergei didn't come, the more she felt she had made the right decision. Meyerhold seemed oblivious. He was his usual, dependable self. He had commissioned a new portrait of her that he hung in his study and showed to everyone who came to see them.

Meyerhold at home, with Zinaida's portrait

Sergei never learned what had happened to his best man. The facts of the Alexei Ganin case would emerge only when the files of the Soviet secret police were opened after the collapse of the USSR in 1991.

According to OGPU records, Senior Investigator Slavatinsky had concluded on the basis of the available evidence, supported by a full and detailed confession voluntarily given by the accused, that all the alleged members of the Order of Russian Fascists were guilty as charged.

Slavatinsky had communicated his findings to the OGPU Director, Felix Dzerzhinsky and his deputy, Genrikh Yagoda, who may well have been amused. The Order of Russian Fascists and other similar organisations, such as the Monarchist Union of Central Russia and the Underground Trust, were inventions of Yagoda's imagination. They were fictions, used by the OGPU to frame suspects whose views they didn't like.

On 25 March 1925, the Secretary of the Central Committee, Avel Yenukidze, signed an order granting the OGPU the right to deal with 'the fascists' as it saw fit, with no need for a trial.

For Alexei Ganin, both of the Chekrygin brothers, Viktor Dvoryashin, Vladimir Galanov and Mikhail Krotkov, the sentence was death. The others were given jail terms of between ten and twenty years.

Ganin would be shot on 30 March 1925, his saint's day, in the Butyrskaya Prison, together with the other young poets from the list. Their bodies were transported to the mortuary of the Yauzskaya Clinic in central Moscow, to be buried in the hospital's wooded grounds. When the OGPU records were opened seven decades later, there were more than a thousand requests between the years of 1920 and 1926 for the disposal of executed prisoners there.

The drama of the autumn had damaged Zinaida's fragile psyche. She spent the winter filling her diary with pages of scrawled reflections. She wrote of the damage she had caused, of her regret for the love she had given up, of her dissatisfaction with the safety and comfort she had chosen. She feared she was turning into a character from Chekhov. She had played so many of his roles, absorbed so many of his lines that they swirled in her head and gave her no peace.

I married the Latin professor, who declines *amo, amas, amat*, but doesn't know what it means ... My heart is a grand piano that can't be used because it's locked and the key is lost.

Sergei and I love each other. That's what matters ...

It isn't all that matters.

Other things matter, too. Self-respect matters, and decency.

I can't go on ...

Who will remember us when we are dead? We forget the sacrifices of previous generations and the future will forget ours ... What seems to us now to be so serious and important will be forgotten.

But can we really say goodbye? Never see each other again?

The strain of our different lives, our lives apart from each other.

The feeling of guilt. Too great a price to pay. I shall love him until the end of my life.

I know he feels all this. It is the same for him.

Too cruel. We can't do such violence to our hearts.

I must talk to him.

It's torturing me ... the decision I made.

I remember our last day together. We went from the flat and walked as far as Tverskaya. I lit cigarettes for him. We didn't talk much. We walked the same streets that we'd walked so many times before.

I shall see all this again, but without him ... without Sergei.

Meyerhold was at the door of her room. She closed her diary and hid it under a book. She felt she was committing some act of treachery towards him.

'Vsevolod,' she said. 'I don't know what is happening to

me. I feel so distracted. I can't remember the simplest things any more; others keep crowding into my brain and pushing them out.'

Meyerhold put his arm around her.

'What is it? What is it, darling?'

'Where? Where has it all gone? I've forgotten everything ... everything's in a tangle ... I don't remember the Italian for window or ceiling ... Every day I forget something more. Life is slipping away and will never come back.'

'Darling, darling ...'

'I'm so sad! I've had enough of it! My brain is drying up; I'm getting fat and old and ugly, and there's nothing, nothing, not the slightest satisfaction. And time is passing and it just feels as if we are moving away from a real, beautiful life, moving farther and farther away and being drawn into the depths. I'm in despair. I don't know how it is that I'm alive and haven't killed myself ...'

'Don't cry, my child, don't cry. It makes me miserable.'

'I'm not crying. I'm not crying ... It's over ... There, I'm not crying now. I won't ... I won't ... I see that we shall never, never go to Moscow! I see that we won't go!'

Nobody told Sergei why he was released. The authorities rarely explained. Terror was reinforced by uncertainty. So, in the same way, relatives of executed prisoners would be informed that their loved ones had been sent to the Gulag 'without the right to correspondence'. In those early years, the phrase was a new one and many clung to the hope it offered.

Most likely, they released Yesenin because he was famous and Ganin was not; because his poems were cherished by millions who had never heard of Alexei Ganin; and because Ganin had written his contempt for the regime in a pamphlet rather than just poetry.

It didn't take Sergei long to discover that Zinaida was with Meyerhold. Late at night, drunk and impetuous, he banged at their door. The building was asleep.

'Give me my wife back! You have my wife and my children! Give them back to me!'

The neighbours appeared and warned him to leave. Next time they would call the police.

When he came back the following evening, they did. Sergei spent the night in a cell.

CHAPTER 38

Sergei had long felt excluded from the jollity of Christmas. Memories of childhood happinesses and the fact that he had first met Zinaida on Christmas Eve made it harder. At Christmas 1924 he was alone, with ice in his heart.

He went to see her in a Meyerhold production of Gogol's *Government Inspector*. Zinaida played the wife of the mayor, a faded beauty who falls for the blandishments of the fake Inspector, Khlestakov.

Sergei had drunk a lot. On stage, Zinaida was laughing, when she should have been mourning, as he was. She was flirting, when she should have been afflicted by the loss of their love. He found it hard to draw the line between reality and representation. When Khlestakov took Zinaida in his arms and began to kiss her, Sergei rose to his feet.

'Leave her alone, you bastard! She's mine! Get your filthy hands off of my wife!'

Ushers escorted him to the exit. In a bar, he drank vodka and waited for the play to end. At the stage door, he said, 'I am the poet – the famous poet, Yesenin – come to see my faithless wife.'

Meyerhold was in Zinaida's dressing room. Sergei raised his fist, but Zinaida calmed him. She told Meyerhold that she would need to speak to him sometime; here, in a public place, was safer than elsewhere. He left them to talk.

Sergei asked why she had abandoned him, a question with no answer. The warning in Marienhof's letter came into her mind. She said, 'You left me for a tart in the past, so why would you not do it again?'

Sergei shrugged. There was such a mountain of misunderstanding between them that he was never going to clear it away. He was drunk; things were too much for him.

'Marienhof was always jealous of you,' he said. 'You know that. He had some stupid, juvenile idea of us being a band of boys, poets together, making music, dedicating ourselves to art and to each other. He just thought it would be like that forever. Any woman who took one of us away would be guilty of destroying the band. But that's not what it's about, Zina. It's not that ... I'm so unhappy. In the middle of the night, I call your name – "Oh, Zina!" You must hear me! Surely you hear me ...'

*Zinaida as Anna Andreyevna, Erast Garin as
Khlestakov in The Government Inspector*

Trotsky and Stalin were destined to clash. In this savage regime, only the victor would survive.

In 1925, the battleground was the future of communism. Marxist doctrine held that socialism could be secured only by spreading revolution throughout the world. Right up to his death, Lenin had remained convinced that global revolution was about to happen.

'The word Soviet has become known and popular everywhere,' he wrote. 'It is the favourite word of all working people. Despite the persecution to which communists are subjected, Soviet power will inevitably, and in the nearest future, triumph all over the world.'

The message of world revolution reached many Western countries after 1917, but years went by and global communism failed to materialise. Enthusiasm faltered. The Bolshevik leadership split.

Trotsky continued to advocate world revolution, with a dogmatic certainty that made the term synonymous with his name. Stalin was more pragmatic. He advanced a new doctrine of 'Socialism in one country'. He proclaimed that the Soviet Union could build communism on its own and, in a departure from Marxist internationalism, appealed to Russian national pride to do so. It was a rewriting of Party orthodoxy, but Stalin had his regiments lined up.

At his direction, the Party Congress agreed that it was Trotsky's dedication to Marxism which deviated from official policy, and that in future it was Stalin and his allies who would decide what was acceptable and what was not. Trotsky's influence would plummet as Stalin's rose. Within a couple of years, he would be expelled from the Party.

Stalin was beginning to airbrush his rivals from the record. Few had wanted him as leader; everyone knew he was manipulative and dangerous, but no one was brave enough to stop him.

At Zinaida's request, they met one more time. Sergei suggested Perlov's, but she wrote to say that would not be appropriate.

They sat at one of the new state-run cafés – known by a number, rather than a name – waiting for the surly waitress to serve them.

'It is *so* lovely to see you, Zina,' he said. 'I thought you'd taken offence at my coming to the play ... I am so happy to be sitting across the table from you. It makes me think of all the times we did this in the past, all the hours we spent looking into each other's eyes—'

'Seryozha,' she interrupted. 'I asked you here for a reason—'

'Yes, love. But just let me say one thing. I'd meant to say it when I saw you in your dressing room, but I was too drunk. I didn't mean to hurt you. I am sorry for everything; sorry that I made you cry. I'm so sorry, Zina. But you know, you know – I'm a very jealous man.'

'Yes,' she said. 'I do know that. And I believe you are sincere in what you are saying. But life has moved on. There are things we can't change. We can't change the past. I want to ask you something—'

'Yes, love. Of course. Tell me.'

'Do you still have my letters?'

'I do. They are precious—'

'Do you remember Tatiana and Onegin? How he could have damaged her by showing her husband the love letter Tatiana had written? You ... you could damage me now if you were to show Meyerhold all those passionate letters I wrote to you; how I offered to pull out of my wedding if you would come back to me ... It would hurt Meyerhold terribly to see I was pleading with you to take his place. It might end my marriage. You won't do that, will you? Sergei, you won't, will you?'

'Good lord, Zinaida! What do you think I am? I may be a

bastard, but I wouldn't do that. I wouldn't harm you. I don't hate you – I adore you!'

Sergei Gorodetsky, the young poet with whom Yesenin had stayed when he first arrived in Petrograd, said that Yesenin's poetic output had become a lyrical novel, with Yesenin himself as its central character. Readers awaited his poems like postcards in the post, bringing them news of their hero's fate. By 1925, the postcards were from the edge.

When Mayakovsky spoke of Yesenin's appearances in the newspaper crime columns, he was not exaggerating. That year's arrest logs of the Moscow Police Department record at least five occasions on which Yesenin was taken into custody, drunk and disorderly, charged with assault and affray or causing bodily harm.

On 9 January, he was detained after an altercation at the Café Domino on Tverskoy Boulevard. He was taken to the headquarters of the 46th Division of the Moscow Militia, where he was found to be so drunk that he had to be rushed to hospital. The report by the medic in charge, Dr A.V. Perfiliev, records that Citizen Yesenin was 'intoxicated, physically agitated, in an advanced state of alcohol poisoning'.

The following day, when Yesenin was interviewed under caution, he could remember nothing. The police made him sign an undertaking not to leave Moscow, pending the filing of charges. On 18 January, the People's Court of the Krasnopresnensky District sent him a summons under article 86 (hooliganism) and article 176 (resisting arrest) of the Criminal Code of the Russian Federation, each carrying a potential sentence of one year's hard labour. When he failed to appear for the hearing, the judge issued a warrant for his arrest.

Similar cases were recorded in February, March and April. All of them resulted in new charges and new arrest warrants, and all were aborted when the accused did not appear in court. Search warrants were issued, but each of them stated that Yesenin was not found at any of his known addresses.

By the spring of 1925, four unresolved cases lay on his file and a fifth, more serious, was about to be opened. Yet another drinking session, this time at a bar run by the publican, Ivan Malinnikov, on the corner of Myasnitskaya Street and Chistoprudny Boulevard, ended in the usual brawl and fisti-cuffs. This time, though, witnesses reported that Yesenin and three companions were heard abusing the Bolshevik regime and making threats against its leaders. When they were brought to militia headquarters, the superintendent classified the accusation as political. The case would be transferred to the Joint State Political Directorate, the secret police, the OGPU.

Sergei told Shershenevich that it was over between him and Zinaida. She had opted for safety first with Meyerhold. He sensed that she regretted the decision – she kept telling him that she was in 'a happy, loving relationship', as if repeating it would make it true. But whatever she felt in her heart, she showed no sign of coming back.

He had pinned everything on making it right with Zinaida,

atoning for past sins, re-establishing the love that could have saved him. Now that was gone. It wasn't a conscious decision to drown himself in drink and anger, but he knew where it was coming from: if Zinaida wasn't there, what was the point in restraint? Drink offered oblivion. A few hours of escape were worth the pain that followed.

Life is sheets and bed. Our life is a kiss, then into the
      whirlwind.

He struggled with the line; sent it to Shershenevich to ask his opinion.

He missed many things about Zinaida. One of them was how she slowed down time. Making love – time stopped; there was space for everything – seeing, understanding, embracing the world.

Life is sheets and bed. Our life is a kiss, then into the
      whirlwind.

He wondered if he should write 'whirlwind' or 'whirlpool'.

It wasn't only in bed. Living with her had muffled time's drumbeat. His life focused. Distractions, the swarm of events *beyond* were shut out. Just living, just being, was enough.

Life is sheets and bed. Our life is a kiss, then into the
      whirlpool . . .

The fear was back. Time returned. Sweeping him towards an end that approached too soon; no time to finish what he needed to do; time speeding up; time running out.

Life is sheets and bed. Our life is a kiss, then into the
whirlpool.

Shershenevich introduced them. He knew Sergei needed someone to steady him. Avgusta, too, was hurting from a failed
relationship.

Did the fact that she was an actress influence Yesenin's decision to take up with her? A leading lady, mentioned in the same
breath as Zinaida?

Moscow knew Avgusta Miklashevskaya as much for her
beauty as for her acting. She appeared in magazines, modelled
for *Fashion News,* sang and danced in cabaret.

Avgusta Miklashevskaya

Miklashevskaya had been the star of Moscow's Kamerny
Theatre, run by the director Alexander Tairov. He was
Meyerhold's rival. His style was classical, old-fashioned, the
opposite of Meyerhold's socialist avant-garde, and very popular
with audiences.

The authorities didn't like him, though. And they didn't
like the Kamerny. A production of Mikhail Bulgakov's satire,
The Purple Island, was denounced for its mockery of the government. Stalin, who increasingly saw himself as the arbiter

of cultural standards, called the Kamerny 'unreformed and bourgeois'. He issued instructions for changes to be made, and denounced Tairov as 'the last representative of bourgeois aestheticism'. Ten years later, such condemnation would have been a death sentence, but Stalin was still shoring up his position at the head of the Party, still subject to moderating influences.

For Miklashevskaya, the professional reverses were accompanied by personal misfortune. She had married young, but left her husband when she fell in love with another man. She and Fyodor Loshchilin, a dancer from the Bolshoi, had had a child before their affair came to an end. Now she was alone, with a six-year-old son to care for.

Avgusta knew Yesenin's reputation for drunkenness and wild behaviour. When Shershenevich mentioned that they should meet, she was reluctant. But she found him charming, sober, courteous and gallant. At each of their meetings, he brought her a bunch of white roses.

For Marienhof, the white roses were a sign of Yesenin's insincerity, proof of his role-playing, a romance *contrived* for the sake of his poetry. Yet his poems for Miklashevskaya were beautiful; wistful lyrics of yearning and regret. She was five years older than he was, restrained, distant, hurt by life and careful to guard her heart.

> Another man has drunk from your lips, I know,
> But what care we for the past?
> The autumn languor in your eyes, the billow
> Of your golden hair may comfort me at the last.
> Now the fall, with its reds and russet brown,
> Is dearer to me than youthful spring,

Than summer heat and loud renown,
The dreams I had, that have taken wing.
When my heart speaks, you know I do not lie;
My soul stills all notions of conceit.
I quell the tumult that broils within me
And lay my wreath of laurel at your feet.
And when September knocks the door,
When willow branches stoop and show the crimson,
I'll gather my possessions and set out once more
To walk the road made bitter by the season.
For go we must – He tells us to prepare;
My companion for the road I wish it might be you,
The only one for whom I care,
My friend, my lover and my sister, too.

Yesenin and Miklashevskaya never lived together, but were constantly in each other's company, beautiful creatures, darkened by sorrow and experience.

At a dinner given by actors of the Kamerny Theatre, Avgusta's former lover and father of her child, Fyodor Loshchilin, appeared unexpectedly. Yesenin rose and offered him his place at the table, returning with a bunch of flowers that he laid between them.

Half a century later, in her ninth decade, Avgusta Miklashevskaya would tell a literary researcher that she and Yesenin never slept together. His love had been pure and noble; a man of exquisite delicacy, with the tenderest understanding of her feelings.

From Miklashevskaya he had hidden the drunkenness and rage and despair. Nadezhda Volpin saw a different Yesenin.

Volpin was young, five years younger than Sergei, a musician and a poet. She said their relationship was a fire that raged out of control. Yesenin devoured her with an animal passion. There was something unbalanced about him, a desperation in his lovemaking, an unassuaged greed of the flesh, as if conscious of time rushing away, striving to grasp what remained. He was extravagant, forceful, rash. 'I permit myself everything,' he told her. She had the impression he was straining to impregnate her, hurrying to leave a trace of himself before the waters closed above him. She fell pregnant at the end of their relationship and gave birth to a son after they had parted.

> Sing, old man, sing!
> Play the goddamned guitar!
> Make your fingers flash on the strings,
> Make her eyes blaze like the stars.
> If you gaze at the glint of her bracelets
> Or the silk that slides from her neck,
> You'll choke in the smoke of the basement
> You'll end up with your life in a wreck.
> Sing, my friend.
> Sing it again and again!
> Bring back the frenzy of morning
> One more time now, just like it was then.
> Make it happen,
> Make it come to her now.
> After all, she'll go kiss another
> As the soil rains down on your brow.
> And I shall sing my life story
> To the sound of a hollow bass chord.
> I've slept with so many women
> I've scattered my seed abroad.
> The world's truth is empty and bitter;

As a child I caught sight of its lies.
It's a story of sex and the gutter,
And the ending is no surprise.
Forget it; forget what I said.
Love's the hardest, meanest school.
Our life is sheets, our life is bed,
One last kiss, and then the whirlpool.
You know me, I go for broke;
If they think they can stop me, tough luck.
You know me, I'll never croak;
The lot of them can all go to fuck!

Restraint was gone, the brakes on his life released. He was hurtling downwards, out of control, willing on the smash that would end it.

He surrounded himself with women. While he lived with Zinaida or hoped to win her back, he had refused the offers of sex. Now he rushed into everything. Women. Drink. Oblivion.

Nadezhda Volpin

Sergei picked fights he knew he would lose, insulted his friends, spat on those who offered him help.

He had an account with the State Bank but paid little attention to it before the crises of 1925. After the break with Zinaida and his arrests by the police, he started to fret about money running out.

He wrote angry, mistrustful letters. He accused Marienhof and his former colleagues of doing him down. He was suspicious about the liquidation of the accounts from the Pegasus Stable, about money from the Poets' Bookshop and the division of royalties from the publication of Imagist poetry collections. He published ill-tempered denunciations of Marienhof and Shershenevich, wrote that Marienhof was a thief. They, in return, sought to distance themselves from their unstable friend in a letter to the newspaper *Novy Zritel.*

> We denounce the reckless, irresponsible behaviour of Sergei Yesenin. It is true that Yesenin was one of the signatories of the first manifesto of the Imagist group, but he was never an ideological colleague of ours. Yesenin attached himself to us solely for his personal benefit. We never trusted him. Following recent events, including Yesenin's arrest and judicial proceedings against him, we declare our unconditional split from him and our firm resolution to have nothing further to do with him. Sergei Yesenin is irredeemably sick, both physically and mentally. In our opinion, that is the only explanation for his behaviour.

The acrimony and reproaches were understandable. They were a function of Yesenin's personal decline, but they were also a result of the times. These were years when people felt themselves under suspicion, spied on by mysterious, powerful forces; when acquaintances were arrested for incomprehensible reasons and friends disappeared without explanation. Of the poets who perished in the Order of Russian Fascists affair, Alexei Ganin and the Chekrygin brothers – Pyotr and Nikolai – had been close associates of the Imagists. Those who remained lived with the knowledge that they could follow. It was not surprising that Marienhof and Shershenevich wanted to disassociate themselves from Yesenin.

Sergei remained incongruously sanguine.

'Why should I care what these nonentities say or do,' he wrote in a letter to his sister in Ryazan. 'Marienhof and Shershenevich don't scare me. Let them do their worst. It is water off my back. They are mice with puny teeth nibbling at a mountain. Their dirty tricks and all their shit-stirring don't trouble me in the least.'

When he returned to the flat on Afanasievsky Lane, he found his possessions in the corridor. The locks had been changed and there was a note from Shershenevich and Marienhof saying it was no longer convenient for him to stay there.

CHAPTER 39

The lights at the Lubyanka burned all night. The OGPU never slept.

The Yesenin case was giving them trouble. Disturbing the peace and resisting arrest wouldn't do; they were going for Article 58 and they wanted to make it stick. It would be harder to deal with a famous poet in the way they had with Ganin and the Order of Fascists. If Sergei Yesenin disappeared with an obfuscatory 'no right of correspondence', people would ask questions, and not just in Russia.

It needed to be public, with Soviet justice seen to be done. Investigators went looking for witnesses who could swear they heard the poet *oppose the legitimate organs of authority* and *publicly insult the representatives of state power*. They started with those who had been in Malinnikov's bar on the night of the offence, then widened the circle to those who had a smart suit and could be trusted to learn a script.

A certain Mikhail Rodkin had been having a beer in Malinnikov's. Rodkin was the boss of a Moscow food production combine and a Party member. He knew the form.

I was quietly enjoying my refreshment when a group of persons unknown to me sat at a neighbouring table. These persons began a conversation about the legitimate organs of Soviet authority. 'The representatives of state power are all scabby Jews,' said the persons. 'I mean, that Trotsky and that Kamenev, they're Yids, aren't they? I bet they're up to all sorts of dirty tricks.'

Unwilling to tolerate such opposition to the legitimate organs of authority and such public insults to the representatives of state power, I addressed myself to the nearest militia post. A militiaman entered the said place of refreshment and attempted to arrest the said persons. The said persons would not agree to be arrested. Therefore, the aforementioned militiaman invited several of his colleagues to assist him.

There was a drawback. Citizen Yesenin had also made a statement.

I was in Malinnikov's bar having a drink with my friends. We are poets and we were speaking about poetry. We never said a word about the Soviet authorities. We did mention that Jews figure in Russian literature. We said Jewish writers were less adept at capturing the true nature of the Russian soul than are Russian writers. We mentioned Comrade Trotsky and Comrade Kamenev only to praise the way they have allowed Russian literature to flourish under their guidance. I noticed that during our conversation, an unknown person was sitting and taking careful note of our activities. I fear his hearing was not very good. He appears to have misheard the compliments we were bestowing on comrades Trotsky and Kamenev as insults. We could not have uttered the insults he claims to have heard, as comrades Trotsky and Kamenev are the leaders of the Russian revolution and deserving of praise and respect. The person who was spying on our conversation had clearly drunk too much beer because he got everything wrong.

The OGPU investigator in charge of the case had been told 'from the top' that Yesenin needed to go down. Witnesses and statements would be obtained.

Homelessness was hardly new. Yesenin had not had a place of his own since he set up house with his first wife, Anna Izryadnova, in 1913. But his reputation as a wanted man meant there were fewer friends willing to give him a bed.

Ilya Vardin took him in. Vardin was a genial Georgian – real name Mgeladze – who had fought in the Red Cavalry. His reward had been a position on the Kremlin's literary committee and editorship of the magazines *Agitprop* and *Red Press*. He had worked closely with Trotsky when Trotsky was the guiding force in socialist culture, and hadn't been swift enough to shift allegiances when Stalin claimed the role for himself. He was hoping his mentor could somehow reverse the downwards slope on which he seemed to be travelling and shore up Vardin's own fortunes.

'Pretty ironic, isn't it?' he said. 'Here's me under suspicion as a Trotskyite and you up on charges of insulting him! What sort of a world are we living in?'

'We're living in a madhouse,' Sergei said, 'where the lunatics have seized control and the sane are in straitjackets. Life has become so random that even the nimblest struggle to keep up. The Party can say black one day and white the next, but if you point it out, you go to the Gulag. The Russian people live in two realities – the dreadful, soul-crushing world that actually exists; and the perfect, luminous world that we all have to pretend we are living in. Even the past isn't safe from the Bolsheviks. They rewrite history so brazenly to suit their own view of what *ought* to have happened. Everybody sees the lies and the distortions, but woe betide you if you say anything.'

'You know what they say about communism, don't you?' Vardin had opened a bottle. 'It has made the future certain, but the past completely unpredictable!'

The two of them drank through the night. In the morning, Vardin said, 'I'm sorry, Seryozha. You can stay here tonight, but then you'll have to find somewhere else. If they know I've taken you in, it'll be the end for me.'

Yesenin put his arm around him.

'Don't worry, Ilya. Of course I understand. I can always go and stay with Galina.'

Ilya Vardin

Galina Benislavskaya was devoted to him. She had been waiting for years, never imposing herself, always ready to help. She was one of those people you barely notice but would miss in a crisis. When Sergei was drunk, she would get him a cab and accompany him home. Perhaps she hoped he would invite her in; he never did. Now she came into her own.

In 1925, Galina was twenty-seven and a virgin. She had grown up in St Petersburg, daughter of a French father who went his own way when she was young and a mother too mentally disturbed to look after her. Educated, then adopted by a maternal aunt and her physician husband, she had applied herself to her studies with a ferocity that spoke of a need to prove something to someone, probably herself. She got the gold medal at her high school, but it was poetry that moved her. She turned down a career in higher education to write. She took a collection of her verse to the Petersburg publisher, Averyanov. It was 1916 and he had just put out Yesenin's *Radunitsa* anthology. When she heard nothing after a month, she went back to see him. Averyanov shook his head.

With revolution in the air, Benislavskaya joined the Bolshevik Party, travelling to Kharkov in Ukraine where she worked as a nurse in a field hospital, was captured by the Whites and narrowly avoided being executed. The experience disturbed her. She wrote of the horror of helplessness she felt before implacable external forces. For the rest of her life she would feel a need for reassurance; and for Galina, reassurance depended on being in control.

In 1919 she applied to join the secret police. The Cheka's Director, Felix Dzerzhinsky, needed female operatives and Benislavskaya had the credentials – outstanding academic qualifications, an exemplary revolutionary record and an obsessive compulsion to control the lives of others. She was a success. She rose through the ranks as the Cheka was rooting out those who dared to challenge its authority, intimidating, imprisoning and murdering until Russia understood who was in charge.

In 1923, she moved into journalism. Unable to find work on a literary magazine, she took a job at the peasants' newspaper, *Rural Poverty*. She gained a reputation for erudite, slightly boring articles. But she hankered for poetry. She was a regular attender at recitals. She got to know Sergei through the Pegasus Stable. She was always there in the front row. She was his most devoted fan.

Galina Benislavskaya

Galina had an apartment and, when Sergei asked, she said he must come and stay there. She would clean the spare bedroom, fumigate the kitchen and get an extra key cut. She could do all that by lunchtime. What about his possessions? Any trunks? How many cases? She knew a man with a horse. He would collect Sergei's stuff and move it to hers. Did Sergei eat fish? She would have dinner ready for seven.

She hoped he would agree to her becoming his professional assistant. She knew a lot about poetry. She had long thought his publishing and business affairs could be better handled. As for his personal life, she knew what was needed to sort things out.

Galina was good for him. Sergei was incapable of running his own life, so she ran it. She took over everything, from renegotiating his publishing contracts to choosing his shirts, from correcting his proofs to ironing his socks. She liked order and she liked to know what was happening. She didn't mind him drinking – she could hardly have stopped it – but she insisted on knowing where he would be, what time he would be home and when he needed to be woken in the morning. And she didn't want other women in his life – that was a rule.

It didn't take years in the Cheka to see that he had enemies, she said. She had the training to look out for him and she would do so.

Most days, he did what he was told, slightly intimidated, lacking the will to resist. They were together a lot of the time. It pleased her to be in charge, but she was hoping for more. Lying in bed, hearing him undress in the adjoining room, she drifted into dreams with her hand between her legs.

Galina

Galina had been with the secret police through all the changes. She had begun when the Cheka was torturing and executing the Bolsheviks' enemies in the Civil War. She was there when it became the OGPU and switched its attention to the civilian population. Her job had been in records keeping. She had remained in contact with her former colleagues.

Vladimir Polyansky was in charge of records for cases originating in the Moscow Police Department and he was a poetry fan. He loved Yesenin's verse. When Galina asked him how things were looking, Vladimir said Yesenin should get out of town if he didn't want to suffer the same fate as Alexei Ganin.

It wasn't easy to convince him. He had survived so far and he didn't see why things should change. She told him that things *had* changed. Someone at the top had ringed his name. He was on the kill list.

Yesenin smiled – they wouldn't kill a poet as famous as him; the husband of the great Isadora, known by millions in Russia and the West.

The mention of Isadora irked Galina, but she didn't let it show.

'You have to go. No debate. Don't even question me. I've looked at trains. You can get to Baku.'

Sergei wanted to know why Baku.

'Because they're still fighting down there. They've got their hands full. Azeris slaughtering Armenians; Armenians slaughtering Azeris, and the Red Army struggling to keep the Soviets in power. It's the Wild West; you'll be able to disappear until things are safer back here.'

Galina wanted to come with him, but he said he would be fine on his own. She bought him the train ticket. She would be counting the days until he came back to her.

When Sergei Yesenin left Moscow on 25 July 1925, he wasn't alone. He and Sofya Tolstaya had been seeing each other while Sergei was lodging at Galina's. There had been a spark between them. A few weeks together in the Southern Caucasus would allow them to get better acquainted.

While he was away, Galina harnessed the relentless, troubled energy inside her to a purpose. She monitored the sales of his books, made sure his royalties got paid – he had been so lax in the past that half the payments had gone astray – and kept in contact with Polyansky at the OGPU, waiting to hear when the heat had gone out of the Yesenin case. At night, she dreamed of Sergei coming back, expressing his gratitude to her in more than words.

Galina, while working for the Cheka

Sofya Tolstaya was the granddaughter of Lev Tolstoy. Yesenin had met her at a literary evening. He was used to recognising the signs of interest in a woman's eyes. For him, the interest was purely literary. He liked the idea of fucking Tolstoy's granddaughter. So he did.

Sofya Tolstaya

They spent a month and a half in the Caucasus. He wasn't exactly on the run, but he was hiding from something and for Sofya, that gave him an air of mystery.

They split their time between Baku in Azerbaijan and Tbilisi in Georgia. Stalin had decreed that Azerbaijan, Armenia and Georgia should be amalgamated into a Transcaucasian Soviet Republic, run by commissars appointed from Moscow. The locals were unhappy. None of them liked it. Tensions rose; resentment of Russia grew. It was the first of many lines-on-a-map decisions by Stalin. Over the years, they would lead to ethnic conflicts in more than a dozen regions of the Union.

Sergei and Sofya travelled on horseback, went into the mountains and swam in the Caspian. They both loved the scenery, the food, the weather and the hospitality. Sofya loved Sergei. He drank more wine.

In Tbilisi, Sergei met an Armenian girl called Shaganeh. He made an excuse and left Sofya at the hotel.

Shaganeh Talyan

He spent a week with Shaganeh, wrote some poems for her. The women were becoming a blur. The poetry, too. The thought that his powers were in decline tormented him.

When he got back, Sofya said, 'We should get married, Seryozha. I know my grandfather, God rest him, would approve.'

Sergei and Sofya Tolstaya

Sergei Yesenin and Sofya Tolstaya returned to Moscow on 6 September 1925 and were married twelve days later.

Galina, who had gone to the station to meet the train, collapsed. She was taken to hospital. The doctors found her disturbed, angry and violent. They knew about her past in the Cheka. They encouraged her to write down the thoughts that were tormenting her and assessed them while she was sedated.

I dreamed of him coming to me, not as a friend but as a lover. A deep, tender feeling of submission.

Why did I let him go away? Why did I encourage him to go away?

I am ill again. Probably seriously; probably for a long time.

I believed in love. I must take myself in hand. I yearn for the feel of his body.

He is a bastard. Despite all his loveliness. A bastard. Despite all his charm. A bastard.

He is a nobody. Such an absence of decency in him.

Does he want me to throw myself from the sixth floor? Should I really go down on my knees to him? Should I beg and abase myself before him? All I wanted was for him to love me. I thought he would understand that.

I was meek and submissive to him, because I thought he was a god. But he doesn't respect me. He's a petty, scheming bastard obsessed with his own ego and fame and success.

Tolstaya is *ugly*.

She's repulsive. I know he doesn't love her. All he's after is her name. He thinks he can turn himself into Tolstoy just by marrying his granddaughter. Everyone is laughing at him and how he's deluding himself.

I mistook him for a good man. I idolised him. I gave him everything that is good and valuable in me.

It makes me so angry. I can't live with it. I must pay him back.

I must give him what he deserves. Him and his whore. He won't like it. He won't like what he's going to get from me!

CHAPTER 40

The Old Man was everywhere. It bugged Sergei. The portraits on the walls of Sofya's flat, the big, blown-up photographs with his stupid peasant smock and white beard. He wasn't a peasant! He was a joke. An aristocrat who 'loved the people'. Ha! Went out working in the fields to show he was 'with the people'; but after he'd finished his bit of ploughing, the real ploughman had to go out and re-do it because the Master's furrows were so crooked! The charade had worked, though. He was as bad as all the others – hundreds of serfs, owned entire villages, got so many servant girls pregnant that he had to set up a school for their kids – yet here he was, loved and venerated in the New Socialist World!

Sergei knew he'd made a mistake. Probably knew it before he married her. She brought her grandfather's name, but she also brought his baggage, and now this dreadful shadow that hung over everything.

Old Tolstoy looked down from the wall with such contempt in his eyes; looked down on him as if to say, 'I've got your number, you little shit.'

The shadow was there all the time. It was crushing him.

The agents came in the middle of November. The OGPU had lined up the witnesses, written their statements and decided the verdict. All they needed was the defendant.

Sergei was out. The agents were surprised. Normally when they knocked on someone's door at 2 a.m., the accused would be asleep in his bed.

'Seryozha is out most nights,' Sofya said. 'It's not that often that I see him now.'

The doctors released Galina unwillingly. She was angry, deranged, and a former member of the Cheka.

When they spoke about her in conference, more than one of them thought she would attack Yesenin and, if she did, might well kill him.

None of them wanted the blood of Russia's favourite poet on their hands. But she was demanding to leave and they couldn't stop her.

Galina Benislavskaya

Sergei knew in a detached way that his life was in danger. And knew it was his fault. The women, the drink; the antagonism and violence; the unforgivable treatment of Zinaida; the quarrels with his friends; the loss of the past, the tsar, the Church, the revolution; the admonishments of Tolstoy in his ears; the realisation that poetry was leaving him. How could he deal with all that?

On 26 November 1925, he checked himself into Gannushkin's Clinic.

Pyotr Gannushkin was famous. He'd been a student of the great Vladimir Serbsky, specialising in social psychiatry, perfecting the modern methodology of clinical analysis then taking the leap of generalising from the individual to the collective. Gannushkin's passion was the study of human psychopathy, the elucidation and classification of disordered personalities, all the paranoid, compulsive, manic, obsessive behaviours he saw around him, the schizophrenia and psychosis, all that the twentieth century had inflicted upon a demoralised world.

Sergei saw it as a refuge. Signing over responsibility for his life to a man who, improbably, claimed to understand the human heart.

A refuge, also, from pursuit. As the West deemed churches to be safe havens from arrest, so in Russia hospitals were held to be off-limits to the police. Being a lunatic bought him days of grace.

Pyotr Gannushkin

Gannushkin kept notes.

> Upon presentation, symptoms of neurocirculatory myalgic asthenia. Breathlessness, precordial pain and palpitations. Invasive sense of fatigue. Extreme anxiety. Fear of effort. Delirium tremens.

In subsequent entries, Gannushkin describes his conversations with Yesenin and makes a provisional diagnosis.

> Patient does not feel in control of his life. Drifting, swept by currents too strong to resist. Possible: Emotionally unstable personality disorder.

The Russian term *sostoyanie affektivno-neustoichivoi lichnosti* would later be known as borderline personality disorder, indicating a 'pattern of unstable behaviour, unstable emotions, unstable sense of self and unstable relationships with others; feelings of emptiness; debilitating fear of abandonment'.

'Perhaps everything in the world is a mirage,' Gannushkin records his patient as saying. 'Perhaps we only seem to one another to exist.'

And later, 'I have nothing left. I love no one. Only my verse remains. I have sacrificed everything for my verse, do you understand, everything … Yet now, my poetry gives me no pleasure. I tear it out of myself and it goes away from me.'

His poetry, the scraps he still wrote, was elegiac.

> Every day now
> I go to the harbour,
> To see off those I never knew.
> To gaze with grief-stricken wonder
> On the smile of the deep,
> The eternal, infinite blue.

With a duster and polish that he took from the janitor's room, Sergei made the rounds of the ward, kneeling before the nurses and female staff, solemnly polishing their shoes. Gannushkin wrote in his notes that it seemed an act of contrition.

State Psychiatric Clinic, 11 Rossolima Street, Moscow (Gannushkin Clinic)

His remaining friends interceded on his behalf. Anatoly Lunacharsky wrote to the judge.

> People's Judge, Comrade Lipkin. Dear Comrade! Sergei Yesenin is a sick person. He drinks, and when drunk ceases to be responsible for his actions. I think it is not worth causing the scandalous trial of a major Soviet writer because of things he says when drunk, and which he now very much regrets. I would ask you to stop proceedings, if this is possible.
>
> Lunacharsky, People's Commissar for Enlightenment

Ilya Vardin added his voice.

> Comrade Lipkin! I wish to inform you that Yesenin is currently in hospital. I second the request of Comrade Lunacharsky. Anti-Soviet circles, especially in emigration, will use any trial to serve their own political ends.

Comrade Lipkin was unmoved. On 28 November, OGPU agents came to the clinic. Gannushkin refused to let them in. He gave them a medical certificate to take back to their bosses.

> Yesenin is sick. The state of his health precludes any court appearance at the current time.

Gannushkin had put Yesenin in a private room. He showed signs of agitation, only partially relieved by medication. Noises and disturbances threw him off balance. The open door of his room – Gannushkin had him on suicide watch – the light that burned day and night, the hubbub in the corridor, the faces of other inmates peering in at him heightened his anxiety.

When Sofya came to visit, he refused to see her. He took a young boy under his wing, a street urchin, admitted by Gannushkin after years of abuse. His blue eyes and blond hair reminded Sergei of himself at that age. He thought back to the horse traders at the River Oka who had taken him to their heart, grizzled, life-hardened men, who looked at him with nostalgia for what they might have been and unspoken hope that he might become it.

One night he got dressed and walked out.

Gannushkin found Yesenin's empty bed on the morning of 21 December 1925. He dispatched his deputy, Dr Alexander Aaronson, to track him down. Losing a famous poet was unfortunate; if anything were to happen to him, their carelessness would have consequences.

Aaronson went first to Sofya Tolstaya's address on Pomerantsev Lane. She said she had heard nothing from her husband. At Marienhof's and Shershenevich's, he got the same response. He left all of them his home and office numbers and asked them to call if they heard where Yesenin might be.

It was late in the afternoon before Aaronson had his first

success. At Shershenevich's suggestion, he went to Yesenin's publishers and was taken to see his editor, Ivan Yevdokimov. Yevdokimov said that Yesenin had been there earlier in the day, enquiring about a contract he had signed the previous year for the publication of his collected works. It was odd, Yevdokimov said – Yesenin had never shown any interest in financial matters. When Aaronson asked what sort of sums were involved, Yevdokimov said a payment of 2,000 roubles had just been made into Yesenin's bank account, roughly equivalent to the average Russian annual wage. Aaronson went to Yesenin's branch of the State Bank, but found it closed. He would have to come back in the morning.

Around midnight, the poet Matvey Roizman called in at the Mouse Hole bar at the junction of Kuznetsky Bridge and Neglinnaya Street. Sitting at a table in the corner was Sergei. When Roizman expressed his surprise at seeing him, he said, 'You thought I was in the madhouse? I couldn't stand it. It's full of lunatics threatening to top themselves.'

Yesenin ordered another beer and a vodka chaser. He told Roizman he had just spent four weeks 'locked up without alcohol'. By 3 a.m., he was so drunk that Roizman had to pick him up from the floor.

Dr Aaronson was back at the State Bank first thing in the morning. He explained to the manager that he was pursuing an urgent medical matter. The manager confirmed that Sergei Yesenin had been there the previous day and had closed his account. He had left with bundles of roubles.

The next sighting of Yesenin was that evening, 22 December. Meyerhold's neighbours at the apartment on Bryusov Lane heard him banging on the door. He looked forlorn. They told him that Zinaida, Meyerhold and the children were away at the dacha, preparing for Christmas together. They saw that he was crying and asked if he wanted to leave a message.

'Tell her ... Tell her I just called to say ...' his hand rose to his face, 'goodbye.'

It is unclear where Yesenin spent the night of 22 December. Next morning, 23 December, he was at the Central Telegraph Office on Tverskaya Street. He sent a cable to Wolf Ehrlich, a Leningrad poet with whom he had collaborated in the early days of Imagism.

Find me flat. Three rooms. Arriving tomorrow. Yesenin.

Half an hour later, he sent a second wire, countermanding the first.

No apartment. Book hotel. Angleterre. Room 5.

By the time Dr Aaronson arrived at the Telegraph Office, Sergei was already at the station, preparing to board the overnight express to Leningrad.

Wolf Ehrlich

CHAPTER 41

Ehrlich met him off the train. It was the morning of Thursday, 24 December and Leningrad was full of Christmas bustle. The Bolsheviks had outlawed religion, submerging the old holiday in secular New Year celebrations, but the trappings remained. The streets were full of decorated fir trees and jolly Father Frosts. Snow was falling, the shops crowded with people looking for last-minute presents.

He went with Ehrlich to the Angleterre, on St Isaac's Square. Room 5 was where Sergei had stayed, years earlier, with Isadora.

In the corridor, he said, 'I used to walk along here, pissed out of my mind. The room was freezing. I hope to God they've fixed the heating!'

They sat and talked. Room 5 was warm; the pipes running from floor to ceiling were hot. Yesenin ordered champagne. He had resolved to embark on a new life, with hard work, no drunkenness and a simple, unsophisticated wife who would help him keep to his resolutions.

They spoke about poetry and regrets.

'I've loved . . . kissed . . . boozed . . . No, that's not it! I'm bored, Wolfie, I'm bored!'

Ehrlich said later that he had been shocked by Yesenin's condition.

> He dwelled on insults he had suffered two or three years earlier. He said his friends had abandoned him, but it was probably because of his own behaviour. He seemed very tired. His nerves would fray as the result of trivial things and he would grow angry. His hands shook; he looked distracted. Beneath his fear and rage, an excruciating spiritual drama was being played out, whose secret it was impossible to guess.

Yesenin got up several times to check that the door was locked.

'They're coming after me from Moscow,' he said. 'I think there's no escape.'

The following day, 25 December, Yesenin went out on his own. He evidently found a shop open, because he returned with a goose, sliced meats, wine, cognac and champagne.

He invited Ehrlich and two other friends, Georgy and Yelisaveta Ustinov, to share them with him. He drank in moderation and spoke of his plans for the future. He said that he, the Ustinovs and Ehrlich should find a big flat where they could all live together.

Later, he said to Ehrlich, 'Would you write my obituary? Don't worry, I'm not going to die. I'll go into hiding. Devoted friends will arrange my funeral. Articles will appear in the newspapers and journals. Then I'll come back from the dead. We'll see what they write about me. We'll see who is my friend and who is not!'

Yesenin spent the next day in his room. In the evening, he recited the poem that obsessed him, 'The Dark Man':

> My friend, my friend
> I'm ill; so very ill.
> Nor do I know
> Whence came this sickness.
> Either the wind whistles
> Over the desolate unpeopled field;
> Or, as September strips a copse,
> Alcohol strips my brain.
> The black man,
> The black, black,

Black man
Sits by me on the bed all night,
And will not let me sleep . . .

Both the Ustinovs and Wolf Ehrlich felt he was speaking from the depths. When he finished, he said to them, 'I'm not here by chance, you know. I am here because it has been decreed. My fate is decided not by me, but by my blood. Therefore I do not complain. I understand nothing of what is happening.'

After his guests had left, he instructed the hotel porter not to admit anyone to see him, nor even acknowledge that he was staying at the hotel. There were people from Moscow spying on him.

Ehrlich came early the following morning. Sergei was elated and agitated. He feared the water heater in the bathroom might explode. There was so much heat and no water. He wondered if people were trying to blow him up.

Ehrlich saw that his wrist was bandaged and asked what had happened. Sergei shrugged and said it was the hotel's fault for not leaving any ink in the room. When Ehrlich didn't understand, he went to the table and tore a sheet from a writing pad. He held it at a distance and squinted at it. It was a poem. He folded it in four and put it into the pocket of Ehrlich's coat. Ehrlich reached into his pocket to read it, but Sergei said, 'No. Wait awhile. Read it when you are alone. There's no hurry.'

The Ustinovs arrived. The four of them spent the day in conversation. Sergei seemed in good spirits. They lit the samovar, drank beer and ate leftovers from the Christmas goose. Sergei fell asleep in mid-afternoon. Concerned about his health and happy to see him rest, the others sat quietly until he roused himself.

The Ustinovs left at 6 p.m. to go to a dinner. Alone with Ehrlich, Sergei had a moment of tears. He took out a document holder, a present from Zinaida. He showed him the inscription she had written: 'Our love will outlive the world and the stars.'

Ehrlich left at 8 p.m., but returned an hour later to collect a book. Sergei was alone, reading some old poems. When Ehrlich was about to leave for a second time, he took his arm and said, 'Wolfie, don't go. If you can, stay with me.' Then laughed it off. 'No. Of course, go. Only, come early tomorrow, will you? I fear being alone.'

At midnight, he went to the front desk and told the hall porter that no one should be allowed to come to his room. The porter noted his instruction, but was surprised to see Sergei an hour later, sitting on a settee in one of the corridors.

When Yelisaveta Ustinov knocked on Sergei's door the following morning, there was no answer. She asked the hotel manager to open it with his pass key. The manager opened the door and went away. Yelisaveta entered the room. The bed was not slept in. She went to the couch – it, too, was empty. The divan – no one. She raised her eyes and saw him. He had hanged himself.

Divisional Inspector Nikolai Gorbov of the Leningrad Police Department made a preliminary report.

28 December 1925. Telephone call from the manager of the Angleterre Hotel, Citizen Vasily Nazarov, regarding a hotel guest hanging himself in his room. Arriving on the scene, I discovered hanging from a pipe of the central heating system

a man in the following condition: held in a slack noose, which was tight only on the right-hand side of his neck. His face was turned towards the pipe. The wrist of his right hand had grabbed hold of the pipe. The corpse was hanging just beneath the ceiling. The feet were approximately 1.5 metres above the floor. Close to the spot where the man was hanging was an overturned night table. The lamp that been standing on it was on the floor. When the corpse was taken down and examined, a cut was found on the right arm on the inside of the elbow. The left wrist was also cut and there was a bruise below the left eye. He was dressed in grey trousers, white shirt, black socks and black patent leather shoes. The sum of 640 roubles in cash was found at the scene.

No photographs were taken of Yesenin hanging from the noose. His body was laid on the couch in the corner of the room, the right arm that had gripped the heating pipe still frozen in its final gesture. His boyish face looked bewildered.

CHAPTER 42

Yelisaveta had summoned her husband. Georgy Ustinov had arrived before the police. He was struck by the chaos in the room. Furniture was upturned, documents scattered on the floor. Sergei's body was still hanging, 'gazing out at the huge, brooding bulk of St Isaac's Cathedral looming beyond the window'. The rope around his neck was the strap from a suitcase he had brought back from his travels abroad. Ustinov was mystified.

Yesenin had not made a noose. He had wound the strap around his neck just like a scarf. He could have jumped out at any time. The corpse was holding on with one hand to the central heating pipe. Why? So as not to fall? Or because he didn't want to die? Had he miscalculated the force of the drop when he kicked the stool away and died by accident? Was he only playing with death? The physical evidence remains; the mind's intentions vanish with the last breath.

Hotel Angleterre, room 5, 28 December 1925

Ehrlich arrived. He had read the poem that Yesenin stuffed into his pocket.

> Goodbye, my friend, goodbye.
> My love, you are in my heart.
> It was preordained that we should part
> To meet again one day.
> Goodbye: no handshake to endure.
> Let's have no sadness – no furrowed brow.
> There's nothing new in dying now
> Though living is no newer.

It was written in Sergei's blood. Ehrlich remembered the bandage on his wrist and the cryptic explanation about the lack of ink in the room. Had Yesenin given him the poem as a warning of what he was about to do? Could he have saved him if he had read it earlier?

'Goodbye, my friend . . .' written in blood

A doctor was called and Yesenin certified dead. The case was assigned the police number 89. The body, wrapped in a bed-sheet, was carried down the service staircase, away from the eyes of other hotel guests. In the hotel yard, a horse-drawn sleigh was waiting to transport it through snowy streets to the morgue of the Nechayev-Obukhovskaya Hospital on the Fontanka Embankment.

The following day, 29 December, the police pathologist Dr A.G. Gilyarevsky carried out an autopsy. He confirmed the injuries noted in the initial report and discovered two others. Yesenin's tongue had been bitten through. And there was a deep wound to the centre of his forehead. It was four centimetres long and 1.5 centimetres wide.

Yesenin's brain was removed, examined and weighed. All appeared to be normal. The same procedure was repeated with his internal organs. There was blood in his lungs. Doctor Gilyarevsky concluded:

> Based on the evidence of the autopsy, my finding is that the death of Sergei Yesenin is the result of asphyxiation, caused by pressure on the airways of the neck due to

hanging. The injury to the forehead could be the result
of contact with a pipe or other external object during the
hanging. The cuts to the right arm and left wrist appear
to be self-inflicted and are not the cause of death. Other
bruises and abrasions are consistent with the body having
hung from the noose for an extended period of time.

Signed: Gilyarevsky, Forensic Expert, 2nd Division,
Leningrad Militia.

Yesenin's body, its organs replaced, incisions sewn up with
mortuary hemp, travelled by train through the night to
Moscow. Thousands greeted him at the station. Thousands
went with him on his last trip through the capital. At the House
of the Press on Nikitsky Boulevard, a banner announced, 'The
body of the great Russian poet Sergei Yesenin lies within.'
Crowds gathered outside, waiting to pay their respects.

Before the room opened, friends and family requested an hour to say goodbye. Death buried feuds. Shershenevich spoke of guilt and regret.

> He foretold his end in every poem, cried out about it in every line. Imminent death was everywhere in his verse. We thought it was a literary theme. We thought it was a poetic device. But to our infinite pain and sorrow, it was the terrible truth.

Marienhof, as always, was perceptive and acerbic, but now with a note of sorrow.

> Sergei put on the mask of doomed lyric hero and couldn't get it off. The mask became the man. It tore his flesh when he tried to rip it away. Sergei Yesenin hanged himself because

his poetic narrative became his life. He condemned himself to play the role and he played it to the bitterest of ends. His life was devoured by the art he thought would save him. Perhaps it will. From beyond the grave.

Far left, Nikolai Klyuev. Third from right,
Sofya Tolstaya. Far right, Wolf Ehrlich

Zinaida, distraught, refused the words of consolation, declined the handshakes. Marienhof, Klyuev and the others had resented the love that Sergei had for her. Seeing him in his coffin, she fainted.

From right to left: Yesenin's mother, Tatiana; his
sisters; Zinaida faints on Meyerhold's shoulder

Meyerhold comforted her. She sat with him as the public were admitted. She watched the outpouring of grief for a poet loved by millions, for a man who had been the dearest person in her life and would remain so forever.

Meyerhold told her everything would be all right. But it wouldn't. Sergei's death began a decline in Zinaida that would have catastrophic outcomes for herself, her husband and all connected with them.

Meyerhold comforts Zinaida as crowds file past Yesenin's coffin

There were poems in his papers. Commentators read them as clues to his death, each of his lovers as a message to her.

> It is too late to dissolve the grief I feel,
> Too late to lift it like the mist
> Above the meadow. Time's wheel
> Has turned; those days are past.
> The lime-tree blossoms are faded,
> The laughter in the fields has gone;
> The nightingale dawns uprooted,
> The clock of life moved on.
> . . .
> Do you not love me? Feel no compassion?
> Maybe you'll say I don't look my best.
> Once, when we loved, you thrilled with passion;
> You held me close, your lips skimmed my chest.
> You'll go your own way now, step out with another,
> Chatting of love as you walk in the town;
> It's then you might glimpse me, your
>   abandoned lover,
> Lingering, homeless, forever alone.
> You'll straighten your hair, your smile
>   sweetly winning,

You'll wave me a greeting, perhaps even a kiss;
You'll bow and say softly, 'Good evening!'
And I shall reply: 'Good evening, miss.'
. . .
When a lover and a lover in the warmth of their bed
Hear the words of my song in the night,
Perhaps they'll think of the soul that has fled,
Of the flower that blossomed and died.
. . .
I loved all the things that embody the soul,
The sweetness of nature, the flowers, the trees,
The aspens, the maples, the cattle, the foal,
The snow-trimmed birch buds that blow in
        the breeze.
I'm glad that I sat, that I looked and I thought,
Glad to have written the songs that I did.
I don't grieve for those sorrows the years may
        have brought;
Just happy I was able to breathe and to live.
Happy I knew how to make love to a woman,
That I slept in the grass and under the stars . . .

When the police closed the case, on 20 January 1926, millions
who loved Yesenin refused to believe the verdict of suicide.
Those who had waited for his postcards in the post, the poetic
updates on the lyrical novel of his life, who felt they knew him
as an intimate presence in their own life, began to advance
other explanations.

Yesenin's room was in a chaotic state – Ustinov and others
had said so. Did that not suggest a struggle, intruders? It
was well known that Yesenin was being pursued by the

OGPU – had he not written about his suspicions and his fears? Was it not likely that the authorities, scared of putting a beloved poet on trial, simply murdered him? They had done it before; everybody knew what they were capable of. And what about the unexplained wounds, the deep gash in his forehead? The photographs showed that it was a blow from a blunt instrument; Yesenin had been felled by an assassin's cudgel. The hanging was a charade, staged to conceal the truth. Even the police admitted that the noose was not tight around his neck. Yesenin must already have been dead. And look at the central heating pipe they claim he hanged himself from – it was vertical, running from floor to ceiling; obviously, a noose attached to it would slip down as soon as any weight was put on it. The authorities' case simply did not stack up.

Theories multiplied. Suspects were named. The Russian imagination is potent and unruly. Yesenin had stood up to the Bolsheviks and the Bolsheviks blamed Yeseninism for the ills of their society. They had a motive and they had the means. The OGPU worked by infiltrating its agents into a victim's entourage ... So who was this *Wolf Ehrlich*? A so-called poet, so-called friend of Yesenin? But in everything Yesenin ever wrote and everything that was written about him, there was never any mention of an Ehrlich. He must have been an OGPU provocateur! He must have got the murderers in – Sergei had told the hotel not to admit anyone to his room, but Ehrlich had gained his confidence and tricked him into opening the door.

Within months, it was an established truth that Ehrlich was working for the secret police – a friend of a friend had been told by a reliable acquaintance that he had personally spoken to an unnamed source who had with his own eyes *seen* the OGPU personnel file for a Wolf Josefovich Ehrlich! It was so obvious ...

And then someone found the *really* incriminating photograph. It turned out that the newly exposed OGPU agent, Ehrlich was a close confidant and co-conspirator with the known Chekist, Galina Benislavskaya.

Wolf Ehrlich and Galina Benislavskaya

Sergei Yesenin at the time of his death was Russia's most widely read poet. He remained so for much of the twentieth century. The fact that the regime disapproved of him increased his popularity.

In the year following his death, tributes were paid by writers and poets. Most politicians, knowing Yesenin was *non grata*, stayed silent. Lev Trotsky, removed from his ministerial posts, but still a member of the Party and a towering public figure, was the exception:

> We have lost Yesenin and the loss is a tragic one. Such a fine poet, so fresh and so full of meaning for the times we live in. His farewell poem is tender and gentle. He left life quietly, without ostentation or anger; not slamming the door, closing it softly with a hand already soaked in his blood. The manner of his leaving will forever illuminate the poet and the man that we conserve in our thoughts.

> It is true that Yesenin wrote poems of drunkenness and hooliganism, that he lent his beautiful melodies to the world

of bars and brothels. It is true that he made scandals, that he played the tough guy. But beneath it, he was the most delicate of men, a soul that was always open, always loving, always vulnerable. His toughness was an act, a mask that he wore as a defence against the inhumanity of our times. He was the most lyrical of poets in an era where lyricism is trampled and crushed.

Yesenin was not suited to revolutionary times. He was intimate and tender; the Revolution is public and cruel. That is the reason his brief existence came to such a tragic end. The poem he wrote in his own blood is addressed to an unnamed friend, an unknown lover. It seems to me that it is addressed to all of us. It seems to me that *every* poem Yesenin composed is written in the blood of his unquiet heart.

Trotsky's star was on the wane. Within a year, he would be expelled from the Party, then from the country, before being murdered in exile by a Kremlin assassin. Yesenin's closeness to Trotsky was another reason for the new leader, Josef Stalin, to hate him.

CHAPTER 44

Galina Benislavskaya did not come to Sergei's funeral. For the conspiracy theorists, it was proof of her guilt. That and the fact that Wolf Ehrlich had wired her from Leningrad so suspiciously quickly after Yesenin's death.

In fact, she had been ill. The breakdown she suffered at the time of Sergei's marriage to Sofya Tolstaya had left her gripped by debilitating depression.

She wrote in her diary.

So, he is dead. Dead of that unbearable, fatal longing. That longing that I myself suffered for so many years. And now that he is gone, I feel once again the longing for him, the same yearning for his presence that fills my every thought. I am the faithful dog that lays down her head and waits forever for her master's return.

Her obsession with Yesenin in death was equal to her obsession with him in life. For the next twelve months, she devoted herself to assembling his manuscripts, overseeing their publication, correcting things that were written about him and writing endlessly about her own memories and feelings for him.

In December 1926, a year after his death, she went to Yesenin's grave in Moscow's Vagankovskoe Cemetery. She had with her a revolver, a stiletto and a pack of twenty Mozaika cigarettes.

She sat by the graveside, thinking, smoking, waiting for dusk. By the time she had smoked all twenty, she had made up her mind. She scribbled a note on a piece of card.

> I have killed myself. I have done it here, though I know it will bring even more criticism down on Sergei. By then, I won't care and he won't care. For me, everything that means anything is in this grave. Because in the end, who cares about those who betrayed him and slandered him and persecuted him? Who cares what people think?

She sat a while longer. On the cardboard from the cigarette packet, she wrote.

> If I have stuck the knife into his grave after shooting myself, it means that I did not regret it. If I regret it, I will fling the knife away.

When the notes were found, by the cemetery keeper who came running at the sound of shots, Galina was lying on Yesenin's grave with a bullet in her heart. She was still alive and faintly groaning. Underneath the paragraph about the knife, she had written, 'One blank.' In the end, she had pulled the trigger five times before putting the live bullet in her chest. The knife had fallen from her hand. She lived another three hours.

Galina's suicide note

CHAPTER 45

Isadora Duncan took Sergei's death badly. She was herself at a low point. She had left Russia and was living in Nice, in the south of France. Sensationalised reports of Yesenin's suicide, including claims that he had planned to immolate himself on Red Square, prompted her to write to the press.

> The tragic death of Yesenin has caused me the deepest pain. He had youth, beauty, genius. His audacious spirit sought the unattainable. He has destroyed his young and splendid body, but his soul will live eternally in the soul of Russia and the souls of all who love poetry. There was never between Yesenin and myself any quarrel or divorce. I weep his death with anguish and despair.

She wrote to Mary Desti:

> Poor little Sergei. I have cried so much over him that my eyes have no tears left ... Myself, I am having an epoch of such continual calamity that I am often tempted to follow his example. Only, I will walk into the sea ...

Over the next eighteen months, Isadora spoke of Yesenin as her last great love. She said it was no coincidence he had chosen to kill himself in the very room where they had known their greatest joy. And she dropped tantalising hints that he might have written her a farewell letter.

Her professional and private lives were in disarray. She drank excessively, indulged in fleeting sexual encounters. In September 1927, sitting with Mary Desti on the Promenade des Anglais in Nice, she said, 'Mary, if you have the slightest affection for me, find me a way out of this cursed existence. I cannot live another day in a world filled with little golden-haired children. Neither drink, nor excitement, nor anything can ease this horrible pain I have carried with me for thirteen years.'

That evening, 14 September, a young man Isadora had met earlier came to pick her up in an open-topped Amilcar sports car. She wrapped her trademark flowing red scarf around her neck and jumped in, calling to friends, '*Adieu, mes amis, je vais à l'amour!*' – 'Farewell, friends, I'm off for some love!' although Mary Desti would later claim she had said, '*... je vais à la gloire!*' – '... I am bound for glory!'

As the car pulled away, Isadora's trailing scarf got caught in the wheels. It jerked her head back with such force that her neck was snapped and her jugular vein severed.

CHAPTER 46

Zinaida's final madness probably began on the day of Sergei's funeral. The signs at first were negligible. She insisted on lifting up Tanya and little Kostya to look into their dead father's coffin. She made Tanya recite a Pushkin poem to him. Others found her behaviour histrionic. She cried and fainted.

After the burial, she took to her bed and didn't work for months. When Meyerhold put other actresses in her roles, she yelled at him. Writing fifty years later, Tatiana would remember how her mother could flip from affection to extreme anger.

She would behave normally – her physical health was good, and for the most part she was positive in her outlook – but it took only a minor setback to destroy her equilibrium. Without warning, she would be seized by uncontrollable fear or grief, anxiety and agitation. One minute, she would be telling us children that Meyerhold was 'a god' whom we must love and to whom we owe everything; the next, she would be cursing him in the most terrible way. Such scenes happen in all marriages, but this was more. One day she looked at him and said, 'Seva, do you know your feet are sticking out of your heart?' The doctors said youthful bouts of cerebral typhus had affected her brain. They said she was suffering from several different manias. Meyerhold said the real reason was that she had been terribly wounded in her soul.

Zinaida took a long time to recover from the breakdown of 1925. She began to act again and the years between 1930 and 1934 were relatively stable. Her confidence returned. She learned to sing. To vary the diet of tragic heroines, she took on slighter roles in operettas.

Meyerhold had been asking permission to take the theatre on tour abroad and in the 1930s they were twice allowed to go to Germany. The first visit, a six-week tour of Berlin, Breslau and Cologne drew big audiences but got mixed reviews. The exception was Zinaida, who was praised for all her roles.

Meyerhold and Zinaida on tour in Germany

The manner of Galina's death resonated with the melodrama of the Russian imagination. It had sacrifice and madness, worthy of an operatic heroine from Mussorgsky, Wagner or Puccini.

She was buried in the same plot as Yesenin; the Russian people demanded it. Benislavskaya had given everything for love; it was Russia's duty to reunite them in – and, possibly, beyond – the grave. An enamelled plaque was attached to the now-shared railings, 'Here lies Faithful Galya.'

Her death had another effect. It was perceived as legitimising – glamorising – the sacrifice offered for love. There were copycat suicides. Young girls who thought they loved the cruel, beautiful man called Yesenin. Others who thought they loved Ivan Ivanovich from the next village.

The authorities were alarmed. 'Yeseninism' had already been blamed for melancholia and teenage suicides. His baleful influence was reaching out again. Stalin ordered all but the most optimistic of his poems to be banned.

Yesenin's grave in 1926; the plaque to Galina, also buried there, can just be seen on the right

CHAPTER 47

By 1934, Stalin had consolidated power in his hands. Rivals had been exiled or shot. Many more would join them in the years ahead.

Stalin's Five-Year Plans were industrialising the country and imposing collectivisation in agriculture. The demands on the workforce were extravagant, in many cases impossible. When norms were not met, the state was merciless. Stealing a handful of grain was punishable by execution. Stalin's faith in the crackpot theories of the agronomist Lysenko had led to crop failures and the return of famine.

The more the country suffered, the harsher the repression from above. In July, the OGPU was renamed the NKVD with a brief to be more ruthless than its predecessors. The arts were pummelled; divergence from the precepts of socialist realism brought punishment.

The poet Osip Mandelstam, otherworldly, sensitive, a writer of exquisite, finely crafted verse, snapped under the pressure. He let rip with a savage expression of hatred for Stalin, the destroyer of art and the hangman of the Russian soul:

> We are living, but the ground is dead
> > beneath our feet;
> Ten steps away our words cannot be heard.

In half whispers we speak of the Kremlin
    mountain-man,
The murderer, the peasant slayer.
His fingers are oily as maggots,
Words fall from his lips like lead weights.
With his gleaming leather boots
And his laughing cockroach whiskers,
He flings decrees and diktats,
Heavy as horseshoes, into peoples'
Groins and eyes and foreheads.
Every killing is a treat
For the broad-chested Ossetian.

In January 1934, Mandelstam read his 'Stalin Ode' to friends and acquaintances, in a state of exultation, with an almost triumphant warning: 'Not a word about this or they'll shoot me.' Within weeks he was arrested and sent to the Gulag. Four years later, he would die there.

Meyerhold knew what had happened to Mandelstam. Zinaida knew it. Everyone knew it. Mocking or questioning the supreme leader meant annihilation.

Like most people, they tried to look away, found enjoyment where they could, went on holiday with the children.

Meyerhold hid his distaste for the idiocies of socialist realism. He bit his tongue when Stalin criticised his productions or offered him advice on how to make them more heroic, more Soviet.

Like his friends Shostakovich and Pasternak, Meyerhold walked an artistic tightrope, balancing the need for outward conformity with an inner core of independence and integrity. You needed to play the game and keep your mouth shut if you wanted to carry on making the art you were really proud of.

In December 1934, the Leningrad Party boss, Sergei Kirov, was assassinated. Stalin became increasingly anxious for his own safety. The search for Kirov's killers was a pretext for repression. The years of the Great Purge from 1936 to 1938 would see more than a million executions.

In Zinaida the seeds of madness that had lain dormant began to germinate. Jealous colleagues informed the police that the Meyerholds were living beyond their means and an investigation was begun. Someone in the theatre's administration forgot to pay Zinaida's Party dues and her Party card was withdrawn. She was convinced there was a plot against her.

Tatiana wrote of the terrible evenings when her mother succumbed to her fears.

> She would shout that all our food had been poisoned. She wouldn't let us eat anything. She said we mustn't stand near the windows, because 'they'll shoot us'. At night, we heard her wake and cry, 'There'll be an explosion!' It took all Meyerhold's strength to restrain her, to keep her from running into the street half naked ... The next day, she would be quiet as a mouse.

Stalin recognised Meyerhold's standing in the world of theatre. That was the reason he continued to offer him advice. He liked most of what Meyerhold produced; the Great Leader's expertise would make it even better.

He didn't like *La Dame Aux Camélias*, though. For Stalin, it was a big mistake to stage a bourgeois love story from the darkest epoch of the decadent West. He didn't buy Meyerhold's explanation that he wanted to expose the hypocrisy of capitalist society's treatment of women. He was categorical: Meyerhold should ditch it.

Zinaida was horrified. She was getting great reviews. Her

portrayal of the delicate, consumptive heroine, Marguerite, had the critics praising her grace and beauty.

Meyerhold said there was nothing for it. If Stalin said it was no good, he would have to close the production.

Zinaida fretted. She didn't tell Meyerhold, but she took it up with the man himself.

29 April 1937

Dear Comrade Stalin,

I have been meaning to write to you for over a year. I have been arguing with you in my head and it seems to me that sometimes you are wrong about art. I have lived in the artistic world for twenty years. You have your own concerns to occupy you and that is how it should be. But in artistic matters, you need to think again. You shouldn't just stick to the things you like; you need to be more open-minded. Excuse my boldness in saying this – I am from a workers' family and I trust my working-class instinct.

I want to say one more thing. I know the truth about the death of Sergei Yesenin. It was murder by agents of an outside force. By Trotskyist agents . . .

With sincerest greetings,

Zinaida N. Raikh

Stalin certainly read her letter. The copy that has survived in the Kremlin archives has his underlinings and handwritten notes. He didn't reply, but he brooded for a long time on Zinaida's lack of respect.

In January 1939, Meyerhold was informed that his theatre was being closed. The Cultural Affairs Committee of the

Council of People's Commissars of the USSR had decided it was alien to the needs and expectations of the Soviet public:

> The Committee states that the Meyerhold Theatre has failed in all the time of its existence to dissociate itself from positions that are in their essence alien to Soviet culture and irredeemably bourgeois and formalist in nature. The Meyerhold Theatre has shown itself morally bankrupt in relation to the staging of plays from the Soviet repertoire.
>
> The Cultural Affairs Committee decrees:
>
> a) to liquidate the Meyerhold Theatre as alien to Soviet culture;
>
> b) to redeploy the actors of the company in other theatres:
>
> c) to discuss separately whether or not Vsevolod Meyerhold may be allowed to continue to work in the theatre.

О ЛИКВИДАЦИИ ТЕАТРА ИМЕНИ ВС. МЕЙЕРХОЛЬДА

Комитет по делам искусств при Совнаркоме СССР признал, что театр им. Мейерхольда окончательно скатился на чуждые советскому искусству позиции и стал чужим для советского зрителя.

В своём приказе Комитет по делам искусств дал оценку театру им. Мейерхольда, который в течение всего своего существования не мог освободиться от чуждых советскому искусству насквозь буржуазных, формалистических позиций. Полным банкротом оказался театр им. Мейерхольда в постановке пьес советской драматургии.

Комитет по делам искусств при Совнаркоме СССР постановил:

а) ликвидировать театр имени Мейерхольда, как чуждый советскому искусству;

б) труппу театра использовать в других театрах;

в) вопрос о возможности дальнейшей работы Всеволода Мейерхольда в области театра обсудить особо.

Decree of the Cultural Affairs Committee of the Council of People's Commissars of the USSR

Meyerhold was arrested in June 1939, imprisoned in the Lubyanka and brutally tortured.

After weeks of suffering he wrote an anguished plea for clemency to Stalin and Molotov.

The handwriting winds round and round the page as Meyerhold tries to squeeze in as much detail of the pain and terror as he can.

They are torturing me. A sick, 65-year-old man. They make me lie face down and beat my spine and feet with rubber cudgels. Then they beat my feet from above, and when my legs are covered with internal haemorrhaging, they beat the red-blue-and-yellow bruises ... it feels like boiling water. I howl and weep from the pain ... I twist and squeal like a dog. Death, oh most certainly death is easier than this. I begin to incriminate myself in the hope I will go quickly to the scaffold.

Meyerhold's death sentence

He got his wish. On 31 January 1940, he was taken to the cellars of the Military Collegium of the Supreme Court. His trial lasted twenty minutes. There were no witnesses, no defence counsel and no right of appeal. Meyerhold was sentenced to death and shot on 2 February.

While Meyerhold was in the Lubyanka, unknown men broke into his apartment on Bryusov Lane. They smashed crockery, mirrors, glasses and windows, but did not steal anything. Zinaida, who was alone in the flat, heard the noise. The men stabbed her nine times in the heart and neck then gouged out her eyes.

The police brought Tatiana to see her mother's body and confirm her identity. Zinaida had lived for several hours after the attack. Medics had tried to save her, but she died from loss of blood. Tatiana asked the nurse who had held Zinaida's hand if her mother had said anything.

'Madame Raikh was conscious,' the nurse said. 'I gave her medical assistance, but she said, "Leave me alone; I am dying." After that, she was delirious. Just before she died, she must have heard the voice of the policemen outside, because she said, "Sergei? – Seryozha? ... Is that you, love?"'

Zinaida in her coffin

CHAPTER 48

On 12 April 1961, when Yuri Gagarin became the first human to break free from the bonds of this earth, he took with him the words of Sergei Yesenin, a homage from one peasant boy to another. Gagarin soared into heaven and declared that he found 'no God' there.

Yesenin would have disagreed. *Vse ot Boga*, he had told Isadora, 'Everything comes from God. Poetry, your dancing – everything!'

AFTERWORD

Sergei Yesenin was real.

For much of the twentieth century he was Russia's most beloved poet. Schoolchildren learned his poems by heart. Adolescent girls copied them in their diaries. Red Army soldiers carried them in their uniforms as they went into battle. Yuri Gagarin took them into space. Yesenin's fame brought him meetings with the tsar's wife and daughters and with Rasputin before the Revolution; with Trotsky and Kamenev and Lunacharsky after it. Like the fictional Yuri Zhivago, he survived the turmoil of war and revolution and lived a personal life of comparable drama. Visit his grave in Moscow and you will find tramps eager to recite his poetry. They expect a little vodka money, but they too love this tender, troubled man, dead now for nearly a hundred years.

But this book is a novel.

I know what Yesenin did and I know when he did it. My book stems from those facts. But it is less a biography than an auscultation of the restless heart behind them. The form implies invention; events, characters and dialogue for which factual evidence may be scarce. It means flexibility with chronology and taking an authorial view on the actions of those involved in the story. I have translated his poems selectively, using them in part, or in the draft form they might have been at when they appear in my narrative.

My thoughts about Yesenin?

He hurt the women who loved him. I would not seek to excuse that. But I opened this book with Mikhail Lermontov's famous, wistful supplication, *We almost always forgive that which we understand.* I have tried to understand Yesenin; I wonder if we might forgive him. Isadora Duncan, one of his victims, wrote that Seryozha should be pardoned his sins because of his genius. Yesenin repeats the entreaty in his 'Hooligan's Plea for Forgiveness'. It doesn't minimise the darkness in his soul, but its prayer is clear – that the beauty of the poetry he created from the ugliness of his life might count for something on the day when souls are judged.

> For all this joyful pain and torment,
> For all this anguish and all the love,
> I ask of you whose time, like mine, is spent
> To pray for me to saints and stars above,
> For all the weight of all my sins,
> For my loss of faith in the power of grace,
> That I might die beneath the icons,
> And Holy Russia caress my face.

For readers interested in what happened next, I append a summary of the fates that befell Yesenin's friends and enemies, his lovers and children, and the public figures who appear, or whose words appear in this novel.

Yesenin's Women

Tatiana Yesenina (née Titova), his mother, 1875–1955

 Yesenin had a complicated relationship with his mother, Tatiana. Nadezhda Volpin (qv) said he felt abandoned when Tatiana left the family to live with another man. 'He said it was something he could never forgive her. I felt how much pain it gave him, even now. He was constantly dwelling on the hurt.' Volpin tried in vain to persuade him to let it go. She pointed out that his poems described 'the poet's mother' fondly, yet he spoke of her so harshly. 'Much later,' Volpin wrote, 'I discovered that the name given to this is schizophrenia [sic].'

Tatiana recast her own memories of her son. In a televised interview given at the age of seventy-nine, she claimed that Sergei as a boy loved his parents; that he was always reading and she had to tell him to put off the light and go to sleep; that, as a famous poet, he was always coming to visit them; that he always brought them presents; that he loved socialism and the revolution; and that he was always reading his poems to the peasants.

Anna Izryadnova, 1891–1946

Yesenin's first wife and mother of his son, Yuri (qv). Yesenin was not a good husband. Anna wrote that he was arrogant and ambitious. He was more interested in poetry than family life. Being a husband and a father seemed a burden. When Yesenin walked out and went to St Petersburg, Anna continued to work at Sytin's publishing house. She stayed faithful to her absent husband and made a good job of raising their son. When Sergei and his new friend, Nikolai Klyuev, came to visit her in 1916, she was welcoming. In a brief memoir, written many years later, she wrote cheerily about what for her must have been a humiliating experience:

> I remember the two of them sewed themselves Boyar costumes, long brightly patterned kaftans [to recite in]; and Sergei wore a light blue silk shirt and yellow high-heeled boots. Some people were advising him to wear a poetic velvet jacket, like Byron, but instead he did what Klyuev told him to do. He ended up looking like the leader of a gypsy choir.

In the years of Stalin's Great Terror, 1936–38, her son was arrested and her life turned to tragedy.

Zinaida Raikh , 1894–1939

After Zinaida's murder, the authorities demanded that the family give up the apartment on Bryusov Lane. They were given forty-eight hours to get out. Zinaida's father rang their representative in the Supreme Soviet, Zinaida's former colleague, the actor Ivan Moskvin, to ask for a longer period of grace. He wanted time for his daughter's body to lie in the flat, before being taken for burial. 'The Soviet people do not want a public burial for your daughter,' Moskvin told him. 'The decision to evict you is correct.'

The following day, Flat No 11 at 12 Bryusov Lane was given to the chauffeur of Lavrenty Beria, the head of the NKVD secret police who was then in the process of torturing its owner, Vsevolod Meyerhold, and would eventually sign his death warrant.

Zinaida's grave in Moscow's Vagankovskoe Cemetery

It was Zinaida's rash letter to Stalin that set events in train that would lead to her death, to that of her husband and to the enduring hardships suffered by her children.

Lola Kinel, 1893–1970

Mrs Lola Shipman

The task of interpreting for a couple as fiery as Sergei Yesenin and Isadora Duncan was both complicated and exhilarating. When Isadora fired her on their visit to Venice, Lola wrote that, 'leaving Isadora and Yesenin was like stepping off a brightly lit stage with the actors on it etched in sharp, clear outlines and with lots of high lights – and jumping into the dark, murky orchestra pit where the people, by comparison, were shadowy, unreal, and half dead ... After Isadora and Yesenin, the ordinary world seemed a little grey.'

Lola travelled via Poland to the USA, joining her twin sister and brother-in-law in Chicago. She married an American, became Mrs Shipman, moved to California and wrote her memoirs.

Isadora Duncan, 1877–1927

Isadora's body was transported from Nice to Paris and cremated there. Her ashes were interred in the columbarium of Père-Lachaise Cemetery, next to those of her dead children, Deirdre and Patrick. A spray of red lilies was placed on a red banner printed with a gold inscription, 'The Heart of Russia Weeps for Isadora'.

For many years after her death, her legacy was kept alive by the Isadorables, the young girls who were her pupils, some of whom she adopted. Three of them – Irma, Anna and Maria-Theresa – gained a reputation as solo performers in the United States, before setting up their own studios at which the next generation of Isadora's disciples would be trained.

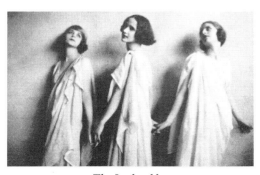

The Isadorables

The drama of Isadora's life and the melodrama of her death made her a natural subject for film. The 1968 movie, *Isadora*, won Vanessa Redgrave an Oscar nomination. The scenes between Duncan and Gordon Craig are affecting, but Yesenin, played by a little-known Croatian actor, is a caricature.

Avgusta Miklashevskaya, 1891–1977

Her relationship with Yesenin in the final year of his life was affectionate and mutually consoling. After they parted, he saw her a final time in November 1925. Miklashevskaya was at home, caring for her sick son, when Yesenin called on her. She wrote that he came in silently and sat in a chair, watching her at her son's bedside. Then he embraced her and said, 'Thank you. That is what I came for.' Later, he sent her a verse from a poem he had dedicated to her while they were still together:

> I did not spare myself for old age,
> For a life of smiles, for resting in the shade.
> How few are the paths I have taken,
> How many the mistakes I made.

Miklashevskaya aged 34 and aged 84

Nadezhda Volpin, 1900–1998

The mother of Yesenin's last child, Alexander Yesenin-Volpin (qv). After Yesenin's death, Volpin had a distinguished career as a translator of world literature (Ovid, Horace, Goethe, Hugo, Byron, Galsworthy). Her memoirs, written in 1980, depict a passionate but unstable Yesenin. He made no effort to care for her or for their son. She says his death was 'like a blow to the chest'.

Nadezhda Volpin with Yesenin's son, Alexander

Volpin is particularly critical of Anatoly Marienhof, whom she accuses of trying to turn Yesenin against her. She describes meeting Marienhof in Moscow in 1939 or 1940. She was surprised by the warmth of his greeting. Marienhof insisted that they should get their two sons together. The boys were of a similar age, around sixteen.

'They can grow up friends together,' Marienhof said, 'just as their fathers, Sergei and I, did. They can recreate our lost youth.'

Volpin did not object, although, she says, she did not believe friendships could be created to order. They fixed a time for Yesenin's son, Alexander and Marienhof's son, Kirill to meet, but the encounter never took place. A few days after Volpin spoke to Marienhof, Kirill hanged himself.

'It seemed to me,' Volpin writes, 'that the death of Marienhof's boy completed the chain of suicides that stretched all the way back to Sergei that dark December night in room number 5 of the Angleterre Hotel. So many young people were taking their own lives in those difficult times, and nearly all of them left their volume of Yesenin's poetry together with their suicide note, open at the page where Yesenin writes, "Do not blame anyone ... There is no one to blame." It is all very well to say, "Blame no one," but the blame, all the same, was always laid at Sergei's door.'

Nadezhda Volpin in her nineties

Galina Benislavskaya, 1897–1926

The victim of unrequited love, and the first of hundreds of suicides inspired by the death of Yesenin. Her passion seemed to legitimise the self-destructive impulses shared by many young Russians in a country where human values were being trampled by repression and intolerance. When Benislavskaya was buried beside Yesenin in Moscow's Vagankovskoe Cemetery, the cemetery management had to cut down the trees around the grave to prevent a spate of hangings. Even today, Russian websites are dedicated to 'tragic Galya', with mottos such as 'the greatest passion' and 'beauty redeems all'.

*New memorial to Galina, replacing the
initial, temporary enamelled plaque*

Sofya Tolstaya, 1900–1957

The daughter of Lev Tolstoy's youngest son, Sofya Tolstaya was
Yesenin's last wife. They were married from 18 September 1925
until Yesenin's death on 28 December that year. In the months
that followed, she collected his manuscripts, papers and documents. She co-founded a Yesenin museum in Moscow, but
the Bolsheviks' campaign against Yesenin and 'Yeseninism'
resulted in its closure after only a few years, with the loss of
many artefacts.

Sofya Tolstaya in 1937

Tolstaya later became the director of the State Museum of Lev
Tolstoy in Moscow and the museum at Tolstoy's country estate,

Yasnaya Polyana. She organised the evacuation of the museum in 1941, just weeks before the invading Nazi forces seized Yasnaya Polyana. She was buried there after her death in 1957.

Shaganeh Talyan, 1900–1976

A romance with Sergei Yesenin while he was on holiday in Georgia earned Shaganeh Talyan a place in literary history. The daughter of an Armenian priest and a Georgian headmistress, Shaganeh was a young schoolteacher when she caught Yesenin's eye. He dedicated a short cycle of poems to her, his 'Persian Motifs', of which one, 'Shaganeh, oh my Shaganeh', became a universal favourite.

> Shaganeh, my Shaganeh,
> Is it because I am from the north
> That I'm ready to tell you everything . . .

Shaganeh, 1930s

Shaganeh married twice, neither time happily, and died in 1976.

YESENIN'S CHILDREN

Yuri Yesenin, 1914–1937

 The child of Yesenin's first marriage, to Anna Izryadnova. The novelty of fatherhood delighted Yesenin, if only for a short time. When Anna returned from hospital with the baby, he had cleaned the flat, made the dinner and written a poem for Yuri:

Yuri, be a Muscovite!
Live and howl in the woods,
Howl 'til your dreams come true!
Long ago, your namesake,
Yuri Dolgoruky,
Founded Moscow just for you!

Yesenin's interest in his son didn't last; he left for St Petersburg soon after. Anna brought the boy up on her own.

Yuri followed his father's career and learned his poems by heart. He wrote his own verse, but kept it to himself. He enrolled in the aviation faculty of Moscow University. The mounting attacks on his father by the regime and the ban on Yesenin's works angered him. After a drinking session with fellow students, Yuri said he felt like throwing a bomb at the Kremlin. The remark was apparently reported.

In 1935, Yuri was called up for military service and posted to the city of Khabarovsk in south-eastern Russia. In early 1936, military police came to arrest him and take him back to Moscow. At the same time, the police raided his mother's apartment and seized Yuri's diaries.

Yuri was charged with counter-revolutionary activities, terrorism and belonging to a criminal group. His interrogator assured him that if he made a full confession, he would be spared the death penalty and sent to a labour camp. Yuri naïvely agreed to do so.

While awaiting his trial, he told a cellmate that he was sure his father had not committed suicide, that he was killed by agents of the state. Yuri Yesenin was executed on 13 August 1937. His mother, Anna, was told the usual lie, that her son had been sentenced to ten years hard labour, 'without the right of correspondence'. Anna Izryadnova-Yesenina died in 1946 at the age of fifty-five.

Yuri was posthumously rehabilitated during the Khrushchev thaw in 1956. The case for rehabilitation succeeded because of the untiring efforts of Yuri's half-brother Alexander Yesenin-Volpin (qv).

Tatiana Yesenina, 1919–1992

Yesenin's first child with Zinaida Raikh, elder sister of Konstantin. Born in Oryol. She remembered the noise and commotion that her father brought into the house and the passionate, stormy relationship between him and Zinaida.

Konstantin and Tatiana

Taken to see Yesenin dead in his coffin, she was confused; the man she saw did not look like her father; she didn't believe it was him. The next morning, Tatiana and her brother Konstantin were at Yesenin's burial with their mother.

> I remember the poetry being read over the open grave. When they began to lower my father's coffin into the pit, my mother screamed so loud that Kostya and I grabbed hold of her, one on each of her arms, and we screamed too.

Zinaida's remarriage to Vsevolod Meyerhold brought stability. Tatiana and Konstantin loved him. Tatiana learned ballet at the

Bolshoi. In 1937, she enrolled in the mechanical engineering faculty of Moscow University, where she met and married a fellow student, Vladimir Kutuzov. Her father-in-law was Ivan Kutuzov, an Old Bolshevik and former member of the Supreme Soviet. Shortly after Tatiana's wedding, Ivan was arrested. Stalin had noticed that he didn't join in the choruses of 'Hail to the Great Leader' at the end of his speeches. Tatiana's husband and his brother were also arrested, as relatives of a political prisoner. Her husband was subsequently released, but his brother was detained for several years because he had argued with the interrogators.

Tatiana was greatly affected by the arrest of Meyerhold and the murder of her mother. She was a young woman, just married, with a younger brother to care for and expecting a baby of her own. When the family was evicted from the flat on Bryusov Lane (see entry for Zinaida Raikh, above), Tatiana and her husband saved Meyerhold's papers, a valuable archive of theatrical history. She kept them safe, despite searches by the secret police.

During the Second World War, she was evacuated with her husband and son to Tashkent in Uzbekistan. After the war, she stayed on, working for the newspaper *Eastern Pravda* and as science editor of the Uzbek state publishing house.

After Stalin's death in 1953, Tatiana set out to discover the truth about the killings of her mother and her adoptive father. It was her efforts that led to the rehabilitation of Meyerhold in 1955 (see entry for Vsevolod Meyerhold, below).

Tatiana wrote about her life and her memories of her parents in a long series of letters to the literary researcher Konstantin Rudnitsky in the 1980s. Tatiana emerges as a woman of great character, sensitivity and independence. She speaks of the years in which the regime traduced the reputation of Zinaida and Meyerhold.

> I inured myself to the calumny. As a child, my mother had made us learn Pushkin's lines: *Fear no hurt, demand no crown; Accept both praise and slander, smile at their abuse, Dismiss the fool and do not quarrel with the clown.*
>
> So when they said terrible things about my dead mother, I was able to tell people the truth: She was a remarkable woman. She had two marvellous husbands. She was exquisitely beautiful. She was intelligent. And she was the leading actress of a great theatre. For many years, it was not permissible to say anything good about my mother. The authorities were intent on wiping out her memory. But I know the truth and the truth is eternal.

Tatiana Yesenina died in Tashkent in 1992. She was the little girl that Yesenin spoke about in the deepest moment of his despair with life. 'I love nothing. Nothing at all ... Perhaps I love my children ... And Zinaida, my one true wife ... My daughter, Tatiana, who's as beautiful as her beautiful mother ...'

Zinaida, Konstantin and Tatiana

Konstantin Yesenin, 1920–1986

The second child of Yesenin and Zinaida Raikh. He was sickly, shy and very short-sighted. Anatoly Marienhof spread the story that Konstantin was not Yesenin's son, although there is little evidence for this.

He was adopted together with his sister, Tatiana, by Vsevolod Meyerhold. Meyerhold taught him to play the piano and Konstantin called him *papa*. Konstantin studied civil engineering at Moscow University. He was not a practical young man and he struggled to support himself. Remarkably, he was helped by Anna Izryadnova, Yesenin's first wife and mother of Konstantin's half-brother Yuri (qv).

'Anna was a woman of utter goodness and modesty,' Konstantin wrote. 'She fed me when I was a student in 1940 and 1941 and she sent me parcels with cigarettes and warm clothing when I was a soldier at the front.'

Konstantin was part of Soviet Russia's campaign to keep the invading Nazi forces out of Moscow. In November 1941, the Germans were within twenty miles of the city centre, already in possession of the outlying stations of the capital's tram network. Moscow looked certain to be lost.

Konstantin served for four years. He was twice wounded, twice decorated, twice promoted. By the winter of 1944, the Soviet Army was pushing the invaders back. The commander of Konstantin's unit and his deputy were killed in a fierce exchange of fire. Konstantin, now a young lieutenant, took charge of the men and led an assault on the German lines. An enemy bullet hit him in the side of the chest, travelling through both his lungs. His relatives were informed that Konstantin Sergeyevich Yesenin had died of wounds received in battle. On 9 December 1944, the Red Army newspaper published a tribute to his courage. He was awarded a third, posthumous, Order of the Red Star.

But Konstantin returned alive. There was no one to greet him. No one had been told of the Red Army nurse who found him dying on the battlefield, who insisted on taking him to the field hospital despite the pessimism of her colleagues. Konstantin was unconscious; he had lost so much blood that the doctors could not find a pulse; but he survived. He was evacuated back to Moscow. When he got there, he found his relatives dead, his sister gone and the dacha they had lived in after being evicted from Bryusov Lane sacked by the Nazis. His father's papers, the priceless Yesenin archive, had been dumped in the barn.

After the war, Konstantin resumed his studies and qualified as a professional engineer. But his passion was football. As a boy, he had been a winger, but his weak eyesight made a career as a player difficult. Instead, he became a statistician, pouring his passion into the compilation of facts, anecdotes, scores and tables. He wrote learnedly about the game. So exhaustive was his knowledge that he was made an honorary member of the Union of Soviet Journalists. His 1968 book, *Football: records, paradoxes, sensations and tragedy*, became a cult classic.

His sister Tatiana told the story of when she was helped by a young man to carry her bags to the check-in desk of an airport. When the young man heard her tell the clerk what her surname was, he could not contain his curiosity. 'Excuse me,' he said. 'Yesenin? Are you by any chance related to the great . . . Konstantin Yesenin?'

Brother and sister, 1970s

Alexander Yesenin-Volpin, 1924–2016

The son of Nadezhda Volpin (qv), with whom Yesenin had an affair in the last year of his life. He graduated with honours from the mathematics faculty of Moscow University and was assigned as a teacher to Chernovtsy in Ukraine. He admired his dead father and resented the official campaign against him. He wrote his own poetry.

Alexander Yesenin-Volpin (right) with his father (left)

In 1949, Alexander was arrested and charged with 'systematically conducting anti-Soviet propaganda by writing anti-Soviet poems and reading them to friends'. In custody, he staged a suicide attempt, possibly as a means of avoiding criminal proceedings. He was sent to the Leningrad Psychiatric Prison Hospital, then sentenced to five years in exile in Kazakhstan as a 'socially dangerous element'. Released under the political amnesty following the death of Stalin, he returned to mathematics and built an international reputation as an expert in mathematical intuitionism.

In 1961, he smuggled a copy of his *Free Philosophical Treatise* to a publisher in New York. His declaration that 'in the Soviet Union there is no freedom of expression, but freedom of thought remains' made him a figurehead of the nascent human rights movement. Nikita Khrushchev denounced him as 'a poisonous, rotting mushroom'. 'He may be insane,' Khrushchev said, 'but we know exactly how to cure him.'

Yesenin-Volpin would spend the following years in and out of prison and psychiatric clinics. He publicly denounced the abuse of psychiatry. The Soviet psychiatric profession colluded in the use of psychiatric institutions – so-called *psikhushkas* – for the detention of dissidents, inventing a bogus condition they called 'creeping schizophrenia'. The rationale behind it was that the USSR was the perfect society; if you oppose it, you must by definition be mad.

The dissident Vladimir Bukovsky said that Yesenin-Volpin's true diagnosis was well-established – 'pathological honesty'. In December 1965, Yesenin-Volpin was part of the intellectual dissident group that organised the 'Moscow Meeting for Glasnost [openness]'. They staged a demonstration on Pushkin Square in central Moscow, at which leaflets written by Alexander were distributed. Undercover KGB agents attended the demonstration and arrested the organisers.

On his release, Yesenin-Volpin became a member of the dissident Soviet Human Rights Committee, together with Andrei Sakharov and Yuri Orlov. The Soviet authorities, tired of his refusal to conform, told him he must emigrate. In 1972, he left for the USA and a professorial post in the mathematics faculty of Boston University. He died there on 16 March 2016.

Alexander Yesenin-Volpin with his
mother, Nadezhda, (right) in old age

POETS, ARTISTS, ACTORS, WRITERS

Anna Akhmatova, 1889–1966

A St Petersburg poet of the Russian Silver Age. Her poetry mixes intense spirituality and themes of physical love. Stalin's Culture Commissar, Andrei Zhdanov, called her 'half-harlot, half-nun'. Her poems remain immensely popular. Her first husband, Nikolai Gumilev, was executed by the Bolsheviks in 1921 and her son, Lev, would spend years in the Gulag. Her epic poem, 'Requiem', is an indictment of totalitarian inhumanity. 'One hundred million voices,' she writes, 'shout through my tortured mouth.'

Alexander Blok, 1880–1921

The leading poet of the Russian Symbolist movement. He was patrician, other-worldly and revered by millions. His poetry offers an ambiguous picture of spiritual and carnal love. At first, he welcomed the Revolution, then despaired of it. In the early years of Yesenin's career, he offered him help.

Thomas Chatterton, 1752–1770

A British poet, remembered more for his death than his poetry. Despairing of life and disillusioned with the world, Chatterton killed himself at the age of seventeen. His youthful tragedy was commemorated in a play by the French writer, Alfred de Vigny, and a painting by the British artist Henry Wallis. Chatterton became the prototype of the doomed Romantic hero, the *poète maudit*, fated by his sensitive nature to suffer and die. Yesenin knew Chatterton's story and was aware that he was himself a *poète maudit*.

Wolf Ehrlich, 1902–1937

The St Petersburg poet who was with Yesenin in the Hotel Angleterre in the final days of Yesenin's life. He became the target of conspiracy theorists who believed Yesenin was murdered and suspected Ehrlich of being part of the plot. Concerted efforts were made to prove he was an employee of the OGPU secret police.

Ehrlich was twenty-three at the time of Yesenin's death and possibly in love with the older poet. He was a committed Bolshevik. He had fought in the Red Army and occupied several Party posts. He was a member of the security detail of the Leningrad Soviet, a position that his accusers said linked him to the secret police.

His later career as a poet and film writer was not distinguished. He was arrested on a trip to Armenia in July 1937, tried under Article 58 (counter-revolutionary activity) and executed on 24 November.

Alexei Ganin, 1893–1925

Alexei Ganin

A peasant poet from the northern Russian province of Vologda, who met Sergei Yesenin in 1916 when they were serving in the military hospital in Tsarskoe Selo. They remained friends and published poetry together in the literary review, *Skify* (Scythians). Ganin was best man at Yesenin's wedding to Zinaida Raikh. He served in the Red Army from 1920–22, but became disillusioned with the revolution.

He was arrested and executed by the Bolsheviks in 1925, and was posthumously rehabilitated in 1966.

Maxim Gorky, 1868–1936

Maxim Gorky

A socialist writer and supporter of the anti-tsarist cause. He wrote novels highlighting the iniquities of tsarist society and agitating for change. Gorky supported the 1917 revolutions, but was troubled by the cruelty of the revolutionaries and their crushing of democracy. He left Russia in 1921 for exile in Italy. He met Yesenin in Berlin. In 1932, he was persuaded by Stalin to return to Russia, where he was fêted and rewarded with honours, a mansion and a dacha. He died mysteriously in June 1936, amid speculation that he was poisoned by Stalin.

Sergei Gorodetsky, 1884–1967

A St Petersburg poet, initially a Symbolist. He served as a war correspondent in the First World War. Yesenin stayed with Gorodetsky for several months when he first arrived in Petersburg. Gorodetsky was a friend and collaborator of the poet, Nikolai Gumilev, who was executed by the Bolsheviks in 1921. Later, he became close to the Bolshevik regime, editing the journal *Art for the Workers* and translating literature from around the Soviet Union.

Sergei Gorodetsky with Nikolai Gumilev before the revolution

Vladislav Khodasevich, 1886–1939

A poet and literary critic. He emigrated from the Soviet Union in 1922, first to Berlin and then to Paris. His book of memoirs, *Necropolis*, contains vivid literary portraits of his contemporaries. He died in Paris in June 1939, following a gallbladder operation.

I came to know Khodasevich's widow, Nina Berberova, 1901–1993, when I was writing my graduate thesis about his poetry in the 1970s. She was a writer of short stories and long memoirs. She returned to Russia for the first time in over sixty years in 1989, while I was there as the BBC's Moscow correspondent. She was a bountiful source of information about the

Russian literary scene of the early twentieth century, much of which figures in this book.

Nikolai Klyuev, 1884–1937

A peasant poet. He had considerable influence in pre-revolutionary St Petersburg. He helped Yesenin when the young poet arrived from Moscow in 1914, and became his lover. They later quarrelled and traded insults in poetry and prose. But each seemed to retain a fondness for the other. In 1922, Yesenin wrote, 'Whatever may happen between us, however much I may curse you, and you me, yet love shall remain.' When Yesenin died in 1925, Klyuev wrote a heartfelt elegy that he read at his funeral. In the book of condolences, he wrote, 'Sergei – I beg, I pray, I wait.'

Nikolai Klyuev, prison photograph prior to execution, 1937

In life, Nikolai Klyuev was spiteful, manipulative and predatory. His reputation as a poet was high; as a man it was low.

On 2 February 1934, Klyuev was arrested on charges of 'compiling and distributing counter-revolutionary works of literature.' The 'evidence' against him was the religious nature of his poems. His homosexuality increased the harshness with which he was treated. The stenographic record of Klyuev's interrogation shows him to be noble and resolute in refusing to recant his beliefs, though he knows it will mean death.

Nikolai Klyuev was executed on 23 October 1937 in a prison camp in Tomsk.

Alexander Kusikov, 1896–1977

A founding member of the Imagist school, together with Yesenin, Marienhof and Shershenevich. He served in the tsarist army in the First World War and was wounded. He later served in the Bolshevik Red Cavalry. In 1922, he emigrated, first to Berlin, where he hosted Yesenin and Isadora Duncan, and then to Paris. He did not join in White émigré attacks on the Soviet regime; he was regarded as sympathetic to the USSR by the Whites and therefore politically suspect. Kusikov stopped writing poetry after the Second World War and died in Paris in 1977.

Alexander Kusikov in exile in France

Mikhail Kuzmin, 1872–1936

A poet of the Russian Silver Age. He was born into an aristocratic family. The overtly homosexual themes in his writing, particularly his novel *Wings*, earned him notoriety. His partner of twenty years was the Lithuanian-Russian poet Yuri Yurkun.

Kuzmin died of pneumonia in March 1936 and Yurkun was arrested and shot two years later.

John Lennon, 1940–1980

British popular music star. Initially a member of The Beatles. Later solo career. Writer of 'The Ballad of John and Yoko'; 'Oh, Yoko'; 'Watching the Wheels Go Round'; 'Jealous Guy'.

Anatoly Marienhof, 1897–1962

An Imagist poet and a collaborator and close friend of Yesenin. The reasons for the falling out between them are disputed. They differed over poetic matters, but the real causes were probably personal. Each seems to have resented the other's decision to get married. It has been suggested that they had a homosexual relationship.

Soviet critics were critical of Marienhof's influence on Yesenin, claiming that Marienhof debauched him. Professor Gordon McVay, the leading Western expert on Yesenin, believes this judgment is harsh, and it is the case that the two men retained some happy memories of their time together. Yesenin wrote:

> Amidst the youngsters and the famous
> You were the very best for me . . .
> Time will pass and perhaps one morning
> You and I may meet again.
> I tremble, for our souls grow hoary,
> Like youth and love which quickly end.

Marienhof feared they would not 'meet again'.

I am afraid ...

People exchange their best friend for some woman.

Marienhof and Nikritina

In later life, Marienhof fell out of official favour. His poetry was not published. He retreated to family life, stayed married to Anna Nikritina and had a cat that he called Seryozha.

Marienhof and 'Seryozha'

His memoirs, *A Novel Without Lies,* speak fondly of Yesenin, although at times Marienhof emerges as a Salieri to Yesenin's Mozart. He retained his animosity towards Zinaida, repeating many of the slighting remarks and dismissive stories he told about her. But he does include his backhanded admission that Yesenin loved her:

Whom did Yesenin love? Most of all he hated Zinaida Raikh ... and this woman, this woman whom he hated more than anyone else in life, her – her alone – did he love.

Vladimir Mayakovsky, 1893–1930

An extravagantly gifted Futurist poet, who supported the Bolshevik Revolution and was regarded as the regime's official bard. He wrote in praise of Lenin, communism, modernity and the rush into the future. He denounced Sergei Yesenin for his nostalgic attachment to rural life, beauty, lyricism and the past.

But Mayakovsky seems to have regretted some of his intemperate personal attacks on Yesenin. He asked for some of his more virulent speeches to be expunged from public record. When Yesenin killed himself, Mayakovsky wrote an ambiguous tribute:

> You have passed, as they say, into worlds elsewhere.
> Emptiness . . .
> Fly, wing your way to starry dubiety.
> No advances, no taverns for you there.
> Sobriety.
> No, Yesenin, this is not me deriding;
> Not laughter but sorrow racks my throat.
> . . . 'Encore!' they shout
> As suicides bloom over you.
> This world is sparsely furnished with delight;
> One must take it from what means there are.
> In this life
> It's not difficult to die.
> Living is
> more difficult by far.

Five years later, Mayakovsky, too, would fall out of love with a woman, the revolution and the world. His own suicide poem expresses similar sentiments to those of Yesenin:

It's past one o'clock. You must have gone to bed.
The Milky Way streams silver through the night.
I'm in no hurry; with lightning telegrams
I have no cause to wake or trouble you.
And, as they say, the incident is closed.
Love's boat has smashed against the daily grind.
Now you and I are quits. Why bother then
To balance mutual sorrows, pains, and hurts.
Behold what quiet settles on the world.
Night wraps the sky in tribute from the stars.
In hours like these, one rises to address
The ages, history, and all creation.

Mayakovsky put on a new white shirt and bow tie and shot himself in the heart.

The first photographs of his body were considered insufficiently elegant. His hair was combed, his mouth closed and his arms rearranged to make an exquisite corpse.

Dmitry Merezhkovsky, 1865–1941

The aristocratic doyen of pre-revolutionary St Petersburg literary society. He and his wife, the poetess Zinaida Gippius, 1869–1945, dominated the influential literary salons that gave the young Yesenin his start in the world of poetry. When Yesenin next met them, they were in exile in Paris. Merezhkovsky expected deference; Yesenin was cocky. They clashed.

In later years, Merezhkovsky developed fierce religious convictions and regarded himself as a prophet.

Vsevolod Meyerhold, 1874–1940

After Meyerhold was executed, the fate of his remains was unknown. A memorial to him was included on the grave of Zinaida Raikh (qv), but his final resting place was not identified until 1990, when Mikhail Gorbachev began declassifying the records of the secret police. Meyerhold's body had been incinerated and his ashes deposed in a mass burial pit in Moscow's Donskoe Cemetery.

Memorial to, 'Common Grave No 1 – unclaimed ashes from 1930 to 1942'

What also emerged from the records is that Meyerhold, imprisoned in the Lubyanka since 20 June 1939, was informed on 16 July that his wife had been murdered the previous day. As well as physical torture, Meyerhold had to live with the knowledge of her suffering and death. It would be another six months before he too was killed, on 2 February 1940. The warrant for his execution listed his 'crime' as espionage for Britain and Japan.

Notice of rehabilitation, 1955

Thanks to the efforts of Tatiana Yesenina, daughter of Sergei and Zinaida, the case of her adoptive father was reviewed in 1955. Stalin had died two years earlier and the new Soviet leader, Nikita Khrushchev, was cautiously exposing the crimes of the Stalin era. Meyerhold was rehabilitated on 30 November 1955.

Vadim Shershenevich, 1893–1942

A poet and founder member of Imagism, together with Marienhof, Yesenin and Kusikov. He translated Baudelaire's *Les Fleurs du Mal* into Russian. In the late 1920s, he lamented the new insistence on collective, civic themes in Soviet poetry: 'Poetry without lyricism is like a racehorse without a leg.' He began to write for the theatre and the cinema. He co-signed the letter denouncing Yesenin in 1925, but later stated that he regretted doing so. In 1942, he was evacuated from wartime Moscow to the city of Barnaul, where he died on 18 May from tuberculosis.

Ilya Vardin, 1890–1941

A Georgian writer and political activist. He joined the Bolshevik Party before the revolution and fought with the Red Cavalry. He was declared a member of the Trotskyist Opposition and expelled from the Party in 1927. Briefly reinstated, he was finally arrested in 1935 and shot in 1941. He was posthumously rehabilitated in 1959.

Mikhail Zoshchenko, 1894–1958

A writer of humorous and satirical stories mocking the absurdities of Soviet society. He served in the Red Army and was wounded in action.

Zoshchenko expressed his irritation with the Bolsheviks' insistence on managing and directing the arts in barely concealed pastiches. When the leadership decreed that socialist art should be accessible to even the simplest of readers, he took them at their word.

'I write simply. Sentences short. Accessible to the poor. Is that the reason I have so many readers?'

The Kremlin denounced him in 1948 and Zoshchenko died in poverty.

Reds

Yakov Blumkin, 1898–1929

Yakov Blumkin, prison photograph

Blumkin's assault against Zinaida was neither reported nor investigated. He was a powerful figure, protected by Trotsky. When Trotsky lost his power struggle against Stalin and was exiled, Blumkin remained loyal to the Trotskyist doctrine of world revolution. In 1929, Blumkin held what he assumed to be a secret meeting with Trotsky in Istanbul – any dealings with 'the Trotskyite Opposition' would mean certain death.

The OGPU secret police discovered that Blumkin had brought clandestine instructions from Trotsky to his supporters in the USSR. They put Blumkin under surveillance and sent an attractive female agent, Lisa Gorskaya, to begin an affair with him. She reported on what he told her. In September 1929, armed OGPU agents came to arrest Blumkin. He was getting into a car with Gorskaya and sped away. The agents followed, shooting from pistols. Blumkin was cornered. As he was taken away, he turned and said, 'Lisa, you have betrayed me!'

Stalin personally ordered that he should be executed. As the firing squad took aim, Blumkin reportedly shouted, 'Long live Trotsky!'

Pyotr Gannushkin, 1875–1933

A psychiatrist. He treated Yesenin as an in-patient from November to December 1925. He seems not to have suffered any punishment for allowing Yesenin to abscond and later kill himself. Gannushkin died following complications from surgery in February 1933. His byzantine classification of personality disorders gained some followers among Soviet psychiatrists, but had little influence in the West.

Anatoly Lunacharsky, 1875–1933

A Bolshevik revolutionary and the first People's Commissar for Enlightenment (education) from 1917 to 1929. Lunacharsky was a man of culture, a playwright, critic and essayist. He was a gifted linguist, who corresponded with H.G. Wells, George Bernard Shaw, Romain Rolland.

He helped Zinaida find employment at the Meyerhold Theatre and intervened on behalf of Yesenin and Kusikov when they were arrested. He arranged for Isadora Duncan to bring her dance school to Moscow, where she would meet Yesenin. In 1925, he wrote to the investigating judge to ask for the charges against Yesenin to be dropped.

Under Stalin he fell out of favour. In 1929, he was dismissed from his ministerial post and sent as Soviet representative to the League of Nations, then appointed ambassador to Spain. He died of a heart attack in Menton, France, on the way to take up his appointment.

Trofim Lysenko, 1898–1976

A Soviet agronomist whose bogus theories were enthusiastically adopted by Stalin. When famine threatened in the early 1930s, Stalin ordered hundreds of thousands of hectares to be sown according to Lysenko's methods. Agronomists who pointed out the danger of doing so were fired or imprisoned. Up to 3,000 mainstream biologists were sacked; some were shot.

The results were catastrophic. Wheat, rye, potatoes, beets and most other crops planted as Lysenko recommended died or rotted. Several million people died of hunger. Deaths peaked in 1932 and 1933. Four years later, crop yields were still lower than they had been before Lysenkoism was introduced.

Vladimir Polyansky, 1880[?]–1937

The official in the Moscow legal records office who tipped off Galina Benislavskaya about the gravity of the charges facing Yesenin in 1925. Polyansky was a fan of Yesenin's poetry. He kept copies of the documentation relating to the cases against him. When he retired, he took these with him. In 1937, seriously ill and with no close family, Polyansky was concerned that the documents would be lost. He wrote to Vladimir Bonch-Bruyevich, Lenin's former personal secretary who now ran the State Literary Museum. On the bottom of Polyansky's letter, Bonch-Bruyevich has written to his secretary, 'Claudia, We need to obtain these documents. The time is not yet right for their publication. 26 October 1937.'

WHITES

Dmitry Lohman, 1868–1918

A brigadier and aide-de-camp of the tsarina, Alexandra Fedorovna. On the empress's instructions, he found Yesenin a post on the royal hospital train. He was Yesenin's commanding officer during his war service. He offered Yesenin a commission in the army of the Provisional Government, but Yesenin deserted.

Dmitry Lohman (left) with Rasputin, 1915

After the revolution, Lohman found himself under suspicion. He was a member of a Russian nationalist organisation, opposed to socialism and dedicated to restoring the monarchy.

The Bolsheviks demanded that all former tsarist officers give themselves up; refusal to comply would mean reprisals against their families. According to Lohman's son, Yuri, his father spent a long time praying, asking God for guidance. To protect his family, he decided to hand himself in. 'I am a Christian,' he told his wife. 'I do not fear death.' Lohman was taken into custody and, with his fellow officers, held as a hostage by the Bolsheviks. When Fanny Kaplan shot and wounded Lenin on 30 August 1918, Lohman was among the first to be executed in reprisal.

Władysław Moes, 1900–1986

The son of a Polish aristocratic family and the model for the young boy, Tadzio, who is pursued by the character Gustav Von Aschenbach in Thomas Mann's homoerotic novella, *Death in Venice*. Mann saw and admired him while staying at the same hotel on the Venice Lido in 1911. Moes was unaware that he had been immortalised until his cousin read a Polish translation in 1924. He fought with the Polish Uhlans against the Red Army in the Russo-Polish war of 1919–1921 and was wounded. He was captured and interned by the Nazis.

Władysław Moes aged seventy-one in Warsaw

The post-war communist regime confiscated the Moes family properties and Władysław earned his living as a translator. He saw Luchino Visconti's film of *Death in Venice* while visiting his daughter in Paris. Moes was not gay. He married a Polish noble-woman, Anna Belina-Brzozowska, and they had two children. Moes died on 17 December 1986 in Warsaw.

Dmitry Rasputin, 1895–1933

The son of Grigory Rasputin, the spiritual adviser of Nicholas and Alexandra. He served with Yesenin during the First World War on board the royal hospital train.

After the revolutions of 1917, he was the target of Bolshevik denunciations and changed his name to Rasputin-Novy. The Bolsheviks confiscated the family home, evicting him and his wife, Fyokla. Dmitry was deprived of his civil rights, including the right to vote, as an 'antisocial element'. In 1930, Dmitry, his mother and wife were deported to Siberia as *kulaks* (rich peasants). His mother, Grigory Rasputin's widow, died on the journey and Fyokla died of TB in early 1933. Dmitry died of dysentery three months later.

Patriarch Tikhon, 1865–1925

Appointed by the drawing of lots just days before the October Revolution, Tikhon led the 1918 Easter parade in Moscow that was broken up by troops. He publicly condemned the murder of the tsar and his family and protested against the seizure of church property. He was arrested by the Bolsheviks, held under house arrest for over a year and threatened with execution. In 1923, under pressure, he signed a prepared statement that he was 'no longer an enemy of the Soviet state'. The Kremlin deposed him and replaced him with a puppet Church leadership controlled by the Bolsheviks. He died on 7 April 1925 and was canonised in 1981. When his coffin was opened in 1992, his body was found miraculously not to have decomposed.

Anna Vyrubova, 1884–1964

A lady-in-waiting and confidante of the tsarina, Empress Alexandra. She helped Nikolai Klyuev to introduce Yesenin to the empress and subsequently to secure a place for him on the royal hospital train.

Vyrubova was arrested after the February Revolution of 1917 and held for five months in the Peter and Paul Fortress. In light of the rumours about her relationship with Rasputin, she was subjected to a medical examination that reportedly proved her virginity. In 1920 she fled to Finland, where she wrote a series of colourful and imaginative memoirs about her time at the Russian court. In later life, she took vows as a Russian Orthodox nun. She died in Helsinki at the age of eighty.

Felix Yusupov, 1887–1967

A Russian aristocrat who murdered Grigory Rasputin, with the help of Grand Prince Dmitry Romanov. After the February Revolution, he fled with his wife, Princess Irina, to Crimea, and left Russia on board a British warship for a life in exile in France.

Yusupov became a celebrity. He wrote a lurid book about the murder of Rasputin. When it was made into a Hollywood film, the producers included a scene in which Irina is seduced by Rasputin. The Yusupovs sued and won punitive damages. The result was that every Hollywood movie since has carried the disclaimer, 'This film is a work of fiction and any similarity to any living person is solely coincidental.'

ISADORA'S CIRCLE

Edward Gordon Craig, 1872–1966

A lover of Isadora Duncan and father of her daughter Deirdre (1906–1913). Craig was the son of the actress Ellen Terry, and was himself a distinguished theatre director. The couple had split up before their daughter drowned. Craig and Duncan stayed in contact and a collection of their letters, *Your Isadora, The Love Story of Isadora Duncan and Gordon Craig* (1974), reveals a depth of affection between them. Surprisingly, in light of Isadora's lifelong insistence that the love of her children and their untimely death had deprived her life of any hope of contentment, Craig claims that Duncan never had maternal feelings.

'Isadora was not maternal. She never showed the slightest motherly tenderness or helpfulness. She tried to dominate Deirdre – her calm with her was not yielding or dear in the least – it was cold and quite unnatural. Strange this, and true.'

Mary Desti, 1871–1931

A Canadian-American socialite of Irish extraction. She was a close friend of Isadora Duncan, and came to Moscow to visit her. The behaviour of Yesenin and other poets shocked her. She was with Isadora in Nice at the time of Isadora's death. The scarf that caught in the wheels of the car and strangled Duncan had been a present from Mary.

Mary Desti died of leukaemia in New York on 12 April 1931.

Sol Hurok, 1888–1974

A Russian born theatrical impresario. He moved to the USA in 1906 and was naturalised in 1914. He was famous for his wry one-liners about the vagaries of working with 'geniuses'. He brought the Bolshoi Ballet and the Kirov Ballet to America for their first tours.

Hurok was fond of Isadora Duncan and sympathetic to Yesenin, his fellow countryman, and wrote perceptively about both of them in his memoirs.

Hurok died of a heart attack in a New York taxi cab in 1974.

Paris Singer, 1867–1932

A lover of Isadora Duncan and the father of her son, Patrick. He was the immensely wealthy heir to the Singer Sewing Machine empire. He and Isadora never married. After Patrick's death by drowning, they saw little of each other. Singer split his time between Florida and England. He was generous to Isadora after their split. He inherited his parents' country house, Oldway Mansion, in Paignton, Devon, which he spent many years remodelling. Singer died in London and was cremated in Torquay, with his ashes scattered at Oldway.

PLACES

The Pegasus Café

Demolition, 1960s

The poetry café and club run by Yesenin, Marienhof and the other Imagists. It was located at 37 Tverskaya Street, on the corner of Maly Gnezdnikovsky. The building was demolished in the early 1960s as part of Nikita Khrushchev's scheme to remodel central Moscow, destroying much of the city's architectural heritage and replacing it with poorly constructed high-rise blocks that became known as *Khrushchevkas*.

12 Bryusov Lane, Apartment 11

The flat where Zinaida and her children, Tatiana and Konstantin, lived with Vsevolod Meyerhold – and where Zinaida was murdered in 1939 – is now the Vs Meyerhold Apartment Museum, with rooms recreated as they were at the time and permanent exhibits of the couple's life and work.

ACADEMICS

Gordon McVay, born 1941

 Gordon McVay is the leading Western expert on Yesenin and the author of the acclaimed 'Esenin: A Life' (1976) and 'Isadora and Esenin' (1980). He was an undergraduate at New College, Oxford, then a postgraduate in Oxford and at Moscow State University in the mid-1960s. As well as his research in Soviet archives, he had numerous meetings with many of Yesenin's friends and relatives and with former members of Isadora Duncan's Moscow dance school. He taught at the University College of North Wales, Bangor, the University of East Anglia, and the University of Bristol. In 2016 and 2017, to acknowledge his debt to Yesenin, Gordon McVay donated his entire archive of letters, books and photographs, accumulated in the course of 50 years' research, to the Yesenin Museum in Konstantinovo. He once remarked that Yesenin had been his companion for over half a century. Having written this book, I am beginning to understand what he means.

Gordon McVay has been exceptionally generous in the help he has offered me, through access to his collection of Yesenin-related materials and his vast store of knowledge about him. He has been an unrivalled source of information about the poet, the man and the times he lived in. I thank him most sincerely. He disagrees with my characterisation of Anatoly Marienhof, feeling that Soviet critics and others – now including me – have blamed Marienhof for debauching Yesenin. He says this is unfair. I apologise to him.

PICTURE CREDITS